To Lynne

After the Quiet

RAY MORGAN

DEDICATION

I dedicate this book to John Brebner. He would have hated the sci-fi premise, but he encouraged me to keep writing and gave me steadfast friendship to the end of his days.

CONTENTS

ACKNOWLEDGMENTS

I want to thank all my dear friends who have taken the time to read my work and still encouraged me to continue by demanding this sequel to, Come The Quiet.

1

OLD SAM

30 A.Q.

The stifling change from frigid fresh air to the smelly confines of the hut struck Bernie in the face like a warm soggy rag. The air stank of wood smoke, leftover food, and dying old people. He narrowed his nostrils against the stench and waded into the clawing close air.

The strong young man endured it to sit and visit with old Sam. Sam was a knower. He remembered the world before the quiet came. Bernie's schooling was the stinky old guy's stories. The decrepit creature who lay in the hut taught him survival. For all of his twenty two years, Bernie listened to and loved Sam.

Bernie spent his time tending their tiny commune of huts. Ten hardy souls depended on the knowledge Sam passed down to Bernie. The only diversion from the tedium of their hard scrabble hunter-gatherer life of primitive survival was to listen to the old man's stories.

Bernie laid a handful of green plants on the entry counter and topped them with three small field-dressed carcasses. A wrinkled, hunched over, thirty eight year old woman, took them. Bernie smiled and wagged his eye brows at her as he handed her a small cloth sack. She grinned her toothless purple gums up at the handsome young man as he turned to the main living room.

"Hah, you're back," Sam's voice cracked through the dense air of the close hut.

"Hey, Sam. I got some squirrel, your favorite and found some mustard greens too. She's cooking it now," Bernie said loudly. He smiled and sat beside the aged man's elaborately carved redwood bed.

Old Sam rearranged himself on the pillow and blanket covered expanse. He crawled up onto the high ground by the backboard against the wall exposing himself shamelessly as he folded into his nest.

"Sounds fine. You got any wine for the old Sam? My throat is parched." Sam grinned, his lopsided snaggleteeth poking out.

As Bernie leaned back, hands up in surrender to deny having any wine for the old guy, the woman broke in. "How about a little fresh boiled tea?" Steaming hot, spoon propelled tea-mugs on a tray appeared. She was always ready with something made into tea. The little sack Bernie brought her carried especially rare tea makings.

"I don't want any of your shit tea!" Sam yelled at the old woman's back. She ignored him.

"I brought tea, Sam. Thank you, Paris," Bernie said over his shoulder to her, "Lighten up you old fart. Jeez. She boiled us water. Goddamn."

"She keeps trying to poison me with all kinds of shit! You don't know," Sam bleated.

"Yeah, OK. She's just trying to help. We can't all be perfect like you. Now isn't that a nice brew?" Bernie asked as they slurped the stuff.

"It's good, it's good," Sam admitted with wheezing smacking noises.

"Now calm down. I brung you tea and supper," Bernie said.

"Pleased to see you. She just ..." he whispered *sotto voce*, "fucks with me."

"I know, I know. You miss Marta and Teri, and the others, don't ya?"

Wispy haired old Sam sat silent and pursed his lips a couple of times. "Yeah. I miss 'em. I'm out of here pretty soon myself." Sam looked in the young Bernie's eyes.

"Old man, you're going quite a bit yet, I think. You're doing OK. Things are working out and we have enough to get to summer I think. All is on course and speed." Bernie smiled at his mentor.

"You went down to the flat," Sam accused. Bernie looked aside to deny it. "Where else you getting greens in March? We're at the edge here and you're not shitting this old hand. No sir. I'm out of here soon and then, it's just you … and them," Sam threatened.

"Jeez! You make everything sound like we don't have plans to go on. Just relax, we're gonna' have a nice dinner and tell stories. You can die tomorrow."

The toothless woman appeared with some small slightly sweet, hardtack-like crackers on a very fancy gold rimmed saucer. They plucked and dipped them into their steaming brew.

"You brought cookies too! Where'd you go? To the ruins?" Sam accused. And slurped the wet cookie.

The tea was a pushy spice mix that pierced through and added to the heavy air in the stick and mud hovel.

"Thanks, Paris." Bernie nodded after the woman.

Sam whistled the hot dripping biscuit to his lips and nibbled at the softened edge, then dove it back into the mug of pungent tea to soften it more.

"This almost tastes like … cinnamon? That's it. This is old. Where you find this little treasure? You been down, I know it. Damn you boy, I told you …" Sam scolded Bernie while he savored the treat.

"Don't you never mind what I'm doing. I get what I need. Like I said, we're not doing so bad." Bernie settled his cold nose into the steamy mist rising from the fancy porcelain cup. He held the place of alpha male and sat his place with the air of assured power.

Cold cool air wafted into the space and the old man pulled covers around his privates. Paris laughed a short cackling bit of glee as several tough looking, raggedy, dirty people came through the loose flap door. A young boy led three grown women each in their late teens who looked like they were in their thirties. They carried a big bowl full of sprouted greens and a small pot of questionable contents. Perfunctorily they greeted Paris and added their meager food to the board. Barely fitting into the tiny hut's space they found places around the room-filling bed to sit for the evening meal and story.

Sam said, "I need to know what things are changing. I mean … so I can tell you the way to do things, maybe it's changing right before your eyes. So you'll be ready."

"Naw, Sam. You don't know what's going on out there. You ain't been out in a month of Sundays. Nothing new out there that you ain't seen already." Bernie dismissed the old man's meddling in the practical workings of tough survival in a broken world.

"Old Sam?" the dark skinned girl Halley asked, "Tell us about the first days? BQ?"

The kid, Connor, jumped in, "Aw. That's nothing good. Tell about Gilligan and the Skipper, and the uncharted desert isle."

"We're safe here and at peace. And you want me to talk about the worst time I know," Sam complained.

Madonna, thin and gaunt with piercing blue eyes set in a filthy streaked face said, "No, no more Gilligan. We heard all the stories of how the magic worked. We know about the flying cars and talking to people far away and the boxes that could think."

"And the TV," Connor interjected.

"You don't tell us about the after the quiet times. What was it like? Where did everyone go? And how you got us away?" Halley insisted. "When the magic stopped."

Sam found it easy and fun to describe the fantastic world full of electricity. It was a time of fanciful visions and super fancy vehicles and flying machines and people going fast fast fast. When he tried to relate the tough times after the quiet came, his mind got hung up. It was a crazy turmoil when the magic stopped and painful to relate. Sam always filled their evening stories with the fun happy stuff from before the quiet: TV shows and super heroes and easy living with lots of food. Fun stories. None of it had anything to do with who they were and where they lived now.

"The day the quiet came. What happened that day?" Halley asked.

"Is that when you met the Baron?" Madonna jumped in.

"And the wicked Baroness?" Connor piped in.

"That day? When I got caught in the city?" Sam thought. "The rules of nature twisted and turned. It changed one day. In one second." Sam looked sad. They all hushed and sipped tea and munched the ancient stale packaged biscuits that Paris served. "I don't wanna," the old fellow whined.

"Please, Sam please," Halley leaned into his space and held onto his wooden stick-like arm. He could smell her strong female unwashed scent. She stroked him gently.

"Yes, please Sam. We so want to hear, how you made the change," Madonna pleaded and batted her big blue eyes at him in adoration as she reached out and touched his leg. The hot caffeinated tea and the beautiful young woman stroking his leg did the job.

"Oh … allright. But, it ain't pretty," he grumbled.

"We know. Oh thank you Sam." Halley cooed in his ear as she leaned and gave him a big wet peck on the cheek. She and Bernie exchanged knowing glances as her job convincing him was done. He'd tell the one story he had never told before.

The old man leaned back, gave a big sigh, closed his eyes and began to speak. He spoke as if reciting some great work of literature that he had memorized. He spoke of the time when the quiet came.

"The first couple of days in the city weren't so bad and the first night there was this big party. It was a waiting-for-the-power-to-come-back-on party. No one organized it. There was no plan to do it. People just pulled out their barbeque grills and hibachis and fired up whatever was thawing in the freezer. I remember the smell of grilling meat."

"Coon and squirrel I bet, and possum," said Connor.

"Sshhh," Madonna scolded him. "What about the people?"

"San Francisco was full of really cool people and at first the holiday spirit was wonderful. Worked stopped, it was an event. That afternoon everyone spent their time on the streets walking home; very orderly and mature, walking home in the street, as if it was what they did everyday. People were put out by the power outage, so, they helped one another, it was a common ill. Everyone was affected, so there was a friendly kind of nervous humor."

"I went home with Eddy to his apartment. Eddy was my pal from work and it was obvious that work was over for the day and the lights were not gonna' come back on. I decided to go to Eddy's and hang there that night. I didn't relish the thought of trying to get across the Golden Gate Bridge that afternoon. It would be dark before I could walk there and then I had at least another twenty five miles to hike home to Foxfoul. I was much more comfortable with the idea of waiting in the city until the juice came back on and then taking the bus home."

At this point, grubby little Connor who had crawled onto the foot of the bed asked, "What's the bus?"

"Shhh." The girls put their fingers to their mouths. "We'll tell you later," as if they knew.

The old man continued, "It's like a big car, Connor boy, with lots of seats."

The nine year old nodded knowingly.

"Eddy and me, we walked to his South of Market Street apartment. He shared it with his girlfriend Allison. She was waiting with a bottle of wine."

The girls looked at each other wishing they had wine.

"When darkness fell we got out store bought candles and the grill and heated up a bunch of hot dogs, some of these microwave cheese stuffed jalapeno poppers, oh they were good. We drank the last two bottles of wine and since there was no power and no TV they went to bed early, Allison and Eddy that is. I couldn't take their noisy humping, so I took a candle and went up on the roof."

"They didn't invite you to join them?" Amber, the quiet sullen girl, asked.

"Not in those days girl, no, we didn't share like we do now," Sam said.

"Selfish," Amber threw back.

"And three bottles of wine." Halley said.

Sam bore on. "Five stories up made a great view of the city. Normally, from there I could see rows and rows of lit-up buildings stretching all the way down to the bay., but when I looked out, the lights were gone. You couldn't tell where the bay started and the city ended. There were some lights down on the ground, some car head-lights were pointed at smoky bonfires in the streets. I could make out a few candles glowing in other apartment buildings. Heh heh, they seemed really lame then."

The old guy closed his eyes and was in an almost trance-state as he related the scene that played in his head.

"A light fog rolled in. It covered the stars and moon and this glow came up between the buildings, from distant streets where car lights shined."

"I thought you said the cars didn't work," Halley said.

"Yeah, well the batteries worked, dee-see, magic, ya' know. But they didn't run. The rest was dark except for some big fires in the distance."

Sam chuckled, "I remember now, I looked downtown and saw some guys hanging from a building by ropes. A fire at the far end of the street lit 'em up. They looked like window cleaners. I thought that was a weird thing to do during a power black-out. I realized they were tagging a whole building face. That was totally beast."

"The whole building?" Madonna, the artistic one of the three nineteen year old matrons, asked.

"Huge tags. Paint, Madonna, remember, we had lots of everything then. They were painting pictures on a big building. I smoked a couple of cigarettes and watched that weird scene. The city had always been light and bustling. Now it was dark."

"And quiet," Connor interjected.

"I tried to fit it all into some world view that made sense. The power out wasn't so unusual, but not to have the cars or buses working was the twist that stumped everyone."

"It was exciting, and me and Eddy talked about it when we walked home. I didn't get it then. There was a lot of distractions and we never got beyond some half-hearted speculation, but now, in the stillness of that roof top, I pondered the world. We didn't know it was going to stay that way. It was unreal, like a dream. It's still like a dream." Sam sighed deeply. "One thing made a big impression that we hadn't thought of and that was the quiet. You are right Connor. It was so quiet. I heard some hippy drum circle way off. The world changed and they sat around drumming."

"Rosers and hosers!" Connor interjected.

"Did you stay up there and watch them paint? What did they paint?" Madonna wanted to know.

"No, I thought Eddy and Allison were done, so I could get some sleep. I was about to go down stairs when I heard the bee. A buzzing angry little bee went by me at high speed, bound somewhere important. A moment after the bee I heard a 'pop' noise. I sat down. The hair on the back of my neck stood up. I shook a little bit and realized someone just took a shot at me."

"With a gun?" the kid inquired.

"Yep. It was a gun."

Dark-eyed Amber asked, "I don't get it. Why did they waste a bullet to shoot at you? I mean, if he shot you from a distance, then wouldn't Eddy or Allison eat you before he could get to you?"

Bernie jumped in. "They didn't eat people then. Someone was just playing around."

"Whoa." Connor rolled his eyes in disbelief.

"They didn't … but why waste a bullet?" Amber was confused.

"There were lots of guns then," Halley said matter of factly.

"What did you do Sam? Did you shoot back?" Connor wanted to know.

"Well, I crawled to the stair well and went down to Eddy's place. I was afraid to relight that candle. It took awhile for me to get down two flights, hehe," he chuckled. "I locked the door behind me and crawled to the couch and curled up and slept. That was my first day."

"Whoa. You almost got ate in the city," Connor squawked.

"He did not. He saw painters tho' didn't you, Sam? He saw painters making art. The quiet came and they made art," Madonna said. She was a quiet thoughtful woman and always making things with yarn and found bits of rope and cloth. The taggers struck her as the important part of the story.

Paris prodded from the kitchen fire, "Go on. Dinner's a while yet."

"Well, the next day people visited and shared the news, except there was none. Bicyclists filled the streets. Some looked like they were already leaving town as their bikes were loaded with camping gear, they were the smart ones. Most bikers were just out on the roads and making a day of it.

"Oh, bikers," Connor said.

"Sshh," Halley scolded.

"Well I don't know what a by-see-jig-list is ..." Connor said.

"Bonfires smoldered. They melted the road. I didn't know you could set fire to the road. There were greetings and discussions between people who were neighbors, but who didn't really know one another. They had only known 'of' each other. People passed in the hallway or on the street or in the little quik-trip grocery store down the street run by the Pakistani family. They barely recognized each other. One certainly didn't know their names or anything about them."

"Didn't they share supper? Or the water in the creek?" Halley asked. She was the leader and oldest of the three women.

"Well, you see, in modern society people didn't spend time with those who were close to their homes. The modern person had networks and communities of people at the end of telephone or internet connections."

They all looked at him quizzically.

"Electronica," Sam said to their faces. He had told them all about these things and always used the term to describe most all the myriad of electrical gadgets and communication means. It was too much to try to explain the multitudinous distinctions between cell-phone and land-lines and CB radios and commercial radio etc. Electronica said it all and they understood the term.

"Look, parents, families, school friends, and just about everyone you knew, didn't live anywhere near you. People flew or drove dozens, or hundreds of miles, to see their people ... for holidays. No one lived just down the street or next door to their own people."

"It sounds insane," said Amber with a scowl.

"That ain't the half of it." Sam sat up a bit, more animated. "Everyone was expected to leave home when they turned eighteen years old and go far away to colleges where everyone's a stranger. They were expected to make new friends and allies and then move to the big city."

"Like my walkabout." Bernie suggested. He referred to the initiation of the teen boys to join manhood in a strenuous trial of staying alone naked in the wilderness for a week. All the boys were expected to fill their place as men by this trial introduction to the world of rough responsibility. "You'll do it soon, Connor."

"Uh, yeah, sort of ... but not really. You became a man on your walkabout and they usually didn't grow up much at all."

"But you said they were eighteen. Who fed the village? Didn't their children starve when they left?" Madonna wanted to know.

"It was different then. You went away, the boys and the girls too. No one had kids until after. Look, just listen, I can't explain everything. You finished 4 years in college then went to make friends away from your people in the city."

"Oh, they started new villages in the city," Halley clarified.

"Well, kind of. Your friends in the city didn't really live next door to each other either. They would go to jobs everyday, miles from their homes, and spend eight to ten hours a day, again, in the company of people they had no other connection to besides working in the same place. People just didn't really 'know' each other. There was no history of shared experience and growth. You were on your own."

"Oh, how sad it must have been." Paris, the ancient thirty-eight year old crone, added from her cook-fire.

Just then the door flap pulled aside and three more people filed into the tight, dark, thick atmosphere of their main hut. Two very rough looking fur-clad men set their sacks by Paris and each gave her a quick peck on the cheek. Paris cooed at the sight of them. An equally rough-shod woman carrying a bow, followed them in. She unlimbered her quiver of arrows and hung her archery on its peg as they all moved around to seats surrounding old Sam in his big wooden bed.

Paris readied more tea.

Bernie asked, "Any good?"

The woman responded, "We got what we went for." She untied a sack from her out-of-place elaborately decorated belt and gave it to Paris before sitting.

"Good, we talk later," Bernie commanded.

Sam looked up from his regal bed-nest, smacking his lips in anticipation of news. "Where'd you go? Tell me about it. Did you see anything new?"

"We went up, Sam. Same-old, same-old," the dark-bearded man, Max, said.

"Oh, up. I see," Sam was disappointed.

Halley interrupted, "Back to the story, people left home and went to live alone and then the quiet came and they were in the city with people they didn't know."

Sam focused on her for a moment and regained his train of thought, "Oh yeah, and now, all of a sudden the only people to connect with were those you could walk or bike to. That was where all the bicyclists were going; to make connections with their people, to re-establish their networks. Man, those bikers were happy about the state of affairs. San Francisco finally became the bike friendly town everyone always dreamed of. But, the drawback to bike heaven was that the traffic had all coasted to stop in the middle of the road. Cars clogged the streets. People were still moving though, flowing along to one place or another," Sam continued with a lilt in his voice as he recalled.

"Me, Eddy, and Allison, we had a talk about what to do that first full day. I remember we had coffee and toasted bread. It was sourdough and there was marmalade. We had to do it on the grill, by hand. It took an hour." He looked at them thinking they might get the irony of having to make coffee and toast over a charcoal fire instead of with a toaster and coffeemaker. "Oh, never mind, anyway, I decided to wait in the city for the power to come back on."

"I remember Allison said in such a matter of fact tone while she puffed her cigarette and jabbed the air to make her point, 'It has to come back on. It always does,' and we conceded her logic. It had to come back on. So I stayed with them and waited."

"It got really warm that day. People tried to do normal things, but it was useless. The shops had a heck of a time selling anything. See, people got their cash from a machine or lived on credit and debit cards. And man, they got frustrated when they had nothing the shops would take as payment."

Connor was wondering how someone could live on a card. He had only a vague idea of what a card might be and was engrossed in the thought of how he might live on top of one. He was in the tale and although nodding as if he knew what old Sam was saying he was lost in fantastic thoughts of a world so gone past that even a card was a mystery. He didn't want to stop the story, so he kept his mouth shut.

"By afternoon the grocery stores got out of control. Mobs assaulted them, dozens of people came in at once and took what they wanted. They just smashed the windows and looted them. They felt entitled to whatever they could grab, so the stores closed."

"I didn't see a cop that whole first few days. I imagine there were few cops who showed up for work and some might have tried to walk their beat and uphold order, but the people took advantage. The streets got mean. The cops were outnumbered thousands to one and they just vanished. Some small shop keepers tried to shoot people into being orderly. It only attracted the wrath of hot head youngsters and got the store burnt out completely."

"Some of the more cohesive and tight knit neighborhoods kept up order, though. I heard that China town grocery stores extended credit to their regular Chinese customers. They even moved their restaurants into the streets as long as food and gas held out. But, if you weren't Asian, you better stay away. Gangs guarded every road and avenue into their neighborhoods as the un-welcome wagon. Those Chinese didn't want the tourists anymore."

"I imagine thousands formed small neighborhood groups. Ethnic and like minded folk who knew each other coalesced. Bicycle people found one another. Friends sought each other out. Before the end of the day most people in the city had found someone else and made allies. Allies are what it's all about."

The young all nodded and looked each other in the eye knowingly. A slight sigh of affirmation rose at the words that held them together. Their allies were in the room with them.

Sam went on, "It was still a holiday. There was no power. No job to go to. People stayed home. Most had a few days of food so they didn't venture too far from home. After meeting the neighbors and roaming around the block there wasn't much else to do."

"They got bored at home with no TV or music and after the last of the grilled freezer food was gone, people ended up eating their irreplaceable food as entertainment. It kind of became a sleep-in, slow-down, read a book, get to know your next door neighbor, and eat that last can of peaches sort of holiday." Sam smiled to himself.

Paris handed a wooden bowl of the grey stuff topped with raw shredded greens to Bernie. "That's a good spot to serve up this tasty stew the girls brought." She ladled out bowls for them all.

Connor asked a question. "Old Sam. What's a 'canapeaches'?"

"Good question boy. I told you he was a smart one." Sam turned and gave the lad his attention. "They were sweet tasty fruits in a metal container, boy. You could keep 'em for a long time until you was ready to eat 'em. Mmmm, they were sweet, and juicy, and deee-liscious." Old Sam leaned back as he remembered juicy slices in liquid syrup from a lost age.

"Eat up everyone. Squirrel is roasting," Paris insisted.

Sam turned his nose up at the offered bowl of stuff. "Well, by the end of the third day most of the people who commuted had walked away from the city and were somewhere on the road to their real homes across the bay. Squadrons of bicycles took over the streets. Some really enthusiastic bike groups pushed cars out of the way in order to make open paths on the street. They worked their way down the avenues and moved a couple of cars then moved a little farther and moved a couple more. Ten dozen people attacked a bus and rolled it to the curb. They looked like army ants, all moving independently with a common purpose as a single blob of committed beings on a single task. Open bike lanes were being made all over. Pretty soon streams of bicyclists flowed along the roadways. The car chaos was being replaced by some semblance of human powered order. Pushing the useless cars out of the way so they could move freely lent stability to people's psyche. The new city paradigm was being established.

Some people smashed in car windows, opened the hoods and pulled the batteries out. They attacked the cars, ripped useful parts out and went scurrying away on their bikes with a battery prize under arm. Some were even going so far as to rob the headlights. It only made sense. Direct current batteries needed direct current light bulbs. Dee-see." Sam elaborated.

The youngsters all nodded. They knew the dee-see power. Priests held it and led sacred processions with the cold lights on high holy days.

"It got hot. Ninety five degrees in the city was unusual. It was a scorcher of a day for August. The fog didn't come in from the ocean as usual. It was a heat wave." Sam looked in their eyes hoping for recognition.

The chill times they were living through did not give them much common ground with the old man. It had not been hot for quite a long time. Their lives were chill and drizzly and grey. Unusual heat was something they weren't familiar with.

"At night bonfires of tires were in the important intersections. The neighborhoods got defined by the gangs. They marked their turf boundaries with fires and gang tags and guards. They marked buildings with their spray paint symbols signs and flags. Lines got drawn all over the city.

The city reeked in the heat. Acrid black smoke of burning tires lay like a pall. It hung on the buildings in the still air. It stank from uncollected garbage and from water systems failing to flush the sewage away." He lay back and closed his eyes against the awful memory.

"Then, news of the coming hard times trickled in on the fourth day. I was sitting on the stoop trying to decide if I could take anymore of Allison and Eddy. Eddy was cool, but Allison was a total poser. She claimed to be a 'dancer'. Her parents footed the bill for her to attend community college and she studied dance. Jazz, and modern dance. She talked a good game, but she couldn't even do a waltz or a tango, and I never, and I mean never saw her dance from joy or for fun. She was a waste, but she fucked Eddy and her parents paid for the apartment. Well, I was sitting there and a bicyclist I knew came up the street."

Sam started acting. He played both sides of his little play.

"'Hey man!' I smiled and waved at Jim, a guy from the shipping department where we worked.

He pulled up short. 'Hey man. How's it going? I didn't know you lived in the city.'

'Yeah, well I'm just staying here with Eddy, you know from operations?'

'Yeah, sure,' Troy said.

'Hey, so, what's going on man? I mean we haven't really heard anything. Does anyone know what's going down?' I asked him

'Oh, dude. The Golden Gate Bridge is closed.'

'Closed?'

'Yeah man, some fascists destroyed the roadway at the north end of the bridge,' Troy told me.

'What?!' I couldn't believe my ears.

'Yeah. Spooky, huh? There's only a small piece of roadway open. They're shooting at people trying to cross.'

'Shooting? I gotta' cross. I mean, like, I live in Foxfoul man. I gotta' get home,' I pleaded with him. Like he could do anything.

'Not now dude,' he said, 'they got snipers on the hills on the other side. They're shooting at people trying to cross. They killed a couple before word got spread. No one else has tried it.'

People trying to go north into rich Marine County were stopped cold. A little concrete demolition and a couple of thirty-ought-six rifles stopped everyone. No one knew who was doing it or why, but now, I was trapped in the city and couldn't go home."

'How am I gonna' get home?'

'I dunno' dude.'

"That's the way guys talked back then." Sam elaborated.

"'There's this huge camp in the Presidio. No one's moving they're just camped there.'

'Whoa. This is too crazy. What about the Marina? Are there any boats still there?'" Aside to his audience, "I sailed the bay with friends and knew how to handle a boat. It was an off chance and as soon as I asked, I knew I was grasping at straws.

'Man, the marina is empty. Every boat is gone or burnt. The docks caught fire the other night and a bunch of boats got torched. It's a gnarly scene man,'

'Well, what're you doing? Where're you staying?'

'Well, I kind of got an in with some of my burning-man pals in the mission. We have a whole building there and it's quite a fortress. 'Turkey Bill' has the whole neighborhood organized and he's controlling an entire city block. It's rad, man,' Troy said.

'Any room at the inn?'

'Yeah, well, I would ask you to come join, but … well, I don't know how long we can go. Food's getting scarce fast. I'm on a scout. We're looking to get on the move soon.'

'Yeah, I get it,'"

Aside, Sam said, "ya' gotta' have allies ya' know?"

Sam's audience nodded at his advisory note.

"'Look. I gotta' keep moving. I'm expected back. You're probably better off by yourself anyway man,' And that was good advice.

'Yeah, hey thanks Jim. Good luck.' I shook his hand.

'Yeah, thanks Sam. See ya'.' Troy pumped his bike and disappeared down the street. I never saw him again. Always wondered what happened to him."

"I told Eddy and Allison what Troy said. They didn't believe it at first. It was hearsay and rumor. That someone would go to the trouble to stop people crossing over the bridge was pretty far fetched. Maybe the people of Marine County were afraid. Even so, how could the authorities allow such a thing? Why would they only destroy most of the roadway? Why leave an open passage? None of it made much sense, but the world was making less sense each day."

The bowl of stew, festooned with bright fresh greens, sat on the edge of his bed untouched.

"You eat," Paris said.

"Fuck-off you old bitch. I'm telling the story here. Besides, I'm waiting for that squirrel, not this shit in a bowl. Christ I can't eat that garbage, you know that. Fucking rabbit food."

"It's good for you," she said

"Yeah, well, I want some squirrel, the nice crunchy parts. You better not burn it either."

Connor boy reached out and took the greens from old Sam's bowl. Madonna grabbed the bowl and split it among the others.

Bernie reached out a tanned stomach wineskin flask to the old man.

Sam took the flask and drew a hearty sip before he choked a little on the bitter vinegar tasting wine. Paris had turned her back to his tirade and tended the roasting squirrel.

"So, me and Eddy spent the day scouting around for food and trying to avoid gangs that were the power on the streets. The refrigerator emptied out in two days, the cupboard in two more. Allison became a raving bitch over running out of cigarettes. No shops stayed open.

The streets became this strange landscape of abandoned cars, buses, garbage, smoldering fires, and barricades. Every neighborhood gang staked out their territory, see, barricades of cars and street debris defined the walkways. They blocked off key thoroughfares, sections of the city were being carved up by gangs. Some gangs were citizen groups, communities banded together for protection. It was getting hard to move around town without running afoul of mean young toughs or vigilante citizens armed to the teeth. People were getting mugged for whatever they were carrying. During day light most main roads stayed open and they were treated as a kind of neutral space, no man's land, and open to travel. The large open space the avenues and boulevards afforded were uncontrollable and therefore became sacrosanct."

The girls looked at one another when he used a word they didn't understand. 'Sacrosanct' ricocheted puzzling glances all around the ring of listeners. No one stopped the man's story. It must mean 'really important'.

"The city really did try to remain civilized. Looking back, it was kind of amazing how long the people maintained their civility in the face of such a maddening situation."

Sam looked at Halley for some support for the change he was attempting to get across to the young. She nodded in sympathetic understanding, but really had no basis in her life to compare. Sam looked to her because she looked so much like her mother, who was Sam's mate from so long ago, and had lived during those times. He didn't realize that she knew nothing of what he spoke. Her looks fooled him into thinking she might understand.

"For the first few days everyone pulled together and helped each other. We shared food. We became a community for just a brief moment in our fast moving hectic lives. We met the neighbors and talked with them. We biked down the open streets together. We made communal meals as the food dwindled. Strains of song drifted up from the thousands of faceless apartment windows. People found reason to tolerate and help one another. Everyone looked up and forward. Remember?" Sam smiled as he gazed into Halley's eyes of compassion.

She knew the old man was a little delirious and she smiled beneficently at him. She scooted a little closer to him on the big bed as he rubbed her thigh. She reflected his love for her mother back to him and waited for him to go on with the story.

"The electricity would come back on," Sam said ferociously. "Everyone knew it, felt it, and no one could entertain the thought that it wouldn't. Everyone supported each other and we were sure that the world would go back the way it was. All we had to do was hang tight and wait a little while for things to get straightened out. Just wait a little while." Small tears formed in Sam's eyes as he fervently spoke an age-old hopelessness to his meager band of survivors and children. Sam snatched the wine-skin and took a deep draught and wiped his face with the back of his hand.

He composed himself. "I tell you, that heat wave increased. The city baked in a hundred and eight degrees. The bonfires of tires rekindled each night, bigger, and more intense. Gun fire increased. Bodies appeared in the street. Fewer people showed on the streets each day and nobody but the wild fire guys after it got dark. It was just a couple of hungry days and it all unraveled.

Allison came home one night with cigarettes. She wouldn't say where she got them or how. She and Eddy had a terrible fight as their easy time relationship soured. I couldn't stand to be in the apartment. I remember that night I went up to the roof and looked at the failing city.

The world was scary. People were hungry. No one had ever really been hungry before. We always had food. Safeway™ was always there.

Gangs raided the warehouses with food in them. The just-in-time economy left the city with only a few days of supplies at most and it was gone." He looked in the eyes of the unbelieving kids that were his legacy.

"You see, efforts by the government, they were stymied at the start. The mayor spoke to hundreds from the steps of city hall and he promised relief. But, he failed to establish his chain of command in time to secure the food and gangs took it all. They set up underground fiefdoms with canned goods as the base of exchange. They took the power. Mobs stormed city hall for the food promised them. Riots destroyed any effort to get it together. In the confusion some fast acting anarchists torched city hall and the main police station. I heard there was a lot of shooting downtown, there must have been hundreds in on it. But, you can't shoot everyone.

Plumes of smoke rose straight up. They looked like columns holding up a roof of smoky haze over town. The last cool fog was the day of the quiet. There was no breeze since then. Very un-San Francisco like." He looked in Halley's eyes for confirmation. "It got hotter each day and cold and clear at night.

I stood on that roof-top and planned my next move. Staying with Eddy and Allison wasn't a workable long term strategy. Maybe after they finished fighting, Allison would be gone. Maybe Eddy would be gone. It was really her apartment. The rumors of the Golden Gate being closed repeated, so how could I get home to Foxfoul? Maybe I could still find a boat at the marina to take me across the bay. But, what did I have to offer someone for a ride? Me and Eddy weren't very good at finding food and we had nothing to trade. Allison at least had something to trade, apparently, she kept showing up with plenty of cigarettes.

As I peered over the parapet a flash of light caused me to wince. A glow shone up from the bay. I couldn't see it directly, but it was obvious a ship was the source of some explosion. I saw the overhanging city haze move up and away from the shore as if being pushed. The shock wave slapped my forehead and knocked me backward onto the roof. My ears burned with the force of the blast. Hot searing air roasted the building front. The sonic crack tore apart the stillness of the night and a rolling boom hammered between the buildings. Windows imploded by the bajillions. Transmission towers were torn off skyscrapers, waterfront buildings instantly collapsed into smoky ruins, old buildings for a mile inland were pushed into permanently crooked houses leaning away from the bay. Huge, round, booming reverberations of the explosion walked across the city. It was the thunder of the end of the world.

On that sixth morning the city was pretty ragged. The sun rose orange and hot. The water front explosions pushed a lot of people into shock. The big one blew-up near the Bay Bridge and rumors were that the bottom deck was destroyed. A filthy burnt tire smell was in everyone's nose. Not a breath of wind. Not a hint of cloud. The weather was hot with brown smog from our burning civilization.

I woke on the roof. My head pounded, my mouth tasted awful and I was thirsty. I went down to the apartment. It was empty. Eddy left me a note. They went to the presidio camp. They were going to Marine County. North to farm land, to happy cow country, to the cool redwoods, to the river and wine and agriculture. They were coming up here to the food. So, I tucked a blanket roll under my arm and head out to cross the city."

"Old Sam?" Amber wanted to know. "What's a mayor? Did he explode the bay-ship?" Her question was so honest that Sam couldn't laugh at its naiveté.

"The mayor was like the Baron is now and no, he didn't do anything to hurt the city except be a big wuss when it came time."

"Oh," she said.

"There was a lot of people moving on the roads to the Golden Gate. I made it to the presidio camp in early afternoon, and I'm telling you, that camp was big. People covered every approach to the bridge. They camped on the highway, filled the woods and the red tiled houses. The parking lots by the toll booth were jammed with tents, the beach and just everywhere you could go was crammed with people who wanted out of the city.

There was this rally happening around the toll booth. A guy with a big cardboard cone bullhorn stood on the top of a box truck yelling at the crowd. He was dressed like the man running the center ring at the circus, I can see him now: black knee-high boots, white fat-thigh pants, a bright green cutaway coat with long pointy tails, and a bright red vest, and bow tie, and a really tall top hat that he kept waving in the air.

'They can't stop us!'

The mob yelled back. 'Noooo!!'

'There are too many of us!' He waved his top hat.

'Yeah!' People waved sticks and bats and guns in the air.

'We can't let a couple of guys dictate to all of us? Can we?' He raised his hands.

'Noooo!' The crowd was filling fast and man, were they getting agitated.

He aimed his mega-phone at me. I could see he wore heavy little round glasses and had a perfectly pointed moustache." Sam made a motion as if to twist his own moustache into a point. "That's when I recognized that it was Turkey Bill from the mission. He was a really cool dude.

'If we move together we can get through! We can overwhelm them!'

Everyone yelled, 'Yeah!' their frustration vented, the mob surged and I got pushed forward. They were really getting worked up.

'We can't stay here anymore!' The ringmaster pointed down.

'Noooo!' A rifle pointed at the sky and went off. 'POW'.

'You guys ready!?' He held his arms out.

'Yeah!' They yelled back at him."

Sam acted out all the roles back and forth like a play in his head.

"'Well then?! We've waited long enough! Come on! Let's go!' Turkey Bill jumped, like a flea, off the truck box onto the cab then onto a car and down into the people. A brass band surrounded him and struck up some really rousing marching tune. Thousands of people seethed between the cars and onto the bridge. It was a march. A movement. Democracy in action.

People were starving and trapped and pissed off about it. They were tired of letting a few unknown people control their lives. That was one of the old ways. They'd had it with the old rules. The old rules had not saved them from whatever this was that they were going through. The rich bankers controlled their lives before and they weren't about to let any rich Marine County bastards keep them from getting to the farm country where they could feed themselves.

I got pushed and became part of the movement. I went there to cross. These people were going to cross. Someone would make it. Might as well be me too. And, you know, you can't win the lottery if you don't buy a ticket, so I merged with the crowd and we stormed across that Golden Gate Bridge."

"Squirrel's ready," Paris called.

"Shusshhhhh," they all said. "Go on, Sam, go on. What happened next?" They were enthralled by a tale about how he crossed a bridge that no longer existed. The span was a broken set of unconnected towers in the middle of the deep swift narrow and violent waterway that separated the north from the south part of the world. It had never been a complete structure for the whole of their lives and a tale about going across it with thousands of others mesmerized them.

"That old bridge sagged and shook with the weight of all them people marching. Tens of thousands of us followed the crazy guy with the funny outfit and his brass band across. It was glorious. I can hear the band. 'bump-ba-da-bump-badda-bump-bump-bump, bump-ba-da-bump-badda-bump-bump-bump.'" Sam rocked and chanted a bit as long gone recollections of John Philip Souza welled up from his ancient memory.

Paris chopped up the bits of squirrel and offered a plate of roasty tasty bits to Bernie. He took a morsel of the hot meat and passed the plate.

"Then, about two thirds of the way across, everyone slowed down and bunched up. We were at the north tower, you see, it was the start of the last section of bridge to cross. Everyone paused in the shadow of those big orange towers. See, from there on is where folks was getting shot.

Then, the guy with the bullhorn yelled, 'We have snipers of our own!' Guys with guns pumped their rifles up and down. 'We are going to make them keep their heads down while we cross.'

'Yeah!' people yelled. 'Make 'em pay!'"

Sam hollered at the roof of the little hut.

"When they started shooting everyone kind of flinched and ducked and screamed until they figured out that it was their own guns shooting. They popped off a bunch. The brass band started up again. There was a lot of noise and we lit out.

The ringmaster guy waved this big American flag and the mob followed him. The road was jammed with cars and that forced folks into single file. That last hundred yards we moved fast. Then the friggin' mob stalled, they hesitated when they reached the narrow gap that was still a road. It was like a tiny bridge.

Turkey Bill yelled, 'Don't stop! Don't slow down! All together! Keep Moving!'

Rifles kept taking pot shots at the hilltops. The mob surged into the narrow open pavement on the right side. 'Keep moving! Keep moving!' he chanted into the bullhorn.

'Keep moving! Keep moving!' we sang.

Rifles kept shooting up at the hills, that band blared away; its base drum booming and them damned horns wailing. It was the most wonderful concert I ever heard. The fervor rose as we got closer to that little piece of pavement. The ringmaster with the flag ran across the open pavement with a mob that pushed forward. The lines of people came together and poured toward that little thirty foot space that was still a bridge. I ran along as best I could. All I could think of was not to fall down. You'd have got trampled. Where the pavement was gone you could see the steel-work below and then, just air. It was a big drop to rocks. People stampeded as rifles shot at the hills. I don't think they really knew where they were shooting, but they kept it up.

I ran right through. We kept running, then jogging, then hiking, then slogging up the grade to the Robin Williams. That's the tunnel, you know? There was thousands of us trudging up toward them big round tunnels.

I never did hear any gunfire from the hill tops. I saw some dead people on the pavement though. The ringmaster guy, in his green outfit, lay kind of disjointed in a little heap at the side of the road. He had some people with him. Someone else took up the flag he dropped. It was Turkey Bill from the Mission. He was a cool guy. I heard he lived and started a group up in the dry hills way up north on one of the lakes up there. Anyway a score of folks got wounded. Everyone else kept going. The snipers did their jobs. It just didn't stop anyone. The band drowned out their gun shots I think.

Pretty much everyone stayed on the freeway. Some folks tried to go down the off-ramp into the first little town. You know, last low ruins," Sam elaborated.

The hunters knew just where he was talking about. It was not a place that anyone went willingly. It was dangerous ground down near the southern tip of Marine County. There were still some very unfriendly people there, pirates and the like.

Bernie had a little bit of squirrel meat for Sam. The old guy snatched it and nodded with pleasure as the tasty roast meat filled his face with joy.

"It was a bedroom community of the city. You know, high rent and rich folk lived there. Little Willow. It had lots of yachts."

They all looked quizzical.

"Yachts, uh, boats fancy shiny boats."

"Oh." They all mouthed as they absorbed the new word.

"Them folks that went that way didn't hear those gunshots either, but they felt 'em. There was this dirt pile across the road with plywood signs warning people to keep out. Them snipers opened up on 'em when they tried to crawl over and they got the idea. They ran back to the freeway and left bodies there.

There was thousands of people marching, maybe more than a hundred thousand. I never saw so many people in my life, before or since. It was a migration. The city was being abandoned.

Those bicyclists raced ahead of the crowd and when they reached the tunnel they slowed down and waited. The long climb up the grade from the bridge to the tunnel was tough on everyone. It was hot. Inside the tunnel was a good place to rest. The tunnel was cool and covered and it felt safe in there.

A clinic of sorts got set-up near the entrance. They had a dozen or more injured.

We filled that place up. It was cool and it echoed. The bikers went to the north end and stopped. Just beyond, on each side of the freeway, were these big signs. You'd have liked them Madonna, they had sparkling glitter and shiny streamers. They were pretty fancy.

But, they said, 'Danger. Stay on the road! Or else,' another read, 'Danger! Off road travel is fatal. Leave the freeway and die!!!', with big orange and yellow skull and crossbones. Them bicyclists stood looking out from the tunnel overhang at the open ground as all of humanity crowded up against them. The road to food and safety stretched ahead. All we had to do was be brave and go out there. And we did, so here we are."

Sam leaned back spent. Bernie gave him another choice bit of squirrel. The audience knew he was done for the night. They all sighed at the story and munched their meager rations while the tale sank in.

Hundreds of thousands of people were pure fantasy to them. The largest group they had ever seen in their lives were in town on a big market holiday when Baron Willem and his men rode through with their flags in parade. Those events happened a couple of times a year and gathered all the folk from miles around. The most that gathered these cold dark days were a few hundred at most and it was usually muddy and there were no bands or gunshots or by-sy-jiglists or fancy funny men with green coats and top-hats.

2

Snood Congress

A.S. +14 Million Snood World Time

Far beneath the surface of Homeworld's northern sea thousands of amoeba-like creatures, intimately clung to audience-rocks anticipating the oratory. In the speech-canyon, they waited for wafting thoughts, floated to bathe their congregation with ideas. Speakers spewed personal excretion from the podium to float in a stream of chemically laden mucous, down the current, through the rock garden of snood aristocracy, and then to the still deeper valley of the general population below.

The oldest and highest order of snood had priority seating at the podium-surrounding rock garden in the freezing deep ocean current and they received the strongest thought phlegm. When it washed over them they were the first to 'hear' the thoughts of the speaker. The viscous concoction was passionate and odiferous. It was repeated and sent on the current to the gathered masses by the snood people and the 'slime-reader-machine'. Downstream, regurgitating snood interpreters reiterated the speech into organically grown slime-readers, immense blobs of flesh-rock organo-borgs which were festooned with orifices. They rebroadcast thought-smell down the river's current. The speech lost little feeling in translation. The oratory was strongly engaging.

In rows of rank and status, hundreds of thousands of individuals' sphincters shimmied in harmony to the speech goo they shared. The thick, reader-gel washed over and scented the crowds. It slathered hints of cultural history and innuendo to define the ideas expressed.

The people reacted as they writhed in a conversation of slime. The crowd felt and heard the speaker's very notion and vibrated their glandular assent to one another. They seethed on the sea floor. This was the Homeworld registry, snood congress.

The speech roiled.

"He has failed to maintain integrity! He has risen on the pillar of culpability to the shallows of consequences!" The unseen speaker spat venomously. "He must be sanctioned before this becomes another moral shame to us all!" He spumed his tirade of oily sputum laden thoughts to the throngs gathered, "the planet known as IV must be taken from him and his negligent Vithlin clan," the ancient snood, hollered into the cold current of the depths, "to be administered by responsible snood!" He was wealthy and his opinion held great weight. "Enough degradation has been visited upon those of us who are honorable and righteous creatures." In his mind he was justified because of the injustice done to him and his family.

The crowds hummed.

"I call for de-registration and an open for-the-taking, re-licensing of IV!" His thoughts floated on the stream of the deep ocean current for miles.

The power of cold current against his back seemed to push the words from him. He had been slighted to the point of retribution. His entire close family had just endured the vacation from hell. They had spent enormous resources and time and bore through the long arduous quiet of the immense journey to IV, for a long-planned and much anticipated retreat, only to have garbage dumped on them.

Duke Sleegat's palatial villa sat just below the continental shelf edge of one of the great river outflows on IV. The water from the river brought delectable sweet organic and exotic mineral tastes to his house. It had done so for millennia. However, the poison resulting from management's failure to monitor the indigenous species had washed over his family, his entire list of guests, and most egregiously, his wife. The awful tasting sludge of some unknown artificially created compounds had ruined his holiday. The family became ill from the vile mixtures that were washed on them and forced them all to endure the enormous ride home after only a very short stay. There had been virtually no recuperation time at play in their vacation home before they had to abandon the foul smelling place and flee. Sleegat's wife had ripped him mercilessly for the fiasco, and because residue rolls downstream, Duke Sleegat was on a tirade to the congressional registry. He wanted payback for the perceived slight. He could think of nothing less than causing his old rival Sloodar and his son, Sloodin, to lose their famous holding altogether. Sleedrack clan would get their due.

Duke Sleegat marked the end of his speech with a single lightning flash of observable chemical light from his body. His emotional end-note of visible light was strongly echoed by his entourage of personal attendants gathered around him. An echoing stroboscopic affirmation by his clan, and other supporters downstream, moved in a wave of light, the visual rippling showed the aged creature's accusations wound their way down the canyon and were replicated and repeated by unseen crowds in the cold dark distance. They flashed back.

The old snood found his way from the podium and nestled into a long held family niche just down to the side of the rock garden and was nestled into his retinue.

Duke Sleegat of Clan Sleedrack was rival to Sloodat and his brother Sloodar; the paternal leaders of Clan Vithlin. He wanted to reopen the licensing of IV so he could dispatch teams and claim it for his clan. He coveted Vithlin Lines' holdings and here was a chance for him to take their prize jewel away from them.

The speaker of the registry assembly took the podium and spoke. "Is there any addition to Duke Sleegat's accusations and suggestions before we pass quarantine on Vithlin IV?"

Sloodat Vithlin, slithered to the edge of the speaker's rocky depression and tickled the speaker shyly to get his attention. Sloodat was a great explorer, common to all as the most prolific space-snood of all time. He had found the Heyameyt string and assisted his brother, Sloodar, in finding and domesticating Vithlin 'Three'. Sloodat ranked high in the ancestral mind of snood and although a bit reclusive, he was known to all of snood-kind. He wrote the book on how to go about finding and taming planets for snood occupation. He had led the race into space. He was a true hero, an original colonizer, and pioneer in the endeavor to find habitable places for his people in the cold reaches of space. All revered him as a true cultivator of rocks in the vacuum for the greater good of the snood civilization. He was a shy and reticent old codger who hadn't appeared or spoken at the registry congress for eons. He was used to being 'quiet' on journey or alone on new planets. Speaking in public was not his thing.

"The registry chair recognizes and yields the podium to our great friend and hero Sloodat," the speaker called out.

The slime of his introduction wafted down the fast moving current into the valley and was echoed and repeated. A sonorous hum of acceptance washed back from the downstream audience as his introduction was accepted and welcomed by the thousands of unseen, clinging to the valley walls in the deep ocean darkness. The snood vibrated their excitement into the water and the audible thrumming and booming vibration came back to him and signaled the general population's interest in his opinion and comments to come. They loved Sloodat.

Sloodat slid alongside and squeezed out the speaker as he slid into the podium depression at the head of the congressional valley. Sloodat was not used to public speaking. He was an explorer first and most lately a simple retiree who only wanted to tend his exotic coral gardens in the shallows of Homeworld's seas. He steeled his nerve and squirted his first slime thought.

"I am Sloodat. I have gone out where no water comforts. I am Vithlin. I support snood culture for my family and for my race." He let that thought ride down the fast current of the valley.

It was a deep cold current of undiluted nature. That was why the congress met at this place of speaking. The arctic cold dropped the salty mineralized water of the planet to the darkest coldest depths at the head of this foremost valley and funneled it into a fast flowing channel at depth to the other side of the planet. This nutrient filled conveyor of water is what kept Homeworld alive and vibrant. It was also the finest place to speak to the masses, hence the congressional official meeting place.

The crowd physically thrummed their approval to his words, "Thrroooommmm," they vibrated their jelly-like bodies en mass.

Sloodat took the welcoming tones into his every pore. They had heard him and they accepted.

"My fine nephew, Sloodin, made IV. He found IV. He built IV. IV is farther than all our endeavors. IV is unique and far and dangerous and different and IV is special!" Sloodat yelled out into the darkness like he was mad. It went to the unseen masses he knew were listening.

After a few moments a steady throbbing hum of thousands of Snood's vibrating their very bodies, to tell him they heard and agreed, came rumbling back up from the dark pressurized depths to him.

"Thrroooommmm."

He unconsciously waved his eyestalk above his dorsal surface to see the unseen audience that he could feel thrumming their approval of his words. A shimmer of light flickered chaotically amongst the hidden folk in the distance. He saw them hear him. Sloodat was gratified that he was being well received.

After a bit, when the rumbling acclimation subsided and they were still, waiting, Sloodat dropped the big one on them.

"Monkeys with machines inhabit IV." He let the single idea roll out into the darkness.

The response was silence. No audible humming of joy came back to him. It was as if he had spoken to nothingness. His eye saw the wave of flashing chemical light march away as the word spread. The emotional shock and surprise at his declaration reverberated throughout the crowd. Thousands of shimmering snood bodies lit up as news of the infestation reached them and unguarded emotional outburst of light rolled along the contours of the sea bottom where they lay listening to him. Waves of flashing anger, exclamation and fear lit up the contours of the depths of the sea and echoed back from the edges. Now, Sloodat could see them covering the seascape to the far darkness. They strongly flashed their incredulity. Not for many thousands of years had the registry assembly glowed so strongly from the gathered folk. The news was devastating.

"Now you know! Planet-Lord Sloodin is cleaning the planet now. He is doing it within the legal bounds as provided by registry law. There shall be no moral shame, but ..." he waited for it to sink into their minds. "We must now wait. As allowed by law I call for a stay."

Sloodat's slimed words floated out on the frigid waters of the profoundly deep waters of Homeworld and were greeted by more silence. The awful image of land creatures, polluting another world that the snood had found to be ideal, was a shocking revelation to them all. Who would have thought that the same thing would happen again? The terrible incident of 'The Kitchen' was, although ancient history to most, still an awful stain on the honor and moral foundation of the snood race. Mistakes had been made before and here it was, again, another chance for terrible spiritual disturbance. If snood acted in the wrong manner another failure of the civilization would befall them all and possibly another great family would be sacrificed to cosmic justice. The loss of IV, to poorly thought out remedies for land creatures, could plunge the entire culture into years of despair and spiritual longing for redemption. The actions taken to remedy IV's infestation must be carefully executed. The law must be followed.

A slow rhythmic chant arose from the unseen crowd. Sloodat could feel the throbbing vibrations of the multitudes questioning him. A reddish hue rose from the masses as their despair rose and a collective mantra prayer commenced to calm them.

"Thrroooommmm."

Duke Sleegat, stretched out a thin tentacled finger to Sloodat and screamed, out of order. "What is being done?!"

The snood masses calmed down a bit and the rolling thunder of their prayer subsided. Sloodat spoke his slime, "Sloodin has activated the magnetic bacteria, as provided by law, to change only his planet and not harm the creatures thereon. They will then revert to their natural state and abandon their efforts of war against us."

Sloodat made some quick calculations with his thought humps and replied with the last of his available strong phlegm. "One hundred and twenty eight is the minimum time slots allowed after Sloodin reports that he is successful in cleaning up the vermin before intervention ... legally." Sloodat pulled in his old ragged edged tentacles that had unconsciously surrounded and held onto the edges of the podium rock and waited for the howling he knew would come. It came, a slow sonorous rolling wail of despair mixed with approval from his friends and enemies alike. With the loud humming vibrations came also enormous flashes of light from the multitude of snood bodies expressing a wide range of emotion: anger, fear, dislike, sympathy, and also colors of tolerance and understanding. The sound was deafening and the emotional light show glimmered into the far distance, but the agreement to the timetable was overwhelming. No one would touch IV.

"Thrroooommmm."

Duke Sleegat's suggestion was out of order and Sloodat's comments forced the registry to invoke a stay. There would be no unlicensed run by anyone to IV. Until the procedures were complete there could be no interference. There would also be no revenue. Only registry sanctioned inspection teams, after the re-licensing had commenced, would go to IV. Sloodin would be left alone to do his work. When he brought clean samples and proof that the monkeys were under control, only then would the planet be reopened for business. It would take time, but time was what the snood had plenty of.

Everyone loved IV. It was the finest and tastiest planet that had ever been found. They lamented the thought of not being able to go there, even if most of them couldn't afford it and only wished they could go. The fact that it was so far out on the rim of the galaxy made it a special treat to visit and gave it an air of richness to savor. It was not the simple, easy to take sort of place one could find near the center of the galaxy. It was arduous to get to, and wasn't simple to stay on, but when there, "Oh wow! What a place!" There were heady thick and succulent rivers full of the organic detritus from rotting vegetation and animals in the deep interior of the land and clear sweet tasting Arctic Ocean currents with a refreshing mix of salty and fresh waters full of fish and all manner of aquatic life. The water's quality was highlighted by amazing dangers. Predatory creatures, who apparently found snood tasty, abounded. It made it all the more desirable. Extremists loved IV. Swimming in her waters was a definite star on one's vacation history. Even after 80,000 solar turns of visitation only a minority of snood could boast of having swum amongst the ravenous creatures of IV without protective measures. IV was a place of legend in their own time. It was the ultimate resort destination for all of snood-kind. A common fellow might work his entire life just to earn enough time slots in order to suffer through the long and terrible quiet to get there for a brief visit. It was the place to go. It was mythical and yet real. IV awaited them as paradise.

Sloodat ruffled his body edges and flittered out of the podium niche as the wailing and emotional body flashing about the de-registration of IV continued. He did not wish to politic any longer. His brother, Sloodin's father Sloodar, was off planet and on a counter core vacation/exploration jaunt and, so, out of reach. He would be livid when informed of all this upheaval. Vithlin IV made a tidy profit for the family. Any interruption in that cash flow would cause disruption to the legacy. Sloodat just wanted to go home and hide in his coral garden. If they wanted more from him or the family they would have to come and look for him there.

The ocean surface vibrated a huge circular subsurface disturbance from the registry congressional assembly howling and thrumming. Waves radiated out from that point on the ocean. No snood saw the surface waves miraculously appear and build as they flowed from the unremarkable spot on the sea, where thousands of their kind vibrated and hummed so far below. Snood don't surface fly much and they don't much bother to use their mere vestige of an eye to look at things. Rings of waves from the outcry below radiated from the open ocean spot and fled across the surface of the water world, unseen.

Sloodat slithered into his small planetary runabout and as soon as the iris door sealed he popped out of the water and flew home to his exotic coral reef garden. The outward rippling flow of waves emanating from the gathering below reached to the horizon.

Sloodat loved to look at things, he was a true eccentric, and he marveled at the unrealized commotion the deep sea conclave caused on the surface. A huge ring of surface ripples ranged out from the undersea congressional broo-ha-ha. He outpaced the acoustically created wavelets of animalistic snood response and watched the glittering sunlight dance off the surface of his ocean as it flitted under him. Marching parallel lines of natural planet wide combers mixed with the out-flowing locally caused congressional outcry in a cross-hatch confusion of conflicting water emanations. The transition zone of mixed wave frequencies passed under him and fell behind and the water returned to the familiar, solemn, uninterrupted planet-wide waves he was used to.

The never-ending waves of Homeworld paraded in even uniform phalanxes of momentum across her face. Their water world vibrated and shimmied in joy at its place in the galaxy. She was close to the core, yet far enough from the nastier rogues of the violent central chaos to remain vibrant and alive. Homeworld rolled with her twin brother moons. Her fluid nature lubricated the wobbly juggling orbit of her and her stabilizing little brothers. The three rocks hurtled around their happy yellow sun in a dance of perfect harmonious display. Shimmering reflections glimmered back from the sea at Sloodat and filled his childish curiosity for looking at things with the immense glory of his own home planet. He understood the unique nature of it all. He had been, 'out there'.

Sloodat knew the de-listing of IV from the active registry put their entire house in jeopardy. Falling revenues would squeeze other assets for output and their load of customers would increase with the revocation of IV from the menu.

The 'stay' would only keep the other clans at bay for so long. The registry couldn't physically stop Sleegat and his cronies from entering IV with their teams to discover any scandalous dirt on the Vithlin Line. They could publicize whatever they found to discredit Vithlin. Sloodat imagined they might even stoop to assisting the monkeys with machines if it meant that Sloodin would fail to re-register and therefore lose the licensing for the planet. He knew Sleegat for the treacherous old manipulator that he was and a scenario where the Duke sabotaged a morally correct effort in order to gain the upper hand wasn't so far-fetched. Perhaps Sloodat needed to distract Clan Sleedrack from interfering until Sloodin could stabilize and re-certify IV as a vacation resort.

Count Sleegin was Sleegat's son. He was a profligate and thin dandy of a snood. There were many holes in his character that could be exploited. If Sleegat was going to endanger the legacy of Vithlin by sabotaging Sloodin's effort at cleansing IV, then Sloodat needed to make some effort toward getting Count Sleegin into notoriety. That was not territory where Sloodat was wholly comfortable. He would put out feelers and call in some favors to find out what the Sleedrack's were up to. If they moved against Vithlin in any way Sleegin would pay the price for his father's folly. Sloodat wasn't so naïve that he couldn't take on the old Duke. He had done it before and he would do it again. Sloodat could gamble on Sleegat's overconfidence. Sleegat would think that Sloodat would want to remain quiet and inactive during the stay while the cleansing period occurred. Sloodat would foster that sense of control on the part of Sleegat to lure him into a false sense of security. Tending his coral garden made a fine cover for his work. Meanwhile Sloodat's spies would find out if Clan Sleedrack was working against them at the edge of the galaxy on IV.

Sloodat almost relished the thought of working while he relaxed in his garden near the surface – a warm water command-post. Sloodat warmed to the idea of luring Clan Sleedrack into a web of treachery that would backfire on them and allow nephew Sloodin to do his recertification work on IV. He was tired and wanted to rest, but he had work to do.

3

Happy Lair

A.Q. Day 4

Early the next morning a trailer load of youth camp gear and their horses were led down the back road to the Christian camp where they belonged. Dawn broke a hazy gloom of grey into the gulley. John banged on the door of the largest house. Jonas, the tall blonde leader of the young counselors answered.

"What's going on?" He rubbed his face wearily. Apparently the fellowship party they sponsored the night before had kept him up late. The house was full of people who stayed on after the fellowship.

"We got your horses back," John told him.

"Our horses? You got 'em back, from where?" Jonas slurred.

Alice came and stood at his elbow. She looked past the older man to Bill, standing at the edge of the sprawling decked porch. He stood tall and confident with his hands on his hips handsomely framed against the forest backdrop.

"We apprehended the bandidos last night. They were trying to steal cattle from a ranch in Fiddlestick." John turned and waved a signal to his men holding the horses, they led them to the camp barn. The little diesel tractor putted by with feed and tack. It was a nicely staged parade.

"Well, what are we supposed to do with them?" Jonas asked. "We're leaving today. We can't take care of them. They're not ours."

"Well gosh, I thought you'd be glad to get them back." John shrugged.

"Well, yeah. We're glad I guess, but now what do we do? We're planning on getting out of here today," Jonas whined.

Bill piped in, talking more to Alice than to Jonas, "Well, the way things are looking I don't know if I would advise you to go anywhere. Those guys last night were armed and um … well, there was a fight. Things are getting pretty scary out there. I am not sure it's safe."

"Look, Jonas. Could we talk for a minute?" John motioned to him to come out. Jonas pulled the fuzzy pink blanket around his shoulders and came out onto the porch. Bill stepped forward and spoke to Alice at the door.

John deftly touched the young man's elbow until they were aside and facing away and couldn't be heard. "Jonas, you are the leader of these people here." John stared into the young man's pale blue eyes. "They need you. They depend on you. You can't be doing things just for yourself here. You can't go running off across the country-side, the way things are getting, with a bunch of girls in tow. Can you protect them?"

"I don't see how I …? The only reason I am in charge here is I've been a counselor here the longest. Camp is over. I'm not responsible for them. I've got to get home. School starts soon and I've got to get home." Jonas rationalized his position. The whiney pleading with his Dad to let him borrow the car crept into his voice.

"Jonas. People are shooting out there. It's gotten bad pretty fast. The power is off everywhere and there are no cars running," John reasoned.

"I don't get it man. Just because the power is out? What's going on? None of this makes any sense." Jonas shivered slightly in the chill of the morning mist.

"We think maybe they dropped the big one," John said.

"You mean the earthquake?" Jonas asked incredulously.

"Not the big one earthquake; the big one bomb. It could knock out the power and the cars. It's the only explanation we have come up with that makes any sense." John was somber.

"You have got to be kidding? I mean that's just not happening. You mean like an atom bomb or something?" Jonas got louder.

"Easy. Let's not panic your people." John took his arm and pulled him further from the door. "They need you to be calm and make the right choices here. Yeah, maybe an atomic bomb. It would explain a lot. The point is, things are pretty screwed up out there right now and you taking everyone on a little hike is probably not the right move. We need to wait and learn more, before you risk everyone else just so you can get home."

Jonas looked out on the redwood ringed glade that was their front yard. Here, nestled in the peace of the old Christian camp, at the bottom of a deep gulley surrounded by huge quiet giant trees, the thought of what a bomb might have done out there, back in civilization, shocked him.

"We need you Jonas. We need you to be strong. We need you to help us save what we have. Who knows, there may not be anything out there to save, and besides, endangering what we know to be safe now doesn't seem to be the answer. We have people to protect and I was counting on you to help lead them." John cut himself off. He let Jonas chew on the words for a minute. Finally the young man turned to the older lion, nodded his head and assented to the suggestions.

"If what you say is true then we can't go now. And, even if you are wrong and we stay here a bit longer it might be better to be safe rather than sorry. But, what if we take the horses into town? We could get there pretty fast and see what's up?" Jonas flopped on himself too easily. He wanted to get away from the camp. He wanted to go home.

"We got word from Saint Rose. It's a shambles. There is no transportation and no word from the bay area. You really want to take those girls and run into the brothers of the murderous thieves we met last night? Please, take care of your people. You are the only one. I saw how you handled the crowd last night. You have a gift. It's your Christian duty to minister to those who need it, here, now." John practically bowed his head to the young man.

Bill glanced over his shoulder and thought his Uncle John was really laying it on thick.

Jonas nodded again in acceptance. "I know, you're right. We will wait. I will do what I can to keep things together." He was disappointed. He wanted to go home.

John reached Jonas' hand and quickly brushed his lips on his knuckle. "Thank you Jonas. Thank You." John then stood up tall and barked at the perimeter where four men appeared. "These men will be here for you. They are good men. We can't let thieves take the horses again can we? They will not get in your way and they'll stay at the barn mostly. I want at least two here, near the houses at all times, so don't freak out. They're here to protect you."

"Do you really think that's necessary?" Jonas asked.

John got that look on his face and stared at Jonas. "Did we just have a conversation?" He said it sternly and with the dangerous tone that cut through the childish doubt Jonas exhibited.

Jonas froze, swallowed and said obediently, "Yes Mr. Ritter."

"Sir ... John," John said flatly.

"Yes-sir ... John," Jonas repeated quietly.

"Bill! Let's go, we have a lot to do today. Alice, good to see you again. You can go back to taking care of the horses now, eh?" He smiled warmly and nodded to her as they turned and marched behind the house where men held his horse. They rode up the hill to the Happy Road lair as it was being called.

Jonas heard their horse hooves pound away unseen. His eyes stared unfocused as he shambled back into the house.

Alice spoke to him as he passed, "Are we going today?"

"Not today. Not today." He stepped over people sleeping on the floor and went back to bed and tried to forget the look in John's eye.

Alice was secretly happy that they might stay a while longer. She liked Bill and wanted to get to know the handsome young man more closely.

John, Bill, and their posse of three, rode the finest thoroughbreds from their raids. As they passed through the stone pillared gate, it swung open for them. John saluted the guards who crudely snapped to and knuckled their brow in response. They rode to the stables in back and dismounted. Men came and took their mounts to be groomed.

John finally toured the barn and the surrounding grounds in daylight. It was a sprawling complex. He could hardly imagine one or two people owning such a large piece of property. Only a few days ago it was not out of the ordinary for just a couple of people to occupy thousands of square feet. There was room enough here for dozens. The yard had sprouted camp tents and a tepee. He walked the perimeter until he at least knew which way was which. Finally overcome with exhaustion, and yawning, he found his way back to the house. Mark directed him to what was once a large walk in closet, now a private sleeping room. John lay down for a few winks and tried to let the rush of the last few days sweep by and leave him in peace. He fell into a deep sleep of the truly tired in the quiet, dark, windowless closet.

In the early afternoon John woke, splashed his face and found his nephew sleeping on a corner sofa. "Bill, call the company."

A call went out and after a few minutes of the word being passed the main room filled to bursting. There were women and kids among the group. They had been arriving all morning. These were the sandwich list people who had been fulfilling minor tasks and recon for Mark and John for the last two days. They had been gathering at Happy Lair with information and pilfered goods and camp gear. The bedrooms of Happy Lair turned into stock rooms: one with toiletries; toothpaste and brushes, soap, shampoo and the contents of medicine chests for miles around, another with underwear, socks, and shoes, and another with canned goods. The largest internal bedroom was an arsenal map room and library. Bookshelves covered the walls and a conference table filled the open space as clerks busily cataloged and organized the stores.

Mark Young, rotund, fifty eight years old, short ponytail and Fu-Manchu moustache, was the king of the roost. He was in his element. He puttered about, setting people to tasks, directing his bureaucracy of household. Upon the call for a meeting, his clerks closed their respective rooms and gathered in the main hall with the rest of the assorted company at Mark's elbow.

When the moment was ripe, John entered with Bill at his side and his three killers in tow. Joe, George and Jack had proven themselves quite ruthless and efficient. John was gratified to have them at his back. He was worried he would have a hard time finding the right guys to do what needed to be done. The cream had risen to the top and John and Mark had scooped them off cleanly. John stepped up onto the raised dining room step. He looked over the motley and varied folk as they quieted.

"Welcome!" he said with a huge smile. "Welcome to Happy Lair. If you don't already know, I am Sir John." There was a smattering of nervous laughter. They had all been interviewed by John and Mark. "I want to let you all know how honored I am to be able to serve you. I shall do all in my power to assure we survive."

He bowed long and slow to the crowd. They became still and silent watching the man bow to them. No one had ever in their lives bowed to them. He had fed them. He had listened to them. He had given them unswerving hope in the face of enormous doubt about the future and here he was bowing low to them.

"I want to introduce some people. You may know them, but I want everything to be clear." John gestured at his young nephew Bill to step up. He put his hand to his shoulder and turned him to face the crowd. "This is William. If you can't find me, William is my deputy. He is my eyes, ears and voice. I listen through him, I speak through him. He is here to help me serve you. Please welcome Squire William." They applauded.

It sounded pretty strange to poor Bill who had never in his life had to stare down so many people much less have them clap their hands for him. He blushed hotly and people laughed good naturedly.

John gestured for Mark to step forward. "This is good Mark." They all broke out in applause and a little cheer right away. Mark was a likable guy and had interviewed and assigned tasks for everyone in the room. He was jovial, nice about everything and people liked doing things for him. He shucked and waved a little and stepped back to the side right away.

John gestured to the sergeants at the side and they came up. "These men are William's crew. They are here to help him. Dave, Brick, Bob, Joe, Jack and George." He held out his hand like a game show girl showing the prize as he spoke their names. They stood chagrined as the crowd clapped. "These fine fellows are here to help us. Please help them do that. A big round of welcome for these guys, eh?" Everyone clapped and a whistle pierced the thunder of applause.

"Now I have some important things to say." John stopped and bowed his head for a moment as the crowd calmed down. "We are starting over. The old world order is gone. The new world order is in this room. We must be very strict about some things that we never really thought much about before. There are no more stores. There are no more factories in China making shoes and toothpaste and socks for us anymore. Our hands are the only ones that will feed us. Understand, the police are no more. This group is the only one who will protect us."

People fidgeted a bit and looked aside at their new allies.

John continued, "there will soon be thousands of starving people coming here. It's not their fault, but they have no choice but to take what we have and to destroy us. We must prepare. Do what is asked of you. Do it gladly. Do it well. If we act in time we will survive this." He paused and let the words stew a little. Everyone stood still and stared quietly at him. They waited to be told what was coming next. John had been the only thing in their lives that was in control for the last three days. They wanted him to tell them what was next.

"Last night we caught thieves trying to steal cattle and horses from a ranch in Fiddlestick. Because we were prepared, we stopped them, and we saved the livestock. Now we have to deal with cattle and horses. Most of us have never done this kind of work. We must now learn to do this. We don't have time to grow crops this year. There may be no food before winter is over and we get a chance to plant something. So, we must become cowboys, and girls." He nodded deferentially to a group of fairly tough looking mountain-momma's standing together. "There are also a lot of other animals out there scattered all over the countryside that are going to be eaten up by wandering hordes fairly soon. We must save them. This ranch, Happy Lair, everyone is calling it I guess, is going to be our main camp. Work parties according to ability will be formed and we have a lot of work to do. Things are just not going to be easy any more, but we must do them if we are to survive."

John noticed a woman standing to the side holding a toddler. They were both red haired. The kid had a real orange carrot top mop of hair. John gestured for her to come forward. He held out his hands as to where she should stand. He saw the young Carpenter boys standing to the side. He motioned to them. Dave Nickel caught their eyes and stepped down and prodded them to move. They stepped up beside John. "This!" He put his arm around the woman with the toddler. "These are what we are doing this for. These children will survive. All of us will survive. We will make it happen!"

Bill stepped out and started a "Hip! Hip!" He tried to get them to "Hooray!" The first one was feeble. People just don't do that anymore and they weren't used to the prompt. Bill did it again. "Hip! Hip! Hooray!" The second time people got the idea and by the third time they roared. "Hip! Hip! HOORAY!" and they cheered and clapped their hands and nodded and smiled and milled around slapping each other on the back. John gave the mother a peck on the cheek and waded slowly through the crowd shaking hands and greeting everyone in the way of the finest politician.

The rally was over. John retired with his deputies to the map room. They closed the door.

"Mark, maintain course and speed?" John lifted an eyebrow at his good friend.

Mark smiled slyly and nodded. "On course, Sir John."

"Anything I should know?"

"All is going well. Goods are coming in regularly and our agents are getting all the unattended stuff for miles. We're on the move to the camps further west." Mark nodded at Bill and Joe, they smiled. "We will be moving stores before dawn," Mark reported.

"Gentlemen," John addressed his three main strong-men, "I am awarding each of you a fort. Each of you will take possession of the three main outposts on the ridge west. They will be yours.'

Mark broke in, "I have assigned assistants who are, at this very moment, collecting your loved ones and their goods from your homes and bringing them up onto the ridge top." Each sprawling mansion was being turned into a chain of lairs. These fellows needed to see benefit from their risk right away. Mark's organization and John's blessing was making that happen. Joe, George and Jack each now commanded large estates that were once only the dreams of those peering in through closed gates. Now the gates were theirs.

The three tough guys beamed with pleasure at the news.

"Thank you John."

"Yes, Thank you, Sir John," they all smiled.

"As always, you are two steps ahead of me old friend, Brick, Bob, anything?" John asked them.

"Not much Cap. We got men working on the perimeter fence and the barn is filling up. Horses are secure and fed. So are the cows. I guess they are dairy cows and a couple of women insisted on milking them. So we got a bunch of folk going up to the meadow and trying to figure out the best thing to do with them. We ain't really got a real cowboy yet, so we're not too sure what to do with them," Brick said.

"I see. Well I will work on that today. Dave? Do you have anything for this meeting?" John gave the teenager his moment.

"I got six more kids together. We are going down to the Christian camp to take care of the horses down there today, if that's OK?" Dave said.

"That's good. Yeah take them down there. I also want you to work this area." John indicated the farms to the southwest on the map. "We need more intel from around here. Take them kids on a horse ride if you can. Nothing spooky. Totally in the open. You got it? You are kids. Make sure one of the guards down there goes with you. They need to learn to ride too," John suggested.

"Will do Captain." Dave snapped a salute. His dark black hair fell over his eye.

"How's the semaphore going?"

"We're all making flags. It's working good. I got a whole string up to Sentimental already. No one comes that we don't know about first." Dave replied.

"Good. Mark, we need six good bicyclists with bikes to volunteer at the firehouse for courier duty to Saint Rose, and not all at once, they are supposed to be freelance and not associated with us. We need to know what's going on there."

"I think I have a couple of guys that will be perfect for the job … Sir John." Mark smiled and cocked one eyebrow.

John chuckled, "I need a food requisition for Sentimental. Bill, would you and Mark work out a package of goodies for today's sandwich recruitment? I am going to do a little ranch inspection. I don't even know where the can is around here yet. I ride in an hour," John commanded.

"Already working on it Milord," Mark agreed.

They all nodded. Not much else to say. The list of things to accomplish was long. There was a lot to do. They filed out and went back to their tasks.

John spoke quietly to the side with Mark, "Milord? I kind of like that."

"I thought you might. Sir John eh? I kind of like that too." Mark smiled a cagy little smirk as they left to their respective chores.

John was greeted like an old friend by everyone he saw. The place was a bustle of activity. Workmen were boarding up windows, building fences, splitting wood, pushing cart loads of lumber around and working in the barn. Mark had been busy delegating authority and assigning lists of tasks to be accomplished. John didn't know any of these people beyond possibly having seen them casually in the post office when he checked his box for mail once a week. Now they were calling him by name and seemed ready to do anything he asked. He didn't ask anyone to do anything. He asked people how they were feeling. What they thought about their task or what was on their minds, things that Mark or John's crew mightn't have thought of. People were owning it. They were taking the entire communal exercise to heart. They were each sharing what they knew toward a common goal. All John and Mark had really done was provide them the script and they acted on it. They had a good idea where they needed to go, at least for the short term.

John came upon group of women he saw at the meeting. He vaguely remembered two of them, but the others were new to him.

They were women together, perhaps lesbians, more than likely they were those who were once known as crones, women past the youthful sexual dalliances with men and having children and the insanity of the modern world and were now trying to find their way through maturity.

Mature women in the post modern world had been confused so severely. Family and womanly ways were, for most of their lives, portrayed as some sort of betrayal of the feminist movement. All their adult lives they had been encouraged to do things that were not the forte` of women. In doing so it had hampered their overall confidence. In the name of post modern feminism they were denied the pride of doing things that they were really good at and suited, by their gender, to do. So they had spent their lives trying to do things that did not come naturally to them and the things that they were inherently good at, remained wholly undeveloped. Now, in their later years they were hamstrung by not being able to easily make their own clothes, nor did they desire to set a good table for the warriors who would fight to keep them safe. They had allowed the empathy and nurturing of their characters to languish un-tuned for so many years that they had become callous. They were not the healers and creators of life anymore. They were merely aging into their maturity. They were dragged from their youthful beauty into the oldness of sagging lives. They should have been secure in a legacy of children and family structure around them. They got older only to find they were alone − alone with others exactly like themselves. These vibrant souls cloaked in pudgy form before him were all near John's age. They were the kind of women he had grown up with. John respected the older women as much as he pitied them. He introduced himself and asked what they were up to. They did not respond overly friendly.

"Hello. How are you ladies today?" John asked casually. They stopped sorting through the sacks of clothes around them.

A cheery little woman replied, "It's a little hot today."

Another less than happy looking woman with some serious jowls spoke, "Do you know who is responsible for … this?" She indicated the clothes.

"I'm afraid I don't know what you mean," John answered.

"Who decided we should sit here and sort through other peoples' laundry? Who thought that was a good idea?"

"Now, Lois, Don't go stirring the pot. He doesn't know anything," Gladys, a thin silver haired woman, said.

"No, I really want to know. Some jim-crack kid who works for Mark, told us if we wanted to be here we had to sort clothes. I think it's a waste of talent, if you ask me," Lois groused.

"Well, what do you think you should do instead?" John asked her.

"Well something less menial at least," Lois persisted.

"I don't mind so much," said Nancy. She threw another pair of jeans on a pile.

"Well, anyway. Whatever the reason for sorting clothes you get first pick." Another woman, full figured Shirley, sporting large out of style glasses, gave her two cents worth.

"I don't want any of these rags." Lois held out a silk blouse in her fingers and let it drop.

"Come on, Lois. No one else has any idea of what's going on. Sorry, she gets frustrated." Gladys flashed a beguiling smile and batted her eyes at John.

"I do not get frustrated! I just want to do something more important. This is child's work."

John listened and then asked, "Speaking of kids, did you hear about the little boy who got hurt earlier?"

"No, was it bad?" Cherubically rotund Nancy peered up from her pile of clothes, genuinely concerned.

"What boy? Where?" Lois blinked.

"He's resting in the barn now. He got a nasty splinter. Do any of you know any thing about doctoring … or nursing?" John prodded.

The women exchanged glances.

"Even if you don't, the boy could use a little kindness. He's feeling pretty sorry for himself; his folks were in the city." John concluded.

"I've done a little nursing." Gladys piped in.

"I think I'll just go see that boy," Nancy said as she rolled over and levered herself up.

John lent a hand to Nancy. "We're probably going to need a hospice or clinic of some sort before too long. Maybe you ladies might find that a more interesting chore." He threw out as he turned and walked away.

The women were resistant to being told anything by an alpha male. They couldn't be told 'to do' anything. If they did do as directed they could blame the task-master for any failings and conclude the idea wasn't any good. But if they thought it was their idea then they might flourish. They were rediscovering their latent skills slowly and on their own. They rode the wave of protection through sheer inability to cope with the possible new world and its dangers. John's hint at the need for a hospital may have given them something to hold on to, at least he hoped so. He let them decide what to do. He didn't tarry, but left them with the planted seed of the need for a clinic. Either they took hold of it and made the idea their own, or they didn't and would, before too long, be left behind as useless. John didn't look back, but he did mention it to Mark.

4

Enclave Spirit

Day 5

Jonas rolled in a tangle of bedclothes as the thick fuzzy blur of his mind slowly surfaced to consciousness. He mouthed sticky goo that coated his tongue and teeth and groggily opened his rheumy eyes to the dark interior of the main house. Last night, the second night of fellowship meeting around the campfire had turned into quite a party. The sacramental wine flowed freely to soothe the stress of recent events and Jonas imbibed a little too much. He sat up on an elbow and cast around the room to remember where he was.

"Oooooooh," a warm lump of bedclothes next to him moaned and tugged at the covers.

Jonas was on the living room floor of the main counselor's house. It was a communal bedroom now. The central heating didn't work, so he and the camp counselors ended up sleeping like puppies in a single clump of mattresses and blankets in front of the living room woodstove. Thick memories of the fire-filled night impinged on his forward planning. He wasn't even supposed to be here. He was supposed to be on his way to a Colorado dorm-room in the seminary.

Jonas realized he was naked and he felt embarrassed. His mind reeled trying to remember what he'd done during the late night debauch. It wasn't like him. Very seldom did he drink, much less get drunk, but the stress of the crazy world and being stuck at summer camp and the heady power of leading the fellowship around the fire and the friendly people, had overcome him. He gave in to temptation and here he was, hung-over in a communal bed, naked and feeling like shit.

A banging from upstairs jolted him to more completely awaken to the wine headache that coated his consciousness in a veneer of pain. Jacob came clumping down the stairs dragging his backpack. At the bottom he slung it onto his back, "Oh, hey Jonas," Jacob said.

"Hey. Uh, going someplace?" Jonas croaked hoarsely.

"I got invited to go up the hill. I can't stay here anymore."

"Well, uh. … what about Kimmy and school and getting back to Arkansas?" Jonas asked. He didn't really give a hoot about Kimmy, he was more concerned with Jacob's path.

"Kimmy is going to stay here for a while until she feels better, but I gotta' get a move on, those guys offered me a job," Jacob explained as he headed for the front door. "Look, they're waiting for me, I gotta' go. I'll see you later. Thanks for everything, man." Jacob slammed the door behind him.

Jonas couldn't formulate any kind of rational conversation. His brain was still thick with alcohol and Jacob's words pounded into his forehead like a physical force. He watched his co-counselor, summertime-friend, go out the door. He waved feebly.

Jonas wasn't sure who was in the bed next to him. He crawled free of the bedclothes, tip-toed around the room, found his pants and the rest of his clothes and pulled them on. He was terribly thirsty. He got water in the kitchen, struck a match to the propane stove, started some coffee and tried to remember what happened after dinner. It was all a blur and he turned his thoughts to getting his hangover taken care of and planning his next move.

He wanted to leave the camp and get on to school. He was expected. It was all planned out. All he had to do was get to Colorado. He needed to leave the Christian summer camp and get on with his life. It was the last year he was going to be a counselor and he seemed to be stuck. The world stopped, with him in summer camp. How was he going to get things back on track when he couldn't even get a car ride out of the redwood gulley? And what in the world got into Jacob that he left so early? "A job? What kind of job could they offer him?" Jonas thought about the old guys who talked him into the campfire sing-along church services. It seemed like a good idea to have a fellowship service before they left for home. That was two days ago.

How he had ended up holding another, and even larger, campfire service for the townspeople last night, he wasn't sure. They showed up and he welcomed them. It was almost as if it was a decided thing. They came to him and he performed. Campfire songs and words of God and Jesus and faith and fellowship flowed naturally from him. The people last night were totally different than the first group. Last night were true Christians. They didn't balk at the invocation of Jesus' name. The first night they wanted it all very general and non-specific. Last night was a good old fashioned, bible banging, revival meeting.

The men on the hill who asked for the first service weren't there last night. They had orchestrated the first night's gathering and for some reason Jonas didn't fully trust them. They were old and although they seemed friendly, now, after the fact, it felt as if he had been manipulated by them. Manipulated to do things he wasn't sure about. He acted on their invitation to hold the dinner campfire service two nights before. It seemed innocent enough. Nothing bad really happened, but he couldn't help feel as if he were being used somehow.

A warm soft body slid up against him from behind. Two arms enfolded his waist and he was being hugged from behind by a girl in a very thin nightgown. Jonas turned to see it was Becky, Bruce's gal-pal. Each of the guys and gals had paired up over the summer. None had any kind of romantic relationship before the camp season, but as the summer progressed and their young hormone laden souls intertwined in the love of Jesus, they found one another. This was all wrong though. Becky and Jonas weren't an item. She was supposed to be with Bruce.

"Oh, Jonas, mmmmm," she cooed and pushed her warm soft body into his every fold, hugging him intimately and close.

He couldn't rudely rebuff her. She clung to him in need. "Becky?"

"Hmmm?"

"Where's Bruce?" he asked gently. He felt her tense up.

She held him tighter, "I don't know and I don't care." She shuddered a little at the loss of Bruce, but knew she had traded up.

Jonas turned and hugged her as he realized they must have broken up and he was now her comfort. He had to help her deal with her loss with the love of Jesus through him. He felt his pants tighten as her sexual odor mixed with the smell of freshly brewing coffee. Jonas held her for a moment longer, bent and gave her a quick kiss on the head and extracted himself from her grasp.

"Coffee?" he asked.

Dark haired Becky nodded and got powdered creamer and a spoon.

They poured a couple of cups and sipped.

"Where's Alice?" Jonas asked.

Becky stiffened a little. "Well, she didn't sleep with us," she smiled slyly and wrapped her bare feet around Jonas' under the table. "Maybe she's with Bruce," she said with acid in her voice.

His seat squirmed a bit as he tried to project outward calm. "I see." Jonas had hoped to get close to Alice from the first of the season. She was blond and pert and just full to the brim with attractive happy-go-lucky exuberance. She radiated good feelings and Jonas had worked to get her confidence all summer. None of them could blatantly act on their sexual feelings for one another while camp was in session. The after season clean-up was usually when hook-ups occurred, but this year, when the crazy world shut-off, things were all messed up. He was hoping to get Alice's address in Utah and maybe go see her during the upcoming school year. He could envision a future life with her— marriage, kids and happily ever after. He didn't push it too hard all summer for fear of putting her off. Now it seemed he had blown it by comforting Becky in drunkenness. He wanted to pursue the question and find out where she was, but Becky didn't seem receptive to any further inquiry.

"You were really marvelous last night Jonas." Becky flattered him. Jonas worried about what she meant. "I mean your service was top notch. I didn't realize you were such a powerful speaker. I think you did better than Richard."

"You think?" She had his interest.

"Yeah, I mean you really got those town people going. They loved your sermon and your prayer made everyone feel so much better. They really liked you."

"There were some strange people there, huh?"

"Yeah, they were really searching and you led them to the Lord."

"I drank too much I'm afraid." Jonas hung his head.

"You weren't the only one."

"I don't really remember it all."

"Nobody noticed. We all needed to blow off a little steam. I mean, the way things are now, what with the world so … different and all." Becky's feet massaged his under the table and she poked her toes up his pant leg. Her feet were cool against his warm calf. She slurped her coffee.

He stared at her. He couldn't just tell her to stop and leave him alone. That would be mean and insensitive. He didn't want to encourage her either. He didn't know what happened between her and Bruce and he was equally in the dark about Alice.

"So what are we going to do today?" she asked him.

"I'm not sure. Jacob left. He said those guys offered him a job up the hill. Maybe we should go up there and see what's going on."

"But, what about the enclave?" she asked.

"Enclave?"

"Yeah, last night you said we were going to make an enclave of spiritual study here. You told everyone. Don't you remember?" She rose and came to him.

"I did?" Jonas was struck. He couldn't believe he had promised to stay here.

"You helped them get settled in the other buildings. There are a whole bunch of people here now. You're in charge of the camp. They cheered you. Remember?" Becky looked at him as if he knew all about it. He remembered nothing about what she was saying. She slid into his lap, wrapped her arms around him and nuzzled her firm young breasts against him. She was warm and soft and smelled of desire.

"Becky …"

"You are in charge now. They listen to you, to us. We're the ones who have to lead the flock." She held his face in her hands and kissed him briefly. "We have our own congregation. This is truly god's work. They want to be saved … and we're the ones that can do it. Isn't that wonderful?"

Jonas was transfixed by the vibrant young woman sitting on him. Her warm bottom heated him up, her words of power took him to a fantasy-world of religious fame and fortune, her caress and kisses pulled him into sexual desire for her dark beauty. He couldn't move and heard himself say, "Yes, it is wonderful."

5

Sleerdin's Curiosity

She brooded, deep dark cold, long quiet still, big thoughts went out from her to 'us', and returned amended. Only short flits to hot vents interrupted her spell of contemplation with 'we'. The situation; as perceived and believed, addressing circumstances assailed upon their selves, their implication and anticipated forward action by their group, was the question. The thought went out. It came back, changed. The idea reverberated amongst the mass huddled on the sea floor. The predicament they were in was analyzed; torn apart, each fact bared, its simplest terms defined, revisited and agreed upon, to each point of logic in the chain of decision, before sent on to be agreed upon or changed, and sent out again. The gatherings' consideration flowed inside a free form mass of chemically communicative slime on them. They clustered tightly. Their encompassing communal phlegm carried the conversation in coded notions of chemical savories and smells and odors of innuendo and metaphoric historical context. The discussion moved in viscous swirls and eddies of current, driven by thought, driven by the spiritual force of their combined will to be 'one'. Driven by their mutual tactical proximity, the vibration of their bodies, an outward manifestation of their mantric exchange of fluid caused them to hum as they contemplated the mess they were in.

"Throom," they vibrated and moved the thoughts held in their shared mucous. It was their process.

Sleerdin pushed the agenda by insisting that the remaining minds on IV be tasked with pro-action. The old snood below, who weren't able or inclined to vacate their posts, normally spent their spiritual time below thinking great thoughts about the universe. To ask them to think about an alien threat was asking them to plan around insanity. They were looking at things on a grander scale. The universe was a known wonder of change. The spiritual thrust for snood, when off the job, was massaging well-worn synapses in their comfort zone. To have a juvenile family pet officially direct their prayers, to consideration of so alien a concept as war, peeved them no small amount. She pressed them by participation. The strength and amount of thought imbued goo could overcome less powerful ideas. Sleerdin spent far more time in prayer with the congregation than she ever had before in her short thousand year old life.

"The planet is ours, registry verified. Water is sacred. The water is changed. The change is not good, it stinks and has mutating properties. The source of the 'not good' is the land creatures. They poison water. We can do nothing 'to' the land creatures, by law. We know nothing about the land creatures, or their motives. Speculate solution."

"War, they attack."

"Invaders, they want our seafloor."

"Stupidity, they don't have a clue what they're doing."

"Vengeance for some slight, and misplaced none the less, for we could have done nothing to them. It's forbidden and so has not occurred."

"Jealousy of snoodkind, after all, we are covetously placed."

"Those poor creatures must live their lives in suffocating warmth, unbearable light, and (always a shudder of revulsion) the dry. How horrible to endure such a hellish existence without the loving fluid embrace of ocean around you."

It was as foreign a thought as they could imagine. To suppose intellect, devoid of wetness, thriving, under their very noses, on the surface, would have been discounted as impossible if not for precedent. It was conceivable for lower brutes to evolve in the gaseous air (their tasty detritus was proof of possibility), but to imagine intelligent creatures who could manipulate elements for production of artificially synthesized poison that they then conspired to send down the rivers to attack, was hard to believe.

It was, however, the conclusion they came to.

There was a history from between the lines. The current Compendium listed a previous incident of similar nature in bare terms. There was an entry, but no location or time of discovery or time of demise. The slime records were very spotty about the myth of the 'Kitchen'. That didn't change the fact that snood had encountered this phenomena before. The saga of the Kitchen lived in song and myth. Snood found the wonder world, it was infested and stubborn, snood devised a remedy, it killed the planet. Shame and remorseful guilt was the lesson.

Now they were confronted with a similar vermin problem, but they couldn't eradicate them. The vermin were working against them and they had to wait for rescue or death in the farthest reaches of the galaxy. Saved by Homeworld or poisoned by aborigines.

It was war, whatever the reason.

The snood clumped together in their pitifully small mass of holdouts. The residue workers left behind to take care of the various villas, palaces and mansions, tour guides and site docents, machine and craft shopsnood who stayed to repair any ships or infrastructure and a smattering of rental and facility service workers, had all come to commune with their own kind. The congregation had gathered out of necessity. No one wanted to turn feral. There was no spiritual support alone. The synergistic feedback loop of mind that a crowd evoked was powerful, and needed a mass of snood to take on strong and rejuvenating qualities. Staying solitary, or in small groups only led to eventual decline and early death for them. They huddled together, the entire known population of the resort planet Vithlin IV, and thought about their circumstance. The salve of contact and mantric chanting was, to their souls and in turn, to their bodies, very therapeutic. Snood could stretch their lives for tens of thousands of years with the power of thought as their fuel. It kept them young and vital. Once away from the mass, the aging process took hold in earnest. A still snood with brothers lived and an active snood alone perished. All of them clung to the other as they worked through the problem of their stranding on the harsh jewel, IV.

"The concept of war is not unknown."

They had fought inter-clan rivalries in ancient times and the sagas recounted those times of woe. The conflicts were only a couple of generations distant, yet there was still a collective memory about it. The real difference, that was putting a wrench in the whole conversation, was dealing with an alien species altogether. How to fight back against pollution of the water that fed their oceans' habitat?

"The enemy are unknown, but not unknowable."

The most prominent artifact from the historically fabled planet known as the Kitchen were the survival spacesuits. They were shaped in an approximation of the creatures on the Kitchen in hopes of assuaging the native's fears when snood attempted to make a meaningful contact with them. That turned out badly, but the suits remained as the only extravehicular method for traversing the surface of the land. It certainly wasn't possible to swim. As ungainly as they were, the suits were usable and therefore could be used to learn about the animals.

The thought progressed.

"In order for the animals to be observed or examined, they must be approached somehow, and that meant someone had to don a spacesuit and go onto the land."

This was a terrible thought indeed. The throoming hum of their vibrating bodies rose to a discomforting level and pitch. Anxiety and fear pervaded the crowd. The conclusions were painful to think about and not popular. Disturbed congregants slipped away to linger in anonymity around the delicious fountain of the volcanic vents. Spewing mineral water gushed, boiling, from the floor and filled the water with tastes and nutrients in their most raw form. It was heady and intoxicating to bathe in the saturated sea. The pleasure centers in each snood's thought humps were massaged with rich pure elements. It was a break from the discussion.

"It was Sleerdin's insistence that we find this thought. Sleerdin wanted pro-action before Sloodin returned with help. Sleerdin has the burden, Sleerdin shall go learn about the enemy. Go Sleerdin, go. Let this mind return to quiet. Return when you have information we can act upon."

The mass of slithery folk squeezed more compactly and practically squirted Sleerdin out of the mass. She slipped into the bare naked water of the cold deep blue sea, hovered there alone and let the residue of her kind wash off her. She thought her own thoughts now. They gave their best. She had her answer. She got what she came for, permission.

She dove down to the vents and kicked up bottom mud as she nudged each snood she could, in hopes of finding collaborators. She needed more than her office crew at Sloodin's HQ and her two sidekicks, to do this chore. That was how she found her team.

—

White puffs of vaporized seawater splashed up and away from Sleerdin's personally grown runabout as she flew headlong through blue wave-tips of the great open ocean. She loved wave skipping IV. Surface-surfing was about as galactically cool and viscerally absorbing an obscure talent as one could get. The skill required was true. Her world's single fat satellite, strong enough to cause global tidal flow, interfered with and twisted control commands. The strong bending of space by the secondary mass near IV made for tricky gravitational surfing. Most snood said, about flying on the most famous jewel in the cosmos, 'Damned big moon!' Driving fast near the surface was tricky and lazy handling, possibly catastrophic. Sleerdin aimed at the coast as her machine bounced jauntily on the bumpy water.

She reveled in the exuberant brisk wash of her underside and squealed high pitched throoms of joy as she bounced along in gleeful abandon. She vibed her way along, humming and steering, constantly veering in control, she flitted from wave to wave, bouncing and caressing the ship with warm water. Her gelatinous body smeared the forward interior of the pressurized fluid-sphere's control surface. It resembled a reef wall, full of holes and rills. Sleerdin was plugged into, and clung to, her surface-surfing-egg. She flew the egg as herself. She felt its skin. She sensed its every jostle, bump, push and pull of the hull as it moved between water and air. She knew how to ride.

"Plugged in, turned on, in tune, riding the fluid of my world," she throomed a song in rhythmic cadence as she flew toward her uncle's office in the shallows.

Sleerdin balanced her vessel's gross apparent mass in dancer's fashion. It was her crucial capsule. She couldn't go galactic, but she could live in it and she flew it like it was a part of her. She writhed and shuddered and chemically teased just the right amount of magnetic field from the toroid band of super-ferro-magnetic dark matter around her to remain between heaven and IV. She blew and sucked magnetic flux through the yacht's skin as through her own and bent space to skip her form-fitted craft as herself along the surface of her gem of a planet, like an exuberant child jumping neighborhood curbs on her bicycle. She hurtled toward the land that ringed her world.

Sleerdin was home-girl on the greatest extra-Homeworld planet known. This was her backyard. She grew up on IV, to her control twist was normal. She'd never been anywhere else. She was a backwoods hick way out on the rim. She'd never acclimatized to any different environment. She was attuned to her planet and, as closest kin to Lord Sloodin himself, technically owned it. Skipping the surface without goin'-a-space was her sport and joy. She could easily space her way about and let the slime-reader run her course from place to place, but she'd have missed so much. Autopilots were handy, but manually flying the surface kept her in tune with home. She tasted greenery from the shore ahead and savored her planet.

Sleerdin knew the face of IV better than any snood in the galaxy. She liked the surface; it was a place of learning, where conditions collided and things changed. The exterior of the planet was her backyard.

The surface wasn't snood-norm. Deep-dark-bottom-dens, were normal. Cold-lying, and being deep, awash in currents of spiritually tasty slow thought, was what regular snood did with their off-time. Strong ideas, exuded by most-thoughtful-elders, wafted philosophical aroma over snood masses huddled on sea floors. When a core communal thought was well tapped, heavily scented ideas teased congregational ooze to gush forth from the masses. Shimmering ideas wafted over the populace on the deep ocean currents. They were compounded, added to, modified and amplified as they washed through a gathering, and re-oozed, stronger and more contemplative. It was marvelous feeling community of mind in tightly frigid masses that worked toward specific solutions. Civilization formed and manifested itself as a cohesive effort through this process. All the achievements of snoodity could be traced to communal thinking. The conundrum of whether or not to venture beyond the resource confines of Homeworld's ocean to explore the cosmos was determined in this way. Every major endeavor of the snood species was addressed through communal thought on the sea bottom. It's a snood's natural way. It was huge and intimate. Snood loved to lay about, massed in phlegm-like slow-motion slithering masses, in almost frozen waters, under enormous pressure, in the darkest pitch blackness at the bottom of the sea, and think about things. With minimal energy expenditure they ate little, moved little, and thought together. They thought great thoughts, lived upwards of a million years, and had dared to explore the far reaches of the galaxy. The learning curve however, for modern snood, who spent time down deep re-hashing great thoughts from the past, was shallow. There just wasn't that much that was new to snood collective thought.

But, out here on the rim of the galaxy, on the ultimate vacation resort planet, IV was a place of myriad new experiences. Sleerdin always saw something new when she surface-surfed. When she went below, she brought new thought. It wasn't always welcomed, so she seldom went down-cold-deep. Sleerdin lived more topside than down-cold-deep. She was a warm water kind of snoodlet, she had to be, to tolerate the uncomfortably tepid shallows. She bore the heat and became used to it because that's where everything happened and where she preferred. Life expressed itself in colorful abundance near the interface to the gaseous atmosphere. The visual stimulus was astounding. Sleerdin delighted in teasing her minds with fabulous colors and the emotionally charged contrasts of IV. Up-top it was hot, but never dull.

A whiff of earthy land-musk filled her minds. She slowed herself slightly and peered to see the familiar outline of islands looming ahead.

Sleerdin followed her Planet Lord Uncle Sloodin's eccentric habit of looking at the visual world. It enthralled her to discern the world with her eye instead of by taste alone. Ever since Uncle Sloodin taught her the telescope, she fell in love with the optical. She took her uncle's weird habit of looking at things to the next level and rarely spent time in darkness, below. It was too slow and gloomy for her down there, there was so little to look at, but topside there was always light somewhere and plenty to see. There were interesting, frightening and inspiring things in the light, so that's where she lived.

Wrapped around the golden eyepiece in slavering embrace, she piloted closer to the deadly land ahead. The edge of the sea was a myriad of snood death-visions, but when respected and avoided was tame and inert. Most snood were terrified at the thought of coming anywhere close to the edge of their aqueous world. It held mystery, was very difficult to taste or smell, and its desiccation was alien hostility to them. The dry, was death most certain. She drooled at the sight of land and its delicious nature.

Sleerdin reveled in the solid contrast of the seacoast. Land was a great puzzle and interested her no end. The telltale odors from land were second-hand because she couldn't taste the terrans directly, only their river-wash scent. She watched them and tasted their effluent. It was her vocation to make sense out of the smells by comparing them with observations made through the crystal eyepiece. Her thought humps batted visions from her eye back and forth with contrasting wispy aromas and she studied them. She spent her life watching and tasting traces of dry things and so, she thought she knew how it might be working. It was all speculation, but no one could disprove her theories about what was going on out in the atmosphere. No one else had ever bothered to study it. The mechanisms at work on the earth were unknown, and although traceable, the latent odors she sampled gave only clues as to what was really occurring. Sleerdin had unusual hypotheses about the land and its denizens, she had to, she was the only one trying to understand the war against them.

Sleerdin, and her uncle's assistant Slingin, worked to train recon crews to use the primitive visual approach. Most of the residue maintenance workers they conscripted, balked. They were suited to their jobs down deep. It was a confusing concept to watch where you were going. Snood smelled and tasted where they were going. They followed trails of scent and odor and were attuned to chemical traces in water around them for guidance. The slime-lines laid down on the floor by foregoers and guides were how they went about. Very few groped about blindly in the darkness of the deep with no slime path to lead them. They were essentially herd animals who followed with noses in the behind of the one ahead. They liked following the slime of a leader. Scent tracks were easy to follow and usually on the path of least resistance. A slime-trail held scent from returning snood that described destinations and so, goals could be anticipated. For a snood to diverge from a pre-slimed way and not know where they were going was not customary. To go where no smell had gone before was a leap from the average snood's comfort zone. To forego smell entirely and use their feeble eye to chart a course, was beyond reason.

"Who leads ahead? How do I anticipate the journey's end?" the rookie pilot complained.

"Trust your eye." The instructor, Slingin, said firmly.

"The horror, the horror! What is that?! I can't smell it!!" The newby pilot, most recently a house residue mitigator, screamed and plunged into the depths for safety. The round craft plunged from sight into the waves.

"What are you thinking, Slingin? You, of all snood, doing the dirty work of that... that, snoodlet." The rookie accused the instructor.

"Smeedor, you have to understand. I do Sloodin's bidding. He is our Lord."

"It doesn't matter what he wants, it doesn't smell right, and I should know, I work in residue." Smeedor argued as he aimed the craft deeper, away from the distasteful light.

"We are the few left here to keep things in order. You must get hold of yourself and help us in this, Smeedor," Slingin reasoned.

"Must I? I already have a job to do and it doesn't include killing myself on the surface." He fled from the control wall of the craft as soon as they reached ocean darkness and huddled near the sleep sockets.

"Look, Smeedor, I didn't want to have to pressure you on this, but I sign your check. You are going to have to do whatever we assign to you. This is a state of emergency."

"I just can't Slingin, my thought humps debate what they see versus what I smell and I get sick, it paralyzes me. I just can't do it. Please let me go back down deep." Smeedor was losing emotional control. His viscous speech-phlegm was thick and tinged with fear and high anxiety. His skin flickered uncontrollably.

Slingin sighed, "Allright, fine, go back to the mansion. I'll find some excuse." He understood the house-snood's reticence. They were creatures of the dark. They were asking too much of simple workers.

"Oh, thank you, Slingin. Thank you, so much." Smeedor was in tears. He slapped the proper patch on the slime reader auropilot with his one extended tentacle. The biological software engaged automatically coded course coordinates and they popped out of the water and straight up to space, safely away from the surface, the planet turned under them and they fell back down to splash and submarine to the mansion docking station.

Slingin hated the chore of training the untrainable to do the unthinkable for an absent Lord on a closed planet. It seemed futile.

When he returned to corporate office on the tropical reef to report, he found it filled with pilot recruits. Slingin hovered at the edge of the crowd and listened.

Sleerdin was speaking to the group. "The future of IV must rely on you, sport-snood, to fly our reconnaissance." Sleerdin smelled Slingin's presence, "Ah, Slingin, is your trainee ready?" She squirted a direct slime of inquiry.

"We lost him to fear, Milady."

Her newly inducted crew, resort surf instructors and dedicated sports enthusiasts who hadn't fled with the exodus, snorted quiet derision.

"As you can all tell, it's been almost impossible to get any of the house-snood up from down-cold-deep to help," Sleerdin continued.

"It's hot up top," one of the macho pilots mocked.

"So much light's not natural," another complained sarcastically.

"My eye? How gauche. I can't see the smell?" Another chided with a sardonic smirk. Mirth slime floated among the team of hard-core wave surfers as they made fun of the wimpy house-snood who couldn't make the grade. The idea of looking at things was uncomfortable for most stuck-in-the-mud snood, but here was Sleerdin, a pushy family-company female, paying them to engage in a juvenile act and practice their sport. To the surf-bums and extreme sporters this was their dream job.

"All right, all right, everyone has their talents. Residue must be controlled. So, that means there won't be enough of us to cover the planet, but we're going to do our jobs as best we can. We can at least monitor the heaviest river outflows and get samples until we can show registry a clean kitchen." They seemed eager, but they were just surf-bums, like her. Sleerdin hoped she was doing the right thing by employing these rag-tag surface-surfers as her defense force.

The surfacers listened and got what they wanted from the lecture. They knew that as long as the planet was delisted they would get paid to skip-wave to their hearts' content on the greatest resort planet in the galaxy. It could be decades.

Sleerdin's crew was a mix of low paid, one-term, employees who gave wave-surfing lessons in rented eggs to high end clientele, some loose-end fellows who had, one way or another, slipped through the regulatory cracks and overstayed their leases, and a couple of young very upscale professional surfing clients who had been caught up in the emergency conscription. They were all going to get to skip waves on IV for free.

Sleerdin droned on. "It's an ugly job and toxins will weigh heavily on you. We've documented mixtures that mimic estrogen-like hormones. These hormones are artificially produced by the dry enemy and the effects could be devastating for us as well as it has been for the local life, especially up the rivers at their source."

The tone took a somber turn.

"So, we have to go up rivers?" One wealthy snood, Sleegit of House Sleegat, asked with a tinge of snobbery. He'd been left behind when his family cut their vacation short.

"That's where we need samples taken, yes."

There was general rustling and some murmured comments.

"That's where we found the worst infestation." Slingin chimed in from the back.

"Skipping waves is one thing, but flying over land … that's a different school of fish." The haughty snob replied.

"We're giving you top of the line wave skippers with full compliments of survival gear." Sleerdin said.

The two rich kids, Sleegit and his cousin Snoogin huddled together and slimed the same thoughts at the assembly. "I have my own yacht, snoodlet," it was a pointed jab to her leadership, and gender, "I'm only here because the law demands it, but the law does not compel me to go over land, nor up rivers."

Slingin was used to dealing with the upper-class and slid into the mass. "Using her eye," he referred to Sleerdin, "she figured out that dry animals were to blame for the sour-soup. She followed toxic odors, from your family's villa, Sleegit, up the river to its source."

The two rich kids pulsed a muted green light of barely held irritation as they clung together as one, in silence.

"She staked out those locations until she unraveled the mystery." Slingin was telling a horror story that snood could barely fathom. "Dark dry land creatures attended a structure connected to ropes that led across the countryside. She followed them." There was a gasp at the thought of this young girl following her sighted course away from water, across landscape. "She found," he paused for affect, "electron pulsing machines, and there were no batteries."

The pilots and surfers murmured at this spectacular supposition. To pilot a runabout over the land, with no water to take refuge in, was the height of dangerous endeavor.

Slingin went on. "She watched them until ... she brilliantly concluded that they created electron current mechanically, and with that force made the poisons." These most intrepid explorers of the hostile ocean surface huddled together in fearful embrace at the land story.

For her to probe into the workings of an alien species waging war against your own kind was heroic, or mad. That one was a real stretch for them, as well as it was for their Planet Lord, Sloodin, when he first heard the tale. Creating electrical flow without chemical interaction and without infusing flux-enhancing bacteria into ferro-magnetic materials was a novel crude leap, it was far-fetched to imagine much of a potential electrical difference and could only be attempted in a dry setting and therefore had never occurred to snood. Never-the-less, the dry animals had somehow figured out how to surge great quantities of very crude current through ropes on land to manufacture death and proliferate monstrous mutations. Recognition that dry animals had power and used it to wage war against snood was revelatory and devastating. What Sleerdin discovered upset Sloodin and caused him to flee core-ward, to Homeworld, to seek help. It stunned the young snood surfers who intended to monitor the horrible things and they lay quietly on the office floor in a mass, absorbing the thought.

"Sleerdin, a snoodlet, yes, was left in charge as chief planetary manager. In her Uncle Sloodin's absence, she'll lead us, a mere cartilage crew, to monitor and document the dry creatures in their war against our beloved wet realm. We will all go up the rivers; we will all do what we must to save our ocean. We will all watch. And that includes you two."

The rich cousins cowered.

"Let none hesitate to follow where a mere snoodlet has gone." Slingin said with gooey finality.

The crowd processed the story and creamed approval of Slingin's speech. They spewed derision directly at the two rich kids for balking at the task. They were in solidarity with Slingin and Sleerdin.

"Let none hesitate," they called out.

After a few moments for the current to clear the water, Sleerdin declared boldly in blue tinged phlegm. "I have been tasked to roam IV and vigilantly watch the enemy. We're trapped on this faraway frontier and doomed to make notes on dry things and monitor sour tasting water. It's not an enviable job, but those were Sloodin's commands. I go forth. Do you follow my path?"

"We're snood enough to follow your slime," they said and throomed a vibratory accolade to Sleerdin. Sloodin's office dripped with blue intent from the wave pilots.

"You know what he said just before he left?" Sleerdin posited to the now rowdy group.

"No, what?" Slidit, the eldest brother of Slidik clan called back to her.

"Keep an eye on them."

For a moment there was silence, then the gathering broke into open laughter and writhed about in a squirming laugh-mass. (Since snood only have one eye each, and it's generally never used, it was funny.) Even the rich boys joined the joke.

After it calmed down a bit she said, "He was sincere. Those are the orders. We'll observe the dry animals and learn all we can about them." Sleerdin was more vested in their mission than any of them, after all, it was her home-planet, she was born here.

Their defense fleet was comprised of rental planet-class sport-abouts. The resorts niche marketed them to wealthy sport-snood who dared to skip the surface of IV. They were the best money could buy and specifically designed for IV. The craft were equipped with telescopes for driving manually and dampened toroids for horizontal travel close to the globe. That was the death defying sport of it. Teasing an egg to surf on IV was not safe. The ocean was finite and line of sight navigation was the only way to bounce the fluid gas interface and miss the hard land at the edges. It took skill and practice to skip the waves on a planet that was notorious for its treacherous gravitational twist on control functions and its innately dangerous hard edges. The surf-bums and elite pro-skippers in Sleerdin's crew prided themselves on their ability to go where they would and do what they wanted on IV. They would ride an extravagant rental regatta.

Slidik Clan brothers Slidit, Slidir, and their brood brother Slidil, lay close to Sleerdin as she gave them their orders. "You three are to monitor the western ocean north of the equator. I know it's a lot, but I haven't any others. You boys are my best and I need you to watch it all. The northern continents have shown the greatest concentrations of the poisons and we believe it is there, we will find the strength of the enemy. If there is anywhere that we'll be able to notice a change in the poison levels it will be there."

"Sure thing, baby." Slidit caressed her pilot tentacle with his own in a familiar pattern. "What ever you say planet mistress." His tiny fingers tickled the underside of her and he smiled as he said it.

"Be serious, will you, Slidit." She hardened her extended arm. They were all four enmeshed in a tangled globular mass of themselves to facilitate close conversation.

The other Slidik brothers tittered at their older brothers' familiarity with the boss.

Sleerdin exuded a mild corrosive acid to discourage their mirth and bring them to the table of sober discussion. She held them tight in her acerbic covered tentacle-like arms as she ordered them as subordinates. Sleerdin approximated the map coordinates to them and continued.

"There are three large bays on this north-eastern shore, the southernmost is benign and of no interest, the two in the north are well infested with the creatures and I want you three to spend the next eighty revolutions sampling those."

The youngest brother, Slidil, piped up. "Eighty revolutions on one ocean? Come on Sleerdin, you know we're the best surfers on the planet."

"Been there lil' bro'," Slidir added, "There are some monstro humps on that coast. And the land is all, like, a big cliff and easy to see. You can't miss it."

The humorous reference gave them all a chuckle.

"Fuuuunnny." Slidil retorted to the jibe about not missing the shore, which would kill. Surfer humor.

Slidit calmed the brothers. "Guys, it is a huge piece of ocean. It's the biggest. There are gonna' be some gnarly chops to be had. Don't worry doll, we'll take your samples." His tentacle snuck into another delicate crevasse beneath her enormous eyestalk.

"Slidit." She said with feigned indignity. She enjoyed his boyish charms and he knew just where to tickle her treat. "You have to go into the big bays," she slimed the locations for them to retrace onto their slime readers in the ships she gave them. "That's where the dry animals spew the worst. We have to establish a baseline of toxin, so we can tell when it abates."

"If ever." Slidir threw out cynically.

"Sloodin, our planet Lord, has gone to Homeworld and will bring relief force to stop their attacks on us. Be sure of that." Sleerdin said almost too firmly. She hoped to believe it herself one day. The devastation of the attacks unnerved her. She wasn't at all sure there was a solution or cure.

The poisons drained down the rivers into their beloved sea, in floods and deluges. Strong traces of concocted hormonal weapons had forced early and rapid change of sexual development and behavior in the sea life. Local sea animals suffered large populations of female transgendering and failed to reproduce a healthy cross section of traits that normally kept the gene pool robust. These populations were now vulnerable to stresses that had been easily resisted in the past. Some collapsed under the strain and entire populations of sea life behaved abnormally, they changed sex. The onslaught was disturbing on a level of coldness that gave any spiritually minded snood the shivers. These dry animals were ruthless in their attack on the sea. They went right to the heart of all creatures' existence, their ability to create healthy offspring who could, in turn, procreate themselves. The offensive was constant and deadly.

"Yeah, right, Sloodin will save us." The middle brother, Slidir, scoffed.

Sleerdin's grasp on him tightened uncomfortably. Small welts burned into his flesh where she held him and increased the acidity. "The great Sloodin, shall I remind you, is my Uncle Sloodin, Son of Sloodar, Nephew to Sloodat the explorer, and we are of Vithlin Line and owners of this planet. Or does Clan Slidik forget who their masters are?" Sleerdin was pulling aristocratic rank on him. She knew she could threaten him and his older brother would let her. Slidit was enamored of the snoodlet and as long as she didn't mess with the youngest she could have her way with the smart-ass middle brother.

Slidir relaxed and hung loosely in her embrace, showing his acquiescence to her superiority. She could have easily killed him in this posture, but she didn't. She valued these guys too much. They were her best surfing buddies. She had to establish the pecking order clearly though. It was war and dissension in the ranks was not acceptable, even from friends.

"Yes ... Planet Mistress." Slidir answered respectfully.

She caressed the other two with the tips of her masculine tipped pilot tentacles and her grip loosened slightly. The conversation was not over. Her thought slime fed directly into them as she carefully squirted her private thoughts. "You three are my core team. You know, I love you all. I hold each of your sperm for my eggs one day. We shall make great snood when this is all over. We shall meld our clans, but I must have your obeisance. You must be the example to the others. If I have you behind me there is nothing the others can question, especially those Sleegat cousins."

They floated neutrally buoyant in still embrace for a few moments. Slidit curled his most sensitive tentacle into her eyestalk fold and gently stroked it with his residue whisking fingers, right where she liked. Slidil, the youngest, curled around her hind-arms and inserted himself into her main residue duct, a symbol of complete subservience. Slidir, the middle brother, who liked her the least and was most likely to cause her trouble, shivered and reached his main pilot tentacle into her feeding mouth. He was showing her that he trusted her so much that he put his life in her hands, if she refused him she could chomp off his main appendage and he would die a cripple. Her four main appendages stroked and flowed over the three male snood she held against her. She touched them all in their most sensitive places with a caress of knowingness and familiarity that displayed her acceptance of their loyalty.

"Good, I accept your service to the cause. Go now and report back here at corporate, once every solar turn, with your observations and samples."

The other snood in the office chamber hovered close by them as they hugged. It was not polite to interrupt their boss and so the other surfers waited quietly as Sleerdin finished her conversation with the brothers. Her speech slime was direct and private, so the other snood had little clue until the end, when the brothers and Sleerdin released what was discussed to the group for digestion. The gathering rejoiced when the solidarity of Sleerdin's core team members shared their intimate pledge of loyalty to her. In the dark no one used their eye. The gathering never saw the ministrations the brothers gave to Sleerdin. Her crew of surf-snood were impressed and fell in line automatically. The most hard-core snood brothers known, were solidly attached to the agenda of their new Planet Mistress, Sleerdin.

Sleerdin's crew flew their wave skippers to every corner of the planet and found land creatures' toxins everywhere. They collected samples from near the great rivers and stored them for their annual meetings.

6

<u>Shire</u>

The first few days after the quiet, John's posse rode hard while his friend, Mark, deftly organized the teams of raiders and a growing cadre of camp followers. The two men forged ahead with a plan of acquisition for their rapidly coalescing group. Captain 'Sir' John, the leader, and his second in command, 'Seneschal' Mark, along with their Lieutenant 'Lords', moved fast. They capitalized on the world changing event of the quiet. They knew there would be only a short window of opportunity to get those things that they needed. Their influence grew as they collected people, stock, and territory. It was a gathering time.

Before the quiet, the daytime ratio of people to houses in West County was low; most drove to the city every morning for their jobs, people were at work, dozens of miles away when the quiet came. Those who survived the long foot-sore hike home found their homes empty, looted, and more often than not, burnt down. The wealthy, non-work-a-day owners who visited their resort homes at high summer, were lost out in the wide world, and had little thought of their deep forest retreats. Their buildings sat empty most of the year. Some estates' status were 'for sale', and likewise empty. The few stay at home self-employed or retired folk, minded their own business and hunkered in until the power came back on. Lots of houses were fully stocked, but empty of caretaking residents. The gathering was easy pickings.

Homes for miles around, in an ever widening circle, were sacked. There was no one to object and occupation was easy. Just walk right in and take what you wanted. The only real barrier was the socially constructed reticence at taking other people's things. Everyone got over that pretty quickly. Every useful manufactured item that would soon be a scarce commodity was pilfered: clothes, soap, toothpaste, drugs, and of course guns, anything that could not be made, was made off with. The loot had to be taken somewhere and a chain of commandeered ridge top mansions became household compounds that formed what people started calling the Shire.

Sir John's key lieutenants were each given a 'Lordship' over a household compound. Brick and Bob, the tough carpenters whom John recruited in the Federal Hotel bar, along with Joe, Jack, and George, the older retired vets who had allied themselves to Mark in the Sentimental parking lot, each commanded squads of willing men and rode out daily from their mansion forts. They stole, ransacked and moved as much livestock, goods, and foodstuffs to their hilltop villas as the day would allow. Distinctive households grew west from Sentimental, on the ridge to the sea.

The forested countryside of West County emptied of structures as the Shire looted and torched a several mile wide perimeter around their core forts on the ridges. The Shire's population grew as these fast moving fellows ruthlessly gathered anything un-guarded and duly noted any food or resource asset for later visitation.

Real estate lots were large in West County and most people couldn't see the next door for the trees. In the first weeks, their work-a-day commuting neighbors' houses flamingly vanished, and then silence — nothing but quiet and a smoldering foundation lingered where once had stood a house the next door neighbor may have visited once or twice, if at all. The Shire's web of information and persuasion expanded. The lure of food, security, and community, drew people hungry for order to them and their forward-looking intent.

Those who sat still and waited for things to go back to the way they once were, got left out of the loop. They found themselves alone as the first week flit by. Food ran out as their days of waiting and watching rolled past. Many of them stayed home, eking out the last remnants of dried rice, canned goods, and water. They waited for the world to turn back on. Homebodies had no idea that they were alone until it was painfully obvious. When the retirees and stay-at-homes bothered to look out their windows they saw people moving on the roads. By the end of the first weeks those peripheral solitudinous souls were sending messages to Sir John, via his kid network, for safe passage to his more sustainable position, or they just packed up their stuff and joined those on the road and hoped for the best. They figured that all those marching people must know something and be going somewhere, and so, they joined them.

Herd mentality was a powerful force when faced with starvation. After the first couple of weeks there wasn't anything left to eat in the house, or in the surrounding redwood rain-forest.

—

Jimmy Carpenter watched his little brother Phillip walk up the driveway to the wide auto turn-around in front of the modern glass fronted house. They had done this dozens of times and it was becoming routine.

The gangly twelve year old Philip walked right up to the front door and knocked, loudly. After a few moments of silence he nervously knocked again. Jimmy watched from hiding. He knew they had to wait until the hesitant people inside got up the nerve to answer the door to a lone twelve year old. This was the most un-nerving time; until they answered, or the kids decided it was empty, so they could descend on the ranch style home and take what they wanted, they had to wait.

Jimmy crouched quietly in the bushes and waited. Phillip stood like a trooper, all innocent kid-like in the porch overhang as if he were selling candy for the elementary school music program. Finally the door cracked open. Jimmy couldn't see the people inside. He had to depend on Philip to make contact. After a few moments the door closed, Phillip turned and made what, to an inexperienced eye, looked like some crazy arm flailing dance steps. He executed semaphore signals to his brother.

"2-o-l-d-g-u-n-g-o-a-w-a-y."

Phillip finished his dance and quickly walked away from the sprawling retiree's home, back down the clean driveway, around the bend and out of sight of the houses' inhabitants before he darted into the bushes to hide with his brother. Jimmy had already given the retreat signal to the other dozen teenagers and kids in the bushes around the house. He could only see a couple of them, and they could only see a couple more, on around the property. Hand gestures flashed around the unseen gang hiding in the woods, quickly, from kid to kid. These folks wanted to be left alone and they were armed.

Of course, Jimmy noted on his map the few fruit trees and any other significant resource assets on the grounds before he and his merry band of gleaning thieves moved off and disappeared. The kids loved this game. They were getting very good at it.

The kid corps proved to be an excellent way to reconnoiter. They were under strict orders to refer all requests or negative encounters back to Seneschal Mark for higher level attention. The corps was only to ransack empty homes. At any sign of resistance, they fell back and moved on. Everyone was suspicious of everyone else.

Shoot first, ask later. Folks hid in their homes for a week or more and waited for the world to turn back on as all the futuristic apocalyptic delusions fostered by the now non-existent TV came to fruition in their minds; lonely folks were leery of anyone. Kids were a good way to make contact. One kid at the door was a non-threatening emissary.

Through the kids, people could approach Sir John to join the mass of people in his household compounds. The initiative of individuals to go it on their own dissolved into a need for company, society, and other folk. If they decided to join the group their final commitment would be to swear fealty and let the Shire strip and scorch their house for the good. Then you and yours and what you could carry, would scurry away to hide in the woods with a ... 'Lord'?

The world had changed. The moment of the quiet was a demarcation point in people's lives. The shock of no electricity was initially borne well by people. Power outages were never a truly dire concern because it always came back on after a bit. Everyone was confident that it would come back on. That was the mindset of society. In spite of all the dire predictions of environmental cataclysm, and the almost forgotten cold war doomsday prophesies, people lived confidently in the twenty-first century status quo of American civilization, that would, of course, continue to blunder forward somehow. Electricity did a lot of things for us so we didn't have to actually do them ourselves. The electrical magic worked for us quietly, dependably in the background, unseen and always powerful and ready. It was the least of our doubts and fears.

We trusted the magic energy juice. It was a certainty. Rotate some copper wire in a magnetic field and you have electricity. A scientific certainty. A lot of things fluctuate in our lives, but that is a fact. It dare not betray us now. It can't refuse to flow along the ugly wires strewn across the land on poles. And now … nothing worked reliably except your hands and feet, and ammunition. Everyone was now faced with laborious daily chores for basic needs, which, only a few pumps and motors did before the quiet.

People were stranded in their useless islands of four walls with growing anxiety and paranoia. It was only ten days when the secondary migration of the hold-out locals and retirees increased noticeably. In the second week a large majority of people decided to move away from their dark foodless homes, towards … help?

Hot days increased, the power stayed off, and as the first couple of weeks wore on, people became much more easily convinced that this was the new order of things. Apparently no one was going to come and turn the world back on for them. There was no radio or TV to assure them of relief. The phone was dead and the car wouldn't start. It was already too late to act. Now they could only react. Canned food in people's pantries dwindled rapidly and the momentum of John's people to move in a positive direction was alluring, even if it was outside social norms.

Not only the houses and their goods in the forested uplands, but the ranches and farms in the valleys below were targets for forage. Each day Sir John and his Lords' posse rode longer and farther from the hill top forts as the ring of gutted houses expanded.

There were still a few farmers and ranchers who actually lived near their own cattle in the valleys below. Young, dark haired, Dave, and his reconnaissance teenage scout troop spread out and put together reports of resources ahead of the marauders. Sir John was briefed on each farmer and dairyman before he rode up. He was preceded by a young boy or girl, of about twelve or thirteen to announce his coming. These youngest teen scouts were young enough to not appear as a threat and old enough to do exactly as they were told. They were initiates into young Dave's teen troop and eager to please.

The teens brought 'good news' to the ranchers.

"Help is coming."

They presented handwritten letters of introduction tied with bright colored ribbon and greetings in official looking script that promised relief and the return of some semblance of normality.

Mark was a crafty seneschal. He had formed a cadre of administrators to produce beautiful official looking hand written missives and letters. Each letter or proclamation was calligraphed in fine handwriting and official artwork adorned the margins. No letter left his seneschalate without a flourish or personal mark of a, sworn to oath, clerk. Mark's files grew and people had jobs tending them. It was organization. Bureaucracy. Heraldry.

People fit surprisingly well into the feudal structure of a corporate organization that was driven from the top down. Most people had worked most of their lives under such a paradigm. They had always thought their lives were their own as they quietly and subconsciously gave their life allegiance to faceless executives above them. Mark used their need to be useful and their modern conditioning to advantage.

They provided the field teams with very official looking letters. It gave the foragers supportive back-up from an authoritative source. They were empowered by official paperwork. Government was really a concept of officialdom more than a visible force. The paper-pushers fell into this structure smoothly and quickly.

Teen corps carried the decorated letters ahead of the men. After summing up the situation and having made their strange little semaphore dance that gave John the all clear to approach, he rode into a farmyard and greeted the owners warmly. He dismounted and shook hands, he exuded energetic joy at seeing the ranchers as if an old friend visiting. He was the long awaited help, security, stability, authority. He had great news and was going to re-establish the world with them. More often than not he used their names, he smiled, came with an open hand, and exuded joy at meeting the beleaguered folk.

Before long they would sit, as John offered that they brew up the ground coffee, and share the fresh baked little sweet cakes that he brought.

"So, it has been pretty tough down here, I gather?" John prompted.

"Damned right," the dairyman blurted. "What the hell is going on? We haven't heard a thing in days." The forty-something-year-old man held out his hands.

"There has been a change. How are you doing with your stock?" John probed.

"It's been a nightmare. Without power we can't use any of the milk machines. We've been trying to get the cows in and do a little by hand, but it's just overwhelming. Millie and I can't do all the milking ourselves. The cows have to be tended to and milked regular or they dry up. It's too much." Seymour Handel complained as his plain faced wife, Millie, clung to his shoulder and nodded assent.

"Well, we are here to help," John assured.

"Great, you have a generator then. If we can just get back on the milking schedule we can survive this." He gave a hopeful look at Millie. She smiled tersely.

"Well, I'm afraid the power is not going to be an easy fix. As I said, things have changed. Everything has changed. The world has changed." John sipped the hot coffee, lightened with fresh cream, and sucked at his pastry. He let the silence linger.

"What do you mean the world has changed? Look, whatever is going on out there is no real concern of mine. I only give a rat's ass about whether my herd produces. No production, no mortgage payment. You get my gist here?" Seymour squinked his face sideways at John.

"Seymour, listen close for a minute. Millie." John looked her directly in the eye. "Things have changed so radically that there is not going to be any mortgage collector. The bank is gone. The power is not just down for a bit. It's gone. Finished. No more." John let his words settle. "Our best guess is that a nuke went off and ruined all the power somehow … Look, we aren't totally sure what happened, but we know what the upshot is, at least for now."

"Oh, Seymour," Millie gasped.

"You can't be serious? This isn't just a local power issue? What? Maybe Iran or North Korea or what?" Seymour got wide eyed.

"We really don't know for sure who or why. We do know that electricity just isn't working. Not anywhere. For anyone. Society has pretty much collapsed. Your milk customers will not be bothering to come get your production."

"Oh my, Seymour." Millie was almost in tears.

"Hold on a second here. You mean to tell me the world has come to an end? The big one happened?" Seymour stared into John. "It's all over?"

John sat still for a moment. He sipped coffee and gave a slight nod. To his side sat his deadliest killer, one of them always sat with him during these friendly conversations, he sipped warm coffee and snacked on sweet cakes while showing a pleasant and sympathetic face.

After a few moments John said. "It has gotten very bad out there. Soon there will be a lot of people roaming across your land, tens of thousands, maybe more. The city folk will soon be out of food and then they will come here. They are going to come marching over those hills, ravening hordes, starving people, and they are not going to want to help you milk your cows."

Lieutenant Lord, George, who had sat quietly aside till now, held the dainty china coffee cup in the remaining two fingers of his left hand poised just below his lips and said, "They are going to cover your green fields like locusts. They'll devour your cattle on the spot. If you resist the slaughter of your livestock for their one night feast they will kill you all."

Seymour and Millie looked at the man with the mocking smirk on his face and missing fingers with horror.

John broke the moment. "Your choice is to face tens of thousands of hungry people alone, or take an honored place in our Shire community on the ridge and be protected."

"Or, of course," George chimed in again with more fearsome foreboding, "You could wait until the Sheriff comes and takes them. You have heard that he is confiscating all livestock you know?"

Seymour and Millie looked at him in bewilderment.

John enlightened them. "The county council set up a stockyard in Saint Rose. They declared martial law and have authority to manage any thing they want. We offer you the chance to continue to manage your own herds," John offered softly.

"They'll take my cows to town? What for? They live here. We are here."

"They are confiscating all livestock do be doled out as they decide," John answered.

"Aw, that's nuts. If they drive them to town it'll take a while to get 'em to milk again," Seymour complained.

"They won't milk 'em man. They're slaughtering," George popped in.

Millie pleaded with her husband. "Oh no! That's not what my folks wanted. We're supposed to maintain the herd. Keep up the stock. My parents spent their whole lives putting this herd together. We have a prize milking herd here. You can't slaughter them! Don't let them take them Seymour. Please, you can't!"

"We don't want to let anyone hurt your herd. We want you to continue the dairy. We have safe areas where we can go, away from the bar-b-que pits and government forces. They're your cows after all," John offered.

"Take my cows somewhere safer? Uh ... well, what about the labor? I've been under the gun these last few days without power. My hands left. I have a lot of equipment and hay, I can't just leave," the independent farmer pleaded.

"I have men for you. They will be under your supervision," John recited from his script. Mark was thorough in providing such a script. Some things you do say, and some you don't.

"And this man here, my lieutenant, George Bentham," John introduced George with a hand on his back, "will attend to your needs personally. On my word I guarantee it." John held out his open hand and looked the previously debt ridden farmer in the eye.

Seymour took John's hand after a moment's hesitation and a glance at his partner/wife to be assured of her support. She tightened her lips and nodded.

"Good then." John pulled two elaborately decorated hand made identical scrolls from his inside jacket pocket. He unrolled them onto the gingham tablecloth and with a flourish signed his name at the bottom of two identical copies in big scrawling script. He turned the papers to Seymour and proffered the archaic fountain pen. Seymour took a deep breath and after signing he gave the pen to Millie who likewise wrote her name at the bottom. George signed as a witness. The darned documents looked like they were made by medieval monks.

John, blew on the ink to dry, gathered his copy and held out the other to Millie, "Excellent. Now I have to get going. George is at your command. His men will take care of your cattle as you see fit. He is your Lord," John declared. He stood, shook Seymour and Millie's hands perfunctorily, turned and strode out leaving his half nibbled cake on the table.

George filled the space John left in the farm kitchen and smiled his un-nerving sideways smirk and shook their hands also. He snatched John's leftover pastry, popped it into his mouth and left the quaint farm-style kitchen. The screen door slammed behind him.

Outside the house John signaled with a wave. He mounted and rode off with his posse around him. There were more farms and daylight was wasting.

Lord George's squad appeared from hiding. Diesel farm tractors pulling hay trailers crowded with scrounging teams, roared into the farm yard. Horsed riders had already been driving cattle from the fields to higher ground. The outcome of the meeting meant nothing to them. They started moving cattle the moment Sir John went into the meeting. A core of minions mustered around their Lord George and, under the peripheral supervision of Seymour at his elbow, began the roundup/stripping of the property.

Sir John rode to where another Lieutenant Lord and his squad awaited in readiness, hiding in the low hills nearby, ready to move onto the next farm.

They rolled across the countryside. Teen emissaries, Lords and their men, the air of authority with papers and smooth talk, all backed with a constant stream of smoking noisy tractors with trailers and old diesel dump trucks which flowed to and from the farms to disappear, laden, into the thick forest above.

There were of course some industrialized corporate factory farms operated by hired hands. Some loyal employees had stayed to take care of the animals they didn't own. They got a visit from John, whereupon they were informed; that the cattle were no longer theirs to care take of and they, in a very officious sounding announcement, were dismissed from their duties.

Mark had a very nice scroll drawn up proclaiming this. John read it with a smile and then held it high for them. Most corporate workers, almost universally Latino cowboys, acquiesced immediately upon hearing the proclamation, paid a cash bonus in worthless one hundred dollar Federal Reserve paper notes, were allowed to gather their things, and go. For the most part they did just that. They wanted to go home and take care of their families. Cash talked and the bullshit … stayed in the fields.

One Hispanic man asked to join John. Jorge. He became the first real Latino cowboy in the Shire. Jorge rode to help his new Lord assemble cattle. He loved working cows and had no real family in America. The funny thing was, it was George's squad that he ended up riding with. Jorge was amused at the thought of having the same name as his new 'jeffe'.

One corporate farm resisted. The foreman was on site the day the quiet came. He was manager of the absentee corporation's shareholders' livestock. John had barely finished reading his proclamation when this company supervisor, Bill Blanching, a hard nosed guy who had plenty of dealings with Hispanic cowboys and tough cattle stockyards in Nevada, started shaking his head and wagged his finger from side to side.

"No. No. No. Who the fuck do you think you are? These cattle are property of Amalgam Corporation and until I hear from ..." John did not flinch, he showed an innocuously bland smile as he turned, pulled a pistol from his lieutenant's hip, and shot Bill, point blank, through the nicely worded proclamation, several times. Bill fell as a sack of rocks to the floor of his cheap trailer office. John tossed the beautifully calligraphed scroll full of holes onto Bill's still quivering body.

When John cut loose, all of his men in the trailer opened fire. Those were John's standing orders. When he shot they all shot. At the first sound of gunfire all of the company's ranch hands that were close enough to the proceedings to witness the act were summarily gunned down. The poor employees had no idea that the gringo corporate lackey had doomed them. John didn't give them a chance to recant any statements of dedication to the now non-existent corporations who had once owned the cows. If John started shooting, it was over for them all. Those were his orders. He was very strict about the killing. None of it would be in passion. It was to be complete, and without exception. It wasn't personal. It was just business. As far as the Shire's men were concerned, the hired hands were mercenaries of non-existent corporate entities and part of a world that no longer existed. Once the shooting began there was no quarter. There were to be no witnesses. There would be no one to report or object. All of the corporate employees within earshot were killed. John insisted on a pacifist threshold of tolerance. Once that was reached the rest were expendable. There were enough mouths to feed and plenty of people left over to afford a few non-witnesses. The Shire could not risk vengeance by people who knew too much and who would only tax the already burdened group. Ten men died at the hands of John's five gunmen that moment. The bodies were quickly piled in the cheap portable trailer office. It was doused in gasoline and torched.

It was all done clinically and fast. No one from the scrounger teams coming down with the tractors and trailers saw the carnage. They had to wait for a signal to approach. It was only the core riders who exacted justice on the obstructers of the future.

Whether acquiescent or conquered, every ranch was burnt after a thorough looting. There was no evidence of their previous existence other than a black smudge on the ground. John wanted only a lack of anything to remain. The demise of the West County ranches as sprawling ostentatious expressions of large scale corporate activities ruled from distant financial considerations vanished. The open country once again became the land of the deer, badger, turkey and sharp-shinned hawk.

John held fast to the simple strategy of 'with us or not'. He had no love lost for the vast corporate farms that had edged out the independent farmer's families. All his life he had watched the small guys crushed economically and taken over and now was the time for that way of the post-modern world to conclude.

Those older families who had tamed and made something of the rough land had been bought out, priced out, and horn-swaggled out of their simple desire to make fine food products from their farming endeavors, so when it came to having to deal with the temporary corporate employees who filled the exploitative niche that the industrial manufacture of bulk resource required, John had no sentiment. It was only business, nothing personal. A gunshot was not a personal statement. It was as officially impersonal as a pink slip, or the devaluation of a paycheck, or the outsourcing of a man's livelihood to an un-named person on the other side of the world for cheap fast profit. It was just more final and real. It wasn't a thinly veiled threat that would cause long-term suffering of one and one's family, it was mercifully immediate.

His men had taken to the slaughter almost too easily. They had all been relegated to service jobs, early retirement, lower wages, and competition with people from foreign countries because they supposedly didn't want to do the work that they had done all their lives and were depending on for their legacy. No one gave them anything except a lack of a job and a devalued life through undeserved competition. Americans were ready to right the perceived wrongs of the late twentieth century, even if it was against people in their own backyard. It was a matter of principle, and the underlying rage, so long suppressed, rose to the surface and expressed itself in mayhem. Thank goodness there were few who openly challenged their authority and the death-toll was relatively low and not so overt as to alarm the sensibilities of the Shire's people as a whole.

John turned his back on the sickness he felt over the killing. It was the only way to succeed. Ruthlessness was a primary strategy that had been used against honest decent guys to disparage them of their legacy and now he was becoming the thing he had despised most. He was now the exploiter. He would try to limit it, but he would not tolerate those who thought their Lexus automobile and fat bank accounts gave them the authority to control his people's fate. John strode from the scene as calmly as if leaving church.

The Shire evacuated the surrounding countryside of livestock. John's roaming bands of scavengers worked the countryside for miles around Sentimental. The buffer zone of outlying houses farms and ranches that were stripped and torched expanded to miles. The Shire's ridge-top compounds grew into bustling villages. Each day more goods flowed in from the consolidated ranches and from collection teams stripping food sources. The grounds of each compound became delineated by a variety of different food processing. Apples were sliced and laid in drying racks created from window screens. Walnuts were stripped, spread on tarps, and constantly rolled to dry. Huge stacks of hay migrated into and through the yards of the big houses. Cattle rumbled through on their way to new hidden pastures further up on the wooded ridges. Horseback riders came and went constantly.

People found small menial tasks that they could focus on. If they were not actively filling needed positions, Mark's household staff assigned them productive labor. Some chafed a little at first at having to muck out stalls, or split wood, but soon folks became territorial about their new jobs. Horse grooms served the Lords' horses and stables. Small knots of women and kids marched the country side and denuded fruit trees and abandoned houses of their useful bits. Bicyclists zoomed in and out the gates on their message running errands. The day time hub-bub was all very serious business and everyone pitched in: people rose with the dawn and kept busy all the day long, food was rationed carefully through communal meals administered by official kitcheners, everyone worked harder and were happier than they had been in their former lives, and darkness brought sleep and dreams of TV shows unseen. Community purpose and security of group displaced thoughts of loss and despair.

—

Alice Gunderson swept the front step of the one room cottage that she shared with young Lord William. She cleaned the dust from their love lair with the broom and bathed herself in thoughts of him at every stroke. She gripped the handle firmly and smiled. Bill Rizzoli had swept her off her feet.

From that very first moment that she saw him hanging out the open door of the last operating car that she would ever see, she was smitten. His hair blew in the wind; his out-thrust, manly jaw sliced into the danger of the crazy ride in the out-of-control machine, as he clung with sculpted arms that made her think, 'guns'. He broke the moment and gazed at her in passing while the quiet auto zoomed by on that lonely road the first day of the quiet. He smiled and winked at her in that fleeting moment and won her heart. He was gorgeous. After the car fled around the corner and was gone she gushed and was just a teensy bit ashamed at herself for having such a visceral reaction to the man.

Then, only a short while later, he and his compatriots came walking up that road to her. She could hardly contain herself. The older man, Sir John, as he was now being called, was the one she talked to. She couldn't face Bill then. He was sent to the rear and she forlornly hoped that the shape of her tight jeans were to his liking. She chatted freely with the elder and told him all manner of things, but her mind was on Bill. He was behind and she knew he must be looking at her. She was embarrassed that she felt so strongly about a guy she had seen only once before as he flew by on that nutty car ride and to whom she was only perfunctorily introduced to on their hike up to Sentimental.

Later the next day he came to the fellowship campfire dinner and they talked. It was like a fantasy. She had been hanging out with

Jonas all summer and here this guy shows up and he is so totally awesome that she forgot all about the shared history that she and Jonas built during their summer of camp counseling and she spent all her time at dinner with Bill. Of course, Jonas didn't even notice, he was playing guitar and singing songs and leading the service.

Bill pulled her aside from the fire and main congregation to the edge of the light. They sat on a bench and talked. She doesn't exactly remember what they talked about, but she remembers the look of his hair and square jaw with the firelight behind him. He said nice things that made her laugh. Before Bill was ordered away by his uncle, they held hands for a bit and he gave her a polite and respectful kiss on the cheek with a promise to return for her.

She felt the brush of his lips on her cheek as if it were a hot brand; a brand of joy that she felt and which no one else could see. In her mind there was a mark on her face where he touched her. She carried it around all the next day as if it were some monstrous blemish that everyone could see and knew where it came from. She blushed at the oddest of times during that next day. She hid her face and turned beet red. Her legs quivered at the thought of him. Her insides felt an ache when she remembered the smell of his manliness. She wondered then if she would ever see him again.

No one noticed. There was no mark on her cheek. No one paid her the slightest attention as she and the other girl counselors hung out the laundry from camp that had been washed, but still needed drying.

The next night Jonas held another campfire service. A lot of townspeople came and on the surface it was much more Christian in nature, but underneath it became a nightmare. There was wine. Someone brought a lot of wine and after a little respectful communion during the service it flowed freely. Jesus did turn water into wine, so the stuff wasn't prohibited, and after the stress of the last couple of days it turned into quite a drunken hootenanny. Jonas played music and people sang and stomped their feet and banged on old buckets for drums and praised the lord on high.

Alice had a few sips, but didn't really get into the spirit of the thing. Jonas and Becky and Bruce sure played the host though.

Jonas promised people he would run a monastery, or enclave, or some refuge for those of the true faith and Becky was urging the crowd of strangers on until they were all chanting "Hosiah, Hosiah, Hosiah," in drunken cadence in the middle of the night.

Alice left them to their drunken party and took to her bed in the middle of the living room floor of the main house. They all slept together near the woodstove for the last couple of cold nights. It seemed natural and was respectful and cozy.

She was rudely wakened by someone in bed with her.

It was Jonas. He was drunk and it was very late and he was groping and grabbing at her in a distressing way. Alice might have responded positively to Jonas' fumbling if he had been sober and wooed her a bit and eased her into a soft and loving place where they could share the bed space in harmony, but no, Jonas slunk like a serpent under her covers and slithered shamefully and without respect up her legs and onto her body heavily. He stank of wine and slurred his words as he clumsily pinched and grabbed at her most sensitive features. The dark sensations of him groping at her formed a foul picture in her mind of someone she did not know and who was foreign on every level. He pushed and thrust against her.

"Oh, Alice. You know I love you. It's you I really love and you're going to be my wife and we'll have lots of babies," he garbled.

"Jonas? Please, don't ..." she pleaded.

"I been waiting all summer, kid. You and me are made for each other. Let's make our baby ... now ... tonight ... whadda'ya say? Hmm?" He stuck his hand between her legs and rubbed up and down. The weight of him was crushing to the girl and she struggled to breathe and keep him from getting a hand inside of her. She clenched her legs and pushed his face.

"Jonas stop."

"You want me. You know you do. I am for you. You are for me. We are for ... me and ... you. You know what I mean." He smeared his young unshaven beard against her face and scraped her soft cheeks as he tried to cram his tongue down her throat. He smashed her left breast with one hand and pinched her sacred gates with his other rough hand. He was strong and forceful. His legs were working to pry her apart and get access to her. It was not mutual. It was all Jonas and the unyielding oyster.

Alice lay there and for fear of offending the guy with whom she had worked and liked and built a decent relationship with all summer she tolerated this assault. She could forgive his desire, as long as it only went this far and he stopped when she demanded. At first she thought she could simply dissuade him, as she had other guys in high school, from sullying her honor, but it wasn't working. He was drunk and selfishly inside his own head so deeply that he was not responsive to her as a human being. He wanted to nail her. He wanted to push his agenda up inside of her. He wanted what he wanted and there was nothing else in the world. She was a receptacle for his focused need. The point of him was to fold her back and part the illusions that her clothing held secret. She was to submit her castle to his battering ram of lust. Her submission would be her fulfillment and he would get his moment of delirious animalistic entrance into her world and be done. It was downright biblical.

Bruce came clattering down the stairs and was yelling, "You're a total bitch, Becky! Piss on you and your shit. I'm outta' here!" He stumbled over Jonas trying to separate Alice from her virtue and startled the whole affair.

"Oh shit!" Jonas screeched as Bruce tripped and fell on him.

Jonas pulled back from his siege at Alice's castle walls to address this unexpected onslaught. Alice curled and scurried out from under him. She quickly groped in the dark for her boots and clothes as Jonas and Bruce yelled at each other.

"God-damn man! You fucking broke my back." Jonas whined loudly.

"What the fuck? Is that you, Jonas? Holy shit man, you're in the middle of the fucking floor," Bruce exclaimed.

"Yeah, well … I was sleeping, man."

From the stairs, "Get out! Get Out! Get out!" Becky was screaming and she threw something that clattered around the room

Alice took the opportunity to sneak out through the kitchen to the back door.

"Fuck you Becky! I'm outta' here!" Bruce proclaimed to the world and slammed the front door behind him.

Jonas hovered in the darkness amidst the tangled bedclothes in a drunken haze. Becky's sobs from the stairs were the only sound left in the big house.

—

Alice paused to enjoy the day as she swept the dust off her tiny porch. The hot afternoon sun carressed her upturned face. She was at home in her and Bill's cottage and they were in love and she was sure that she carried his child. She was truly a Lady in waiting. Bill's Uncle John was the Lord of the Shire and Bill was his second in command. She was the next Lord's wife in all, but ceremony. Bill kept her comfortable and well cared for. He had arranged the little house for them to be alone and not have to share the main house with others or sleep in a tent in the compound. She got plenty of food and when Bill was away on his missions to protect the Shire, a guard was left to watch over her and assure her needs were attended to.

Her life had changed so dramatically since the quiet came. She was supposed to return home to Utah and start community college in her backwater town. She didn't have any idea what she would have studied; general education for the first couple of years until she decided on a major. That was the usual path. Probably clerical or computers or maybe she might have gotten ambitious and gone to the nursing college in the next town. It was a hazy future that would now, never be. There was no getting to Utah. There was no community college anymore. There was Bill, the heir apparent to a Shire of survivors in the coastal woodlands of Northern California, her mate, and her new life as a mother to be and Lady of the manor. She sighed her contentment at the fairytale life she was now immersed in. She had left the old world behind easily. The complications of modern life fell away and were replaced by things that she truly enjoyed more; cooking and cleaning her own house, and taking care of a magnificent specimen of a man. She was a natural at these things. No one had ever let her think that she would ever become simply a housewife and supporter of a provider. She was supposed to have education and a career and make it on her own out there in the world until some appropriate fellow came along who was her equal and they would be partners in life together. The modern way. They would both work and share the bills and eventually plan a family and it would be all laid out in advance with no randomness or chancy speculation and all totally equal.

'This is better,' she thought. 'I am a kept woman, I am in charge of my household, I am a princess.'

Alice Gunderson put on a pot of tea and sat down to mend her man's torn clothes as she awaited his return from the frontier.

7

Freeway North

After that insane run, through sniper gunfire on the Golden Gate Bridge, a long tiring slog up the hill and confining walk through the white tile-lined highway tunnels, the crowd huddled under the overhang and stared out uneasily at the open freeway ahead. The roadway stretched ahead of the refugees from the city. A cluster of bicyclists stood at the head of the plodding river of humanity from the city. On each side of the freeway ahead, framing the open lined road space, were large hand painted signs with glittering streamers.

"Warning! Leave the highway get shot! Stay on the road! Or else," the crude signs proclaimed.

The crowd rested quietly. They were near the top of the highway's steep traverse inland. The barren concrete expanse stretched away, up the grade, to the top of the ridge and disappeared beneath a pedestrian overpass just barely visible ahead. The road's edges were clearly delineated by the four foot grey, K-rail, concrete walls that lined the sides of the freeway. Occasional bits of flagging could be seen fluttering along the top of the roadside cement walls, more warning signs.

It had been a traumatic slog up from the bridge. People were ready for a little break before they trudged down to the next bridge north, at the town of Grist Gulch. The car strewn freeway ahead peaked and then aimed down, back to sea level. It was all downhill from that pedestrian overpass ahead, a tantalizing goal.

Another plywood sign read, "Danger! Off road travel fatal. Stay on Freeway or DIE!" Crude skull and crossbones were spray painted on them.

Little Willow, the rich enclave of techno-super-rich and venerated Portuguese family fishing money, was the small town that spawned the signs. Mansions and clapboard Victorian homes dotted the steep lush hills down from the freeway to the marina-fronted town. The little burg perched on steep bluffs facing eastward into the sheltering bay, a maritime community at its core, and the first sheltering cove inside the Golden Gate. Dickson Bay and Little Willow were famous for their excellent natural boat harbor. Little Willow was a boat town at its heart.

Quaint as it was, the town was apparently armed, organized, and very dangerous. Some form of militia defended the town. The freeway bypassed it on the hill above and the effort to keep the refugees from the town was well coordinated. They couldn't allow tens of thousands of desperate hungry people from the city into their town. The chokepoints from the freeway on the hill into town were easily defensible.

It was common knowledge that the exodus marchers had been fired upon as they crossed the golden gate bridge. Word spread fast. A tough young man in the clinic area at the southern entrance to the Robin Williams tunnels, lay dead in a pool of blood from a bullet wound. He made it all the way up the hill to the tunnels before he finally collapsed and died.

The word went back, stay on the highway, or else.

Would the warning signs be honored? What of peoples' destinations off the freeway? How far did the Little Willow militia hold sway on the freeway?

Most of the people leaving the city had only vague notions about what they were going to do when they got across the bridge and into Marine County. They knew that there were farms and cattle and vineyards to the north. They may have had friends or acquaintances in Marine county or farther north in the coastal and wine country resort towns. They knew there were no food sources in San Francisco to sustain them. They never imagined that the people of Marine County would be resistant to them. It hadn't really occurred to them that they wouldn't be welcome.

Here staring at them, the only obstacle to their continued march North, were hand painted warning signs. Each person had to make the decision to leave cover of the freeway tunnel and march up one of the two concrete troughs of freeway. It would be dark soon. The tunnel was filling up. There were a hundred thousand or more still crossing the bridge behind them. Word was through San Francisco that the bridge was open and the city was being abandoned. A multitude made for the bridge and a vague notion of safety.

The sinuous snake of humanity trailed over the glittering ocean narrows on the grand old reddish suspension bridge, up the grey concrete grade of ten wide lanes of freeway to the tunnels, a slowly undulating trail of army ants, each loaded with whatever belongings they could carry, streaming from the city. Huge plywood warning signs faced them at the end of the tunnel. The way forward was dictated.

"Get off the road and die."

Would the signs be honored? Would the imprecation, that staying on the road, be safe?

The surreal murmur of ten of thousands of people slogging along in the reverberating tunnel took on a strange low key roar. The shuffling feet, suffering moans, and a louder subtly distinct, group sigh, became ubiquitous as the space filled up with the crowd. Both of the coming and going tunnel tubes filled with people from the shimmering city by the bay, and they came to a stop at the open northern mouth where ten lanes of openness out into space, clearly declared to be 'under the gun', faced them. They were held up by no obstacle other than their own fear.

When the people behind, hiking up the grade, couldn't get into the perceived safety of the overhanging white tiled auto tunnel because of the hesitation of those ahead, a protest arose. A roaring one-voiced holler of hundreds echoed, as those behind, still in the open and hoping to reach the tunnels, were smashed against those stopped in front of them. The crowd hollered to the front to keep moving. Roaring waves of voices of the people rose up and washed forward through the mass of refugees. The tunnel echoed with the cries of those behind to those in front.

"Don't stop! Don't Stop! Keep moving. Get moving!! Don't stop! Don't Stop! Keep moving. Get moving!! Don't stop!" The chant rang out from the rear and the lament was taken up by those in the tunnel.

The echoing force of the chant reached the front-runners. They couldn't discern the words until the chant worked its way forward through the crowd to them. The hundreds of leading bicyclists mounted up and with a yell took off out onto the car lined freeway.

"All right," yelled a small blonde woman. "Break's over. Let's go." She shouldered her pack and bravely trudged out of the tunnel's safe confines.

The herd started moving again. The tunnel served as a bottleneck. The natural proclivity for humans to shelter and rest caused people to stop and set a spell. The entire stream of people moving up the road was slowed as the backup rippled slowly down the hill to the bridge where the missing bridge pavement held the flood of refugees in check.

Tens of thousands marched out of the city, over the bridge and up to the tunnels. Thousands marched out from the tunnels and onto the exposed and tree lined road.

Suddenly, a loud barking clatter of machine gun fire brought cries and screams as people hit the ground cowering and dodging. The fire was from behind and raked the edge of the road ahead of them all. Three short, timed bursts hammered out. The guns fell silent. They were obviously not aimed at people. The bullets were clearly a warning and it was heard by everyone.

In the following silence an authoritative voice could be heard from somewhere on the hill above the tunnel opening.

"Keep moving! Don't Stop! Stay on the road! Stay on the road!"

People crawled out from under cars where they had ducked and moved nervously and more quickly up the modern multi-lane super highway. No one was willing to defy the rules. Everyone, all one hundred and seventy five thousand, stayed on the well defined roadway north. The town of Little Willow was by-passed by the people from the city. The freeway north gave them hope and they took it.

The bicyclists pumped out of the tunnel and up the final slope to the overpass. There were more warning signs, but no people, and no gunfire. They crested the pass and pointed down the highway to the north. The bikes strung out as they picked up speed and zoomed away and out of sight of the walking hordes.

The crowd stayed on the road and marched. The city emptied into the country. A couple of hundred thousand people hiked to where new lives awaited them. A mass movement of the most literal form. They abandoned their city, on foot.

-

Wayne, leaned into his crow's nest, bobbing twenty feet ahead of the incongruous jumble of vehicles in parade known as the 'Arc'. He perched on the plank bowsprit with a firm grip and a hand in signal to the bulldozer driver behind to assure vehicle clearance.

The driver could barely see where he was going due to piles of goods and people on the bulldozer. Driver was tucked away because the first week's furor had claimed several drivers. He was now protected from being an easy target, but his view was narrow. It gave him only a few degrees of clear view directly ahead, but he could see Wayne, perfectly.

Wayne was his eyes and so the 'dozer's as well. He was the guide. Where he pointed, the caterpillar tractor aimed; it rumbled on, because once moving, a stop was of concern to the hundreds of passengers as well as the roamer community that walked with the machine and therefore an alert. Wayne smiled blissfully ahead as his hand waved at driver behind.

Allying with the bulldozer and its retinue had slowed Wayne's escape from the city and forced him into a coalition of strangers that had more security than roving alone, but which moved slowly. Food got scarce fast and most everyone was still trying to get home and was hungry. They felt stuck in the east bay. They felt the futility of sitting still and waiting for help in the starving cities. People were on the move.

The construction crew that first left the city with the old diesel vehicles, had attracted riders who became allies in common cause. People wanted to go somewhere, so the initial exodus group of trucks and buses and earthmovers had broken up and moved in different directions.

Wayne helped form a mobile community with the bulldozer earth moving machine at its core. His only reasoning being they were the ones headed to cross the bridge to Marine County and the north coast, hence home.

The ground vibrated and the steel treads clanked, loudly heralding the massive thing: its heavy blade of iron hanging out front gave it gravitas, its rumbling engine hammered steadfast, thumping each stroke and spewing a lone column of black exhaust. Its insistent and regular pace hurtled the contraption slowly onward. The caterpillar bulldozer was no longer the naked dirt pusher, it was festooned with an incredulous mass of humans and their home-made version of transit-vehicle. They clung as parasites to its back and yet, were nothing to the strength and ability of the diesel wonder. It was geared to move massive amounts with ease. Tons were its normality.

The rolling bulldozer-treads underneath were barely visible under the burden of creative hitch-hikers. Over the last two weeks quite an elaborate superstructure sprouted on, and behind, the ancient puffing monster. Steel I-beam outriggers stuck out and supported an elaborate platform which sported a long train of a tail: a short fat fuel-tank trailer, then daisy-chained wheeled platforms, loaded to the gills strung out behind, and finally a silver-shiny rounded Airstream travel-trailer ended the snaking train.

Over one hundred and fifty human passengers, forty dogs and cats, chickens and exotic birds; mixed in with the odd assortment of bundled belongings and make-shift weaponry all swayed and teetered above the chuffing old iron.

It appeared as an untidy clutter of gravity defying jumble. The box-like 'house' of riding humanity was constructed of netting and lumber and rope-lashed branches and patches of sheet-metal and lots of hanging things, and flags. Big flags up top and lots of little pennants grew from the bristle of walking height spears that proclaimed, 'Do Not Walk Here!' Riders perched atop the constructed growth clinging to the strong stubby machine at the heart of their land-ship.

Wayne was headed home, at one and a half miles per hour; slower than he could walk.

He had gotten out on the wrong side of the city. His work-buddies convinced him to stay with them for the evening. Wayne sometimes stayed at Noah's house in Oakland during the work week to ease his commute. He followed them home to the east bay. The power would return tomorrow. It was like an earthquake, sure it's disruptive, but tomorrow everyone goes back to work and civilization resumes.

They had all worked for an old skinflint, determined to drive his 'illegally' polluting old earth moving equipment as long as possible, so Wayne, and the people he was working with that day in the bottom of a skyscraper basement pit, were a crew. Getting out of the city on their machines was a natural act for them. It gave them power.

They owned iron contraptions that provided pure raw power. For a little bit of diesel, canola, corn, olive, or pretty much whatever oil, the noisy iron would run in spite of electricity. Wayne rode a relic into the future in order to get to his past.

Who knew it would last? At first they were one of many rides out of town, now they were one of the few things moving at all.

The only mechanized vehicles were diesel-powered, so Wayne's bulldozer became home.

He got stuck trying to stay alive with the 'dozer crew. For two weeks Wayne dodged and weaved and defended the 'dozer. He defended all the trucks and equipment at first, but they drove off on their own path or broke down, or were destroyed by overzealous coveters, but he stuck with team-dozer.

He wasn't an operator, he was a carpenter, but he worked with the guys and there was a bond. He proved himself as loyal guard to them and their machines from the beginning. He rode up front that first day and, in a barkers voice, called loudly, "no ride, keep walking," as they made good their escape from San Francisco. To those who ignored his words he brandished his twenty ounce long-handled framing hammer. In the following days several other fellows were shot or injured around him, but Wayne was unfazed and held the front quarter of the bulldozer as his domain.

It had taken them two weeks, but they were finally moving toward his home.

A crunching groan squealed from the blade as they shoved another car aside, the whole concoction lurched and creaked. The freeway leading to the Richmond Bridge was cluttered with cars. The blade angled at its severe limit to shrug the obstructions aside. A mob of wanna' be riders and trying to prove their worth to the roving village, ranged ahead to relieve parking brakes, neutralize transmissions and possibly steer the cars aside.

The 'dozer trod on.

Wayne's anticipation rose as the approach to the bridge, framed by hills littered with earth tone oil storage tanks, came ponderously closer. The Servus Oil Co. refinery spread around them.

His mind wandered to the maintenance of the machine. He wondered how many of the large fuel tanks littering the landscape had diesel fuel. It was a useless thought, as they were quite replete with diesel from initiation dues to join, and with the ever-moving bulldozer-bus-trailertown heading to cross the Richmond Bridge, there was no more concern on his part for the dozer. He would shortly leave the east bay and go home to his wife and son in Slocoma County.

As they passed through the road-cut, the bridge crept out into the cleft of horizon and Wayne's heart skipped a beat. The bridge stretched across the gleaming water and drew him. He wanted to jump down and run to get there as soon as possible, but he knew he had to let the power of the 'Arc', be seen so to lessen their chances of being fired upon. The screen of car movers range out and ahead to the toll-plaza buildings.

The base of a major bridge was critical territory. There might be a toll.

People exacted payment these days, usually in food, from anyone they could, for whatever they had. Defending a major bridge seemed a valuable possession. Wayne nestled into his crow's nest and scanned diligently as they rolled closer.

The bulldozer nudged another car aside. Wayne saw no hint that any force occupied this territory. The cars hadn't been moved and there were no barricades or makeshift forts. The approach to the toll plaza came into view and the elevated causeway stretched up to where the steel girder bridge loomed in the distant sky.

As the hills fell away the tension mounted. The whole of the company was on alert, crouched and obscured in their nest of gear behind plywood shields with weapons on guard. The cut through the hills was a perfect ambush and everyone felt the possible threat above them.

The monstrosity clumped on, resolute, until the gridlock of cars at the toll plaza forced Wayne to signal left where he saw the less dense employee parking lot, then signaled for a stop and the entire collection shuddered to a halt.

The tractor puff-puffed the exhaust flapper in a tink tinging counting of rpm's. The machine was never turned off.

Driver secured the transmission, applied the foot-pedal track locks, then dropped the blade to the road.

They had finally made it. Wayne and several dozen others wanted to cross to Marine county and this was the bridge to get them there. He was a little wary that there was no one here and the approach unguarded.

From behind and above, "Stanley, get out there, recon that span!" Noah bellowed as he pointed out from his umbrella'd conning tower above the dozer.

A group of men dismounted from the first trailers and, armed to the teeth, sped off and over the bridge.

8

Three Stones

Dave Putnam's steel-toe work boots clunked with a metallic tinking sound against the bent steps of the rattletrap dump truck that belched smoke and vibrated raw fossil fuel power in front of his house on the hill. He handed his camp-pack with sleeping bag up to the armed men in the dumper and climbed up into the small cab.

Dave lived in the ritzy upland section of Saint Rose. The well-to-do had bought up the hills above town and built gated McMansion developments for their wealthy kind. Dave gave a quick look at the beautiful portico front porch where his socially elevated wife stood with their thirteen year old daughter waving good-bye. This was worse than deployment overseas. This was a journey into the unknown. He gave them a bright smile and waved. He hoped it wouldn't be his last look.

"Welcome aboard councilman," the driver hollered over the loud banging of the hammering diesel.

"Thanks, just Dave."

"What's that?" the driver asked.

"Dave, just call me Dave."

"Oh, yeah, hi, I'm Ricky. Used to be Just Rick, but since the outage I'm Ricky again," the stocky blond man said with a beaming ear to ear grin. He turned to his driving and ground the long unused gears into position with a 'clunk' and shudder. He gunned the old engine and eased out the well-worn clutch, the truck skipped and lurched a couple of times and rolled out the sweeping driveway of the upscale home. He gunned it, double-clutched and up shifted; Dave held onto the hard metal dash and cracked seat with white knuckles. The journey was on.

"This is a hell of a machine." Dave said loud enough to cut through the engine's roar.

"Yeah, we were lucky to find one that had no electronics. It's illegal as hell; no smog control, or computerized injectors, or any pollution or efficiency stuff. It doesn't need any electricity to run." Ricky laughed. "It's perfect!"

"How old is this thing?" Dave noticed the lack of padding on the dash, radio, or seat belts, much less air-bags.

"Nineteen fifties, I think. Sheriff was excited when we found it. We commandeered it from a farm and now it's our armored personnel carrier. When you council guys said you wanted to make this trip and this thing turned up, we figured it was a perfect fit. Better than a front end loader." Ricky said. He popped it out of gear and they freewheeled down the long road to the freeway that would take them south.

The truck quieted and picked up speed to an uncomfortable rate, "Going a little fast aren't we?" Dave asked in fear.

"Yeah, well we gotta' conserve fuel. Not much diesel available." Ricky twisted the old wheel from side to side just to maintain the road and avoid the few stopped cars.

Dave's eyes got wide as the deputy swerved around obstacles and pointed the clattering thing to the side of the highway. On more than one occasion he thumped up the curb and mowed down a small landscape tree as he took the sidewalk. When the road leveled out, Deputy Ricky Berniski ground it back in gear and dropped the slipping clutch.

"How'd you draw the short straw?" Ricky asked.

"As the only county councilman with recent military experience, I got tasked with this dubious chore of assuring compliance by the only military authority in the county to assist our local government in its defense. I'm on my way to take up the position of government liaison to the Coast Guard." Dave repeated his orders.

"That sure sounds official, but what does that mean?" Deputy Berniski asked.

"Well, we have a request for the Three Stones training facility down near Eggtown," Dave said.

"Oh, yeah?"

"We're joining the coast guard. So, we gotta go make sure they know what to do," Dave elaborated.

"I figured it had to be pretty important to send me and the guys with you. Well, hang on and we'll get there." Rick hollered as he swerved onto the freeway on-ramp south.

The clattering old machine roared along the shoulder and squeezed through narrow openings between cars. They made their way south to the Three Stones Coast Guard Base.

Dave went over the orders in his head. Suppressing a civilian population was what the modern army had trained him to do and after Iraq and Afghanistan he had a good idea about how to go about it. They may be fellow citizens, but they were still just civilians. At least this time they spoke the same language.

Dave ruminated as the loud smoke belching monster wound its way to the far reaches of the county on its ominous mission.

The sound of the diesel truck as it roared through the main gate of the government facility got the attention of the whole camp. They came out and lined the road just to see a working machine.

Ricky pulled the thing to a grassy knob and parked at the lip. He was going to need a nice long down-slope to get it running again. He turned it off and as silence blanketed the scene and the sound of the past faded there was an audible groan of disappointment from the crowd of young cadets.

After brief introductions, Captain Julius Herzog, U.S.C.G., invited councilman, Dave Putnam, into a small candlelit office.

The county council, a group Julius had never had many dealings with when the world was normal, had sent him an official councilman-liaison. It wasn't so far fetched to imagine that the first contact he got would be from the county council. He was a little put off that the word wasn't from the closest town, Eggtown. He knew the mayor there. The local county council was further away and sent their message couched in as official a manner as might be managed; a guy in a dump truck driven by a deputy sheriff. At least they had mastered machinery.

A small contingent of armed cadets stood guard outside the door. The sharp looking young recruits eyed Rick Berniski and his disheveled looking deputies.

Julius called out, "Callahan."

A crisp neat young man entered the tiny office which had once been the receiving office for the PX bowling alley complex. Julius moved here because this room had exterior windows and was adjacent to the dormitories and close to his students. He had also moved his family out of the large Commandant's house, that sat separate from the main cluster of buildings, and into the dorms. Julius wanted them all close by. He didn't have a phone or walkie-talkie to contact his people anymore and the big house was exposed on the periphery.

"Bring us some coffee would you? Or, would you prefer tea?" He directed at Dave.

"Coffee would be good, thanks."

"Mr. Putnam, welcome to Three Stones."

"Thanks Captain, I have a message for you."

"I imagine you do."

Dave dug into his knapsack and gave him the letter. Julius took the medieval looking wax sealed communiqué. He had to crack it open to break the seal. It was nicely worded, hand-typed and personally signed by several people, whom he had only a vague recollection of.

Julius read their plea/command.

"This says I am under your authority."

"We are the only civilian governmental authority that we know of so far. We've sent out couriers to Sacramento and to other points, but none have come back, yet." Dave elaborated.

"This says we are to act as if we are at war. Martial law."

"That's right. As you can see we have the local judicial and council governing bodies in agreement. There is a legal precedent and we are imploring you to assist us in maintaining order."

"What exactly do you expect me to do?" Julius asked.

"We've had reports from the south. At this moment there are tens of thousands of people from San Francisco marching north."

"Are they hostile?"

"The city has been abandoned. They have no supply."

"My supplies are limited. I have no way to supply them. You seem to be the only one with a working truck." Captain Herzog explained.

"That's not what we're asking. We've already sequestered cattle and stores from the gardens and ranches to the north. We are maintaining order in Saint Rose. Things are stable and we can offer to include your people in the supply loop. The council will keep your men fed and in the food chain."

"In exchange for what?"

"We need you to mobilize. It has come to our attention that you have a substantial armory." Dave said.

A knock at the door and cadet Callahan came in with a tray of coffee service and arranged cookies.

"Thank you, Callahan."

"Aye aye, Captain." He excused himself and left.

"Cream, sugar?" Captain Herzog asked as he poured.

"Yes, please."

They took a moment and savored the hot brew. It was a comforting reminder of continuity in the world.

"Cookie?" Julius offered. "Chocolate chip I think. Someone's been holding out." He smiled at the suggestion that one of his people thought enough to hide cookies for just such an occasion.

"Look, Captain, we don't want to take your armory."

"That's good, because you wouldn't get it." He smiled enigmatically.

"What we are proposing is that you set up a perimeter."

"A perimeter?"

"That's right. County resources won't allow for an incursion of such magnitude without suffering debilitating harm, your base included."

"So, you don't intend to incorporate these people from the city into your protection? You want me to take care of them?"

"Take care of them … in a way, I suppose. We don't need you to feed them from your stores. How can I put this?"

"Please be plain."

"All we want you to do is stop them. Stop the migration from the city."

It sounded simple, but the implication was ominous. The council tempted him with full bellies and sustained support. It would be to his benefit. All he had to do was keep hordes of ravenous riotous uncouth civilians from crossing into the county. Stop tens of thousands from swarming across the broad rolling grasslands that had been the kingdom of many happy cows. Prevent masses of urbanites from marching across the wide open hilly fields that separated the refugees from the lush food resources of the northern county.

"Keep them in Marine County, or rather, divert them to the central valley, east. There are food resources there and they would reach their own natural level of ... subsistence." Dave said quietly.

"Is that what the phrase," Julius read from the letter, "proper biological level of sustainability means?" They both knew that meant level of starvation.

It had been ten days since the quiet came and the base stores were close to depletion. He knew that he had to start foraging on his own or find a substantial supply of food to sustain his men. He had an army to feed. The prospects of him gleaning enough from the surrounding country for a continued campaign of any kind seemed remote. He had already gotten reports that the local Sherriff, or whomever, had essentially denuded the surrounding countryside of livestock. Where cows and sheep once grazed in abundance there were now none. There were now empty miles of grass to forage from and Julius was pretty sure there weren't enough deer and wild turkey to feed his people.

He had waited for communication. He had erred on the side of prudence. Days passed in quiet before he realized he was the most powerful military force in one hundred fifty miles and he had made no move to gather local resources for his group's survival. Stealing local livestock wasn't in the manual. He had waited for word from above, or improvement of situation, or simple resumption of electrical power. They had been reduced to the emergency ready-to-eat meals in their store house and that was going fast.

Prolonged periods of no supply were not in the plan for the military of the future. It was all aimed at rapid deployment and 'as you go' inventory. There was no internal mechanism to support the nutritional needs of the troops under his command. Contractors handled all the day to day food needs of the base and they just didn't keep extra food on hand. They brought it in on an as needed basis. This put the Coast Guard training station and Captain Herzog in a precarious position. It made him vulnerable to the demands of minor local officials with a few pounds of beef.

The one thing that Julius had that no one else did, was the armory.

He had to make a command decision, the one decision that defined the career of a man, either brilliant and ballsy or infamous and stupid. He could take his force and do something to preserve the status quo with it, or let the tide of humanity wash over him and be as forgotten as the multitude who would starve to non-existence around him. He had no evidence that there was anything besides the county to help him and his men. The only thing nearby that was in abundance was the grass that dairy cows normally ate, redwood trees, vineyards and marijuana patches, all the way to Oregon. There were no other large stores of food besides those that the county council had apparently already secured. Once the hundred thousand or more from the city from the south rolled over them there would be nothing left. Ravenous hunger would take over the mob and they'd eat it all. There would be too many to govern, too many to stop. They would be the ruling mob. By sheer numbers they would decide what the county should do with their survival stores.

Julius couldn't be placed in such a position. His character wouldn't allow it. His wife and daughter were with him. He wasn't fighting for any other cause than for his family, in his country, for survival of the species. He had an army at his command and he wasn't going to squander that one power that he held in his hand.

"Look, Captain, you're a realist." Dave reasoned, "you know that five hundred thousand mouths from the city will destroy us all. The uncontrolled multitudes will strip the land. Then, we all starve together. You know this." Dave let it sink in as he gauged the crisp white uniform's reaction.

"What you're proposing is … well, quite insane. How do you expect that my people can stop thousands? It's ludicrous to even think that. The job is too big. The space too vast."

"We understand that. There is a plan." Dave held his hand aloft.

"What sort of plan?" Captain Herzog asked dubiously.

"Right now, a convoy of trucks is gearing up to assist. We have a lot of deputized men. We intend to establish a border south of Eggtown, on the other side of Egg River. That leaves only the west side." Dave fished in his knapsack and unrolled a map. "Here, they can't cross the river after we blow the bridges. It's on this side, where you are, that is open. They are going to funnel this way when it's obvious that they can't continue up the highway. Now, see here?" Dave pointed, "This line of ridges heads southwest. It's a natural barrier. The valley beyond is deep and steep and runs all the way to the sea. We intend to take this ridge, with your help, and maintain a buffer zone there."

"A buffer zone?"

"The convoy is bringing signs, billboards, lots of them. We intend to mark the opposite ridge with them and enforce it. We can fire warning shots all the way across this valley and keep them from even getting to us. The point is, we want to encourage them to head east to the central valley. Or, go back to the city."

Julius studied the map and the red markings on it. It was a crazy turn in his career.

Dave continued, "We did this in Afghanistan. There were a lot of places where we denied access, just by warnings and threat. We didn't have to shoot that much. They went a different way."

Julius sat back and buried his nose in the cup of coffee. He allowed the warmth to curl around his face as he cogitated.

The county was rich in agriculture and he was almost out of food. It was simply a matter of numbers of mouths versus numbers of things to eat. The food factories in the central valley of California were the true repository of the city's nutritional needs, but this was not the valley. They couldn't come here and expect the quantity that the central valley had to offer as staple. It just wasn't possible. The county was a tiny part of the food needs of the city, lots of wine, a little cheese, a few organic niche market cattle and pigs and sheep, but little else in quantity. The hordes were coming. He knew it intuitively. It was simply a matter of numbers of people and their needs.

What would he do about it? The decision loomed. There was little time to ponder. He had to commit to a decision to stymie the flow of population into the food rich land or suffer the inevitable.

"Callahan," Julius called.

The bright young cadet appeared in the doorway.

"Call the Chief Master Commander, please."

"Aye,aye," the pink cheeked seaman replied.

—

Commandant Julius Herzog, U.S.C.G., strode through the dark and cavernous bowling alley towards the other end of the Post

Exchange complex. His boot-fall echoed dark and hollow from the hardwood floor, but his tread gave only a faint echo in comparison to the cacophony and rumble that the lanes normally resounded to at this time of day.

There were no bowlers here now. It was just an unlit space between the PX and the utility storage rooms at the back of the swimming pool. The pass line between the ball return and the bowling lanes was the clearest path across the dark cavernous room. He walked the obstructionless fault line. He strode deliberately through the space, knowing there was nothing in the gloomy darkness to trip over, just polished hard wood floor. The mission was forefront in his mind as each lane, perpendicular in front of him, became a lineal course of intent. The ends of the lanes became a directional symbol in his mind as he looked down on them. It coincided with his conclusion. Sometimes going against the grain was the easiest path. He had one pragmatic course to follow.

His echoing foot steps cut into that thought for a moment and the latent nostalgic reverberation of pins crashing in front of an onslaught of hurtled black balls niggled at the edge of his mind. The bowling alley held the sounds of its purpose well into the silence of its disused and present future. He could almost hear the balls hitting the boards and rolling sonorously to their explosive impact. His dedicated and well timed boot steps surrounded him in the comfort of familiar sound. He liked to march where he was going. Balls rolled, pins crashed. Progress was made.

In the new now, there were no bowling sounds.

The quiet had come and mechanical sounds had passed. Only noises of their own making came to the fore. Natural sounds. Nothing contrived nor insinuated was conjured subliminally onto the memory of man now. Only sounds that actually occurred and were not falsely generated, impinged on a fellow's consciousness. Latent electronica lingered as extra noise in peoples' minds, or perhaps the sounds of a bowling alley. The repetitive electronic extra noise of the old world faded away into 'before the quiet'. What a person thought about what was happening around them had vastly changed from that of a connected world perception. Being stuck on a particular course didn't get any refined distraction or doubt interjected and an idea could go forth unhindered in its rationale; righteousness of purpose. Whole thoughts formed and forced action to occur in ways that, if there were more perfect knowledge, could have been avoided. The good of the many over the good of the few.

That's what the recruits called the event: the Quiet, Before Quiet and After Quiet. BQ and AQ the cadets said.

Although Julius assimilated information quickly, the realization that not only had the electricity stopped, but the fact that it wasn't coming back on took several days to sink in.

The timeline had been altered. His charges realized it quicker than he. When Julius came around to that least desirable yet pragmatic point of view he wasn't happy.

Two thousand five hundred sixty one recruits and another eighty staff people had been under his care when the electricity stopped: when communication with command had ceased, when the world quit, when he had been thrust back into the world that his great-great-grandfather had lived in, when steam and horses and simple human might were the main forces that ruled the planet. With no command authority other than that of the human voice: no power, no overwhelming force, no shock and awe, no communication with those outside of a day's ride or walk, no ability to call others in order to gauge the state of things, nothing outside one's own ability to command and control on a personal level, Julius maintained the cohesion of the school.

In the last week Julius re-established a command network that relied on line of sight visual and audio communication. Semaphore classes became mandatory for the entire command. It was almost comical to see formations of uniforms standing face-to-face waving their arms at one another. They looked like human tick-tock clocks, facing each other off in some sort of silly graduated movement duel. They were talking. Not a sound uttered. The flapping sounds of their hands flitting to the next letter. They counted off the time of the new world with their waving arms; slower, quieter.

He spent his entire life always changing and learning a new way. He had learned how to make the electronic world work and serve the ends of the United States Coast Guard. He had prided himself on his ability to mold himself into that modern world and learn all the new fangled fancy little things that were thrown at him. He had always been in a constant state of change. Apps and laptops and wi-fi and smart-phones and remote vehicles and satellite feeds and every new way that the electronic world had twisted. He kept the curriculum updated to make his tenure, as the Commandant of the premier Coast Guard training facility of the world's greatest power, relevant. And, now it seemed, it had all been for nothing. The core of his curriculum was as useless as a screen door on a submarine.

He strode through the quiet echoing space that was once a bowling alley and was now a fairly useless piece of wood floored warehouse. He couldn't even get enough light into it for anyone to bowl. There were no windows. He toyed with the thought of a series of mirrors in the middle of the day. A dozen mirrors, human pinsetters, and ball retrievers.

"Enough!" he yelled to himself as he dismissed the fantasies of the now past world.

The local county council, the only official entity he had received any communication from, had given him commands, requests. In response he mobilized his men in defense of the only status quo that he was aware existed.

He'd had no contact from high command in the Coast Guard, or from the federal government, as to what he should do to assist in this time of obvious national need. Things were slower now. There was no electricity nor radio nor any other electronic communication device operating and the closest nexus of command and control would be San Francisco, or Fairfield, where there was an Air Force Base. No word had come his way. They were a long ways off. There was no communication at all. He had been on his electricity-less own.

His boots echoed through the bowling alley, through the utility storage rooms and he strode out onto the wide parking lot where his men were assembled.

As soon as the Commandant appeared at the doorway, a command was hollered over the heads of the eager recruits on the concrete parking lot and they all snapped to attention. Twenty six hundred bright, young, strong, and educated men and women stood in long straight lines before their leader.

Julius marched in the most militarily precise bearing of his life. The eyes of all those upon him stiffened his back bone and regulated his marching cadence. He took his place directly in front of the formation of neatly uniformed youngsters.

"At ease," he said.

"At ease!" his third in command hollered out and the entire block moved as one into a disciplined and forced position of structured relaxation. They stepped apart from their attention and folded their hands behind them with an audible clapping sound.

Julius spoke quietly to his subordinate, "Command Master Chief, get us a semaphore interpreter up here. I want them all to understand exactly what I am saying."

"Aye aye, Captain," Billy Zane replied. Billy was Julius' operations, go to, everything, guy. The executive officer was on a trip back east when the quiet came and so was out of the command structure. It was Julius and Billy running the whole show.

Silence enfolded the formation as a soft morning breeze, scented with pasture and ocean smells, graced them all with fresh and heady cool air.

Julius stood looking at the fine group of young people in his charge. He was supposed to train them in search and rescue and to interdict violators and infiltrators to our great country. They stood awaiting his command. They were eager to be told what to do.

Julius took a deep breath and began. "Good morning."

They replied as one. "Good morning sir."

"I have bad new and good news." He let it wash over them. They waited in silence.

"The bad news is … we are at war. We are cut off."

A slight moan and sigh went up from the youngsters. They all imagined they had joined something bigger than themselves, and that something bigger would be able to come and make sense of any situation. There would be support from the great American nation no matter how bad it got. Now, their craziest rumors of the world having abandoned them were true. They were not going to be relieved or deployed or rescued.

"The good news …" Julius let it linger as they quieted down and listened.

"Is we are in command!" he hollered as if it were a revelation. It worked, there was a smattering of a cheer.

"I have received orders," he let it resonate. The formation was eager for information that wasn't pure barracks scuttlebutt.

"We are to mobilize our force." They listened with a little shuffling of feet. "We are to mobilize immediately. Petty Officers! Form your squads!" Julius almost screamed. Several non-commissioned officers stepped forward in crisp coast guard dress white uniforms and began the process of carving the twenty five hundred plus young people into units that would serve the future purpose.

Until that moment, the grades and direction of any individual was determined by their ability to fill the search and rescue and interdiction needs of a larger naval and air force that was already deployed and at sea. Now, the older and more experienced middle rank non-comms started hollering out names of men and women according to their predilections for the coming action.

Soon, small groups formed at the edges that were, at first appearance quite sexist and politically incorrect. The women recruits were herded away from the groups of macho minded and more blatantly hard charging young men. Knots of highly charged young men coalesced into seething mobs of chanting and cheering squads who jumped and yelled enthusiasm at the taunting of the petty officers who egged them on and yelled exciting encouragement.

In only a few moments squared formations of people began marching off into different directions. The hardiest heaviest and most arrogant group of hard chargers was marched straight to the building where the arms were stored.

Although a Coast Guard training facility, Three Stones held quite a large arsenal. This group of tough and macho young men was marched to the doors of that arsenal. The others were formed and marched around in a strange formation that seemed to merely delay their visit to the armory. It was a glorious display of authority over people who had acquiesced to follow orders of persons they had never known previously and who, merely at the hint of officiality, made them the dominant dictators in these folks' young lives. They chose to follow and follow they did.

The first group of heavy and arrogant men marched from the armory laden with heavy machine guns. Teams of two carried the steel. The second group, hot on their heels loaded themselves with boxes of ammunition for those guns. Each group armed themselves alternately with heavy M-2 fifty caliber and lighter M-240 machine guns. They marched, following the hollered orders of the older non-commissioned officers who had been training recruits for, in some cases years, around and round the stiffly standing Captain Herzog, who stood stock still through this entire parade.

Finally, the group of the female cadets who brought up the last of the parade, hollered their higher pitched cadence loud and strong in response to the queue chant their one petty officer, Sheila McCutcheon, led them with. She hollered out and they followed as they marched at the periphery of the real action where the men were being armed and marched off to ready themselves for their assignments. The women were left on the field armed with M-4 carbines.

The lawful authority of the county was now militarily enforced.

9

Teen Teams

A rag-tag group of kids, between the ages of thirteen and seventeen, sat the dry grass meadow in a semi-circle around Squire William as he explained their mission.

Squire William, was the name his Uncle John, or Sir John, as he was called, had given him. He was just Bill Rizzoli, public school educated early twenty-first century twenty year old. He didn't want any more school and so, didn't go to University for the big degree after high school. He took a couple of community college courses at his mother's insistence, but she had no idea how he could apply himself. She was a single mom, retail worker. Her horizons were made from TV shows and a couple of Hawaiian vacations when she was young. Bill was just an ordinary guy who worked for a Hispanic landscaper and partied with his friends and hung out. He had just happened to be at his uncle's house the day it all went kaflooey and ridden the crazy old guy's coat-tails into this crazy future where he was the heir apparent to a bunch of post-apocalyptyic nut-cases hiding out in the woods.

Now, here he was, leading a bunch of teenage guerilla fighters. He was nervous about getting up and telling people what to do, but they were younger, and looked up to him, and hung on his every word, and they feared him. Bill took heart as he looked over his cadets.

The younger kids were in camp under the tutelage of the women doing household chores: picking, sorting and drying fruit and nuts, washing clothes, cleaning horse stalls, and mending clothes that were wearing out too fast. Little fingers for little work. The older cadets were already herding cattle from one upland meadow to another as well as out on recon and riding with the men. The stamina they brought made them perfect candidates for the leg-work.

The in betweens, were here with Squire William, learning the ropes of recon, small game hunting and code communication with flags and mirrors. A dozen of them ringed around in a motley array. Most had parents in the camp and were reasonably attired; a few were orphaned by the quiet and were pretty disheveled looking and a bit dirty. All had some kind of weapon; a sharpened stick, a big kitchen knife, a couple had bow and arrows, one kid had a golf club. There were lots of feathers and dangling bits of colored string and little shiny baubles. Kids decorated themselves far more than before the quiet when fashion was dictated by the TV and other school kids. Now they were free to be whoever they wanted. There was no cool role model being crammed down their throats. There were headdresses and cloaks and camouflage. Their upturned faces were attentive to the two young men standing above them in their ring.

"Allright everyone, listen up," black-haired Dave barked out, "this is Lord, Squire William," he emphasized the title, "he is the voice of Sir John. He has graced us with his presence to set out our new squads."

The kids looked at one another in curious anticipation as the thought of new squads sank in. It was the choosing of teams before the game.

"Each group will muster under their new squad leader and get their first mission assignments. Squire William." Finished, Dave Nichols, seventeen years young and the kids' direct commander, stood to the side. He had been instrumental in forming the kid corps. Dave had worked them intensely for the last week into able reconnaissance.

Sir John, had put this cadre of teens under his nephew, Squire William (Bill Rizzoli), as his first independent test of leadership. Sir John knew that trial by fire was the best way to see if one could fill the bill. He had always wanted his nephew to excel and thrusting him into a leadership role would be the only way to tell if his trust and hopes that his nephew would be able to rule, were misplaced or not.

Bill and Dave, had been with John Ritter, and his old friend Mark Young, since day one, and although Bill, was a few years older than Dave, the younger was a trusted and efficient commander in his own right. The two had talked beforehand and Bill was doling out assignments in his new guise as Squire William, their liege lord and commander.

"Hello all. I have a roster for the groups." Bill fumbled with the rolled up sheet of paper. "Group alpha: Phillip and Jimmy Carpenter."

Dave motioned them stand to the side.

"Ethan the crooked, Blessed Jason, and Jim the thin is your Sergeant." They gathered in a clump.

Jim the thin, a tall lanky youth, sported a wispy goatee and almost shoulder length black hair. His pointed and bony face gave him a slightly sinister look. He smiled and stood up tall in front of the guys, Alpha.

William continued, "Group Bravo: Half-ton, Stone-cold, One-hair, and Jackal. Oh and Jackal, your little sister Ella is with you."

To the side a little girl jumped up and screeched in glee. She wasn't sure she was old enough to be in recon. Her brother Jackal had told her on many occasions to 'go home', and rake drying nuts, but she had tagged along stubbornly

Jackal moaned a little at having to keep his kid sister in tow. She was feisty and quick witted and drove him crazy at every chance.

Jim the thin, was happy he was Sergeant, but he rankled a bit because his best friends were all in group Bravo. He was forced to manage guys he hardly knew.

"Group Gamma, you're with me: Brendan high-star, Rufus the red, and John-Paul. We ride today Gamma, so get your gear. The rest of you, Captain Dave, has orders for your deployment."

The groups stood together in the meadow, proud and tall. Two weeks before they had been in high or middle school and rode big yellow school buses to boring classes that ill-prepared them for the modern world and gave them not a clue about how to go about surviving in a primitive one.

They had come to the Shire quickly and fulfilled their need to be amongst a company of like-minded people of similar intent and purpose. The kid corps had taken them and trained them non-stop for the last week and a half, in the arts of line of sight communication and signaling, wood lore and stalking and camouflage and pilfering. They'd already been on many forays to glean from unused fruit-trees and to make contact with reticent hold-out retirees and ranchers. Their previous lives had been so entirely supplanted with the new world that they were unrecognizable as cell-phone talking, video-game playing, mall-rats. They were eager to take over the new world. They were ready and were being given tasks of importance that bred responsibility.

They stood around William and Dave as a tiny army of clear eyed youth. They were the Shire's eyes and ears.

"Alpha, you guys are to relieve the riders on Sentimental road. Jackal, Bravo group is to deploy on the southwestern corner at the Olsen farm. You know, where the forest finally ends and the vineyards start before the ridge? You guys are to report any incoming activity post-haste, that means real quick. Set up a line of communication with your flagmen ..."

"And flag-girls." Ella piped in.

"And, flag-girls. We need intel for the invasion from the south. We can't have a bunch of people stomping through our lands just higglety-pigglety."

Everyone laughed.

"Now don't do anything stupid. We have to relieve the older men for more important stuff and this is our chance to prove we can do it. Any questions?" Dave stared them all down.

They shrugged their shoulders and wagged their heads no. They were young and smart and on their own and they knew, just everything.

"I have a question." Jim the thin ventured.

"OK, Jim, shoot."

"How about horses? We should get horses." Jim crossed his arms as he had seen more mature people do when they felt they deserved something.

"Well, we don't get any. But, any horses you find are yours." Dave dismissed the query. "Anything else?" He looked around. "Good, now get to your stations and I want reports to start filing in every morning and night and if something happens, right away. You got me?" He peered at his young charges. Most nodded their understanding. Ella snapped to a farcical pose of attention and executed a comical stiff handed British-style salute.

In only a few minutes the clearing was empty, but for Dave. He watched the forest edge as each of the groups vanished into the thick woods, then he too ambled from the meadow and started the hike to his next meeting of new kid corps candidates.

10

Talk To Me

Don Shelby, Fire Chief of the tiny unincorporated village of Sentimental, sat behind his tiny formica desk in the back of the cavernous empty fire house. The trucks had been outside getting washed when the quiet came and there they stayed.

Don had led the campaign to upgrade and replace the old obsolete fire engines with modern, electronically controlled, state of the art, fuel efficient, trucks. Now, there was no way they could be started. The computer controlled injector and fuel pump systems were integral to their operation, so they would not work.

The fire chief spent the last two weeks coordinating emergency efforts to relieve suffering of the people of the village. The volunteer firemen had always been a strong and fundamental part of the local community fabric. Don stayed on duty at the fire house since the catastrophe had started. His wife had left him years before, his kids were grown and gone, the volunteer fire station was his life; he even slept in the back of the station.

Don worked diligently, during this present crisis of no electricity, to organize housing at the Y.M.C.A. community center next door and to assure that the tiny clinic was manned for any medical emergency. It wasn't difficult. The Y.M.C.A. facility manager didn't live in the area and left the day of the quiet. She had told Don to do whatever he felt was right. The clinic ladies also left, but one, who lived nearby, came in each day to see what she could do.

Sentimental was not an incorporated town and so, had no police or town council or any of the basic governmental services that one expects from a town. Don was about all there was. He was the only real official connection to the authority structure at the county. Fire Chief of the volunteer fire house was about as high as you could get out here in the far reaches of west county.

The only other real power structure in Sentimental were the business owners. They owned property and controlled the small downtown tourist-trap of a village. They made their desires known to the county when they needed to, and the rest of the time they did what they pleased. Many of the property and business owners didn't live in Sentimental. They were far gone and the old family run businesses were operated by paid manager surrogates. The day of the quiet, found most of the powerful owners absent.

Don had gotten no instruction from those local power players as to what they wanted out of this mess. They were in Hawaii or Mexico, or living in their high-rises in the city. They were absentee owners and were now non-owners by dint of their absence and inability to communicate or get to their legacy cash cows.

He concentrated on organizing communication to the county council. Since little had really occurred since the quiet came Don had become quite bored in his garage. As a firefighter he was used to being bored, but with no telephones or radios, nor a siren to call his men to emergencies, it became a long slow tedious wait until the next horse or bicycle rider from Saint Rose returned with a new message.

A few of the local horsey folk turned up the first couple of days to help, but they were soon disenchanted with the long thankless ride to town and back. There were no accommodations for them in Saint Rose and the county council seemed uninterested in anything they had to communicate. The horse riders had all pretty much bowed out of the daily rides and left Don with a few hardy bicycle riders to maintain the connection to the only civilization that existed.

It was a perfect vacuum for Mark Young and his Shire organization to exploit.

Shire bicyclists reported to Don. Five young men and one young woman from Sir John's camp doubled the volunteer bike corps already established. A relay rode to Saint Rose and surrounding villages each day.

The riders planted by the Shire, copied and relayed every message back to their seneschal, Mark, at Happy Lair. Very quickly the messages were reduced or changed outright. The Shire exerted its influence through Mark's scheming input. He loved the game of twisting the ignorant to his purposes for a change. The status quo was so used to being in the know that it was easy to bend their reality with a few believable un-truths. He only told them what they wanted to hear—that things were going well. From Mark's perspective they were going well.

Don had gotten some word, second and third hand, of horse thieves and cattle rustlers. He dispatched notes to the council of those nefarious happenings in hopes of some professional police assistance. There were also reports of house burnings, Don wanted to respond, but there was little he could do with no functioning equipment and only a bell to rally the firemen. He noted all these things to the council. Don waited on the county council to send him some help. He did his job.

The Shire intercepted, read, and changed the S.O.S. missives into reassuring statements of law and order and a docile and complying populace. Requests for assistance by the firemen and their small Sentimental town core were replaced with offers to help the larger town of Saint Rose.

Mark Young sat at his small outdoor desk on the patio of the large hilltop mansion, Happy Lair, overlooking the valley of Sentimental below. He chatted quietly with one of their most trusted Lords, Joe Billsop.

"Joe, I have a 'very particular' chore I need done." Mark emphasized and Joe picked it up.

"Sure thing Mark, what is it?" Joe asked as he sat backward on the hard steel fold out chair across the table from the rotund and cheeky administrator.

"Seems there are a group of bicyclists who are spreading lies and false accusations against our people to the county," Mark laid out.

"Really? Are they some of our people?" Joe lifted an eyebrow.

"No, they aren't. Our guys are doing a bang-up job getting the word out and keeping us in the loop. No, we could handle them here at the Shire if that were the case. No, I am talking about some of the volunteer do-gooders that Fire Chief Don has talking to the council. They're causing some serious disruptions and may be dangerous," Mark continued. "We need them to …uh,"

"Vanish?" Joe offered.

"Well, I see you grasp the situation. Good. Yes. Our com lines are compromised as long as they are shooting their mouths off and we really can't have that." Mark wrinkled his brow and looked over his reading glasses at Joe.

"I understand fully Mark. Don't worry. It's done. Is that all?" Joe was quick and wanted to get on with his day.

"Well, you must understand that there has to be … no trace …" Mark hedged.

"Mark, I get it. It'll be done." Joe got up and slapped his trousers of dust. "Do I need to tell John?"

"No. John is already apprised. He's approved the action." Mark looked up with a pleasant smile at the Lord who led the elite group of killers and ranch raiders.

"Good. Hey, see about getting some nice women up to our house. It could sure use a little cleaning and I have men who could use a little company. OK?" Joe tilted an eyebrow at the heavy-set older man.

"Yes. Of, course. I'll see what I can do for you, Joe." Mark gave his close lipped reassuring smile as he reached a tiny cup of espresso coffee from the table.

Joe nodded, strode to the stables, mounted, and rode off with three grim looking men at his heels.

Mark sighed a bit of relief when the man left. It was a heady chore to ask of a man. Joe scared Mark, but as long as he kept his head he could get the murderer to do his bidding like a lap dog. Mark sipped the thick black bitter coffee and turned his thoughts to the next task brought to him by the diligent clerk who appeared at his elbow with fresh missives and papers to peruse.

—

Freelance volunteer bicyclists mysteriously failed to return from their daily forays to Saint Rose. The Shire sent more cyclists. Soon, Mark had complete control of the fire chief's communication to the county council.

John and Mark knew all about the sheriff's livestock seizures and the council proclamations legalizing them. People were used to their cushy twenty-first century lives. They couldn't fathom a world where the quiet and darkness would remain in perpetuity. They allowed the authorities to prevail. They got in line and bowed to the badge of the sheriff and the power of the council. The outward appearance of order calmed people. The populace eagerly embraced any form of visible organization by uniformed groups that exhibited a modicum of control. It held up the illusion of the status quo, and that was all that people really had any interest in holding onto. A semblance of normality.

The local volunteer firemen felt strongly about following the lead of the council and they responded eagerly to bogus requests, placed by Mark into the communication stream, for assistance to Saint Rose. Responsible west county firemen and their families packed up their sleeping bags and started the long hike to town. Their sense of obligation to authority led them away from Sentimental.

People depended on the government to establish communication and restore power so things could go back to the way they were. For the first two weeks it really looked like the power structure of the county council and the city of Saint Rose was going to maintain order. The populace was compliant in their shared adversity. People pulled together and for the most part, obeyed. Sir John and Mark operated freely in the power vacuum of this false sense of order and security.

Communication to the most central village in west county was now controlled by the Shire. Sentimental was the hub of the west county in terms of strategic locations. It sat on the top of the main east and west running ridge that divided two main watersheds and connected directly to both villages that controlled access between the interior and the sea. River Mountain, to the north, sat astride the great Rushing River, it controlled one of the few bridges that crossed that mighty little river, and the only road in the north from Saint Rose to the ocean. To the south, Fiddlestick, lay on the only other easily accessible east-west highway to the town of Bowditch by the sea. Control of both River Mountain and Fiddlestick meant an effective denial of access to the people of the interior to a huge section of the coast. The only other access to the coast was by means of a road from the far southerly town of Eggtown. That was a long and lonely road over some of the most lush and verdant grasslands in the state. It was easily watched and, originating in Eggtown, was not readily available to Saint Rose. Eggtown had its own agenda.

Sir John's forays ventured far and wide and pierced deeply south into Eggtown's rolling hills of greenery. His control stretched north, far beyond the Rushing River, as his rovers forayed into sparsely populated state parkland. His position effectively gave him control of access to the sea for a one hundred mile stretch of the coast.

—

The Lord's riders had stopped for a brief nap and lunch at the southern edge of the great forest before the open rolling grasslands. John sat, leaning against an ancient gnarled oak tree, on the small knoll. He quietly munched a Gravenstein apple in one hand and bits of smoked salmon in the other. It had been a hard morning ride and John was weary to the bone. Bill, his bright young nephew, came riding up the incline, swishing through high brown grass, to visit his busy uncle.

"Uncle John!" Young Bill called as he dismounted at his uncle's lunch camp. The two big lumbering dogs from the Creek House came loping up from behind, ran past Bill and right into John's arms. They pawed and slobbered their master in warm greetings. They'd been following Bill on his wide ranging recon chores.

"My good young Lord William," John called, mostly for the benefit of his men as he had never called his nephew William, "get on over here," John beamed.

Bill pushed the dogs aside, flopped down next to his Uncle, Sir John, and took the small canteen offered. "Hey, Unk. What you doing down here? Checking up on me? All quiet on the southern front." Bill offered up as a casual report of the status of the boring border of open country.

"Well, I was just taking a little swing down here to your end, to see you, and check it out." John smiled at his only relative.

"My guys told me you were here so I thought I'd come greet you. Nothing gets by us. Welcome to the southern plains." He boasted to his uncle as he reached some of the old guy's lunch. "Man this is good salmon, can you get us some of this?" Bill asked. "We're getting sick of beef."

"I'll see what I can do, young man. I guess you are keeping it all under control down here, not that there's much going on," John noted.

"Everything is copasetic. Not a thing for miles. We got heliographs south and all the way to the edge of Eggtown. Since the coast guard guys took up on the south ridges there's been no movement at all. They got their border set up and we're kind of watching their backs. I don't think they even know we're here. The guys are getting tired of looking at nothing." Bill reported the system of mirrors and semaphore lookouts posted on the frontier.

"You keep 'em active, Bill, believe me, they're going to come. The city is starving for sure and we need to have a heads-up about them before they arrive. It is not a matter of if, it's a matter of when. I'm counting on you," John warned him.

"Of course, Unk. No one moves that we don't know about." Bill assured his uncle.

"I'm counting on you, Neph. We're all counting on you. If they get to us when we aren't ready then this is all for naught. They'll eat us up like soup."

They sat silently and munched salmon and cheese and tart apples together. The other men ranged around them under the big old tree and napped in the shade while they enjoyed a few minutes of not sitting their horses. The days had become unbearably hot and the lack of cloud cover sent everyone into afternoon siesta paralysis. Doing anything the least bit strenuous during the afternoon swelter was near impossible, so they napped in the shade of ancient oak trees.

"Unk?" Bill stared through the dry oak canopy above him.

"Yeah, Neph."

"You know Alice and I are together now, and ..." he got wispy.

"And ...? You get her knocked up yet?" John asked bluntly.

"Wha ... noooo. I mean, I don't think so ... maybe."

"There you go." The old guy chucked Bill in the arm and grinned. "The only reason for being on the planet is to have kids. You guys deserve lots of 'em. Hope she likes her little house."

"Yeah, she does, uhhh, I really like her, Unk." Bill backpedaled into feigned embarrassment.

"I know you do. I'm really happy for you two."

"It's just that ..."

"What?" John looked out from under his broad brimmed hat at his scruffy tough looking nephew. The young man's budding beard had filled in the boyish features and given his jaw a hard line.

"Well, there is this other guy," Bill started.

"Yeah, and ...?" John raised an eyebrow.

"Well, I talked to him and told him to go find someone else to bug. He told me some things."

"Things?" John asked.

"Yeah, he said he didn't think a good Christian girl should be with a guy like me. He said he knew what we had done and we were going to hell."

"Did you punch him out for being rude?" John tucked his face back under his sweaty hat.

"No. Alice was nearby. He walked off. I didn't know what to say."

"I see. Do you think he has any hold on her?" John queried.

"I don't think so. She wasn't mad at me last time I saw her. He might though. It's been a couple of days," Bill elaborated.

"What's his name?"

"Unk, I don't want to blow this out of proportion. Just leave it be."

"Then why did you tell me?" John asked. "If this guy is willing to threaten some kind of blackmail against you for a girl then he may be a loudmouth security threat."

"Well, I guess so. I didn't believe him."

"So you think he was blowing it out his ass just to get a rise out of you in front of Alice?" John asked.

Bill hesitated a moment. "Yeah, I guess."

"Is this guy a rider or camp-follower?" John asked from under the covering hat.

"He's no rider. He's one of the Christian guys from the camp."

John pulled himself to an elbow and dropped the cover. "Well. If you think this guy could be a threat to the Shire, then I suggest you deal with him quickly and completely." John suggested.

"What do you mean?" Bill asked.

"You can't allow some crap-head little camper to dishonor you publicly and get away with it." John said.

"Oh, it wasn't really publicly, he was whispering and it was just to me." Bill tried to soften his accusation.

"I see." John said. "Look, I want you to keep an eye on this guy. He may be a threat. We can't have campers going around with information they shouldn't have; spreading it all around you know."

"It's not like we've done anything wrong. The only bad stuff has all been self-defense, so it shouldn't matter." Bill said.

"It matters if some piss-ant is shooting his mouth off to the sheriff in town about us. So far, we've kept this all pretty tight-knit. We can't afford a war with Saint Rose, not with the hordes coming. Either one would destroy us." John warned.

"Oh, come on Unk. You really think one guy snitching to the sheriff is gonna cause him to send deputies out here? To do what, arrest us? Hah! For what? Collecting a few cows that were out of his reach anyway and burning a couple of old barns?"

John realized his nephew had not really been in on the nightmare inducing forays. Bill had always been in the rear-guard, watching the back door, and he missed the worst of the bloodshed. Bill had no experience of how bad it had turned. The riders had all kept their mouths well shut, so that even the trusted nephew wasn't aware of the heinous cold blooded acts that had gone down: thoughts of the innocent Hispanic ranch hand, pleading on his knees in the dark, before he was put down, haunted John, or the incredulous look on Bill Blanchard's face when John punched holes in his chest for arguing the corporate line.

"This is the kind of thing I need you to keep an eye on, Bill. It's the little stuff that'll kill ya ..."

"You can see the big stuff coming. I know, I know." Bill parroted his grizzled old uncle.

"Well, I say marry her as soon as you can. Get her trained right taking care of your house, make her a grand Lady. She'll forget all about idiots like him," John advised.

"I guess so. Bill agreed, looking down at the tinder dry brown grass.

"Keep up the good work here. Remember, they will come and we need to know about it fast, OK?" John smiled and chucked Bill in the shoulder with a soft punch.

"Sure thing, Unk."

"We got to get going. No rest for the wicked." John gave Bill a big quick strong hug and perfunctorily waved at his men. He mounted and they grunted their displeasure at having their siesta cut short. They followed.

The two dogs, AB and CD stood, but held their ground at the prospect of more running. They stood next to Bill as his uncle John rode off.

Bill tilted a small hand-held mirror while holding his fingers out in a 'V' as an aiming guide. When he got a flashing response he pulled semaphore flags from his saddle bags and did the weird flag flapping dance. He peered through some small binoculars across the grassy expanse to his contact. Then he walked to the north side of the old oak and did the same. He had done his duty and checked in with his men. All was calm they told him. Bill walked back under the tree and laid out his blanket. He fished the clear glass bottle of vodka from his saddle bag. He tipped it to his lips and savored the heady liquid.

Everything in his world had been turned upside down. His girlfriend was lost out there somewhere. His mother was equally lost. In the hopes of finding them he had left specific instruction with all of his teenaged semaphore communication reconnaissance group to keep an eye out for them. Bill's youthful charges had nodded earnestly when he described his mother and girlfriend. They might be coming up from the south, but when his guys turned away, they shook their heads at the futility of trying to remember such vague descriptions at their vast lookout stations.

In Bill's mind, he was sure they could isolate and identify the dearest people in his life because he had so fervently described the women and pictured them so clearly in his mind's eye. If anyone had the chance to find lost family or a lover in this crazy new world, it was him and his bunch of scouts. They had the entire southland approaches to the county, and the Shire, covered and under watch. His guys and gals could find them. They had to be coming north to meet him. It was only natural to presume that the significant women in his life were on their way to find him. All he had to do was keep a sharp lookout for them and welcome them into the fold. Uncle John had given him the means to not only find them, but to have them protected and welcomed to the Shire when they appeared.

He swilled the vodka freely in the warm afternoon. It warmed his insides and cooled his outlook. The eighty proof juice seeped into his mind and soothed the pain he felt over having lost the anchors in his life.

His mother had nurtured and protected him from evil and from the nasty consequences of his poor choices. All his life, whenever something marginal or bad had occurred, his mom had counseled that he set it aside and pretend to everyone that it didn't happen. This led Bill into a world where he kept things secret. It was just too difficult to share things and so, he denied their existence. That was his mother's way. Put on a good face and don't let even those who are closest to you know you are having trouble or a hard time. That left Bill in a place where whenever he had a set-back, he was so embarrassed by it, that he didn't seek help. He glossed it over and went on as if everything was just fine. The problem was that things were not just fine. Things may have gone terribly wrong, but because it was 'private', and we shouldn't share the burden, people who loved him and may have wanted to help, couldn't. No one was aware of his situation and therefore couldn't offer ideas or suggestions about how to work out the problem, or how to cope. Isolation in adversity was his reality and now that the world had fallen to pieces he shared his trauma with the only friend he had, the bottle. Bill chugged as if the answer lay somewhere inside the transparent glass structure holding the elixir. All he had to do was drink enough of the liquid away to illuminate the solution.

He'd take care of that meddling Jonas and set Alice up in grand style. She was one tight sweet piece of bible-banging fun. Sexual readiness seeped from beneath her façade of nice-girl camp-counselor persona. They had already done the deed and Bill wanted her to be his new confidant, at least until his mother or girlfriend showed up. Alice was the only thing good about the entire apocalypse; her and the free liquor.

Bill lay back in the quiet solitude under the old oak tree in a sea of brown dry grass and although exposed and alone, he felt comforted and whole with the rosy glow of drunken numbness. He nodded off and slept the afternoon away.

—

The weather nagged at the edge of everyone's experience. Daily temperatures soared relentlessly into extremes. It was hotter each day and colder each night. With no more jet contrails interlacing to make the familiar late afternoon haze, the sun's radiant energy fully penetrated to the ground and become trapped there by the high levels of carbon dioxide that had built in the atmosphere during the industrial age. The particulate pollution and vapor trails from the eighty thousand flights over the United States each day had offset the warming of the atmosphere by the greenhouse effect. The shiny high altitude clouds reflected substantial amounts of radiant energy back into outer-space before it could be trapped by the carbon dioxide. Now, the atmosphere was free to act as the climate models had been predicting for the last fifty years. The heat bore in every day and each night the lack of artificial cloud cover, created by the airplanes and pollution, allowed an unseasonable chill to permeate. Hundred degree temperatures in the day and near freezing temperatures at night became the new normal.

California grasslands dried out in the late summer. That wasn't unusual. Freezing nights and the lack of fog in September was unusual.

The thick fields of grass had not been sheared, nor processed into hay fodder bales for the winter. The pastures flourished with the pre-quiet late summer rains and were lush and full. There was forty miles of open grazing country between the remaining forests of west county and dense woods of Marine County to the south. The grasslands were a huge buffer zone of pasture.

In the north, cattle had been effectively pulled off the land by the ranchers and the Shire and everyone else who thought to corral the beasts. In the south, the animals were left to their own devices by dint of their freedom from the harassing four-wheeled machines that the modern cow punching ranch-hand used.

The cattle of Marine County were generally the property of hobby ranchers who had made immense amounts of money and were living out their romantic dreams of the good-life. The old family farms had sold out to these carpet-baggers when they had the chance.

Old family farms and ranches didn't stand a chance against the onslaught of the modern money reality. They stupidly bought into the idea that debt and borrowing money from the banks was the only way to stay afloat. That didn't pan out so well and when the movie stars and financial wizards who manipulated the system, and who had made some serious bread in the industry came along, they jumped at the chance to get out and get on. The kids of the old ranchers were seldom interested in staying on with dad and his grubby old cattle, and all the stinking cow shit that plagued the memories of their youth. They had gone to college and learned easier ways to suck money out of the system than trying to raise food the hard way. That was just antiquated. So, when the hobby ranchers showed up, mom & pop sold out and went on the one big vacation of their lives.

What the old codgers didn't realize was, that having their cattle and their land was the ultimate paradise. They had a reason to get up in the morning and they had gratifying chores to do during the day. This is what kept them healthy happy and moving forward. Their gardens were lush, full and green. Their larders were packed with wholesome canned veggies and their lockers stored with the best aged meat on the continent. They were in the middle of the greatest heaven on earth that could be gleaned from the land and they let the TV and media internet world convince them otherwise. They were led to believe that what was 'out there' was far better than what they had in their hands. They sold out. They left.

The animals faired well under their new owners, but they were mostly just hired hands who didn't really give a hoot about whether the livestock survived the year or not. It was a job, not a vocation.

The quiet came and the planes stopped making high altitude sunscreen and the temperatures soared and the grass of paradise dried out.

—

Bill laid in an almost comatose blacked out state of bliss. There was no joy in his bliss. It was a bliss of nothingness. A bliss of not feeling the pain he felt he must endure because it had all happened to him. He was the universal focus. It was all aimed his direction, with the explicit purpose of thwarting his happiness. He medicated himself into a stupor and slumbered in the deadened unfeeling joy of not being in so much pain for a minute. It was an alcoholic nap.

Small glittering flashes insistently beamed from the far ridges to the south. Bill saw nothing and he and the two dogs slept into the warm afternoon.

126

11

<u>Surf Snood</u>

A.D. 1932

Slidik Clan brothers, Slidit, Slidir, and the youngest brood sibling Slidil, worked the northern great ocean. They viewed lights ashore and avoided them. There were massive steel creatures of machinery that swam the sea surface and they avoided them. They worked for Sleerdin and they avoided her. They sampled the stinking water, as was their duty, and surfed and skipped great ocean waves in their high-end planetary runabouts to their hearts' content.

Their three orbs, flew in a slash formation, Slidit, the oldest, in front, Slidir, the middle, behind and to the right, and Slidil the youngest brother, trailing him a bit in-line. They matched the angle of the ocean swells, so they hit them at about the same time. Following in a typhoon's wake they surfed their personal western sea. The waves rolled long low and evenly spaced. Three spumes of spray pulsed upward simultaneously as they punched through the tips of the massive hills of water, together. It was a move they had practiced. They appeared as one unit moving across the sea.

It was great fun.

Patrolling their beat gave them the time and freedom to get creative with their surf antics. When the far-flung global patrols gathered, which was rarely at first, they 'wowed' the others with a few simply timed stunts. They eventually worked the flying spray and jumps into choreographed exercises. The other snood of Sleerdin's 'cartilage crew' were delighted and it became a competitive sport between them. The Slidik's had started a fad sport, performance competition in: timing, altitude, speed, angle of bounce, splash height, formations and craft flips and rolls became a popular intra-mural game for the overworked and forlorn cartilage crew left on IV. The Slidik clan brothers had inadvertently invented team sport wave-surfing, IV style.

IV was far enough out in the backwoods of the galaxy for such a childish preoccupation to take root. The young snood had access to very expensive rich boy's toys and it was a natural evolution for them to turn an elitist extreme sport into well honed practice. The high end wavecraft afforded them the tools and time to exercise their creative talents. They could get minor damage repaired, paid for by planetary coffers in the name of maintaining the fleet necessary to monitor the resort world, and the shame and embarrassment of engaging in sighted activities was out of the view of registry and priesthood scrutiny. It would have been prohibitively expensive, and socially frowned upon, anywhere but on IV.

The three brothers were the preeminent wave skippers and they never tired of skipping new formations and routines to wow their comrades at the annual gathering at corporate.

The Slidiks became used to the finite oceans that prevented them from blasting about endlessly. Their Homeworld was without continents, but IV's oceans were ringed by hard land, so there was concern for collision. Not only did they have to be careful about the edges but also each other. The wing-snood had to keep an eye on the formation leader's signaling flashes of hull light and also on the next wave. The lead watched for, and timed, waves. He flashed and trusted his brothers to follow at a safe distance and they trusted him to keep from piling them up on the stone fence that ringed their play-tub.

Inside their ships, each was wrapped around their telescope in focused embrace, plugged into their control panel, humming and squirming their way along, while constantly shifting view to keep up on the visual clues as they flew. It was strenuous and exhilarating.

The Slidik brothers had previously never had time, nor money to wave-skip beyond occasional jaunts for maintenance checks of the rental fleet they were employed to manage. As rental valets they could only skip very occasionally and for short moments. Now they could fly as long as their stamina and spiritual duties allowed. Now that the planet was evacuated and they were conscripted into Sleerdin's fleet they had their own run-about yachts to command. They'd gotten their pick of the fleet and flew the company craft as often as they liked. It was only required for them to do their rounds, take samples, and observe the enemy, but they loved thrills. So they skipped a great deal.

The main constraint on their flying time were the required spiritual chanting down cold deep and the imposed night of the solar day, can't surface surf in the dark, and mustn't neglect prayers.

The typhoon left steep, green-grey, uniform hills rolling in lines that were perfect for skipping in the grandest style. The three, in line, popped synchronous splashes high and close together. They stretched the limits of safety to within a few hull lengths of each other.

Slidil thrilled at a quick glance askance to spy his brothers in close proximity. They wobbled in aerofoil turbulence; rivulets cascaded from their colorfully lit hulls, poised against the sky in joyous abandon.

It stopped his hearts to see them in such adventurous poses.

Their ships' interiors were slimed in bliss as they skipped on the tops of marching mountains of water.

They flitted across the storm's ripple.

Slidit flashed signal for a staggered formation and then, a red flare as danger loomed.

Slidil didn't see Slidir respond in kind and swung his view forward just in time to see the hull of the warship.

Slidit dove as soon as he pulsed the red warning and vanished, Slidir whipped at eyelevel over the deck of the steel creature, Slidil watched, aghast from astern, as he swung aside to avoid hitting the thing.

Slidir's colors flashed surprise, resentment, and then anger as he turned in an arc to return toward the lumbering pile of iron and dove under it.

He must have turned the magneto toroids to full circular flux as the water jumped up and vibrated around the floating lump of a ship, then plunged beneath the waves as the water under it came apart and became gas.

The box of metal's buoyancy failed as the water boiled out from under it.

Slidir was really pissed off about almost hitting the monstrosity. He was more volatile than the other two and in a fit of anger sucked the thing to the bottom of the sea.

Slidil hovered and watched.

The machine belched a puff of smoke, stick-like structures onboard waved frantically, and the red dot on a white flag flapped defiance as it was sucked beneath the heaving and turbulent water.

The sea shrugged and went back to its never ending surge from the just passed storm. In only a few moments Slidir could be seen floating in its stead. Slidit joined him from below and Slidil sheepishly flew to them and nestled up against their yachts. A slight magnetic field for docking and the three stuck together, just under the surface on the high sea in broad daylight. It was a common maneuver, they often rafted up to discuss their exploits or next attempt. They bobbed on the heaving fifteen meter swell.

"The bastards tried to kill us!" Slidir was yelling as he slid outside in the caressing chill water of the tempest tossed sea.

"What the hell are you doing!?" Slidit hollered back as he swarmed his younger brother. "We're supposed to observe, we're not suppose to 'do' anything to them!"

"You saw it. They attacked us. I was just defending myself." Slidir made up his version of events. He swam out of reach of his brother.

"It was barely moving." Slidit rebutted as he chased Slidir in agitated circles.

"You saw it, Slidil, it got right in our way deliberately." Slidir tried to get little brother on his side.

Just then a huge oily glop of fuel oil boiled to the surface as the tanks below were crushed by the pressure. They were surrounded by a slick of black stinking petroleum.

"Ahhh!! Tar!" Slidil screamed as he swam out of the mess. His brothers did the same.

They couldn't understand his anguished sliming-speech due to the stench of the oil.

Slidil found himself alone in the open ocean, separated from his brothers, separated from his ship and in Meerbock territory.

He dove in an attempt to cleanse the goo from his body.

It was too deep to easily get to the bottom and scrape himself, he might lose track of his ship altogether, unacceptable.

He circled the ugly mess and eventually found Slidit and Slidir together, wrestling and still yelling at each other.

"How are we going to get our ships back now? Huh, brother? Answer me that?" Slidit fumed.

"I hate them, I hate them, I hate them!" Slidir yelled at the cosmos. His stinking oily bile of enmity mixed freely with the oil around them.

"Lotta' good that's gonna' do. Go on, yell. You're the one that caused it, not them," Slidit accused and slapped at Slidir with his main tentacle.

"Well, we just go get 'em," Slidir reasoned a poorly framed solution to retrieving their craft as he evaded his brother.

"How, gel for brains? I'm not letting that greasy stuff into my vehicle, no sirree," Slidit declared adamantly.

Slidir was at a loss. He knew they couldn't just leave their ships abandoned, they'd never find them again, and they'd suffer the wrath of Sleerdin for losing them. He clearly felt her mouth on his main tentacle. They could wait for the oil to break up, but that might take days, weeks, and the predatory Meerbock of IV were voracious on the open ocean where little food was to be had. Swimming in clear water at the edge of an oil slick for days and nights with ravenous Meerbock was out of the question.

"We could tow them out of the oil." Slidil said.

"Oh, but the stench, it's bad in there." Slidir recoiled at the idea of going back into the messy pool.

"We're already soiled, we might as well do it while we're rested. The spill is finite. We can get them out here in clear water and clean enough to enter."

Slidit squirted admiration on his littlest brother. "Slidil is right Slidir, let's do it." He snagged his brother in a sucking embrace and pulled him toward their ships.

"Oh, residue," Slidir moaned.

The three snood gulped great quantities of clear water and plunged into the oil spill.

It took some time for them to find their yachts and when they did, Slidir's iris hatch was ajar.

"Damn the dry! Damn the heat! My boat's fouled!" He cried out.

"Good," said Slidit, "You can enter and tow us all out of here."

Slidil laughed at his big brother's predicament. He had started the chain of events and was now paying for his temper. Slidil usually paid for his older sib's anger, now it had fallen back into his own crevices and Slidil and Slidit were taking a little joy from it.

They clung to their yachts and rode the waves to their height and then down into the dark troughs, as their middle brother gently teased the three rafted ships through the water and away from the oil spill.

"Keep going, nice and easy we're cleaning as we go," Slidit spit a call into the open hatch of Slidir's boat. He knew it must be awful inside with oily gunk on everything. The oldest and youngest of the Slidik brothers scrubbed with as much secreted chemical wash as they could muster up while water sloshed over them.

In the clear and up-current, Slidir came out cursing. "Those nasty scum are going to pay for this. I am starved and everything aboard is foul. Throom me brothers." And with that he slipped away and dove, naked, into the depths.

"You don't think he's going to ...?" Slidil asked.

"I don't know. He was pretty sour. Who knows. We've never tasted one. It might be good." Slidit posited.

It wasn't long before Slidir returned with the body of a seaman. He flopped it onto the deck of the awash craft and the brothers ringed around to examine their despised enemy. The creature was far less imposing than they imagined.

"It doesn't look dangerous." Slidil said.

"What kind of skin is that? It peels off easily." Slidit pulled at the clothing of the sailor.

"You don't eat the peel." Slidir said as he ripped the body naked. "Oh dear," he said as all was revealed. "Is that an eyestalk?"

The brothers groped with their tentacles and adjusted their one eye to examine the details.

"It can't be, it was covered up. And besides it has eyes, two of them, on this bulb on top, like the life preserver suits." Slidit sounded knowledgable.

"I wonder what such a tiny tentacle like that would be for?" Slidil wondered.

"It doesn't look appetizing." Slidir said.

"Nothing 'looks' appetizing bag brain, just try it." Slidit derided.

Slidir swarmed over the man. He secreted just enough digestive juice to melt some of the flesh for a sample. "Not bad. Not bad at all." He squirted samples for his kin.

"Mmm. Kind of sweet," said the older.

"Tastes funny." Slidil said.

"An acquired taste." Slidir was more sophisticated in food from IV. He had tasted just about everything he could get his tentacles on.

The three swarmed the corpse and in only a few minutes dissolved and ingested the navy man. They spit out the bones to plop in the ocean around them.

———

Taiji Mizuki floated on the turbulent sea. His life jacket had dragged him to the surface. He saw no one else from the deck-gun crews. They had made fun of Taiji for always wearing the cork jacket and now he seemed to be the only survivor of the attack. At least he was alive.

He had just finished breakfast when general quarters rang.

In a hurried scramble he manned his station as machine gun loader just in time to see the incoming enemy aircraft.

His gunner, Tamako, let loose a stream of 7.7 mm rounds and the first plane disappeared into the sea.

The second flew at them and Taiji ducked instinctively as the attacker flew over the deck by only a few feet.

The next thing, the ship sank in the cold water of the Taiwan Strait.

His world had turned upside down in only a few moments; warmth and camaraderie, the battle he trained for, and now, desolation and frigid cold.

Wind whipped spray pierced his brow as he lifted high on the swell, salty green water burned his eyes and forceful wave-top spume stung his face in the bright afternoon sun.

There wasn't a cloud in the sky.

The storm had passed.

It left behind a monstrously churned sea, and Taiji, bobbing alone.

He blinked and sank down the backside of the swell, into the trough. He was carried down swiftly, like a leaf in a river. The painful spray ceased, a quiet moment of relief stole over him as he rode between cliffs of water. He looked up from his dark well to the towering hills of water above him, and spent a moment in peace and stability at the bottom. It was calm and quiet and didn't feel insistent in any way. The foothills of moving liquid hovered above and gave him a second to compose himself. He saw himself in a gulley in the middle of open ocean. He could look down the valley to wonder at the uniformity of the massive movement of liquid about him.

Waves.

Enormous, waves.

The water seemed as tangible as the hills around his father's farm in Fukushima, except, it was on the move, constantly.

He pondered what to do next, to survive, then he was drawn back up the next hill and thrust into the piercing wind again.

The never-ending repetition of ocean waves would time his death knell, over and over, again.

At the top he saw a long way.

He sank into the deep trough.

He lifted to great heights.

He fell again, into despair.

Taiji was propelled toward heaven and sucked into hell with each passing wave. He bobbed as a bug on the stream, washed to wherever the world decided.

He hugged himself closely and tried to preserve body heat.

He was alive and could go on. He watched for others or debris that might help him.

Relief came in form of an oil slick. The spray lay down, as just upwind, where the ship must be, rose a sizable pool of fuel that calmed the seas.

Taiji saw something moving where the *Sarawabi* had been, rising out of the oil slick, as if trying to escape the polluted water: giant jellyfish. Large amorphous globs of transparent gelatin like creatures, with writhing tentacles flopped about on the surface and began sliding magically through the water as if riding on some platform.

Taiji could only get glimpses as the turbulent sea lifted him to see clearly and then hid him from the mysterious phenomenon. Each time his view cleared he saw them move farther from the oil filled water. He tried to make sense of the vision. He had grown up on his father's farm, but had also spent time down at the docks and was well acquainted with most things from the sea. He had seen whales and porpoise and giant squid and huge ocean fish dragged up onto the quay for butchering, but he had never seen anything like these creatures. The salt spray strung his eyes but he kept staring after them.

They dragged one of his shipmates into the open and in only a few moments consumed him.

Taiji's blood ran cold.

If they saw him he would be the next course. They spat the man's bones high into the air, some fell near Taiji. He lay very still. Tears streamed from his eyes. Taiji knew his end was soon coming, but he could not keep from watching the hideous monsters eat his compatriot. They finished their grisly meal and disappeared.

Then his entire body vibrated with a deep rumbling sound that came up from the depths of the ocean to penetrate his core and added to his violent hypothermic and fear induced shivering.

"Throoom."

Three spherical shapes, the enemy airplanes he had thought, rose silently from the water and hovered in a formation just above the wave tops.

The craft didn't move as the waves fled under them and splashed the hulls as they marched by.

In another moment they took off, straight up. Slow at first, and then accelerating at a constant rate, they rocketed away and vanished into the darkening sky.

Taiji bobbed helpless on the seething sea and waited for death to rescue him from the nightmare.

12

Emissary

The forest swallowed the plip, plop, plip, plodding clack of steel horseshoes on hard asphalt as the cavalrymen spoke quietly and shared a little lunch on the hoof. Saddle leather creaked under their weight as the horses trod on languidly.

The men snacked on jerky, hard cracker, dried fruit and washed it down with a little canteen water. They were wrapped in the comfortable and familiar sounds of their own progress, rhythmically soothed by the power of their passage, on their loyal mounts, and protected by their uniforms and badges on a mission of import. There was no time to stop for lunch. There was also no great hurry. The urgency of their mission wasn't one of haste, but rather one of gravity. Their orders were to meet and establish face to face communication with the fire chief of Sentimental. It seemed to be a good time to slow down and take advantage of this easy milk run foray to West County. They normally had much more intense and stressful duty and were glad for the trouble-free road and languorous mission. They clip-clopped through the woods and would arrive when they got there.

The two young Hispanic deputies, Jose and Edgar confidently followed their squad leader Sergeant Michael. He had led them through numerous hectic and chaotic victories since the quiet. The men rode with easy swagger. They knew what they were about. To the West County folk they brought the awesome badge of the

Sheriff. Their rescue mission was to help organize the poor disheveled rural people who, would surely welcome them.

The authoritative sound of horse iron tapping the road under them instilled an air of command unto and around them.

Control.

Order.

Cadence.

The equine cacophony ricocheted off the trees around them and their advancing animals. The hoof-beat, moved as one and announced them sharply into the quiet two lane country road ahead. The four horsemen came around each automobile tailored curve of the western wooded rural road into thicker and older verdant enfolding rain forest. The lush green surrounded them and bathed them in peace, calm, and confidence. The deputies paraded down the corridor formed by tall redwoods that lined the road. They dozed through the dappled shadows and into the warm yellow slanting sun.

Sally got a piece of four day jerky from Michael and had fallen back a little as she chewed on it and swigged her canteen.

She thought to herself. "I ride with my men."

Sergeant Michael Sullivan, with the cute dimples and disarming smile was her loyal devotee. Sally had found a relationship of platonic and flirtatious respect with Michael.

She was older, he was vibrantly youthful.

He thought she was an inspiring, full, and exciting woman, so much more than the flighty and superficial girls of his own age.

She got tiny butterflies when the testosterone charged young man came near her.

Young women just didn't know the power they had. Sally knew her womanly power, and she used it to effect. She read him easily. She smiled and played with and rode with and led Michael and his men. They were hers. She made them all feel powerful. They made her far more powerful than she had ever felt in the 'before the quiet' part of her life.

Michael's broad square shoulders floated magically in front of her, his tight round butt perched lightly on the saddle over his horse's rounded behind. He sat his mount well, framed by his equally well sat men arrayed in front of her.

His presence drew her and her romantic thoughts of desire and let her slip into a dreamy state of yearning for a man. She admired the backs of these three masculine guys that Sheriff had sent with her on this diplomatic waste of time. She could smell their piquant and deeply alluring odor mixed with the horse sweat and green damp of the forest. She chewed her lower lip, leaned forward into the saddle horn and felt the gait of her mount under her.

The two fellows, Jose and Edgar, followed Michael assiduously. They were his protégés. They were all young, good looking, strong, virile, and most important, obsequious to her judgment.

She was the power figure; the consultant, the knowledgeable one, the adult. She wasn't totally sure why it worked, but she was careful not to let it be sullied by any disrespect. She played the 'County Animal Asset Officer' to the hilt, but in her mind she was the commanding cougar in charge. A lioness and her minions. The future demanded an encouraging nudge in the right direction when things were so muddled. The destruction of the status quo demanded a bit of confidence in order to maintain any air of sanity and Sally had found a clear path through the craziness of the new world. She played the cold bitch in charge and it worked.

Michael and his guys lined up with her intent and made it happen. In a given situation, Sally could see what was missing or what was being done too much or where the current move just wasn't working, and then made a decision that Michael and his guys could productively act on. During the livestock confiscation Sally directed them and then quietly migrated to the periphery of the action as the tough young deputies put themselves into the breach. Her powers of perception were strongest when the tension was high and she watched it play out in front of her. She could discern the next move and she fit right into the maelstrom of people and chaos of animals. She inserted her social authority judiciously and directly to the young men of the Sherriff.

They were tough deputies, initially trained by the U.S. of A.'s military might, but they needed to be told exactly what to do. She kept it clear what she expected at each expropriation/raid.

When they first rode up to a ranch she was asked what she thought about the approach? She obliged and gave them her take; they, more often than not, took her suggestions and observations. It was the personal touch, coupled with the legally warranted confiscation of people's livestock, that allowed the Deputies to make successful polite and friendly incursions into people's yards. It became a matter of course. Sally proposed and they imposed.

To each of the men she rode with, she gave the time of day to, in private, so as to keep them believing in her. Her moments of personal touch were doled out to each of them at one time or another during the course of their dirty, gritty, stinky, chafing, workday. She spent her time making sure each and every one of the guys she was riding with had gotten a measure of personal interaction and meaningful eye contact.

She took a moment with Jose as he led the horses to water and grooming. She stood close and whispered encouraging words, letting her sweet soap smell and the touch of her lips momentarily on his ear as she congratulated or gently chastised him.

She made sure she touched and spoke to each man privately each day. Every man got a moment or two of her directing attention. She displayed her female admiration for him, each, alone, to all of them. No matter how many men she rode with. She found time to spend a moment with them all.

None of it was overtly sexual, but the smell and ministration of a strong female lured them to loyalty. Since the 'quiet', she had endeared herself to every deputy the Sherriff had put near her. She didn't have to do anything overt. There was no 'putting out' in the modern sense of the word. She just ingratiated her wily mature female self to them and told them what to, or, not to do. They followed her lead like a pack of heavy, dangerous, well armed puppy dogs.

The men appreciated her and responded well to her strong female authority. It was refreshing to be around a woman who knew what she wanted. They acted on her suggestions and didn't worry about feelings and diplomacy and couching every little thing they said in sugar coating so as not to offend.

Sally gave and took honestly. Her criticisms were short and sweet. She was on a mission to get the animals she had only seen on paper and these men were her tools to do that.

The deputies had a mission to do something their training had never really prepared them for and this gracious woman was making it easy for them.

She somehow got a chance to offer solutions when the round-up went roughly and things got hectic and frazzled and close to violent.

She always had a simple note for those who couldn't get the cows, or ranchers to do what they wanted as they corralled the resource that were, by decree, the county's asset. They deferred to her judgment or authority when the bluster of brute Sheriff force wasn't enough.

The combination of the tough para-military police force tactics and Sally's diplomatic tempering of them with a cool assured approach worked well.

When they rode on a ranch she spent a moment to get the eye and give a nod to the guys risking their lives to legally steal the cattle and livestock of the citizens of the U.S. of A. They nodded back in turn to her and rode into danger.

They had run livestock for three weeks and were now on a long diplomatic mission as emmisaries.

The sound of their four horses' steel shod hooves on the asphalt road banged off the bark of the trees around the advancing animals. The hard steel percussion on pavement announced the four horsemen on the rural road.

So far, luck had been with them and she was feeling pretty good about herself and what she had going with Michael, Jose and Edgar. She smiled enigmatically as she stared at their tight young masculine flanks.

They had ridden all day and were bored with the long ride that had finally become monotonous. They were swallowed by the heavy forest jumble of hills and gullies of the scrunched and wrinkled coastline of the west coast. The humplety-bumblety hills just inland from the sea where the Pacific tectonic plate mashed against the shoulder of the continent was a perfect place for a fog harvesting forest of redwoods. All day they had headed out the one central road of the three possible paved roads to West County. The four of them plodded along into the glaring late afternoon sun and deep long shadows. They rode their trusty mounts onward and followed the never ending serpentine bends of the road, up and over hills and into occasional deep cool shadow filled gullies.

It was late in the day and the horses had gone farther than usual without turning back. They had gone beyond the edge of the plain. They had pierced the wood. The sheriff's and county's authority had only been able to exert itself on low hanging fruit thus far, and that meant that only the easy to get to ranches that they could reach in a morning and wrangle in a day had been their focus. No one had had the time to venture beyond the fringes of the flat expansive plain that was Saint Rose's farming legacy; the shallow basin formed by the Rushing River's watershed.

Up until then there had been no reason to ride that far in a day. The edge of the plain was it. Once you hit the woods it was rough and heavily forested. It hadn't been worth the effort to try and find any large amounts of cattle there. There had been plenty to take in Saint Rose basin proper without having to go mess with all the minimal outlying populations. The horses knew this by daily habit and were ready to turn and head for home where pleasant groomers waited for them with tingling curry combs and sweet bags of oats. It was getting near stable time.

They had been on the leading edge of an army of Sherriff's cavalry collecting livestock and helping to secure the foodstuffs that Saint Rose needed in this time of war. Now they were on a little overnight trip.

The deputies chatted,

"These folks wanted to live way out here by the dad gummed river, well, it's going to take us a bit to come fix things for 'em." Edgar mocked their use of time in his slight Spanish accent.

He was bored with the trip. He wanted someone to face down and hustle for their animals. That was what he had gotten used to doing as an 'after the quiet' deputy for the sheriff. To him, this whole mission was a demotion of sorts. No adventure, just a boring ride to the far side of the newly geographically challenged world that they lived in, with little at the end of the day's trail but a cold rough bed in the forest.

Up until now they had gotten to spend every second day in the hangars at the airport: luxury, grooms for their mounts, dry quiet real beds in warm dark rooms, with pillows and hot wash water, he got used to being catered to a little. He was going to miss his hot grilled steak for supper.

"Come on Edgar, we're gonna' find nothing we can fix. No comida. Nada. We bring nothing but our word that things are what they are." Jose smirked and hung slovenly off his saddle. He let both legs hang on one side of his horse for a change-up and to stretch and change position from the constant riding astride. He wanted to rotate his saddle sores a little.

It was just his and Edgar's luck that they spoke Spanish and were Michael's go to guys.

They had been going since dawn and everyone relaxed in the staccato click-clack of the sixteen hammering steel shod hooves on the rigid roadway. Up close, their party was quite loud and pronounced and audible, however, the road wound around and back and forth and back again. The effective distance of hearing a horse, or a few, riding up at a walking pace was about 75 yards, that's if you sat still and were listening.

Only bike messengers had regularly run the road from Saint Rose as far out west as Sentimental, but they had recently come under suspicion. No official sheriff's, or county council's emissary had made direct contact with the people in the west of the county. The Bike messenger corps had been the only communication connection.

The county council felt it needed to have some independent verification of the information they were getting from the fire chief in Sentimental. It was almost unbelievable that the people of West County were doing OK. So little was asked for. The county council was happy they didn't have to expend any of their precious resources on the extraneous people outside of town, but a few disturbing and disparaging reports had come in from independent and unverifiable sources that forced the hand of the council to take the action of at least sending a recon team, to ascertain the status of the people on the western side. The news from there was almost too good to be true.

Hence, the recon team of Sally, Michael, and his two vaquero deputies. They rode confidently into the friendly and welcoming forest of West County.

Jimmy Carpenter, all of fourteen years old, sat quiet by the side of the road. He watched and waited for them. He knew they were coming. He could just see his little brother Phillip on the other side of the road, up and hidden amongst branches of the bay tree. They each sat quiet and waited. They knew the deputies were coming. They had the camouflage net set on the telephone line across the road in place and waiting. They watched the uniformed men ride through the trap, past them, and disappear around the bend in the road ahead. The Sherriff's men never looked up. Jimmy got up after the horses disappeared and waved at his little brother. Phillip stuck his tongue out at him.

Jimmy was internally furious with his little brother. This was serious and Phillip was pushing it. He waved again.

Phillip acted like a monkey in his tree and walked down the angled trunk of the old Bay Laurel with his arms waving wildly like a chimp.

Jimmy had to wait for his little brother to do his monkey thing and reach for the trigger line. At the bottom he turned and both the boys pulled together.

Two opposing trucks rolled from their hiding places aside the road and pulled the net down across the roadway. The S.U.V.'s had been laboriously winched up into the woods and poised on inclines to roll to the center of the road and instantly block it. They rolled silently and smashed head-on into each other at only a mile or two an hour. The net they pulled along the phone wires above wasn't thick or physically tough. It only looked like it was impenetrable. Most of it was cloth streamers that had no structural integrity in the least. The curtain of woven deception fell across the roadway and made a wall of what appeared to be a fairly solid and entangling barrier.

They had waited for two days for someone. Jimmy and Phillip were the youngest kids in the posse. The others were up the road at the narrow cut around the bend. He and Phillip were only to stop any retreat. They were not to engage anyone. It was horses they were after. It was only horses they were expecting to deal with. Jimmy readied his lasso. He was going make himself a hero and get a good big mount to replace the beat up old camp horse he had been riding.

Old Mazey was ok for a first horse, but he had outgrown her. He was almost a man now. He needed a man's mount.

He waited at the side of the road, ready.

Jim the thin also waited in a nest of fragrant bay leaves, poised, ready, peering at the horsemen in the crosshairs of his scoped .223 bushmaster rifle.

His group Alpha guys were invisible, as was he, in the trees surrounding the open spot in the road. They waited.

Jim the thin waited a lot. He set things up and, then, waited. Jim let his breath out slow and noted the lax attitude of the uniformed troop coming into his bushwhack. They advanced too far into his fire zone, openly and without alert; textbook.

Waiting, was how Jim made it through middle school as the white kid in a world of brown, how he kept from getting pounded for being a geeky guy all his life, how he weathered his father's alcoholic rages, waiting was how he survived. Jim found out early in life that standing still, was usually his best option.

Standing still and being still.

Not interjecting.

He waited and it came.

Of the myriad options of action: forward, back, left, right, up, down, say something, say it forcefully, or say and do nothing at all, Jim found that not moving nor speaking worked statistically the best. No response at all was not only the path of least resistance, it was the pregnant pause that many people blundered into and spilled their true agenda, to Tim's advantage. If he let the space lag a little, people would invariably tell him what he needed to know. When it didn't work and he was left in silence he always had an out. He could shrug ignorance. People forget 'nothing happened' instances, but Jim usually got the informational goods and learned enough for the incident to net him something positive that he could use in the future. His innocuous self-positioning ingratiated him to people. He portrayed a pleasant subservience by not taking the lead and by letting others spew their most present thoughts.

Over time Jim ended up with a large cadre of loyalists. People let Jim lead by virtue of not leading. The major drawback was that he seldom went forward on his own initiative. He had never excelled at anything and led a life of having things happen to him instead of making things happen.

Jim liked waiting for the culmination of the ambush. It was old hat to him, even before the quiet.

Jim waited for the opening that inevitably came. If he stood by and waited for that moment, he could be ready and act. Those little points in time which really made a difference were the stuff of Jim's world. He waited until his minor effort made the maximum effect to his goals and then he acted. What served him well in school, served him well now. Let someone else go for the glory; let someone else open their mouth and get pounded while he made away with his hide intact.

Jim waited, he and his 'men', poised to capture horses. Better than a video game. The colors were crisper. The sounds of the forest were fuller and more interesting. He had been waiting for his chance to really make a difference and get the attention of Sir John. Now, he had a perfect ambush that would net maximum effect for minimal outlay, relatively risk free.

They seemed to get awfully close in those couple of minutes.

The three men and one woman sat up and heeled their mounts as Ethan, a crooked-nosed kid, brayed through a handmade cone of poster board, "Halt! Dismount. Do not advance further. Halt your horses. Dismount. Do not advance further."

All three men controlled their horses, swung to ready positions, and drew their side arms. The person in back merely held her hands aloft as she stopped.

"Dismount. Dismount. Dismount." Jason yelled from the opposite side of the road.

"Halt. Dismount. Drop your weapons." Ethan's hollow booming cone amplified voice hollered clearly to the men.

Deputy Michael yelled out in what sounded like a feeble response to the slightly amplified onslaught. "We are sheriff. Show your selves! Show Yourselves. We have the force of the law."

Deputy Jose and Edgars' horses wheeled to each side of the road as they brandished their pistols.

Jason stepped out onto the roadway opposite the mounted men with his hands at his sides. It was totally outside protocol. He was exposing himself dangerously.

"Halt. Dismount. Drop your weapons!" Ethan yelled again. The sheriff's deputies reflexively focused on and pointed their pistols in the direction of Ethan's hidden voice.

Jason got their attention when he yelled at them, "Hey, you heard him…"

One of them whirled and took a shot at him. He hadn't seen Jason come out onto the roadway and was startled when he yelled.

Another shot rang out from behind them and Edgar collapsed from his saddle and like a bag of sand fell onto the hard black roadway.

Jose started firing wildly into the thicket where Ethan was hiding and spurred his mount as Jason dove for cover.

Michael spurred his horse and joined in the fusillade that Jose was pouring into the thicket.

Sally sat stock still on Garnet, eyes wide as the all too fast gunfire flared around her.

Several rifle shots loudly echoed on the tree-lined highway.

Jose hit the ground scraping along as his boot hung in the stirrup and his horse swept by.

Wild horses fled the scene.

The rifle fire was much more concussive than the pops of the deputies' pistols.

Sally reacted only when Michael swung his open palm at her as he sped by in the other direction.

She turned tail and started to follow him as three tiny punching bits of metal placed themselves in a neat pattern in front of her, into his beautiful back.

He disappeared and she fled.

It was a sprint to the end of the straight spot in the road where the bend would shield her.

Garnet's hooves clattered on the asphalt and Sally ducked low and rode.

She rode for all she was worth.

She let her beautiful horse friend carry her from the insane instant death that had popped into the world.

She felt the terror as it crept up her back and tried to find a target on her.

She dodged and wove and steered Garnet on the course of a hopefully safe path.

The assassins were behind and unseen.

She ran.

The popping report of the guns at the ambush filtered back though the forest. At least a dozen or more shots were fired. They didn't sound like gun shots. They sounded like bad sound effects; sort of comical and not in the least bit deadly.

The Carpenter boys looked to one another across the gulf of the two lane black top. Philip grimaced and waved his twelve year old monkey arms. They were ready to do their duty for Sir John. They crouched in preparation with coils of line and lassos for the retreating deputies' horses to come running back down the road.

Capture horses.

Jim, feared the worst and held a sixteen ounce framing hammer tight in his fist. Just in case. The hammer and a thigh long bowie knife were his pivotal weapons. They had taken his dad's guns away from him and left him with only hand tools. It had burned in his brain when the men told him to dive and hide if there were any danger. He could handle himself even though he was relegated to hand tools.

The horses' hooves slapped and echoed as the ambush victims' mounts came running back down the road on their way home; riderless.

The first horse balked at the road-block curtain across the road, Phillip jumped out and lassoed.

Jim, stepped to the edge of the black-top and waited for the next horse to come into his hands.

Three mounts came running around the corner at full run.

Jimmy waited until they balked at the screen of obfuscation before he made his move.

The first two came up short, saddles empty, but, the third horse was being ridden deliberately.

The creature wasn't fleeing or loose. It was under command by its rider.

Jimmy had his lasso thrown over one horse and a second line at his feet in preparation to get the next animal when he realized there was a wild eyed woman staring down at him from the third mount.

She skid to a halt as her horse reared above the youngster.

The hooves of his agitated captive and the frantic animal above him hit the pavement.

Jimmy looked up at the rider as he scampered out of the way of the deadly hooves that slammed the hard road all around him. Sparks flew from the skidding iron shod animals.

Young Jimmy and the frantic woman locked eyes for an instant before she yanked her reins aside to get off the seemingly blocked roadway in favor of the tangled woods.

She was escaping.

Small bees whizzed around Jimmy as he watched her bolt off the road into the scrub.

He heard the pops of the gunfire, it registered on his psyche that they were shooting at her and he was down range. Angry bees whipped and slapped on the tree trunks following the crazed woman on the flying horse.

"Goddamn you a'holes quit shooting! We are down here!" Jimmy screamed up the road at the overexcited bushwhackers.

Jimmy bolted off the roadway and into the woods where the woman had plunged on her horse. He had to try to follow her.

He raced down the steep slope skidding and sliding as he creatively fell into the gulley that had swallowed the angry eyed woman and her horse. He bounded and slid through ferns and layers of leaves as he slid on a tree dodging toboggan ride down the rough, forested, dirt slope.

Almost at the bottom of the gulley Jimmy stopped and listened.

He heard an awful sound. A sound of unholy agony reached up into him.

He tightened the muscles in his face, shook his head, and as he relaxed his clenched jaw, he listened carefully and homed in on his prey.

The agonizing scream of the horse pierced him.

Jimmy turned right, closed his eyes and let his ears tell him where the sound came from. He turned slowly, then froze at the awful sound of the injured animal.

The horse was screaming in agony from down in the bottom of the ravine.

He thought he could hear the cries of the woman mixed with those of the injured animal.

Young Jimmy Carpenter, moved toward the sound and found them.

They had fallen over a large redwood log and the horse had apparently broken a leg.

The woman was standing on the log above the broken horse and holding the reins. She was entreating the horse to rise and be good once again.

The horse squirmed, tried to get up and screamed in high-pitched agony as the pain and reality of the destroyed leg came into the here and now.

Jimmy watched the woman in fat-thigh riding jodhpurs and a khaki bloused shirt stand over the animal with a pistol in her hand.

She cried and yelled encouragement to the poor creature.

There was nothing he could do, but watch helplessly.

She was armed, he was not.

Her horse was making an awful racket and she hesitated to put him out of his misery.

The moment froze in time.

The wood was so peaceful and this scene had taken over and turned it into a scene of chaotic anxiety, despairing agony, and pain.

The woman, screaming and crying, shot the animal in the head. The pistol shot resounded and faded into the sounds of the forest.

The animal's cries of pain and lung filled wheezing, abruptly ended.

Jimmy watched the scene as a melodrama ... like TV. It felt unreal.

She stood on the log in a slight haze of the smokeless powder of her ammunition; staring down at the friend she had just been forced to kill.

"Don't move!" Dark haired, dark eyed, Ethan called from up the slope. "We got you covered. Put the gun down. Put the gun down ... Now!!"

The woman didn't seem to hear anything. She just stared down at the horse she had just shot.

Jimmy climbed onto the end of the huge log and walked carefully toward her.

Jason and Ethan advanced clumsily down the steep ravine slope, guns ready.

Jimmy crept up the log towards her, his hammer held loosely.

The woman did not register his presence. She stared into the terror of her beloved Garnet, broken, bloodied, shot dead by her hand. The memories of her love for the animal filled her senses.

Jimmy walked right up to her and was within reach of her pistol when she slowly turned her head to him.

"Please, Lady. Drop it. They will kill you. Honest. Come on. We don't wanna' kill you. Just give me the gun. OK?" Jimmy looked up into her tear filled eyes.

Her chin quivered. Her power drained and she sobbed.

"Drop it Lady!" Jason yelled at her from only a few feet away. "Drop it or I gotta' shoot you!" He threatened.

Jimmy took the distraction as an opportunity and made a quick move. He hit the shiny chromed .357 magnum from her hand with his hammer.

She recoiled in pain and clutched her hand as the pistol fell into the blood filled hole where her Garnet lay and slithered out of sight.

"Don't move I swear I'll blast you lady!" Ethan yelled from the other end of the log where he shakily aimed his twenty-two caliber, bolt action, long-rifle at her.

Jason moved to her at ground level with his gun pointed at the small of her back.

She whimpered in pain as she crouched down onto the log and held onto her newly injured hand. She sobbed and blubbered uncontrollably. Her tears came welling out and she turned her face to the sky and howled her anguish.

The teenaged boys froze and stared.

She wailed to the unseen Gods about her pain and loss. She wept uncontrollably and a tragic drama, of a quiet unfeeling forest that echoed all of the pain and anger and confusion that a single woman could evoke, played out.

The catharsis held them all in its grasp and they felt sorry for her, and her horse, and were ashamed at themselves.

Sally slowly looked up at Jimmy.

He was upset by her raw outpouring of grief and wanted to get away from the embarrassing scene. He stood over her with his hammer raised. He was poised to hit her again. He shook as he stood above her. There were tears streaming down his cheeks.

She looked up into the eyes of the kid. He was maybe fifteen years old. He had the look of an old man in a kid's body. She composed herself and wiped her tears. She wanted to see him clearly.

He looked down on a broken grown-up. He had the power. He had taken her power and he held it now.

She took deep breaths and composed herself. "OK. I'm OK now."

13

Bowditch

A.Q. Week Three

The Shire Lords rode constantly. Each squad of men grew as they acquired more horses and support. The highest priority for John's Lords was to commandeer diesel powered vehicles and old discarded antique farm equipment. All machinery was under John's personal command. None of it rolled without his express permission. Diesel fuel was dear and finite.

Jack Brown's mid-ridge compound, dubbed Brownsville, became the machine shop. A large steel shop building, hidden in the woods behind the five thousand square foot house, became the official motor pool.

Seneschal Mark, had set Jack Brown and his mech-heads onto the task of creating battle tanks from the dump trucks and highway equipment. Jack and his men got carried away with the idea and created a variety of attack machines. Compressed air powered wrenches were modified into starter motors; steel plate was bolted on the front and sides of the cabs and engines, and large angled cow catcher blades adorned the front bumpers to smash aside obstacles. To the regiment they added a couple of large front end loaders that sported steel boxes hanging off the sides as gun turrets and steel plate with eye slits all around the cabs. They painted them black with garish red teeth on the scoops. The side yard of Brownsville filled with mechanized armor.

The technical problems were immense. All of the metal construction had to be done by hand or with torches and oxyacetylene was scarce and dear. They were limited in that; powered saws or welders used magnets and needed large amounts of unproducible electricity to function. Even punching holes in a quarter inch piece of steel plate became an arduous task. Rivets were reinvented from existing scrap in lieu of welding and drilling of holes was minimized due to the amount of effort involved. Prenineteenth century technology, long unused and mostly forgotten, was now the modus operendi.

The only relief of modernity was the solar panels and wet cell batteries. They could charge the lead acid batteries with solar panels, but the only use was a little light and warming the glow plugs in the diesel machines for starting. The DC power would not drive any power tool, they had magnets.

John forbid the use of battery power for so trivial a purpose as profligate and wasteful lighting. The energy was held in reserve to warm the cylinders of the massive machines so compressed air could start them. Light was an extravagance that could not be afforded. There was plenty of daylight to accomplish the tasks before them.

The solar cells and batteries worked and no one knew why they did and the magnets didn't. Initially there was a lot of discussion and some experimentation to try to make some magnets from the small battery sources remaining, but these efforts ended in short order and they got on with the business of operating without the electricity. All metal seemed to now be non-ferrous; in that, it would conduct current, but would not hold and propagate any magnetic field, therefore no electric motors.

One of the technical challenges Jack's team overcame was a cylindrical well pump powered by a shaft coupled to a power take-off from one of the front end loaders. Most wells were fitted with electric pumps that lived in the bottom and pushed water up to the surface. Suction pumps were good for a maximum of thirty two feet of altitude and were laborious to operate. They had plenty of small suction hand pumps, but getting a large volume to move in a short time was best done from the bottom up. They finally perfected a pump that they could move easily and drop into a shallow well or tank quickly.

On the seventeenth day after the quiet, John led a force to the coastal town of Bowditch for fuel.

Bowditch sat on the very edge of the ocean surrounding a perfect natural harbor. It had been improved with a breakwater and channel dredging and it was a valuable place of refuge for the local fishing fleet. The town had been a fishing hub for more than a hundred years and despite the efforts of modernity to destroy subsistance forms of production and locally based food gathering from the sea, there was still a small core of the fishing culture that survived.

The majority of the townsfolk were now vacationers and retirees and people who had no need to depend on the ocean for their livelihood, but who enjoyed it and reveled in their romantic notions of Bowditch by the sea.

Recon had reported a serious schism between the fishing community and the 'land lubbers' of Bowditch. There was a single road that ran around the curve of the bay to the head of Bowditch peninsula where the marina lay. The majority of the commercial fishing boats were moored there and the sailor folk had cut the road with barricades and were keeping the land folk away and at bay. The fishermen realized their power of being able to provide transportation and food and were not about to accede it to a bunch of needy insensitive land folk.

There were only three sources of diesel fuel in Bowditch. There was a tank at the marina, one at the Coast Guard Station on the narrow sand spit that comprised the southern boundary of the bay and the lone land side gas station on Highway One. All of the tanks were underground. Recon reported the locals were using hand pumps to get at the diesel in the service station. Jack's shaft powered pump should allow them access to this fuel.

At dawn the rumbling of tractors hauling tanks and a makeshift column of five large machines roared down the steep back road and onto the highway north of town. They moved unimpeded through the town to the gas station and parked, chuffing and popping their diesel exhaust into the early morning light just peeking over the steep hills surrounding Bowditch.

The ground tank access was opened and the pump carefully lowered into the dark oily depths of the tank. In only a few minutes the pungent fuel was pouring into the squat old water tanks serving as their fuelers.

The three armored and crenellated dump trucks surrounded the gas station in defensive positions. Each bristled with armed men. At the very outside of their perimeter lone guards stood in brilliant orange crossing guard vests with stop signs to warn away anyone who might interfere or even question their authority to take the fuel.

Roscoe Jarvis, a local man, retired from the highway department and generally mister good citizen, came walking up to the orange vest crossing guard. "Good morning young man."

Jacob held out his hand and stated sternly, "Don't come any close mister." He had been a counselor at the Christian camp when the quiet came. He felt strongly about the state of God's new world and was a loyal soldier of the Shire.

"Well I just was wondering what's going on." Roscoe walked right up to him.

"Really mister I'm serious. Those guys in the truck have orders to shoot." He backed away from the elderly guy with his hand out to stop. "If you touch me they will shoot you. Please stay back. For God's sake."

Roscoe stopped and put his hands up and out where they could be seen clearly. "Ok. I was just wondering … who are you guys? And, what's the deal? Are you from Saint Rose?"

"Mister, I can't really say. I'm just supposed to warn you to stay away. No one is allowed any closer," Jacob told the man.

"Are you guys from the council? Or …?" Roscoe looked quizzically at Jacob.

"Look Mister I told you to stay back, now move back some or them guys are under orders and I don't want to see you get hurt. Please Mister," Jacob pleaded.

"Well can't you tell me who you are? I am Roscoe Jarvis. I live here. You guys just come riding in town like you own it and start taking stuff. Well that just isn't right. At least you can tell me who you are." He tried to smile a little.

"Really mister." Jacob was backing up with his hands out and open. "Please, just go will you?!" He was getting loud.

Roscoe took another step toward Jacob and a shot rang out. The asphalt at his feet popped up a little divot. He stopped and looked down at the hole near his feet and then turned sheet white.

"I told you Mister." He was almost in tears. "Please go away. They won't let you get near me."

Roscoe Jarvis, retired road repair crew supervisor, stepped backward slowly, sucked in a breath, turned and walked away.

He was shaking like a leaf.

An uncontrollable wash of fear swept over him and he could barely continue standing. He felt like he was going to fall down.

They had shot at him. They almost killed him.

The back of his scalp itched where he was certain a bullet was going to enter at any moment. He walked around a building and out of their line of sight.

As soon as he was away, Roscoe crumpled down onto the ground and puked the last of the canned beans he and his wife had eaten for breakfast. He stared at the pathetic vomit that was all he would get for food that day. It took him several minutes before the shaking subsided enough for him to scurry out from cover and head for home.

He suddenly had a deep and strong yearning to see Gloria, his wife. Just to hold her, and be in her company. Roscoe Jarvis high-tailed it home with tears in his eyes.

"Hell, it isn't my fuel. What do I care?" he said to himself as he picked up the pace and left the unknown men to take the fuel of Bowditch.

14

Score

The ghostly shadow of a big old mutt came in and out of view as he sniffed and snooped and investigated while Sam waited in the blind, watching.

Sam lay comfortably in the thick dry grass at the lip of the rise. He spied Atilla through his binoculars. Atilla 'cased' the place as Sam lay still in his vantage point. He waited for the large brindle colored mastiff to find something that would spur him to leave this place and move on, or to investigate further.

The lumbering animal ranged dutifully around the grounds below him, his nose led him in circles.

Sam lay under an oak tree in the dry grass since early morning watching for inhabitants or visitors. He had a clear view of the steel corrugated roof and front door of the cement block structure below. A small loading dock and closed steel roll-up door at the rear of the building faced the hillside he was on. The road side of the warehouse had three small office windows at second story level that looked down on the abandoned cars of long gone employees. Sam watched and waited.

Atilla came and went.

The building's shadow shifted from left to right. It was that time of day when returning residents might appear. He didn't want to be caught inside, or outside for that matter, when they came home from their daily foray.

He waited.

It was a warm afternoon and until he was sure the coast was clear he stay put. Sam didn't understand what it was about the building that compelled him to want to see inside. It wasn't that different a building from so many others that he regularly bypassed. He'd hiked all day and when he popped over the lip of the hill and was confronted by this unremarkable building, sitting in its hidden spot below, he felt a need to see inside. It was a long ways from any town and looked industrial in nature. It drew his attention. He lay still and watched.

Images from the last couple of weeks flashed in his mind as he killed time and let the dog do the legwork of snooping around. It had been a harrowing time since his exodus from the city.

—

Sam had followed the crowds of thousands out and across the great Golden Gate Bridge. They fled the starving urban hell-scape for hopeful future lives in the abundant agricultural Mecca of the northern counties.

The city had depended on a tenuous transportation system for its sustenance and when that ended the people who loved their fabulous San Francisco couldn't stay. They didn't grow food there. It was a big city, at least by west coast standards, and the inhabitants did not produce, but mostly consumed. It was a death trap. Those consumers moved in one massive mob towards the promised land: happy cow country, wineries, artisanal goat cheese, free range chickens, rolling green pastures and progressive tolerant and welcoming vacation resort towns. Tens of thousands crossed the famous bridge into Marine County on their way to Napa and Slocoma to the north. They remembered the wonderful times they had experienced on summer holidays and how the wine tasting and eclectic restaurants soothed the stresses of their workaday urban hustle and bustle lives. It seemed like the right move. They had a connection to the north. It was their kind of country.

The happy cows were sixty miles north though, and they had to cross Marine County to get to them. There was some cattle country in Marine County, but it was mostly far to the west. A few small herds were near the freeway and this picture of food on the hoof lured them north. The refugees were fixated on the beautiful rolling countryside of Slocoma. There the cattle were part of the sightseeing show. Vineyards and green pastures dotted with happy cows. That was the picture in their minds' eye.

Swarms of people rolled into the suburbs of Marine county where the well to do, who wanted a little more elbow room than the city offered, lived in their sprawling and spacious homes. The masses from the city had intended to just pass on through, heading farther north, but the suburban sprawl of Marine County and the lovely tree-lined thoroughfares drew them from the confines of the freeway. They were already a bit hungry and the fairly well off and the super-rich, whose luxurious hillside homes and estates were in full view from the highway, had pantries full of goods.

No one really thought too hard or long about what sort of reception they might get from the predominantly white upper class who had shielded themselves from the riff-raff for so long. The city-dwellers were of the delusion that they were just as good as the Marinians. All one had to do was make a million: sell some software coding or an app that tickled a lot of people's treat, or get a fat insurance or divorce settlement, or win the lotto, and you were in. Afford the big house and you were the same folk, our kind of people.

For years the people of Marine County had kept themselves in a somewhat sequestered state. They had made it very clear that they were different from the rest of the bay area. When the Bay Area Rapid Transit project in the 60's had been proposed to link the cities and peoples of the bay area with a modern commuter rail system, every outlying area to San Francisco had embraced the future of light rail, but Marine County turned the project down flat. They even went so far as to rip the old existing rails out of the ground and rezoned and rebuilt over them in order to preclude any future attempts at bringing trains back. They just didn't want to be subject to the rest of 'those people'. Of course they never said it out loud, but that was the underlying sentiment. Even though the Golden Gate Bridge had originally been designed to have a railroad slung under its superstructure to connect the city to Marine County and to the future, it was not to be so.

—

Bees buzzed around the few remaining flowers on the steep hillside below Sam. He marveled at the intense ferocity of their actions. They seemed very energetic and far more numerous than he could recall. A swarm of bees were working diligently to harvest the nectars from the meager flora. Occasionally one or two would buzz him and flit in front of his face, back and forth, scrutinizing him with their bulbous eyes. Sam ignored them until three of the creatures hovered in front of his face and stared him down. They acted in concert. They were thinking alien insect thoughts about him. One more came and took position and one left. And again another came and replaced one of the bee sentries. They were a relay team of scrutiny.

"Shoo, go away. I am not a flower." He half-heartedly waved a hand at the little buzzers They evaded him and with blurring speed dove down and out of sight.

"I wonder what the hell that was all about?" Sam asked himself and chuckled a little. Entertainment was rare and seldom, he took it where he could.

—

A hundred thousand people, or more, had streamed into the neatly landscaped and quiet neighborhoods of Marine County. Convoluted streets wound in artistic bends and circles that reflected the whims of wealthy developers and tortured topography and not according to the conventions of ease, efficiency, or simple grid patterns that might promote access.

The mobs stayed on the concrete lined freeway until long after the warning signs on the roadside near Little Willow ended. Their initial reception on this side of the bridge had been dire warnings, gunfire, and admonishments to stay on the road and not deviate. They had done just that until it was obvious that the signs were well past and behind them. They flooded over the perceived boundaries of the freeway edge, defined by the ever familiar concrete K-rail barriers that were designed to reflect errant autos back onto the roadway and which delineated the modern super-highway. People inundated the affluent suburban neighborhoods.

Long columns of marching people appeared between the hedges of the narrow private streets and lanes. The masses were propelled by their sheer desire to go and find sustenance that allowed them to continue another day. They stayed together at first and merely gawked through the openings made by elaborate gates in the foliage. They could see winding driveways into fantasy landscapes that were carefully tended by immigrant and ethnic labor.

The people of Marine County espoused diversity by never insisting that they be taken care of by their own kind, they just didn't want the hired help to live anywhere close by. A contradiction, in that they didn't want a train to allow people easy access, but they did want their hired help to be on-the-spot and ready, even though they had to come from the other side of the bay. That's where those poor struggling souls could afford to live on the cheapo-wages the wealthy paid them for their back breaking efforts. However, the gardens were beautiful. The grass was perfectly green and coiffed. The flowers and shrubbery were artistic and elegant to see.

Swarming people breached the perceived barriers that the setting denoted. They had never dreamt of going onto such properties, except in their wildest lottery winning dreams. When the first gate was pushed open they poured in. After that first one, gates were opened in a regular fashion. As more and more crowds swarmed from behind, it became a survival imperative to be the first one inside these homes for whatever was there. If you weren't there first, there were thousands behind you who would take what you left and sharing was getting to be an obsolete concept.

The older, white, previously respected upper-middle-class who lived there were appalled at the blatant disregard for their property rights: lawyers especially. Their entire careers had been based on protecting the rights of property.

The average man had been duped into thinking that some constitutional document guaranteed his personal rights to be treated fairly. The attorneys knew better, and had spent their lives assuring that those with accumulated wealth and property were protected above all else. That was what made the modern world work. We have and we dole out as we see fit. The common man was still operating under the belabored impression that there was some fair playing field, and that if only he would serve the system and do his time that eventually he would be rewarded and finally taken care of.

Naïvete of the masses.

Now they were at their gates. The litigation attorneys, who had made millions on fine points of law that left most scratching their heads at the insane amounts of money awarded by bringing minor vindication to others, were under assault.

The well trimmed privet hedges didn't seem to have any effect on these interlopers' sense of privacy. They ignored the long held belief that he who had the gold made the rules. The regular guy from the city was in the front yard. Some of these financial and legal wizards had sense enough to arm themselves when they had the chance. They did so out of a legitimate fear that eventually the system of paid enforcers who kept up the perception of protection would break down and they might have to fend for themselves. What they didn't count on was that there would be so many of them. Dozens, hundreds came into the yard and beat on the front door asking for admission to the kitchen. Some self-entitled wealthy fired on the crowd. That's when fires sprouted up as the enraged people afoot exacted their justice on the trigger-happy nouveau-riche.

—

Sam chewed a once-sweet stalk of browning grass as he watched the dog's antics.

The canine was great. Sam had seen Atilla lead enemies away from him as if running away, only to return later after he had led them away. It was either that, or the dog ran away when confronted and finally found his way back. So, he was either a really smart dog or just bored, skittish, and dumb. It didn't matter to Sam as long as he didn't lead anyone back to him and betray his presence.

So far, so good.

The mutt adopted Sam after he crossed the bridge from the city, in the suburbs of Marine County. His collar tag said his name was Atilla and Sam was fine with that. At first Sam let the big creature hang around as a ready food source that didn't need to be carried or defended. But, as the days wore on they bonded. And as long as Atilla kept finding things for them to eat he was safe from Sam.

—

Sam wasn't interested in ransacking rich folks' houses. He lived in Foxfowl in Marine County and his path was on the road to his apartment.

When he got there the front door was kicked in and it was empty of food. His things had been gone through. There wasn't much except an old kitchen knife and an antique aluminum army canteen from his father. It was the only item he had from his Dad. It had always been heavy and cumbersome and he never used on any camp trips. It had always been merely a decoration. It was now useful. He scrounged some socks and underwear and a sweater, jury-rigged the ancient canvas canteen cover on a belt and left.

There was no reason to stay there. It was just a box that he once lived in.

He rejoined the exodus north, but on his own terms. Foxfowl was far to the west of the northbound freeway and he would have to backtrack a dozen miles to reach it. He decided to head due north and go right up and over the rolling brown hills. There were few roads and it would be a hike, but he couldn't see wasting time merely to get back in line with tens of thousands of others on the highway. Besides, he had just about had it with the hard concrete and city surroundings. He knew where there were walnut trees and other meager sources of food.

He hiked into the hills to lush happy cow country.

This was sprawling land where movie-makers and wealthy hobby farmers had locked up acreage for their ultimate get-aways and perfectly controlled vistas for shooting country scenes for the film industry. There were small relatively unknown enclaves of trickling brooks and berry bushes and remnants of a few defunct orchards. He wouldn't have to compete for canned goods if he could forage enough. Sam figured he could make Slocoma County in just days if he worked at it.

He had made it too, except there was a border.

When he topped that tall hill and was confronted by the large plywood sign he couldn't believe it.

"Go Back, No passage allowed. Violators will be shot".

These were brand new, crudely painted signs. They looked very much like the signs that lined the freeway when they first came across the bridge. He could see the fresh dirt around the posts. He scanned the opposite hillside ahead and could barely make out the rifle nests.

Sam didn't want anymore buzzing bees flying at him, so he headed east.

After a full day hike he came upon large crowds of people moving in his direction. The refugees had met the border on the freeway and were moving west to find a place where there was no more border.

Sam sat down at the top of a hill and waited for the first of them to reach him. One of the first was a tough looking fellow in bare feet. He walked right up to Sam and sat down.

"Hey man," the guy said.

"Hey," said Sam.

"You're the first one."

"The first what?"

"You're the first person we've seen this far west. I've been trying to out-walk all these bastards and get to the coast."

Several other young men strode up and walked right on past them. Sam looked up at them as they filed by. They all walked just down from the lip of the hill, out of sight of the northern border rifle nests.

"Looks like you got ahead of me." The barefoot fellow smiled at Sam.

"I came from that way." Sam indicated behind him.

The barefoot guy lost his smile. "You're coming this way? What for man? There's nothing back there except millions of people, man."

"Well, I was hoping to find a way north."

"We all are, man. So, you're telling me that you can't get around these signs."

"I guess so," said Sam.

"'Well that really sucks dude. We thought it was only Eggtown that wanted to keep us out. I been hiking all day. They barricaded the bridge across the river and shot at people, so everyone fell back out of sight and, as you can see, we're hoofing it around them."

"I'm not so sure there is an 'around them'." Sam wrinkled his brow and took a tiny swig from his canteen. The other fellow's eyes followed Sam's every move. He was thirsty.

"Yeah well every time someone tries to go over this hill they get shot at. We gotta' go around."

Sam put away his canteen without offering any. His hand fell to rest on the sharp steel bar he had found and carried in his belt.

The barefoot guy got up and said, "Well, I'm going to the ocean anyway. There's just too many people back there to deal with."

Sam looked up and saw a long line of people hiking the ridge top game trail towards him. He rose and turned and followed the barefoot guy. West.

—

The late afternoon sun had warmed him to a state of slumber. Sam dozed off in the dusty golden straw of his grass bed. He dreamt and slept fitfully.

Atilla came in the darkness, crawled into his arms and they spooned in the moonlit nest.

Nightmares danced at the edge of his mind. The carnage of house breaking and gun fire and trying to stay alive. Multitudes of people behind had driven him onward and ahead to the coast. He was among the first. He got first pickings. He followed the barefoot youth; he swirled amidst the events of lucky moments of stealing and harrowing seconds of ear shattering explosive gunshot death at his elbow. He found the dog. He pulled a shotgun from the hands of a dead looting comrade, he ran, he hid, he ate vermin and bugs, and he lived on.

He lived in the present.

The cold woke Sam just before dawn. There had been no movement, so he slunk down to the building, skulked around the side, sidled to the front, and glimpsed in the window. He found it clear.

Atilla shoved his head against Sam's legs and forced his way into the building with him.

It was unusual these days to see glass front doors still intact. It meant someone had left it unlocked.

The glass front door led into an entry lobby with a retail counter. The lobby was small. A heavy metal door led into the interior of the building. He knew his entrance would flash dusky early morning light into the darkness beyond, so he stepped through the door quickly.

Atilla moved with him.

He crouched down just inside the door. It was a dark cavernous warehouse, a relic of the overabundant twentieth century consumer oriented world, frozen in time.

Sam let himself sense the place. He smelled the cool air. A musty odor mixed in with a whiff of plastic, rubber, leather goods lying about— consumer goods. Department store smell mixed with death.

Everything was mixed with death these days. Everyone alive on this twentieth day after the quiet had seen someone die recently.

These days, dying was so much easier than it used to be. Death added to the quiet. The dead are silent, except for the flies.

Sam sensed that something had happened here that was not good.

Something had happened everywhere that was not good.

There was no sound. No flies, nothing.

He crouched and cradled the pump twelve gauge shotgun. His trigger finger caressed the noisemaker as he scanned it around and pointed it at everything his mind processed and identified. He panned the gun from right to left as he discounted things to fire upon.

His eyes adjusted, the dark interior resolved and he could barely see shapes. There were some scurrying sounds deep in the aisles.

Rats.

Sam made a gesture to Atilla and the dog crept forward into the gloom of the building. Sam kept his shotgun ready as Atilla disappeared. The old fellow was hungry and began a hunt for the rodents, snuffling.

From the balcony above, a faint glow of light filtered in through the open second story office doors. He waited patiently as the diffuse light brightened with the rising sun and his eyes adjusted to the darkness.

Sam realized the warehouse was full of shoes.

Mounds of shoes, piles of shoes, loose and boxed, men's shoes, women's shoes, kid's shoes, dress-ups, sneakers, boots, you name it, there were lots of shoes. Hillocks of shoes lay where they fell from the tall shelves stretching back into the recesses of the cavern. There were other things in the space. Bundles of rags or lumps of ... something he couldn't quite tell.

Sam sat perfectly still, listening. 'Who would have thought that this lone building way out here between towns, hidden off the road just a bit, would have shoes inside? It must be some kind of hub warehouse for a chain of shoe stores,' he thought.

A creaking tic, tic, tic, started from above and behind as the sun touched the steel roof and it expanded with heat. The noise made Sam nervous and he decided to move on the upstairs offices while the racket banged away.

He stepped quietly and in cadence with the tic, tic, tic, and occasional banging pop of the heating roof plates until he reached the top of the stairs.

He moved along the balcony walkway that led to the office doors. The doors were all open and he slow-stalked, carefully and listened patiently, before entering any of them. He worked his way cautiously through the second story offices. One led to a storeroom and restrooms that smelled of old un-flushed shit. All of the offices were in disarray and showed signs of people having camped there.

From each of the office windows he could clearly see down on the parking lot and glimpsed the roadway through the trees. He moved back to the overlooking interior walkway and squatted low surveying the open space that stretched out below him.

There was no one here.

He was alone.

Sam's mind worked on the sight before him.

What was the importance of the discovery?

What cosmic telltale had led him here and compelled him to enter this place?

The importance of his find began to sink in.

Everyone thought it was just a power outage. No one knew that the world had been turned off. They might have guessed something was seriously wrong when the cars in the parking lot wouldn't start and they had to walk home from this warehouse in the boonies. No one really knew what we were all in for that fateful August afternoon. Who could picture a world in which nothing electrical operated, a world in which everyone was now constrained to associate only with people who were physically near by? No radio, phone, or internet communication existed. All those people at the other end of community network connectors were now too far away to contact.

Twenty days ago, ground transportation was reduced to horses and carts, bicycles, old diesels (if you could figure out how to start them), or your feet.

Who had a horse or a cart?

He had seen one diesel truck working and it baffled him as to why it would work and everything else wouldn't.

Steam was a power source, but who had steam powered cars, or steam powered anything?

Bicycles were a good answer to the transport problem, but they got their riders killed. Foot-worn walkers with guns didn't hesitate to take out a fancy biker for his wheels.

Walking was the way to get about now.

Sam whispered to himself. "If we want to connect with people, we have to walk. If we are out of food, we have to walk. If we want to survive, we have to walk. Walking away from, or walking to, is our new mission to make a connection, or eat, or escape. Millions of people from foodless cities are moving and their shoes wear out. I can be the one with shoes. A big stock of shoes right here ... I'm rich!" He fantasized with a chuckle, but his next thought was sobering.

How could he make this work? He would have to be smart if he wanted to keep it and parlay it into something. This was where he could make his fortune. This was the stuff of king-like riches. Since the quiet, everything was getting scarcer and everyone had to have shoes eventually. Shoes wear out.

He needed new shoes.

He looked down at his ratty shredded tennis shoes.

'Someone else might find the warehouse. Does someone already have a stake on these shoes and they just aren't home right now? Will they come back soon? Am I in a trap? Should I move them to a less conspicuous place? How could I do that? Could I take and sell some shoes and still return for more without arousing suspicion from curious customers, or others who might claim the shoes? Could I fortify this place and set up a store of sorts? How would I advertise? What do I charge?' Sam wondered.

Attila hopped over a pile and dug into the darkness.

'I've never seen so many shoes,' Sam thought as he peered into the space beneath him. It would be quite a job just going through them so that he knew what he had. Inventory. It seemed quite daunting in those terms. There must be thousands of pairs of shoes here. Tens of thousands. He looked out over the rows of shelves receding into the darkness below. The regular supply of ready made footwear from Indonesia and China had vanished with all the other accoutrement of civilized global trade, leaving only what was in front of him.

"I'm rich!" Sam yelled. The sound of his own voiced startled him and he squatted at ready. He whistled for Atilla.

The dog jogged up the stairs. Slobber dripped from the creature's hanging jowls as he delivered a large rat.

Sam chucked the dog under the chin at the offering. He made the range motion again and Atilla turned, loped down the stairs and went back into the piles of shoes.

These days there was a new value system. It seemed such an odd, yet natural concept. Things actually had very serious worth associated with them. The supposed value of any one thing was no longer an arbitrary valuation by persons unknown. Who says, it is this number or that number I'll give you for that thing I want. What was always called a 'free market', now seemed like a rigged, hostage market. The price of things had always been immutable. You either paid what they wanted for it or you didn't get it. There was no wiggle room. No haggling. No freedom.

One couldn't say, "It's not really worth that much, so I'll offer you this much for it." The modern corporate systems were rigid. To Sam, it now seemed that what he was told was a free market was really a ransom system. People who didn't know you, decided how much your money was worth and what you could get for it. You never got to decide. The only decision left to a worker before the quiet was to spend or not to spend the trifle they were given for their life work.

Now, after the quiet, people didn't want numbers for things anymore. They wanted other things. People wanted food mostly. People wanted a dry place to sleep. People wanted new shoes and they wanted to stop shivering in fear. Their wants were simple and yet, not easily satisfied. They had little to trade for their needs. Their modern skills were no longer valuable. There was always room for haggling. What one considered valuable before the quiet wasn't necessarily so valuable after the quiet. If one was too intransigent about what the other wanted there was always the distinct possibility that they might shoot you for it. Then you'd get nothing and they would get it all. Everyone had some incentive to trade goods.

They were hungry, afoot, and moving.

Now, Sam wandered the countryside to find anything to fill his gnawing gut. He never got to sleep in a bed anymore. He had gone several days at a stretch without any food a few times already.

He kept hearing sounds that couldn't be there: rock & roll music, people calling his name, telephone ring-tones, and he once thought he heard a siren. He jumped like a scared rabbit at any noise.

Every day he had to exhaustively stalk his way through the countryside on the lookout for danger and opportunity. Sam was getting tired of foraging in fear.

The rat would be a nice meal.

The value of things had changed so much that his life seemed not real. Since the quiet it became a more intensely personal relationship between worth as a human life and the things he wanted to have. If he found food, he had to move faster than the other guy. If others were being killed it was a good time to skedaddle. Due to wear and tear, his feet became a great focus, and so, of great value to him. Having shoes could make him rich.

It had been a very bad month as far as Sam's value was concerned. He never had a huge wad of savings, but there had been a bank account, an independent retirement account, and some limited assets. All told about twenty thousand dollars in funds. Add in the big screen TV entertainment center and his motorcycle and that brought his worth up to about twenty two thousand dollars. He had a nice apartment in the village of Foxfowl out in Marine County and a decent creative job in the city. By all accounts he was doing all right.

He couldn't have bought a house, but he sure could have purchased a car, or a small boat, or a plane ticket to just about anywhere on the planet. He had credit.

He compared last month's stuff to what he had now. Today his current assets were a single pack load of gear, a shotgun with limited ammo, and a big eared dog who brought him rats for supper.

He beamed in the glory of what the shoes might buy him these days.

The logistical problems presented too great a task for Sam to fully address. He did know one thing for sure; he could get some new shoes now and if lucky, come back for more.

Sam climbed down the stairs and into the warehouse gloom. The first few rows of shelves had been overturned. He worked to where he found good hiking boots and tried them on until he found two good pairs for himself. He gathered a good collection of boots and sneakers. He tied each pair into as small a bundle as he could and lashed them to his pack frame.

Sam walked away from the warehouse, his pack festooned with an odd collection of boots and sneakers, dead rats swung from the pack by their tails.

Atilla trotted alongside with a shoe in his mouth. His slobber covered prize was a woman's high heel; a bright blue six inch stiletto with a shiny red sole. Sam wondered if Atilla's master may have been a mistress.

A broad grin took over his face as he hiked back to high ground. "I'm rich!" he said out loud.

Sam fretted a tad as he hiked across the rolling yellow grass hills of California and towards where he guessed the next town might be. The new weight of his pack reminded him he carried treasure. He felt vulnerable and powerful. His happy feet carried him quickly up the hill.

"No risk, no grist," he told Atilla.

Huge populations were on the move. Enormous crowds were out looking for food and shelter and they suffered. The smartest were the ones who looted early and moved fast. Sam would trade with some of them.

"We're rich." Sam said to Atilla.

Atilla loped ahead through the dry knee high grass and Sam followed.

15

The Snitch

For the last two weeks Jonas and Becky worked feverishly to organize their church of light. They brainstormed ideas until candles burned low at night and started pitching ideas again each morning as the coffee perked.

The villagers who were Christian, and followed the prophesies of the second coming and of the gospel, behaved as ready servants to the new church and its mission of realizing the light again. A return, or second coming of the magic that lit and filled the world with wonder was a popular idea. The rhetoric of the modern Christian church described the hope that their light would return.

The loss of electricity wore heavily on the people and deflated them of purpose.

The opportunity to do something creative and productive gave them hope and joy and helped them feel a part of something and not so cut off from the modern and insane reality that they were once so adhered to.

No matter what the chore that Becky or Jonas came up with, there were glad hands to do their bidding and make it happen.

Solar panels and batteries were collected from any and all locations: house tops, road signs, and autos. Garments and vestments were stitched by whole cadres of women and kids willing to do their part. Labor filled the void.

Prayer gave them solace.

Meager communal meals were thrown together from what could be gleaned, and was solemnly shared. There wasn't a great deal lying about, the Shire had scoured the land and the pickings were slim, but Jonas had a powerful tool to amend the meals with, prayer.

The limited food made each meal a loaves and fishes scenario. Jonas spoke eloquently and led them in song and filled his followers with heartfelt sentiment before they got their few spoonfuls of rice, greens and beans. The belief of the lord's protection and divine care for those who were fervent and pious made the limited fare for supper merely an adjunct to the whole food of his sermons. The heartfelt beseeching of the Lord for sustenance of spirit and his promise of the return of the light filled their bellies as surely as their meager portions.

Becky trained Jonas. He took the training gladly. The results were instantaneous. He didn't know these people to whom he was ministering and they didn't know him. All of the impressions they had of him were the ones he was giving them. There was no prior image to dispel or cover over. He was new to them and so, was reinvented as a very important spiritual person in a short time. When he spoke, they listened.

Jonas honed each speech and vocal utterance to sincere and profound meaning. On Becky's urging and coaxing, he spoke less and yet, filled it with more. He made no casual banter. There wasn't frivolous joshing or goofing around. When he spoke it had to have weight. The less sound he made, the more he made a noise amongst his people when he spoke. Becky coached him and stood close. She would nudge him gently when he began without thinking, or didn't wait a good three to five seconds before he said anything in response to anyone. He took on an air of gravitas.

To lighten the mood they framed the sermons with song. Familiar songs felt good to recite and they filled a great deal of time. Jonas was comfortable leading the old stand-bys and it wove a thread of continuity through the services. It also helped to quell the grumbling stomachs while they waited through the sermons for their supper.

The old Christian camp became a communal village. The new congregants abandoned their far scattered homes to come live close to the source of their sustenance, spiritual and otherwise. The buildings were full of households and newly formed groups of people who worked together to serve the Lord, and Jonas. The water tank on the hill made it possible for them to luxuriate in the abundance of fresh water, for the time being, and the proximity of Steelhead Creek and shelter of the great redwood trees provided cool retreat from the heat 'out there'. There was still a good supply of propane in the great tanks and although the amount of food was finite, the general collapse of the world as they knew it seemed far away. They prayed and sang and worked at the chores Jonas and Becky concocted and the enclave grew and solidified.

Jonas sat quietly in his new study, what was the second story main bedroom in the big house, and gazed out the window as he waited for his minion to arrive.

The camp was bustling with activity. A stockade fence was being constructed on the other side of the creek by some of the men and older boys. A large cluster of women and children occupied the picnic tables where sheets were spread out and being altered. Robes were being made for ceremony. The bed linen of the camp provided an abundance of usable white cloth for this use.

A large tick-tock clock clicked loudly and the rustle of Jonas' newly fitted red robes of office were the only sounds until the clumping of his ten o'clock meeting made its way up the stairs.

The knock at his door signaled that it was show-time.

"Enter," Jonas said curtly.

The door creaked open and a fairly thickset fellow in dirty jeans and rough out jacket slipped into the room and stood before the regally red-robed and stiff backed Jonas.

Jonas made a simple gesture at his head and the fellow pulled off his knit wool watch cap.

Jonas smiled slightly.

As soon as the fellow's face broke at seeing Jonas' smile, Jonas again made a movement with his hand of a sweeping gesture down; as if he wanted the man to sit, but there was no chair. For a moment the young man looked sheepishly confused. Jonas held up both his hands slowly and softly and then cupped them down indicating the man to lower himself.

The fellow bit his lips and knelt.

Jonas smiled his pleasure again and nodded.

The man lowered his head at the approving nod and sighed relief. When he looked back up, Jonas' face had a quizzical look as if to ask the fellow to speak.

"Uh ... sir."

Jonas looked displeased and the man fell silent.

Jonas spoke. "Bishop," was all he said.

The fellow nodded understanding. "Yeah, uh, your Bishop ... ness, I'm here to tell ya' that I did what you wanted." The rough guy looked up at the beautiful blonde man smiling so beneficently at him.

The clock, tick-tocked loudly.

—

Since Frank's most recent DUI (driving under the influence) arrest, he had relied on his bicycle to maintain his sanity. The modern world just wasn't set up for guys like him. Frank Dillon was the kind of guy who just couldn't keep track of anything like a bank account or an electric bill for long. Managing his affairs beyond the cash in his pocket was beyond him, although he didn't think so, and outwardly he seemed to be the kind of guy who could handle it, he couldn't.

All his life he had spent great effort trying to get control of things presented to him, however the post-modern, twenty-first century world was not to succumb to his sense of order. Never, had more than a few months gone by, before he again made extremely bad choices. Then, he needed help.

He needed help to move, again. He would ask for rides to his 'program' meeting, where, he gave away all of the few hundred dollars he could scrape up borrowing or doing yard-work, to the state program as his penance for making bad choices. He asked to borrow money, he asked to crash on your couch, he asked if you could get him some work. He always needed help.

Frank was a gregarious guy. Frank moved in a lot of circles. He was friendly and could make people laugh and he just so happened to look like movie star John Travolta. He had a big heart and a huge capacity for laughter and smiles. Frank had the talent of being able to tell right away what you wanted to hear. Initially everyone liked Frank.

On the other side of the coin Frank always needed something. He eventually tapped everyone he met. He had to spread it around a little bit. He could only get so much generous charity from any one person with his charm and disarmingly rugged good looks and smile. It quickly wore out with people. Frank owed hundreds of people.

He always stayed fed clothed and housed. He just couldn't stay out of trouble. He couldn't maintain a place or manage his personal possessions for very long. His existence at liberty was always tenuous. The State had, through its long arm of law, been acquainted with Frank for many years. He had spent a year or more in the 'big house' in Chuckwalla Valley. It may have been the result of bad choices, but there, he was clothed and fed and had a dry bed.

Frank was comfortable in heavy physical labor. It was the one thing when he actually felt that he accomplished something tangible. He knew rakes, shovels, picks, hammers, nails, big boards, and saws. If it was tough and heavy work he knew what he was about. Between bouts with the law he hustled his body to contractors and little old ladies for carpentry and yard work. There had even been a couple of short stints as a short order cook. When he worked hard at a single rote task he reached a state of bliss and was productive.

The life of tough labor had taken its toll on him. He had experienced a series of job related injuries over the years and although he healed, he was constantly nagged by minor pains. An addiction to alcohol only added to his discomfort and as a result of the chronic aches in his body and in his head, he took painkillers. He had become quite addicted to them and it distracted him to no end. He was always looking for more pills. Not a medicine cabinet was ever left unsearched.

Frank's life had been out of control for so long that it was normal for him to not know where dinner was coming from or where he was going to sleep next week.

The only time he truly felt in control of his own life was riding a bike. In his meager, fringe, edge of society life, the only moments Frank knew where he was going was when he was riding. It was the only time that he got relief from the circumstances of his life. The air in his face, the grips in his fists, the whirring wheels and gears, all assured him he was 'going somewhere'. Somewhere to complete a task. A single task. There might be a thousand things to do, but at that very moment he was en-route to doing one thing. It made him feel better than any other time in his day. He felt in control and on a mission and moving towards something … or running from something. He was moving and it felt great. It was his specialty.

Bicycle riding, sharing modern roadways with automobile traffic, is a chancy and dangerous journey. Frank reveled in his ability to react to the vagaries of the road. He zoomed through neighborhoods effortlessly and flew along the boulevards and avenues of his town.

He had once tried to live in 'The City'. San Francisco had chewed him up and spit him out, so now he was back where he grew up. He knew his hometown neighborhoods well. They weren't just unfeeling streets to ride through. Each had a distinct and separate feel that reminded him of some past event. Saint Rose was familiar territory.

The road quality and amount of traffic were Frank's criteria for route choice. He preferred to cut through residential areas rather than on the thoroughfares. He was duly apprised of the danger. He personally knew dead bicyclists and had weathered previous brushes with cars and immovable objects. Those events made it very clear who was going to win the collision. Automobiles were his bane. They were hard, fast, and quiet. They came from behind. They snuck up and zipped by quickly. The gust of after-blast, the turbulent air-wake, was a tangible and real force in Frank's everyday life.

The car blurring out from his peripheral vision and speeding away, ahead of him, was his moment of , 'Whew! I almost didn't get killed again! I am brave. I go on.'

In the blink of an eye cars flashed by him, in any instant he could be dead.

A milli-second snuffing out.

So fast, so quick, so instantaneous that there was only afterthought, you lived, yet again.

It became routine. It was the norm. It was insane.

Frank, in his macho, bravado, movie star good looks way, was the glorious bike hero, deftly wheeling through town. He knew the calm tree lined back roads and landscaped residential neighborhoods intimately. He courageously braved the evil and relentless boulevards, where herds of cars blasted by to get from one residential neighborhood to the next. He sped through town.

Saint Rose had grown from post San Francisco 1906 earthquake times when the entire town lay down and then burned in submission to the gods of the Earth. It was a mix of early twentieth century box and craftsman style ranch homes at its core and farmland that had been swallowed by rows of town homes, condominiums, and apartments sprawling to the peripheral trailer courts and rural old farms of the rich shallow valley.

Frank could get across the sprawling suburbia in short order. He was strong and in his element when riding. In truth, he didn't really ever need a ride from other people, if he could keep a bike, but keeping a bike was as difficult as keeping anything else in his life. He lost them regularly. He found them just as easily and the concept of ownership was, in his mind, a grey area.

Frank survived in the periphery of society. He made it from one day to the next, just barely, but that was enough.

The haze of painkillers and occasional bottles of wine allowed him to swim through the time of his life.

Then came the quiet. The quiet changed everything for everyone. The world that made sense to the majority seemed to stop. Electrically operated gadgets failed their masters and refused to obey. The status quo flipped on its head and the minority, those who dealt with life on simpler terms, found themselves in a world that suddenly made more sense to them. Those that could walk were the mobile ones now. Those that did not depend on fancy gadgets and motorcars and electronic entertainment to get through their day were all of a sudden perfectly at home. Those that were wealthy and steeped in the post modern high tech world were lost.

Frank didn't even notice the quiet at first. He was riding his bike across town to try to borrow money from a new acquaintance in order to pay off another.

The loss of electricity didn't stop the wind in his face.

It didn't keep him from jumping one of his favorite curbs near his old junior high school.

It didn't make his movement through life abruptly change like it had everyone else.

Frank was feeling his mojo and cruising along.

It took him a few blocks and crossing College Avenue for him to get suspicious that something different was afoot.

The stop-lights were out.

All the cars coasted to a stop.

People stood by their fabulous gleaming rose-red Beemers, and silver Lexus SUV's, scratching their heads.

Frank rode on.

The events of the last week and a half had brought him out here to the edge of the new world. His parents had retired and lived in a huge house they had built in the hills above Sentimental. Frank gravitated back to his parents, who eschewed his company and had just about had it with his inability to be a regular person who could hold a job or keep a place to hang his hat.

Word on the street was, safety lay with the sheriff. The 'man' was the dominant force and the only group visibly moving forward.

Joining the Sheriff's Department wasn't Frank's cup of tea, the Hispanic neighborhoods were downright dangerous to even be around, and when his stomach growled, the open road to his folks' house beckoned.

Of course, just because the world had turned off was no reason for his aging parents to finally forgive all the years of pain he had given them. They were both well educated and had held positions of status in the government and civil service and college communities. Dad was an engineer and Mom was a teacher. It was a complete mystery why Frank had turned out to be such a bad egg. When he showed at their doorstep, they gave him a plate of food and asked that he please leave them alone. They had bailed him out dozens of times and even gave up on visiting him in prison. He always told them how he was going to change and do the right thing. The words were the right words. The deeds never measured up. He just couldn't do it. No one knew why, the least of all Frank.

His road to hell was paved with good intentions.

He was who he was, and he acted out of impulse and immediate gratification. Loyalty and long-term planning and delayed reward weren't in his bag of tricks. Getting something for the pleasure of his company was his bailiwick. He didn't have friends because he liked them, he had friends because they would do stuff for him. He did stuff for them, it was a fair trade he figured.

—

Frank knelt on the thin carpeting of the dark dusty smelling office in front of the pretty long-haired blonde man in the shimmering ruby red robe. He had done a simple chore for the guy. He expected return. It had been promised to him.

"I found them and I told them about them guys and ..."

Jason made an outward cutting gesture with his hands.

"As I promised," was all Jonas said. He reached out and placed a small plastic medicine bottle on the table.

Frank took the bottle. "Thanks." He rattled the bottle and frowned. "Is that all?"

Jonas stared into Frank's now dangerous looking eyes, "There is more for you to do. All in good time."

Frank knew he was being played, but for now, a bird in the hand was worth it. He was itching to open the bottle and eat the pills.

Jonas rose slowly and his voluminous red robes rustled as he moved to stand above Frank. He very slowly moved his hands to each side of Frank's head. His face shone with forgiveness and joy and gratitude.

Frank froze as the weird guy touched him.

His touch felt electric.

The hair on his neck stood on end when the man's fingers felt into Frank's scalp.

Jonas turned his head up to the ceiling of the shabby wall-papered room and said, "I heal you of all your sins, I bring the forgiveness of our Lord into your heart, I invoke the power of the almighty spirit to lift you from your pain and to anoint you with God's grace. I accept your act of obeisance as tribute to our church and welcome you to our cause. Say amen."

"Amen." Frank heard himself repeat.

"I hold you as acolyte of our eternal light, keeper of our hope and brother of radiance. Say amen"

"Amen." Frank echoed.

"Do you accept this honor?"

Frank was taken in by the man's words. He could only think about taking the pills in his hand. "Yeah, sure."

"Then, by all that is holy and good and righteous, I accept you Brother Apostolus. Say amen like you mean it."

"Amen." Frank said loudly.

"Rise, Apostolus. You are now with me. You are no more who you were. You are the hand of God." He lifted Frank to standing.

Jonas spoke in a whispering voice that held great excitement. Then, Jonas knelt and took Frank's hand and kissed it, quickly. He rose and swished his rustling noisy red robes to behind the desk where he arranged himself and sat regally.

"Go see Becky, Sister Rebecca. She will attend to your needs." Jonas held out his hand bearing a large gaudy purple stone in a ring. Frank looked at it and didn't know what to do.

"I am your Bishop now. You may kiss my ring."

Frank did so quickly, more in order to get the heck out of there. 'Man this guy is out there.' Frank thought as he clumped back down the stairs to his bike. 'But I got my meds.' He fumbled the cap off and slurped two of the big red capsules. He was a little disappointed that there were so few in the bottle, though.

He was a new believer in the Lord. The coming of the quiet and rejection by his parents had landed him in this camp of Christians.

He had heard all the witnessing he cared to in jail. It was an interesting crutch that he didn't really understand, but one that had fed and housed him and given him some slight solace during times of trouble over the years. He hadn't really been able to buy into the Holy Ghost and son of God thing so much, but the soup and a cot and warm words of reassurance had worked for him in the past.

Now, the Lord would provide his needs.

The chore he did was a small thing. He found this Colonel guy on the south ridge and told him about some fellows messing with the horses from the Christian camp. The Sheriff's men were friendly and eager to listen to him. He had to show them a hand-drawn picture of the brand on the animals and a vague description about where they could find them and leave it at that.

Too easy.

He found himself in the main hall of the camp with a bowl of warm steaming gruel in front of him and a really nice looking young lady attending to his needs. She had brought him there the minute he emerged from the large house where Jonas sat in his study. Unbeknownst to him, Rebecca had signaled the girl to take him in hand and make sure he was made to feel safe and at home with the brethren.

Jonas threw the switch that he had wired into his office to illuminate the camp with the little battery power they had. He gazed out the window at the lovely lights.

The enclave lights sparkled as dusk gave way to the darkness of Satan's world.

Jonas felt great relief and tension at the same time.

He was incensed that Alice had spurned him so rudely. He wanted her to stay righteous and she turned her back on all that was good, to go be with that philistine, William.

Jonas offered her the world. His entire world, his love and protection and he would have pledged his troth to her.

She rejected him and the way of the light.

It wasn't really her fault. Jonas found it difficult to blame her for very long. He loved her.

He blamed that little shit, William; him and his thick arms and his oh, so charming smile and that fake laugh.

Jonas saw them together at the first fellowship gathering and it burned him, no end. That William guy just waltzed in here and beguiled her with some spell. He took her righteousness and sullied it. It was his fault.

Now, the fault would find its true home.

Alice would be free of 'Squire William'. She would come to her senses the minute he wasn't there with his horses and guns and men around him.

The sheriff would take him out of play and show him for the horse thieving bandit that he was. As soon as she sees what he really was, then she would cut him loose and return home to Jonas and the enclave, to where she belonged, with him. The sheriff will put the little shit in jail and she'll see that he was just a jailbird all along.

The lights in the compound gleamed and started to dim slightly as the batteries had not charged sufficiently in the deep gulley.

Jonas didn't care. They shone and let his people feel normal for a few minutes during the evening meal. They loved the lights and would follow him to keep the hope of their second coming alive.

16

Count Sneegin

The day of the Quiet

The high speed exploration egg fell out of cold-cold hyperspace with barely a shudder as it fell through the light speed barrier, the pull of gravity thawed it and activated alarms to awaken Sneegin to the worst end of quiet in his life. The liquid drop of spacecraft hurtled into system gravitational pull that warped its shape velocity and feeling of stability.

Sneegin came out of his quiet in a foul mood.

He looked forward to getting out of the tight sleep socket. The quiet chamber was not custom made to his form and he felt out of shape. He'd been crammed in, during the twisted strangeness of light speed, for the extraordinarily long quiet period required to get to IV. He oozed out of the cocoon shaped hole slowly and unfolded his severely compacted self. He couldn't open and stretch fully as he barely fit in the cabin of the tiny fluid filled ship. It wasn't a journey across the cabin to the control panel sockets, he bumped into the reef shaped wall of the ship's interior as he stretched out. He never fully extended from his nest, the size of the craft prevented it. He had reawakened to a reality of being confined in the smallest of pods in the farthest reaches of galactic space.

Its exterior was cold, frigid as the depths of space. The inside was close and stuffy. It was the smallest, fastest pod made, and so his mass was low and it travelled very fast. It was a Spartan vehicle, but very modern and very fast. With any luck he might have even beaten Sloodin back to IV.

Count Sneegin's father dispatched him to IV as soon as word went round about Sloodin's foul up.

"I haven't had a moment to clear up my bar tab at the club," he tried to reason with his headstrong father.

Duke Sleegat rushed him to the launch bay. "I'll take care of it. You have to go before anyone knows you're gone. In the name of Sleedrack, you have to get there before that whelp Sloodin does." The iris door slammed shut before he could argue further.

The hastily organized trip crammed him into the tiny pod before he even had a chance to announce his trip to his friends or cancel engagements with his favorite snoodlets. It was apparently on automatic pilot, as he didn't touch a thing and the press of acceleration sloshed him right away.

The Count pried himself from his comfortably cold, quiet, niche socket to wrap around the slime reader in hopes of feeling this gem of a planet before he arrived.

The famous resort planet IV had been a family favorite vacation spot for ages. Sleedrack Clan were one of the first families to lease ocean on IV. The family villa was a joyous place of gathering. Sneegin had been there as a youth.

The clan travelled en-masse in their Magna-travel 7000, a monster of a recreational vehicle spaceship, complete with multi-level lounge reefs and custom sockets for the entire family. After the faster than light quiet in the RV spaceship the Sleedracks would swarm in the large open salon pond for love and reassurance. The whole family was there to touch and talk and process the dark cold quiet of interstellar ravel. It was never so terribly arduous with his loving family close around him to ease the anxiety of the insane quiet in hyperspace.

Now, Sneegin, was miserable. This end of quiet was torture. Enduring the long quiet after the immense journey alone was a burden. Waking to the solitude of deep space and uncertainty tested his minds. There was no reassuring slithering against his mother and aunties and lesser cousins to soothe and heal the erratic thoughts that the quiet inevitably induced. He had to sing the mantric tunes alone, solo, and without any support. Sneegin whined a vibratory complaint. He felt the high pitched echo of his keening against the walls of his high speed explorer egg.

He fell towards IV.

He knew Sloodin, Planet Lord of IV, of course, they had met a couple of times when on vacation, but the Vithlin niece that was left in charge was a stranger.

This could work to his advantage.

One of his cousins was already on planet. He was a playboy surface-surfer bum and all Sneegin had to do was contact him as an ally.

He dreaded having to stoop so low as to consort with his ne'er do well cousin, but a job was a job. Sneegin could team up with his cousin as a lesser friend and hide his fame.

Then he could sabotage their effort at re-qualification and file for re-licensing.

Sleedrack would get a portion of her majesty, IV.

It was about time someone cracked the Vithlin egg.

He plugged into the control surface and felt the input. He sensed the great solar furnace powering the system and teased IV out of the background.

It lay on course as the slime reader's pre-programmed guide instructed.

Sneegin was not an explorer. He was a dandy and a playboy. He was rich and spoiled and never had to 'do' anything in his entire life to justify his existence. He was the Duke's prime offspring and heir to all of Sleedrack.

He let the machine take him where it would, which was the family villa in the northern hemisphere at the mouth of one of the tastiest rivers on the planet. Sleedrack Palace was well known and unknown. No one went there except family and they leased scads of ocean shelf around it to remain residue free and unperturbed by lookie-loos or nosy neighbors. Sleedrack Villa was famous in its own right and yet, hardly a scent of its true grandeur was smelled by the common populace.

Sneegin felt the changes in gravity, temperature and radiation as he passed into the orbit of IV.

The smells of water and ice and salt and their movement washed him, interspersed with scratches of dirt, minerals and forests and the deadly awful dryness where sea was not.

He could feel these things.

He molded onto the control surface more tightly as the pod fed his curiosity.

He sucked the feelings and senses from the pod into himself.

He smelled the emulations that the pod synthesized in approximations of its data stream.

The spaceship recreated emanations from the planet into information that Sneegin could easily understand. He hadn't bothered as a youth, in the RV, to taste IV closely. It was just the vacation house. He played with his cousins and made light of life when they approached IV. He hadn't spend time plugged into the slime reader to ingest the upcoming destination, droll pilot toil.

He didn't really know that much about IV. He thought he did, of course, he bragged about the wonders of IV as if he were a denizen, it made him exotic and special to all the snoodlets and hangers-on, who he was constantly surrounded by back on Homeworld.

Now, he was engrossed in the wild array of smells and tastes pouring into him from the reader.

He pulsed and unconsciously 'throomed' audibly as the delicious mix of strangeness filled him.

IV was far more complex and interesting than his less mature self had given it credit for.

The tiny egg fell into a deteriorating orbit.

He punched the delay swatch and the slime reader's predetermined coordinates reset, orbit reestablished and entry delayed.

Sneegin wanted to savor the raw data awhile longer.

He lingered in space, at the edge.

He felt the seething seas under him. He tasted the mix of land and ocean combine in savory concoctions of tasty delight. His gelatinous body swarmed around the reader more tightly.

He wanted to whet his appetite more before he splashed.

The comforting cold of the ice caps and disconcerting warmth of the tropics swirled together in his minds.

His heavier outer tentacles unconsciously writhed pleasure, as their tips, delicately inserted into actuator hollows on the artificial reef, touched controls to rotate his pod to focus outer hull sensors at particularly delicious spots on the globe below.

Saliva dripped from him unabashedly.

He secreted a slimy coat of joy and pleasure and desire and wanting and downright lust for the planet, all over himself.

Time stood still for Sneegin as he descended into a self-pleasuring phase of consciousness. Sneegin massaged the centers in his two mind humps with a back-and-forth tossing of the sensations that he derived from the savory data that the machine spat out for him. 'After quiet' derangement held him in its trance.

Long quiet affected the strongest snood deeply, explorers sang mantric calming chants in defense, but Sneegin was not prepared for the onslaught of sensory stimulation.

He over indulged on the input.

His minds lost their hold on mission.

He shuddered and fell into a vibrating orgasm of anticipatory excitement at going toward the desire of his hearts, newly seduced.

He bathed himself in the residue of his thoughts and clung to the reader.

He consumed its stream of informative phlegm. He writhed and vibrated and 'throomed' his joy to the cosmos and spumed his orgasm into the fluidsphere of the miniscule boat.

His moment of delight was interrupted by hot, sour readings.

Between him and the heavenly globe of IV, a streak of burning organism impinged itself.

Sneegin roused himself from internal ecstasy and re-focused on the indication under him.

He followed the streak of fire as it skimmed and bounced and burned on the edge of gaseous atmosphere. The readings told him it was of snood origin and was most likely a craft burning. Someone had made a fatal error and was falling to planet surface badly. Only the failure of a slime reader and its divergence from the preplanned course through the vicious gravity cross-current set up by the enormous moon, would cause such a catastrophic failure. The slime reader was always on a record mode as he tracked after the strange meteor to its final resting place in the middle of a land continent, far from water.

Whoever was trying to splash on the most fabulous of resort planets in the known galaxy, had just died as far from the sea as one could be and still be on planet.

Sneegin pondered sadness as it mixed and tempered his previous exuberance.

One of his kind had suffered the worst possible fate, burning to death.

He had felt it happen right in front of him.

He tasted the charred surface of that poor spacesnood's capsule.

He sensed the fight for control as the egg spun out of the relative safety of cold space to the horrible and terrifying dry land below.

Sneegin shuddered anew as the realization struck him.

He remembered the task he was set to. This wasn't a brief summer visit to camp. This was a mission of the utmost importance, a dangerous one. His clan depended on him to thwart their foes and bring home a portion of IV that they could bank.

Clan Sleedrack had for far too long been in the backwash of Clan Vithlin. His father's feud was his also. The legacy smell of ancestral memory drove him to feel ambition for this task. He had at first balked and outwardly resisted his father's suggestion, but he knew deep down and now, after absorbing the planet from his enlightened state of consciousness and exalted frame of minds, that he was Sleedrack and Sleedrack deserved IV as their own.

He would fix Sloodin's mistake in favor of his clan. His glory would lead the new flow of proceeds into regal Sleedrack and away from rank Vithlin.

His minds worked feverishly at the prospects of taking over an entire planet. This was the time to work this over and form a plan of attack that would work.

Not just work, but overwhelm.

Sneegin didn't want any rework.

He foresaw the complete dispossession of IV's license rights.

He formulated the seeds of a plan to make IV his.

"Thanks, Dad," he said aloud. His bright blue, tinged purple, mucous thought floated briefly in the confined space and was then, sucked into the thumping filter feeders.

Sneegin smiled his formless amoeba-like way and shone a string of radiating chemical lights marching around him and out his tentacles in the pitch black interior of his blind droplet of space chrysalis as it plunged on autopilot to IV. He was transformed, from recalcitrant dissolute, to determined crusader. The quiet had twisted and molded Sneegin's minds. He had tasted the sweetness and felt the sludge. He had found his calling, destroy Vithlin line and become the new king of Sleedrack and planet Lord of IV.

The egg fell to earth in a completely contrived way, every force of nature negated by the intense field from the toroid shaped Snoodalus drive, as it moved in concert with physical forces to minimize friction and collision and slipped into the atmosphere. The sphere glided along magnetic flux lines and flowed along with hardly a shudder as it flew towards the family villa coordinates and splooshed next to the shallows made by the Mississippi River outflow.

Sneegin blushed and shivered at the refreshing cool water around him. He felt the craft's every sensor intimately as waves of wonderful water, that first engulfed and then surrounded him with the enfolding love of the sea, rinsed away his thoughts of alien and hostile vacuum.

Its path wound straight to the doorstep of the palace, and there, the pod stopped its programmed course and opened.

Sneegin cowered in his comfortable dark cell against the prospect of instant release into the wild. He had arrived at his property.

It was his house and he should feel comfortable swimming inside, but he hesitated.

Anxiety at rapid change, even if from stark encapsulation to luxurious accommodations, daunted his minds.

Sneegin clung inside the spacecraft until it started to clean itself. Filter pumps spasmodically thumped and pulled at parts of him not firmly stuck to the control wall.

Native wrasse fish nibbled at the edge of the open door as delightful odors of snood residue wafted out on the current.

Chill and pungent nectar found its way into him and the sumptuous feast awaiting outside sent tempting messengers of smell to torment him.

He was torn apart.

His minds argued strongly.

Waves of childish light flashed up and down him as the internal debate raged.

Quietly in the egg, he felt as if held dearly in the spawn cluster, comfort, safety, connection to home and family, where one of his minds believed he should be.

His other mind raged to flee the small, confining, filthy residue filled shell, and go forth to take and conquer.

In an unthinking pulse of instinctual flight, Sneegin burst from his ship into the warm muddy water. His impetuous spurt propelled him directly into a heady mix of intoxicating mud on the bottom.

He spurted again reflexively in another direction to clear his palate. The mouthful and body covering sludge he plunged into, surged into his system before he could manufacture a defense.

It was out of his ken to chug the strongest mud-liquor of the known universe.

He spurted a dozen times in random directions to free himself of the heavily saturated water.

Organic rotting detritus from the land sent Sneegin into paroxysms of drunkenness.

He plunged into the mud repeatedly.

With each pulse he yelped. "I've got to escape! Clear water, clear water, clear water, there has to be a clear way!" Purple green glops appeared with each outburst and lifted his message to float above the roiling cloudy fog of concentrated scent in the mud.

He worked the cloud and traced out lighter concentrations until he eventually found clear current.

"It's so gooooooood" Sneegin spoke in a clear, thick loud, phlegm call.

His squirt of chemicals appeared vibrant blue and shimmering green iridescence as they rose from the cloud of deliciously intoxicating mud that he had gotten entangled in.

He rose free from the mixed bottom water into a clean clear current of unspoiled sea water.

Night had fallen and some ignorant creature was making a lot of racket in the mud and it smelled in distress and ready to eat.

Sneegin never saw the Meerbock that took him.

17

Repel Boarders

Sheila lay inside the dirt rampart of the nest she and her cadets had hollowed out in the top of the hill to house their machine gun.

Her vision was amazingly clear considering her battered condition. She couldn't raise her head from the gravel; she couldn't feel her legs and her arms which were, she was sure, both broken. She could only stare at the place where their main weapon had been and the rumpled body of one of her assailants amongst the scattered ammunition boxes.

Smoke wafted by and the smell of fire and cooked meat filled her bloodied nostrils.

Her glorious career hopes in the United States Coast Guard, to rescue sailors in peril and to interdict the bad guys and enemies of her beloved country were all dashed. She was the defeated leader of an overrun outpost. Her command had bolted at the onslaught and left her to man the post alone for the last climactic battle.

Ruth and Julie and Bethany and even her most loyal and devoted lover Kit, had all left her. They left at the moment that they were trained for, at the moment of truth, the moment when the men were separated from the boys, except none of them were men, or boys. They collapsed at the moment when it was do or die.

They died.

Sheila's last breath would be the acrid smell of defeat.

She snorted at the thought that they ever imagined they could have stemmed the tide of humanity that washed over them. She made a wheezing sound that whistled from her blood filled nostrils. A sharp pain dove into her brain when she breathed hard.

The events were clear in her mind, a fiasco from the get-go.

They had all been so proud to be in the military. The United States had spent enormous resources to convince young people that a career in service was honorable and patriotic and that being generous and not self serving would enhance their lives immeasurably. The young believed the hype.

'Be all that you can be. Defend Freedom. One man army. So others may live.'

Fabulous sentiments. Great rhetoric.

None of them said, kill people wholesale, or murder the children, or follow orders blindly because that is what they expect of you.

The scenes of her last day on earth had none of the ring of patriotism. There was no pride in a job well done, although they had done their job quite efficiently and with a fervor that Sheila now felt sick about.

Her pride tasted of dirt and blood and bile.

—

A truck brought them, in their crisp uniforms, to the last hilltop near the sea. They were redeployed from the Captain's military police to man a border outpost.

The men from the county sheriff unloaded the heavy gun and stacks of ammo, then left Sheila McCutcheon and her all female platoon at the end of a long line of outposts on the new frontier.

The old dump truck and men rode across the valley to the southern ridge and posted the large plywood signs that would be the border.

All she and her squads had to do were fire an occasional warning shot if anyone poked their head over that ridge and tried to cross the mile wide valley between them. She and her squaddies dug out perfectly defensible positions on the last mile of frontier, mounted their heavy machine gun in their main position and proceeded to make crude, but tolerable camps on the north side of each of her six checkpoints.

They held the position at the end of the line, near the sea. It practically ensured they were in for a long tediously boring assignment. There would be a lot of watching and waiting and trying to maintain discipline.

Commander Herzog had spoken to Sheila privately before they deployed ten days prior.

"Please, come in Petty Officer." Captain Herzog stepped aside to let the sharp looking young woman into his spartan office. "Have a seat."

She sat, stiff backed, in the hard metal folding chair. The seat was warm; she was the last of a long line of interviewees.

Captain Julius Herzog had briefed each of the outpost leaders personally. He asked his charges to enforce a new border, a new frontier, where the haves were drawing a line in the dirt, and the have-nots were being directed away from their natural desire to go where they would.

The county powers-that-be felt there just weren't enough food resources available in their jurisdiction and the interlopers from the city needed to go east toward abundance. The inland central valley of California was the nut, fruit, and vegetable supplier for one third of the entire nation's needs. That area could surely feed the people from the bay area until the crisis was over and supply chains resumed. The county could not.

The equation was a simple one. The hordes from the city needed to look elsewhere for their sustenance.

Three Stones Coast Guard Training facility was tasked with convincing them to move on. The county facilitated this endeavor by supplying billboards and trucks and supplies and reinforcements to the coasties.

Julius Herzog merely needed to keep his command in line and get them to toe the line in dissuading the onslaught from flooding the county with their ravenous maw.

"Petty Officer … Sheila, I'm going to be counting on you to perform above and beyond the call here. I need you to anchor our watch station near the coast. You'll be the last of our long line of defense." Julius spoke in a quiet and kindly voice.

"We have established watch posts all the way from Eggtown to the sea. That will be your place, nearest the sea." Julius pointed at a spot on the wall map. "It will be a quiet outpost and one that may not, in all likelihood, see any activity. The civilians from the city are on a rampage. They are flooding across Marine County as an uncontrolled mob; looting, pillaging, and generally denuding the land of all its resources. In so doing, they are destroying our civilization, our way of life. We must dissuade them. We must channel them to go where there is resource for them to consume. Am I making myself clear Petty Officer?"

"Aye aye sir." Sheila responded. Her blue eyes glinted in the slanting light that filtered through the venetian blinds.

"Good, now we have posted channeling signs and symbols and clear instructions to assist in their understanding of the need to migrate east. But, in the event that some refuse to heed the lawful quarantine of the county and insist on invading government property to destroy the lawful inhabitants' life and property here, we must act. Unfortunately we have few tools at our disposal. So, it is with grave intent that I task you with the job of repelling boarders. Persons who attempt to cross our buffer zone will meet with the severest of penalties. We have no choice. Understood?"

"Aye aye sir. The peace must be maintained." She regurgitated an appropriate response.

"Now, I don't anticipate that there will be much incursion in your sector. I fully believe that the most egregious of the mob will concentrate here, near Eggtown," he stood facing the wall map, "and that we will prevail in dissuading them from moving north. I fully believe that our efforts to convince them to head east will be successful." He turned back to her, his crisp starched white uniform rustled. "So, I must ask you to take this mission. Do you accept?"

"Aye aye sir." Petty Officer, Sheila McCutcheon, snapped to attention and saluted.

"Good, very good." Captain Herzog returned her salute in the most formal military manner, then he faltered slightly and held out his hand. "I give you my blessing. May God go with you."

Sheila looked down at his hand for only a second, then took it in a most firm and manly manner. "Thank you, sir. We'll do our best, Captain." She executed her best snap turn and exited the sparse little receiving office that the captain was using as his command HQ.

She swam in heady thoughts of an important mission ahead of her. She was assigned only female cadets and although it was against regulation for them to be segregated on sexual lines she could find no stomach to object. She would take those women with her and they would do their jobs.

As she walked across the compound back to her room, the memories of how she got here in this place touched her: the last three years spent training in the most elite service group in the world, her college education in internet technology at Iowa State, her busy party-less high school years in the tiny farm town in the middle of the country's corn ocean where she was valedictorian and honor student, the down-home all-American style party her family threw when she left to join the Coast Guard. She never really had much of any boyfriends and after a few encounters in college with sharp and vibrant young women she realized she would probably never be with men.

The distractions of her life were minimal and she focused on tasks well. It served her as she rocketed to meet every goal she had ever made for herself. Her dream was to become a highly placed military consultant someday. It was a strange goal for a girl raised in the corn belt of Iowa to make a career in the service dedicated to the sea.

She thought that perhaps this moment of combat experience would fit nicely into her plan. It would give her an air of legitimacy.

Her command loaded all their gear into a noisy old dump truck that hot afternoon and drove across the entire county to their post.

She and her squad spent the next two days getting their emplacement ready. They dug and shoveled and filled the sandbags provided and checked their field of fire. Before the truck and its three deputies posted the large plywood signs across the small valley, Sheila asked them to stand up a few smaller signs for range markers while they were there. When the sheriff's men finished their chores they took off down the road with a wave.

Sheila and her 'men' set up a nice camp against the back side of their machine gun nest. They had been given one of the largest and oldest weapons in the arsenal. It was a browning fifty caliber heavy machine gun. Normally such a gun would be mounted on the bow of cutter or on a tank. It weighed almost eighty five pounds without a tripod and once in place was not easily redeployed. Once set, it stayed. It was a rapid firing mini-cannon that threw a one half inch in diameter bullet over a mile with fair accuracy. And it was loud. They were also armed with versions of the M-16 assault rifle. There were piles of ammunition boxes that came off the truck. They toted and stored and for two days made ready with little rest.

When they had finished they sat and listened to the wind.

The beach was clearly visible to them and in their field of fire. Sheila had each of them pop off a couple of rounds from the big gun at the beach and the opposite hill. It was a deafening concussive weapon.

Early on the morning of the fifth day out, the dump truck reappeared. It rumbled up and a lanky Deputy got out and called for Sheila. She was ordered back to camp for some briefing.

Petty Officer, Sheila McCutcheon, quickly got into her uniform and hat and climbed into the old machine. The meeting was a rudimentary intel briefing regarding supposed disposition of the mobs to the south. It was perfunctory and told her nothing new, except that Eggtown had imploded with political infighting over the wisdom of denying or accommodating the refugees. It meant little to her group on the far end of the line. Before she left the main base she wangled some candy from a pal in supply and got a water barrel filled for her troops. They would love the chocolate.

On the way back they stopped and dropped squad commanders at their respective posts.

At one piss stop, Sheila found an interesting gathering. On the side of the road were four people on their knees with their hands trussed behind their backs. Their heads were bowed down. A couple of them sobbed audibly.

Sheila approached the Sheriff's deputy on guard.

"So what's up with these guys?" She asked.

"Local bandits. We caught them on the ridge. They tried to run but we got their horses." The deputy said, gesturing at two men earnestly butchering a couple of the beasts in the grass.

Sheila noticed the contents of the prisoner's knapsacks were strewn about on the grass. There were binoculars and some miscellaneous camp gear, and semaphore flags.

"Is this their stuff?" She asked.

"Yeah, loot they pilfered from local homes. Looters get shot. Ya' hear that boys, shot," he directed at them.

The two sobbing figures burst into wailing and crying.

Sheila realized they were young teenagers, barely more than children. "So why would they steal semaphore flags?" She asked the deputy as she examined the semaphore flags. They were homemade.

"How the hell should I know? Look, we caught 'em, they tried to run. We know their kind. Sheriff is real clear about looters and horse thieves."

Sheila looked at the deputy's uniform and realized he was not a well trained professional peace officer. He was some sort of posse conscript.

"So, where is your commanding officer? I take it you're not in charge here." She asked the man.

"The Colonel's up the hill looking at the set-up. When he gets back we gonna' post these boys like advertisements. No horse thieves in this county allowed."

"Hey!" The sheriff's deputy driver of her truck hollered. "Load up. We're going."

Sheila wanted to confront this deputy more and talk to his commander, the Colonel. The truck started to roll without her. She turned and ran, grabbed the outstretched hands in back and jumped on.

She wondered about the encounter. If the horses they stole were shot, it was a pretty counterproductive apprehension. They were only kids. They had no real loot to speak of, and why the homemade semaphore flags? There was a lot more to the story and that dolt of a guard wasn't interested in it. She felt queasy about the mere idea of trying and possibly executing those young boys. At least there was a rule of law and the county court system would find the truth about them. The guard was talking tough to scare them. But, what did he mean by 'post them like advertisements'?

All night the lousy intel meeting ate on her. She was itching for some real time intel about her sector. The next morning, she and her second, Kit, hiked to the signs on the south ridge. She placed more range markers to shoot at. She didn't want to destroy the big sign any more by practicing on it. While there, she scoped the surrounding countryside that was denied to her view from their nest.

The rolling hills to the south were bucolic and peaceful. There was no sign of anything, but ever expanding countryside. Sheila swung her view to the east and tried to follow the lay of the land where the border ostensibly was. She saw some markers near a set of sign posts. She couldn't quite discern what they were with her sixty-five power binoculars.

"Kit, let me see that spotting scope would you?"

"Sure thing." Kit unlimbered her pack and produced the long cylinder.

They lay under the shadow of their border warning sign at the top of the ridge. The breeze blew warmly off the grasslands interior. The continuous heat made the grass brown and it rustled in the lightly moving air with a shushing sound.

Sheila set the short tripod and focused the high magnification monocular scope. She was trying to see objects a few miles away and the shimmering heat made the air waver, as well as her heartbeat made it an exercise to be still enough to see through the tripod mounted eyepiece. Sheila breathed deep several times and finally let it out half-way. The view steadied.

Sheila couldn't believe her eyes.

"They're crosses." She said.

"Crosses?" Kit asked.

Sheila rolled to the side. "Here, tell me what you see."

Kit hunkered down behind the scope and breathed slowly. After a minute four crosses swam into clarity. The prisoners were being advertised. At the very peak of the ridge, spaced for maximum coverage, the sheriff's men had crucified their prisoners and posted them to show that this was not the way to go. Go somewhere else, or else.

Kit wondered out loud. "I wonder if they shot them first?"

"What difference Kit? They were kids!" Sheila hollered to the winds. "Oh, God. What kind of bastards are they?"

"Civilian police have jurisdiction." Kit threw out as a lame rationale.

"Don't say anything about this to the squad." Sheila commanded. "We are going to deal with this, but the rest don't need to know. Understood?"

Kit nodded. "Of course, I won't say anything."

Sheila was now determined to file a report at the soonest opportunity and find who was responsible for this outrage. Even if they were horse thieves, they deserved a trial, due process. She got up and stormed down the hill, back to her outpost. Kit followed.

In the quiet shade of her tent, Sheila wrote a scathing report about the encounter with the deputy and his prisoners. If she had not taken the initiative to go on the recon foray she would have never known about the crosses and their terrible burden. Now, the burden was on her shoulders. She was carrying those sobbing boys with her. Her imagination as to the horrible time they must have had before they died, haunted her. The report stretched into several pages.

Sheila wished they had some contraband liquor so she could have a good stiff drink. They were too good for that. They always had to prove themselves better than the men just to be seen as anything near equal. There was no contraband and the only solace was in each others' company.

Sheila filed the papers into her small briefcase with their terse written orders and her military manual of conduct and went out to brief her squad.

"Hey, everyone, gather round." She called out. As they collected from their few boredom fighting chores, she implored them. "Sit, at-ease. We need to talk."

They arranged themselves around the sand-bagged pit holding the enormous machine gun.

"Allright, Kit and me went over to the south ridge, as you all know. From there, the view of the approaches are very good. I am now asking for a volunteer for the first shift, to go and set-up an early warning station. We need to know before anyone gets there if and when they are coming." She let the silence dictate who would volunteer for the beginning of their vigil.

"I'll start," said Bethany. She was a thin plain faced girl from Texas. Her drawl was soft and she wore her long tawny hair tied and twisted into a tight bun that stuck out from the back of her head. The only time she ever took her hair down was in the shower and after drying always tied it back up and put it away. None of the young women were very large and Bethany was the smallest. At four feet six inches she was a wisp of a girl, wiry and lithe.

"All right, Bethany. You're first. We'll draw straws to see the order. It'll be four hour watch until dark and then we split the dog watches so only two hour watches at night. Any questions?"

"Semaphore flags, Petty Officer?" Bethany asked.

"Yes, and take your firearm, a red signal flare and plenty of ammo and water. Set-up under the sign directly across from us so we can see you at all times. When you need to signal us, take a couple of steps down so the enemy can't see you." Sheila elaborated. There wasn't much else to it. "Report any one coming. That is all."

Bethany saluted and took the rucksack that Kit had used for the first recon. The high powered spotting scope was not in it.

A couple of boring days passed.

The first signs of action were subtle.

There was no signal and their recon outpost couldn't be seen as the dawn broke.

"Petty Officer." Julie called into the tent.

Sheila rolled over and smacked the sticky taste of her night with Kit from her mouth. "What is it sailor?"

"Recon is gone Ma'am."

"Gone? What do you mean gone?" Sheila was up and moving.

"She is not in sight."

Where was Kit? Sheila hadn't seen her since they had fallen asleep in each others arms.

"General quarters," Sheila replied.

Julie stood fast for a moment.

"I mean now, sailor.   General quarters!" She yelled as she pulled on her clothes.

Sheila clambered up to the lookout. They were signaling to Michael Murphy at the next outpost up the line when the first fusillade of rifle fire came. Angry bees went singing by and a couple of plops of dirt hopped up around them.

Sheila knew their recon was down from that moment, was it Kit? What happened to her?

Murphy's outpost kept signaling the 'all is well' message. Sheila's message to him changed; from her need to a file report, to, they were under siege.

Apparently he didn't believe her and kept sending silly responses. "Worry wart, chicken chicks, get glasses …"

She tried to tell him they were under fire. She had no idea that there were thousands of people on the ridge opposite her, just out of sight.

He didn't make any positive acknowledgement of her warnings.

"What an ass." Sheila said when she decoded his messages.

"Should we send someone there?" Julie asked.

"No. No time. We need everyone here. Tell him he is on report."

"Aye aye." Julie said and started waving her flags at her unseen counter-part.

More rifle fire poured in. There was no warning and their source was unknown, as if they didn't know it was coming from the other ridge. The bullets buzzed in silently upon the wind and peppered the hill-top around them. Little puffs of dust spurted up and until a couple of the rounds hit hard surfaces, it didn't feel dangerous.

That's when Ruthy went down. She took a shot to the side of her head and deflated onto the spot where her feet were. Not a peep from her. No dramatics or flailing arms or spurting blood, just 'click' and she turned off.

They all dove for cover. That was the signal that the game was on. But, nothing happened. Just rifle fire, and they couldn't hear the report from the guns that shot at them.

Silent, deadly little bits flew around them occasionally. There was no one to shoot back at. The mob's snipers were arranged along the southern ridge.

There was no single location to aim for. That was the advantage that Sheila's group did not have. They were at their machine gun nest, an obvious brown spot of freshly turned dirt and sandbags. The enemy had only to shoot in their general direction and they might hit something. Sheila had nothing but a non-descript ridge-top to fire on.

The pot shots at them continued through the day until dusk.

The night was a harrowing and stressful time. They had no electric lights to illuminate the field. Thankfully it was a full moon and the scene was bathed in the glow of a cold and unconcerned moon.

To keep the area free from incursion they fired star shells from their flare gun. It bathed the valley with an eery green light. They occasionally fired the big gun, not full auto, but single rounds towards what might have been movement. The muzzle flash was a beacon and drew some fire. They shot it very sparingly.

The first night was tense, but the dawn brought them safely into another day.

It was obvious that whoever was over on the other side was not organized enough, or dedicated enough to risk an assault. For all Sheila knew there might only be a handful of guys with guns trying to draw more forces from up the line in order to weaken it. It was all speculation. She had no idea what they were up against.

Where was Kit?

She wanted to call out for her.

She remembered their last encounter.

The afternoon after she and Kit came back from their recon mission, Sheila lay on her cot and took a fitful afternoon nap.

"Sheila." Kit said softly as she entered the musty canvas tent.

Sheila opened her eyes to the very hazy light of early dusk. "Yeah, come in." She beamed joy at Kit's soft and beautifully round face.

Kit came and sat on the edge of the cot. "How're you doing? Holding up OK?"

"Yeah. I'm OK. What's the sitch?" Sheila took the girl's hand that lay gently on her leg.

"All's quiet. Nothing to report. I don't think any one is ever going to come this far west. Hell, we're all the way to the beach." Kit assured.

"Wouldn't surprise me." A moment of silence passed between them as their hands entwined and caressed the other. "I'm gonna' report that bastard for those crosses." Sheila said.

"I know."

"It's awful, but ..." Kit started.

"But what?"

"Maybe it'll keep anyone from coming here. If they see those things they'll go back the other way. They'll never get here." Kit conjectured.

"Yeah. Maybe." Sheila sat up with Kit's helping hand and they held each other's arms more fully.

They had been together before, once in the barracks and also on a short trip to the city for a weekend. They ended up in a Lesbian bar and finally in the house of someone they met in the bar. It was intense and fun and meaningful and dangerous. It would destroy their careers if it came out. They had to play the hard tough macho chicks who were still interested in men sexually, but could never act upon it either. It was a strange world that the female service member lived in.

Sheila pulled Kit close and they breathed each others' breath for a moment and then kissed. It was a kiss of soothing pleasure, a kiss of consolement, a kiss of comfort in the midst of uncertain insanity. It was a kiss that brought a little normality to the stress of what their new reality confronted them with. It was love in the face of despair and hatred and mean-ness. It was a balm and taboo.

—

Sheila lay in the smoky ruin of her command and chuckled at the outrage she had felt over those crosses. Little did she suspect that it was the least of atrocities. It may have been a kindness to those young fellows. To be shot quickly and cleanly and have their bodies maybe serve some useful purpose before becoming one with the earth again.

She coughed and her chest hurt sorely. She knew someone had stabbed her during the fight. She had momentary flashes of his face, a wild eyed man with some kind of sharpened piece of metal. The image in her mind was animated in nature.

He launched over the parapet like a latter day Conan, spittle flying from his snarling mouth, his weapon high and ready to strike at the foe, orange flames rising behind him and framing the scene in a weird surreal flickering horror movie.

He was inside her range of fire, right upon them, she looked up from the gun she was still trying to fire. His weapon must have been as red-hot as the surrounding hellish landscape because it burned when it went into her.

She was the victim of a sword thrust.

Again, she was amused at the macabre thought and a single chuckle hurt immensely.

Sheila's curiosity grew.

Where was Kit?

She felt she had to look over the edge to see where her command went. If only she could raise up a little she might know their fate. She tried to move and was met with piercing pain from multiple places.

Sheila engaged the little mind-tricks she had used all her life to dull reality and allow her to operate when in great discomfort. She started the practice when as a young girl she had the odious chore of shoveling out the stables. She hated the job. It was shit shoveling. She disliked the smell and the squishy glop under her rubber boots and the rote physical labor. She trained herself to zone out and disregard her feelings, both physical and emotional, in order to endure her task. She used the tricks on herself during boot camp and during those other times when the unendurable needed to be endured.

Sheila willed herself to move.

The stabbing pains from her obviously fatal wounds were excruciating. Her head lolled to the side and her face ground into the hard canvas of a sand bag. She could not orient her body with her mind. It was a numb throbbing mass of loose and cut nerves.

Sheila heard loud moaning. It was an awful gut wrenching sound from the depths of hell and despair and pain. Some tortured soul was being raked over hot coals and having their flesh ripped by nasty ogres in a dungeon somewhere. The wailing struck Sheila to the core. She could only imagine the agony that was the source of such a mournful sound.

Sheila willed her body to roll and with tremendous effort she heaved herself up the short sandbag wall to peer over the top to where she thought Kit might have gone.

The awful cries of pain renewed and when her face fell onto the sandbag she realized it was her own voice shrieking.

The rough taste of the dirty bag cut short her efforts to move any more.

She had attained her goal.

She could see over the lip of the emplacement.

She scanned the unknown landscape and recognized none of it. In the distance she could see flames and clouds of smoke rising up from the rolling grassland. From her to the flames was blackness, smoldering light absorbing black charcoal. A huge grassfire was raging on towards the north forests and to the ocean.

She remembered the fire now. It was behind the people who attacked them. It pushed the thousands to come at them. The invaders swarmed over the top of the southern ridge by the thousands. She had no idea there where that many people hiding there, waiting to come at them. They had camped behind the ridge, out of Sheila's sight. They swarmed like ants over the hill top and into the valley no-man's-land.

Julie tried to deter them by firing the fifty cal when they appeared.

She wanted to pay them back for killing Ruthy, and … Kit.

She wanted to fulfill the orders she was given.

Repel boarders.

An acreage-covering crowd of people came at them from across the valley. They were insane to charge. They must all be possessed, or on drugs. They fired their guns at the horde. No sane person would willingly face the gunfire pouring onto them.

In between deafening bursts of her machine gun, pert-nosed, high-cheeked, blonde Julie hollered, "Zombies! Kill the Zombies. Die you bastards! DIE!"

Their M-16's made light chattering against the booming hammer of the fifty-cal as the women lost their rational reasoning and gunned them down. It was obvious that they would never be able to kill that many people coming at them, but they kept firing.

There was no deterrence.

Rolling black smoke crested the southern ridge and the twenty mile an hour hot wind from the interior of California, known as Santa Ana, fanned the grass fire. They were fleeing certain death by burning. Several thousand people fled certain immolation and ran, straight at the Coast Guard outpost. The flames caught up with any who faltered, or hesitated.

Julie overheated the big gun and it quit firing. Sheila was about to call a cease-fire as she finally understood their predicament, but the people in the front were not going to stop. They were fleeing the fire behind them for their lives and very angry at having to endure slaughter at the hands of their fellow countrymen.

"Fuck this!" Julie hollered when the gun ceased operating. She jumped up and bolted.

It took only a second for Bethany to follow.

Sheila foolishly tried to get the gun to work again. She realized she couldn't depress the muzzle enough to fire on the hillside under her anyway.

She reached for her M-16 just as the wild-eyed man came over the top and stabbed her.

She blasted him when he pinned her to the ground and fell next to her.

When she awoke, Sheila peered at the blackened scene and tried to pick out some sign of life, or of Kit, or of anything she recognized. She couldn't.

She had been borne into a new world of grit and scorched earth.

She focused on the landscape and realized the ground was littered with charred bodies. Small lumps of blackened corpses as far as she could see. The fire had chased down practically everyone and taken their life force up into the heavens with its black thick smoke.

She smelled cooked meat.

Sheila recalled her Dad tending the BBQ grill for her going away party. The tablecloth was red and white checkered, the grass was vibrant green and the beer in the old wash tub was frosty cold. Her friends cheered her and toasted her efforts to become something other than a farmer in Halor Iowa. The future was pretty bleak for the youth of her home town and she had to leave her mom and dad and brothers and sisters to their lives in corn country while she flew off to great adventure. She was the oldest and she was supposed to go away and make good. It was the American way.

The seered burgers were delicious and the beer was cold and refreshing that day.

18

<u>That Day</u>

A.Q. Fourth Week

The county offices in the administration complex were a tumult of frenetic and chaotic activity as messengers flew in and out and deputy and police uniforms milled nervously with drawn weapons and crowds of civilians milled around with all too important concerns that must be attended to yesterday. The dust filtered light in the chambers of the almighty council was disturbed by the hub-bub of people moving in and out and up and down motions and gavel banging and some yelling in the corners and people throwing papers at one another, all in a futile attempt to make some sense of the situation.

The news was that the county was under attack.

The border effort in the south had failed and uncountable hordes were descending on the town of Saint Rose with a vengeance. The border had been a colossal miscalculation and had only served to harden and galvanize the hordes heading to 'happy cow country' for food. Eggtown's liberal and more philanthropic citizens had opened the bridge and tried to welcome the tens of thousands on the freeway into their town.

'We can accommodate our fellow human beings. We must,' they thought.

The strategy had worked in welcoming the mobs of undocumented immigrants from south of the border over the past thirty years or so. They had absorbed them into the fabric of society without any dramatically negative repercussions. The lawns were kept up and the restaurants had plenty of dishwashers. There was room for everyone.

The efforts of Eggtown's mayor to hold the line with his thin militia and support the border, encouraging those from the great city to the south, to go east into the central valley, where large quantities of food that would sustain them lay, collapsed. His ranks came apart when the bleeding hearts infiltrated his lines and tore down the barriers south of town. Eggtown was the weak link in the chain.

Unbeknownst to the good folk of that commuter laden town was the fact that over two hundred thousand people had ranged themselves along the southern ridge line. They were only held in check by the county's hastily erected signs proclaiming the limit of their travel. They had ravaged the communities of Marine County. They slogged overland to the edge of the county's tolerance. They dispersed along the wide ranging frontier to the sea. Eggtown saw only a small portion of the people trying to get to the food resources that they had.

The enormous swarm of people ranged across the grasslands of northern Marine County. They denuded the land of livestock. They ransacked any and all houses that they encountered. Resistance was futile.

There were mobs and mobs of them.

They had formed groups of loose-knit tribes. The conquering instinct formed in the collective mind of people without any intellectual bidding that it do so. Each, automatically found a place in the melee to get something to grab onto: a cow, some canned goods, a garden, a chicken, anything that might sustain their immediate family and needs. Like locusts, the huge crowds seethed over the countryside and devoured it.

There were those who futilely fought against the onslaught, but to no avail.

They were over-run.

People died in the taking and people died in the giving. Discussion about the plight of the homeless and less fortunate was not in the daily conversation. Chase down the cow, kill it, and start a fire was the daily desire. Defending the kill was the next step, and the tribes formed. Bypassing, or burning the houses that stood in the way was the sub-agenda. Eating was top priority. Property and rights associated with that concept had vanished with the lights and sounds of the old world.

When the masses finally reached and were confronted by the message of intolerance that the billboards of the newly created border inferred, they had reached their limit.

They did stop, however and camped against the southern lip of the ridge-top that provided cover from the great machine guns on the opposite hills. Only a few were shot at or killed before the word was spread and complied with. It was the encampment at the foot of the Golden Gate Bridge all over again. For several days they made camp and waited.

They waited for … they knew not what. Some sign, some go ahead, some OK, you are in this and you have to act now, moment. People will wait until they are forced into action. They won't go running helter-skelter into a situation of immediate danger if there is any chance of waiting it out and surviving. The Jews of Europe suffered this during the holocaust. Easily they outnumbered their guards at all times, but the action of pro-action was far too great a personal risk when waiting to see what might happen was still an option. And, so the people camped out of sight of the heavy machine guns facing them and they waited. They waited and starved. No one would move unless they were forced to.

It had been hot since the quiet. The sun bore down on the Earth and dried it out. The air was still and no freshening breeze broke the unnerving calm.

Maybe it was a camp cook fire, or maybe it was deliberately set to spark a little motivation in the people. It didn't matter.

The fire came. It came as a hint of haze from whence they came. It was at first seen as a break in the hot dry days in the form of weather and coming rain. A rumor flew through the camps as hope sprang anew. The people were eager for good news. The clouds of smoke were mistaken for rain clouds and that was enough to sustain thoughts of cool and cleansing water from the sky. No one moved. They saw the cloudy smoke and they waited.

It wasn't immediate.

It was large though.

The entire southern front was burning. It moved north, slowly. There was no wind to speak of and the grass lit up in its own fashion and scorched the ground at the speed of a walking man.

When the grass-fire came within a mile of the encampments there was concern.

It wasn't rain.

It wasn't moving slowly any more. It sucked huge amounts of air into its combustible jaws and was now creating its own wind. The fire was roaring and moving to devour all that was in the way.

Still, the people did not move. They could see it was coming. They could see that it stretched from the coast to far inland. They could fathom the implications behind a wall of flame coming at them, but they couldn't figure out how to overcome their fear of those terrible guns ahead of them, and which had placed a monstrous bogey-man of hammering warfare noise in their heads. They stayed put.

They watched it come. They waited with some hope in their post-modern heads that 911 would send helicopters and fire engines and tankers full of flame retardant to save them. They clung to the vestiges of the world long gone. Intellectually they all knew they had to get a move-on, but they waited. They waited almost too late.

When the orange flames became visible on the opposite ridge, an audible gasp arose. The monster manifested itself as something they could now actually see. The billowing smoke was benign and somewhat innocuous looking, but the flames themselves were active and vibrant and threatening. The flames moved them.

Hurriedly the camps struck.

They moved along the ridge, toward the sea, and not over it into the sights of the guns.

They shifted west. The problem was that there were miles of people camped along that ridge.

They moved into other people.

They ran into others who hadn't seen flames and weren't spooked by the oncoming disaster.

The mass hysteria flared up as surely as the combustion behind them and the mobs stampeded.

It appeared that the ground itself had decided to move. It flowed along like lava. Thousands of fleeing people kicked up dust and trampled one another and fled the terror at their heels. Unlike horses or cattle, people have no compunctions about trampling things beneath their feet and a trail of broken bodies was left in the wake of the movement. A seething mass of humanity roiled across the countryside towards anywhere that had no fire.

A new holocaust began when the flames finally overcame the people and forced them over the ridge top into the forbidden territory covered by the guns of the border patrol.

The end of the world was at hand and the sound of the collective agony of their situation and then the abrupt cacophony of gunfire went up to the heavens and echoed into the coming dusk of that day.

—

Georgie Stapleton, tall, with a square jaw and broad shoulders rushed through the maze of rooms at the County Administration building: overturned chairs and papers littered the floor, window blinds hung at odd angles, people rushed about gathering their few camp things as they fled. Georgie made for his grandmother's cubbyhole closet that they had fashioned into an apartment. He burst in as she poured a cup of tea.

"Granma. What are you doing? We gotta' go!"

"Well, what does it look like I'm doing? It's tea-time. Here sit down for a minute and have a nice cuppa'," white haired Georgia Stapleton invited.

"We haven't got time for this."

"Oh, pish-posh. Always time for a nice cuppa' tea. Calms the nerves." She smiled at her rugged young grandson and held up a saucer with broken cookies.

"But, Granma ..."

"Sit!" She finally said with stern note in her voice.

He knew he wasn't going to get anywhere with her until he humored her a bit. He sat down and dunked a cookie fragment briefly.

"Now, isn't that better?" The old woman cooed. "All right. Now that we have settled a little, tell me the news."

"They're coming, the town is overrun. We have to go." He blurted out.

"Go where? Home? There is nothing in the house. We moved all the food here. And my tea service, and my pillow." She pointed out contritely.

"We have to get out. They're on the rampage. It's open warfare. It's all gone mad." He tried to reason.

"I see. So the border plan hasn't quite worked out?"

"Worked out?! It failed. The border plan was a disaster, some colonel and that idiot Dave Putnam started a frigging war out there, and lost it. The whole city is at our doorstep and they want revenge. We have to go." Georgie plead with the stern woman. She was thin and aged, but she was the most stubborn person he had ever met. Only he seemed to be able to cajole her to action when all others could not.

The council had abandoned the admin center and fled to find protection with the Sheriff.

They left her to her stubbornness.

She sat still and pursed her lips. Wrinkles radiated from her mouth and as her eyes narrowed, crow's feet radiated. "I see. So, we couldn't save them from themselves?"

Georgie watched the grand dame of Saint Rose as the reality of their plight sank in. He just wanted to get her on the road where they might live another day. "We can't save everyone all the time Granma." He used one of her old adages against her.

Sounds of gunfire popped in the distance and punctuated the nervous silence.

Georgia Stapleton, architect of the post electricity rescue of Saint Rose and the county, sipped her tea.

"I've got a truck waiting Granma, we don't have any more time."

"Finish your tea Georgie, and we'll go." She instructed.

He slurped the cup down quickly and crammed the rest of the cookie bits in his mouth.

She gathered herself: put on a jacket, slipped her feet into some galoshes, grabbed her double-barreled sawed-off shotgun and said, "Grab my knapsack," she pointed, "well, come on."

He followed her out.

On the step of the building they were rudely greeted by a deputy sitting in the driver's seat of an ancient diesel bread truck. He was nursing the engine to keep it idling. He held two six shooters on a knot of people who were obviously threatening to take their transport.

"Goddamnit. You took long enough!" The deputy yelled. "I almost left you." He gunned the noisy engine.

"Put those away." Ms. Stapleton commanded. "You people, come on. We'll all go."

The deputy looked at her in disbelief, but holstered his guns as they clambered into the truck. A man holding a toddler, several women and half a dozen school age kids ran to join them.

"Gracias, señora." The Hispanic man said as he trundled his family into the truck.

"Si, si, muchas gracias abuela." The man's wife said with large thankful brown eyes.

Georgia sat shotgun with her shotgun. The old machine roared a black cloud and lurched from the last known seat of organized government.

Civility collapsed. Their efforts to maintain order had worked well and the people cooperated with one another and with the authorities and were saved, until the city people arrived.

Sequestered in the rural outback made it just barely possible for Saint Rosians to survive and go on from the loss of their electrically powered lives, but the rest of the world wouldn't stay away or go away. There were just too many mouths and too few resources. It was an age old problem that had, until the quiet, been tenuously resolved by the expenditure of huge amounts of petroleum and coordinated with the magical electricity. Once that magic was gone all the oil in the world wasn't going to cure the near term shortages. Starvation drove millions to the countryside.

The cities emptied.

19

Atilla's New Friends

A.Q. Month Two

The odds for staying alive one more day were better when he avoided roadways and dwellings. Sam quickly learned that patience and evasion were good skills to nurture.

He had watched road buddies boldly enter buildings and not come out.

Then what do you do?

Go in there after them?

Sam thought not.

Sam preferred to wait.

The patient dog also eats.

He spent his time avoiding conflict, watching. He stayed off the road. He stayed out of houses. He saw a lot of things happen that he was glad to have merely witnessed. Sam was still alive. Being able to stay out of the way was a valuable skill. After so many near misses he felt exposed every waking hour. A low profile was the new paradigm. A scene was not the thing to be the center of.

Keeping enough food in his gut was a chore of late.

Staying on the move and away from people who were mad at you because of hunger was proving difficult. At the periphery of his thoughts he suspected it wasn't sustainable to continue foraging alone.

The first two weeks Sam rolled with the army of two hundred thousand displaced folk from the city.

There was food to be had in the wealthy suburb and bedroom communities north of the golden gate bridge. The hordes swarmed over the wealthy neighborhoods in Marine County, even though there were well armed suburbanites there who felt they owned their property and the goods inside their high-priced homes. Roving thousands from the city thought otherwise. It was not fair for some to eat while the rest starved and no amount of rational argument or high-minded concepts like property rights were going to stand in the way of hungry stomachs that felt entitled to eat everyday. Christian charity evaporated with the canned goods and civilized behavior vanished as people's innate competitive nature took over. The ultimate motivator was enacted, many mouths and not enough pie to go around. Everyone got pretty testy about their hunger.

People just weren't as friendly as they used to be. If you resisted the home invasion by the rif-raf in your yard and they took offense, they shot back. Eventually you and your family were over-run, your house looted and invariably torched. If, however, you shared your food with the multitudes of strangers, they guarded your house from other refugees until your food ran out; which was in hours and you were then fortunately alive and able to join in the exodus north. You became one of the hungry wanderers.

The rich neighborhoods of Marine County became well landscaped ruins as the ant-like masses from the city swarmed over the land.

Anymore; Sam kept on the move, quietly, and it always took him all day to cover any distance. At an instant Sam might fall down and out of sight. He'd gotten good at going to ground. Any depression, hole, bush, or gutter to lay in as if dead, would do. He sometimes ran for all he was worth.

Moving was the constant.

Every day of his new life was full to the brim with things he had to find: food, clean water, a safe place to take a dump (if he ate the day before) and a place where he would wake up after sleeping. Staying alive was a whole new lifestyle and pickings were slim out here in the hinterlands. He had lived through the crazy slash and burn of the close quarters of the suburbs and now, was alone and in open country.

The night of burning gave him opportunities for advancement and he took them. The awful fire and the insane onslaught of the people into the guns left a void. There was a moment when he could move undetected into the north country he was aiming at. His terrible night of groping amongst charred bodies and avoiding border patrols was a memory he wished he didn't have.

Sam, and his trusty big headed mutt, loped through rolling hill country interspersed with oak trees and vineyards as far as the eye could see. He liked wide fields of view and each rise presented a new landscape to scope for threat.

He knew the vineyard could trap him because moving against the line of the rows was a snare of wire and grape vines. He would have to crawl or roll under the bottom wire to get to the next row– then, to keep going laterally, he would have to do it again and again. So, moving against the grain, to escape the vineyard, would be slow and difficult. Moving down the line of least resistance was a clear path between the rows.

At the vineyard edge he scoped with his compact binoculars.

Attila, his dog, loped ahead, below the level of the vines and only a shadow, deliberately, down the row of grapes.

Sam's current field of view was excellent for a half mile or more and he could clearly see the end of the row far ahead. He scanned the large space across fields ahead, then he moved. The slight downward slope allowed a nice jogging gait for little effort and Sam moved down the line of grapes easily. He found himself enjoying moving through the cultured grape vines.

He and his trusty mutt, Attila, moved deliberately and in silence down the long lines of seemingly endless grape vines. He reached out a hand and raked in a few raisins. He stuffed his last good plastic bag in the pocket of his fatigue jacket with the sticky mess. Some of the grapes were hard some were mushy some were perfect raisins some were a little moldy and some were wine. His pace matched his chewing. He never stopped reaching out and stuffing as he moved down the row. He moved steadily, quickly, and slightly hunched over while stuffing his face and his jacket pockets.

It amused him in a harmonious way. The gait of his movement coupled with chewing the sweet wine-like goop as he the snatched at the little dark clusters in a sort of musical cadence. It seemed like a song.

Step chew, step chew, grab grab, step chew, step chew, grab grab.

He chuckled and smacked his lips around the froth of grape pulp in his mouth. He continually spit out large cuds of seeds then stuffed fresh, almost raisins, into his messy face. He sucked the essence from the mass and spit.

Happy moments are cherished more when your life is mean and short.

For a brief subsisting moment Sam felt true happiness at his place in the world.

He was making it.

A break in the rows appeared ahead, slowed his pace and he dropped into a stalk.

He quit gathering, yet chewed on, his cheeks full, and his face smeared purple.

He scanned the perimeter quickly and then crouched. The entire horizon behind and to the side was continuous vineyard.

He sat still.

He had zoned out for a minute while in his eating and walking reverie. Snapping back into the now, he froze and peered ahead with his binoculars. He crouched low with his head barely above the level of the vines. Looking ahead over the lip of the rise to the end of the row and some buildings below he spat out a wad of grape mess, it trickled down his front unnoticed.

Farm buildings flanked by a line of trees that signified a road below, blocked his way. Beyond, thick heavy redwood forest loomed. It denoted the end of open country and of the vineyards.

He spat his mouth clean of crunchy masticated grape seeds and listened.

Atilla was no where to be seen. He was already down there.

Sam lay perfectly still in a low spot under the vines for a full fifteen minutes. He had all day long. He studied the farm buildings and roadway through his binoculars, as best he could, and waited. He watched Attila cross his field of view in front of the barn several times, back and forth.

'Scout Dog' to the rescue, Sam chuckled. The damned dog did a good job of looking over the whole place. He went into the buildings, wherever his nose led him. After a while Attila came and sat down in front of the barn door, in clear view, and then he lay down and took a nap.

"That's my cue." Sam muttered. The coast was clear.

The dog had found nothing of direct threat or food source. Dog siesta was the all clear signal.

Sam jumped up and moved quickly down the slope the last eighth mile to the end of the row. Sam didn't head for the buildings. He made for the forest across the road.

He didn't want to enter the buildings. Doors and windows were broken and he just wasn't in the mood to find another butchered family of corpses today.

He wanted the cover of that forest around him. It looked inviting after all the open space he had been in. The scattered oaks had been scant cover in the wide open rolling hill country and the dense forest looked safer.

He stepped out of the vineyard at a run.

He ran right by Attila and kept on running right through the barnyard, through the gate, across the asphalt road, and plunged into the trees.

Attila raised his head and watched Sam run by him. After a moment he grudgingly heaved himself up from his cozy warm dust bed and followed the man away from the empty farm and into the dense forest.

—

They watched him come over the stark contrasting hilltop. Lines and lines of grape vines wired on posts covered the open ground to the horizon. They could see anyone moving on that hillside. He had appeared as a black dot.

He was a cautious one.

After a good hour he got up the moxy to run across the farm and into their hands.

They had waited and were to be rewarded.

The spider and the fly.

"Look he's coming!" Stone said in a sotto voce whisper to his clan brother hiding in the redwood bush.

The older boy, Jackal he was called, (his real name was Jackson Thurdling, and had always been Turdling at school), nodded and hefted the heavy trip net.

Sam ran right past them, on a mission for cover.

Three of the five other boys hiding in the brush, jumped out, raised long pennants on sticks, all a different color, and waved them wildly at Sam when he was well into their little trap-space.

He found himself in a small open flat spot with few exit options. It was a little bottleneck in the wood. Sam came up short.

Seventeen year old 'Stone Cold' as he now insisted, (his real name was Benny Harrison, but that fell away with the demise of the distracting electronic world that treated him as a creature out of place), was already behind Sam matching speed and with a whipping motion the net shrouded the interloper as he hesitated at the flags in his face.

The older teen, Jackal, jogged in from the side and with a long strait stick whapped Sam viciously right across his shotgun toting forearm as he tried to raise it.

The gun jumped from his fingers and seven teenage kids jumped him in a grand tackle.

"Got ya!"

"Yeah!!" they yelled. Sam collapsed like a sack of gravel at the combined weight clinging to him.

"Get the gun! Get the gun!" The mass of Sam, trussed up, clinging kids, and rope netting, squirmed and rolled for a moment.

"Dude, you wanna' die? Lay still or we can just kill you now," the curly black haired Sergeant Jackal, the leader, spoke clearly from the side of the fray.

"Kill him!" a spindly, fuzzy-haired, twelve year old girl, Ella, hollered from the mass of arms and legs.

Sam squirmed some at the sound of a little girl sounding her vote for the 'Lord of the Flies' scenario. It was such a sweet innocent sounding voice that carried such heavy razor sharp suggestion.

Attila came loping into the forest glade; he hesitated for a moment only, then came right over and started licking Sam on the face.

The kids didn't let go, but they squealed when the monstrous animal came at them.

Sergeant Jackal, stood calmly and trained his big black revolver on the dog.

"Goddamn it, Attila!" Sam tried to yell.

"Get him. Get him." The kids urged the dog on. They started laughing as the dog slobbered all over Sam's netted face.

"Let them take your gun or we'll let the dog keep licking you … then we'll kill you." Jackal said, quietly pointing the huge looking, forty-four caliber, magnum revolver, at Sam.

The end of the threatening black pistol in the hands of this skinny serious kid flipped a switch in Sam's brain.

Sam relaxed.

The kids untangled the shotgun and knives and ammo from him as they trussed him up with the net.

"Look what he's got." A thin wiry kid said. "Shoes." He pointed at the bundles tied on the pack.

"Understand. Killing you is easy. So, do what you're told." Jackal stepped back as the kids prodded Sam to his feet.

"Where'd you get the shoes, dude?" the earnest thin young man barked.

Sam glared at him from under the net.

"Fine, be that way," Jackal said.

"Look, sneakers," one boy said as he cut loose his new oversized prize.

"Leave the shoes for the Master. Stone, One-hair, take the high view until the night watch," Jackal commanded.

"You bet sarge." Stone Cold shook flowing golden blond hair from his face and slapped his smaller partner on the back.

One-hair, (so called because although he was already going bald, he sported a single thick braided ponytail) smiled a tight lipped recognition of the task and the two teenage toughs jogged off and vanished.

Sam's hands had been trussed behind him with a large zip-tie. He waited for the next shoe to fall, so to speak, when he felt a sharp poke in his ass.

"March," one of the boys commanded.

The murderous talking little girl stepped in front holding a string attached to the netting that he still wore on his head.

She gave a tug and took on the air of leading a prize pet. She occasionally looked back to make sure he followed obediently.

Several others followed close behind with sharp hand-made spears rigged with the flags that had startled him at the clearing.

Attila had taken a shine to the kids and seemed to be enjoying their new company. The procession marched into the dark woods, away from the vineyards, the road, and the bright open country sunshine.

"You turned out to be a great help." Sam said to Attila.

The dog looked up for a second then fell back out of sight.

'Well this is a new turn of events,' Sam thought, 'captured by the children of the future.'

They wound through the forest of thick tall trees. The uneven trail wandered through tall green ferns and wasn't worn by frequent use. Occasionally the trees gave way to open sunshine filled clearings that were heavy with scrub-brush. The girl held branches and let them go, to slap Sam. She must have been doing it on purpose as she continued and held them until their strain was at maximum before she let fly.

"Hey," Sam piped up, "quit hitting me." He got a jab in the kidney from behind.

"Shut-up. Keep walking."

Sam guessed it was not their usual path and it almost seemed like they doubled back a bit. They must be trying to keep him from realizing the way. The way got steeper and he found they were on a tailored switchback up a grade. When they reached the top of the hill they stopped at a small rock outcrop.

The leader pulled out a small mirror and flashed back the way they had come.

Sam couldn't see the reply, but they seemed satisfied.

Jackal ordered a heavy-set pink cheeked lad to man the post on the rocks. "Half-ton, you make here tonight. I'll send supper for you guys."

"You got it sarge," the barrel-chested boy said breathily. He may have been about fifteen years old, but he had the bearing of a grown man. He wore a vicious looking butcher knife on one hip and carried a spear with a green flag. He sported a fur-lined skull-cap and dark green army blanket cape. He unlimbered his rucksack and got out a pair of short handled signal flags. He did the same routine with a tiny mirror that Jackal had done and then stood on the big rock and waved his flags vigorously at his unseen counterpart.

Ella yanked on the net-leash. "Come on, you," she barked.

They hiked for a couple more hours. The sun rose high in the sky and heat bore down through the lofty canopy of redwood trees. Deeper into the heavy woods they went: up hills, down into steep gullies, winding paths around rock clusters and hopping over trickling streams.

Sam lost track of where he was.

The path was sometimes well worn and smooth from foot-traffic. Sometimes they diverted and walked over untrammeled ground where the meager tufts of grass under the trees stood up strait until they stepped on them, as if they were the first to have ever passed there.

Twice they passed oncoming traffic. Ella yanked his leash to the side where they stopped for a moment.

The first, a group of women with a gaggle of kids, strode by going in the other direction; they were laden with knapsacks and moved lightly as if the loads were not heavy.

The second were men on horses.

"My goodness, look what our little Ella has caught." The lead horseman said.

The little girl stood, tall and proud at the side of the track, with her captive on leash. "In service to our Lord John," she said as she made a graceful bow and sweep of her arm.

"May your path be smooth shield-maid." The elder man, third in the row of horsemen, said with a chuckle.

Sam opened his mouth, "hey man, just what the …?"

He was abruptly cut off when the thin spindly fellow with curly hair whacked him from behind with a spear shaft.

"Silence slave! Sorry, Sir John, he has no manners. We just caught him. He'll learn." He raised his spear to hit Sam again.

"Easy now, Jack, don't damage the goods before we learn how good they are."

The horseman spoke to Sam. "Young man, listen to my squires. They have saved your life." John looked to his vassal. "Why did you capture him Jack?"

"Well my lord, he was carrying these." Jackal jerked at Sam's pack and untied a pair of brand new boots. He held them up to the horseman.

"Really? Nice. Steel toes," John admired.

"He has more, Sire," Jackal added.

"Do tell? Take him to the pit straight away. Deliver his pack and his story … if he has one, to Senschale, Mark. Young man, like I said, these loyal squires have just saved your life. I just hope you're worth it." John pulled a small chocolate bar from his pocket and tossed it to Ella.

She beamed at the treat and gave a little bow to her lord.

The cavalrymen turned tail and clip-clopped down the path.

"You see how he saw me." Ella squealed. She broke the chocolate bar into three and shared with her two compatriots.

Sam wasn't offered anything. He could smell the processed chocolate the second she broke it open. When she wafted it by his nose handing it to Jack, Sam's mouth gushed saliva. He swallowed and licked his lips at the memory: soothing, brown, silky, sweet chocolate.

Sam couldn't believe the scene that had just played out before him. It was like a ren-fair moment only, after the beating, more real and painful. Those were lords, these were squires who called the leader sire, and he was their slave. They were warriors on horseback and he was a captive of their loyal subjects.

The heat of the day and long hike into the woods accentuated the distance he felt from the real world. The modern era had truly ended and now he was being led like a beast of burden. The hard plastic zip-ties cut into his wrists. He pondered the worrisome reference to 'the pit' and he didn't know what they had added to his pack but he staggered under the weight.

What was ahead for this day?

The little girl took a nibble on her treat and yanked his cord. Sam lurched forward and trudged on, dutifully, behind the wisp of a girl who reeked of the succulent chocolate smell of a world gone.

They hiked for an interminable time.

The day wore on and Sam lost track of where they were and what time it was.

His gut was gnawing a hole in his backbone as he hadn't eaten since the rats from the warehouse and the sodden half fermented grapes worked on his bowels. He felt the need to fart, but he daren't for fear of squirting down his leg. He hiked on and clenched his butt-cheeks at every step.

It became a grueling slog for him.

The kids leading him stepped lightly and didn't have a care in the world. They were on their way back to the warmth of base camp with a treasure in tow. He was their prize. He was carrying their kit and they were pleased as punch about the day.

Sam smelled wood smoke and the group stopped for a moment and arranged themselves to look a little neater. They must be getting close to the final destination.

Sam hoped it wasn't going to be a cooking pot or a firing squad. He had seen a few and wasn't eager to be a participant.

A pit sounded ominous, but it meant he would live for another day.

They wanted him.

Maybe this was the way he would become rich. His knowledge of the shoe warehouse might save him. The cavalry lords seemed mighty interested in the contents of his pack and the boots. He was carrying gold and they wanted it. He had to steel his nerve and figure out some way to parlay his meager knowledge into a place of wealth or power or both.

Sam had never in his life been ruthless.

He was a follower.

He didn't lead the pack, because all his life, every time he had tried to lead the charge he got shot down. Of course, in the modern world, that only meant that he was subject to some kind of ridicule or public scrutiny that dissuaded him from continuing on that course of action. There were no firing squads in high school, but the biting scorn of his peers had felt like it. Sam distanced himself from those who could penetrate the chink in his personal armor and ended up being a warehouse monkey for an audio video company. He could hide in the warehouse and put together the lists of A/V equipment without supervision and therefore avoid any criticism of his methods. He had always gotten the work orders as accurate as he could, but that was just a logistical exercise. It wasn't personal. He liked it that way. No feelings were stomped as they were by an overly critical girlfriend or bullying enemy. He filled the orders; life went on, he clocked in and out, he was happy. Poor, but happy.

Now, in this crazy post-apocalyptic world, he was on his own and to achieve any goal, he had to decide to get into, or to avoid situations of very personal participation.

Now, he had to exert force and his will towards getting fed and to finding refuge.

Others mightn't agree that he should be fed with their food or sleep nearby and conflict arose … daily.

Sam's stomach growled and churned with the weight of the half rotten grapes he had stuffed into his maw earlier. His anal sphincter screamed a leaking warning to him to find somewhere to drop drawers or the leg would be wet.

He sucked in his breath and kept walking as the tiny parade stepped out of the tight confines of the forest and entered a huge, open compound.

There were dozens of people scattered in organized knots around the perimeter of the yard area. Each group was busy with survival activities. People were: chopping wood, sawing logs, stacking hay, hanging clothes to dry, raking nuts on the ground, and a myriad of other things to make the necessities of life a reality through their labor.

The little girl, Ella, stopped and flicked his leash.

Sam came up short and almost shat his pants right there. He wanted to tell them he needed the latrine, but the earlier painful whack of the spear shaft from behind forced him to hold his tongue.

When he dared to look up he saw a rotund man in his fifties, Fu-Manchu moustache and thinning hair pulled back to a comical pony-tail sticking straight out the back of his head, come marching right up to the group.

The man jiggled in his enormity and was flanked by a couple of thin fellows who kept a close eye on their chief every second. When he marched, they marched, when he turned, they turned, in unison, when he stopped they stopped a respectful yet handy distance to each side and a little behind him: attendants, lackeys, body-guards.

Sam wasn't sure, but he didn't really care at this point. He was about to shit his pants and collapse under the weight of his overloaded pack.

The heavy fellow beamed a bright welcoming smile at them. "Report, squire Jack. Why do you bring this man to us?" Mark asked of the dark haired youth.

"I ... uh, well he has these." Jackal stammered a moment as he formed a reply. He held out the bundled pair of brand new boots.

"And you think this is enough to bring him here, to show him where we are?" Mark put his hands on his hips and pierced the thin fellow with an enquiring glare.

"Our lord, Sir John, sent us up. He said the pit until we can discover his worth."

Mark took a step forward and eyed the other shoes tied to the pack. "Strip him. Bring the things to stores. Put him in the pit for now. We will find out what he knows later." Mark sounded so imperious, then he softened, "Good work, Ella, you have done well."

He chucked the beaming little frizzy headed girl under the chin and smiled.

She peered up with an adorably cute cherubic face and batted her glistening eyes at the old man.

"As you speak, milord," Jackal replied with a stiff clenched fist to his breast sort of salute.

"Come on you," he barked, and led Sam away from Mark and Ella.

Mark dug into his pocket for a sweet treat of some sort to give the angelic and murderous little girl.

In a moment Sam's pack was unclasped and yanked from him.

"Take your boots off." Jackal commanded.

Sam started to object, but Jack's spear was already poised on high to brain him if he showed any resistance.

Sam sat and grudgingly unlaced his boots. He was already remorseful about losing the brand new boots. They felt so good and comfy on his worn and weary feet that he was having a hard time bringing himself to take them off.

When he was barefoot they marched him to the edge of the large open encampment, right to the edge of the woods, straight to what, too quickly appeared under him, a dark pit where he was summarily shoved into from behind.

Sam didn't have a chance to react.

The darkness opened under him, he lost his footing, stumbled and fell into the hole in the ground.

He felt only a moment of free-fall, bounced off the dirt wall and slammed into soft moist ground.

He registered an uncomfortable moistness in his trousers. The jarring fall into the pit had loosened his bowels and he laid, ears ringing, head swimming and trousers full of liquid grape-juice-shit on the wet earth.

The ground was cool and he liked the relief from the awful unseasonable heat of the hike.

He wondered if it mattered whether he had a load in his pants or not.

He decided it didn't and he lay still and slept, or fell unconscious.

Atilla appeared at the lip of the pit and decided it was a perfect time for a nap. He lay down and snoozed. As far as he was concerned, everything was fine and his master was safe.

—

Jim the thin had finally done something in his life. He had taken the bull by the horns and gotten his guys to create and execute an elaborate ambush.

He sat in the luxurious sunken living room of Happy Lair and waited for his audience with Sir John. He was beaming. He had netted three horses, a valuable prisoner and no one got hurt, except the enemy. He thought he had done pretty good for his first command. This was going to set him up in his career with the riders. This was the kind of thing that marked one for greatness.

Mark Young, the Shire's administrator, tugged his fu-manchu moustache as he entered the room. "The Lord will see you now." He held open the hallway door to the innermost map and arsenal room.

Jim had only heard of this room. He had never been inside. He stood up, straightened his rumpled coat and with head held high, entered.

The walls were lined with maps. A large table in the center took most of the space. Chairs ranged around the table. On the far side sat Sir John.

"Stand there." Mark directed the opposite of the table from John.

"You are Jim the thin?" John asked.

"Yes, milord." Jim bowed his head and gave a polite bow.

"You commanded Alpha Recon?"

Jim stood up tall. "Yes milord." He stated clearly.

"You are responsible?"

"Yes milord. We took three excellent horses for your stable … with no loss milord." He boasted.

Silence reigned for a full minute. Dust motes were visible hanging in the sliver of sunlight that slipped by the heavy drawn shades.

"Who told you to execute the plan?" John asked.

"Squire William assigned me to the post milord. The plan was mine."

"So, you are the one who decided to bushwhack three deputy sheriffs on my road?"

It didn't sound as good when Sir John said it as it did in his own mind. "They drew and fired milord. We had no choice, milord." Jim was feeling his backpedaling hackles raise.

It was like his drunken father demanding of him if he was late home or not, when it was obviously past midnight.

Mark couldn't hold his tongue any longer. "Do you realize what you've done?"

"Acquisition?" Jim said shakily.

John said evenly, "he has no idea, Mark. I'll tell you boy."

The boy reference brought back his hated father.

"You may have started a war. You have killed officials. Worse yet, you have bragged about it and made it public. You have captured an emissary from the county council and paraded her in fetters through our camp. You have done all this on your own volition, as if you are the only one who will reap the consequences."

"Oh, he will reap consequences John, if I have anything to say about it." Mark blurted out.

"Mark," John said, cutting him off.

Jim's face was stone. His eyes were slits. He was being dressed down for doing what the Shire did every day. He had been set-up. That damned Squire William had practically told him to do the deed. He showed him the truck barricade that was set for the trap. He told him to make sure no one got past. He put him in charge of the main ridge road from Saint Rose. Everyone knew that the Shire was taking animals from whatever source they could. How could Jim be expected to maintain an outpost without arms, and when armed without bloodshed? What was he supposed to do when those deputies started shooting? Wave flags at them. He came into this room voluntarily to get a promotion, favors, some thanks.

"I thought I did a good job." Jim squeaked out.

John said, "I don't know whether I should kill you or not."

Jim turned white and a warm flutter rose in his abdomen and crawled up into his face. His ears turned red and he realized he only had a pocketknife, the only thing left from his hated father, to defend himself with. A mythology of ruthlessness was firmly planted in Jim's mind and he had no doubt that John meant what he said.

"I thought I was doing the right thing." Tears burned Jim's eyes as he struggled to control himself.

"Uncontrolled initiative is dangerous to us. Do we eliminate everyone who tries something that causes us hurt? Or do we try to learn from our errors in judgment?" John asked rhetorically.

Jim's emotions at having this conversation with his executioner got the better of him and he blubbered out, "We try to learn," he sobbed and bit his tongue.

"I don't think he's teachable," Mark declared of the youth.

Jim nodded at John vigorously to convince him that he could learn.

"He's teachable," John told Mark, "he just needs a reminder to slow down and do what he's told."

Visions of the awful pit flooded Jim's imagination.

He put people into the pit.

He didn't go there.

He could die there, filthy, alone, cold.

He looked forlorn and felt lost to the world.

"Get a hold of yourself, Jim-boy." John ordered.

Jim the thin, gasped and hung at the edge of bawling out loud when John used the hated childhood derivation of his name. It's what his father did to put him in his infantile place. He felt sick to his stomach.

"What will you do to make this up to me?" John queried the guy with a lifted eyebrow.

"To all of us," Mark chimed in.

A couple of awkward moments passed before Jim realized he was supposed to answer the question. "I'll do anything, Sir John."

"Kneel before you swear to me Jim. You obviously have taken this all a bit too cavalierly. I need your fealty. You get it?" John seethed at the young man.

"On pain of death," Mark said clearly. "Repeat it," he commanded.

"On pain of death," Jim mewled.

"I swear fealty to my Lord John, and no other," Mark said.

Jim repeated his words, "… and no other."

"Now, because you have caused me such trouble, what are you going to do for me?" John's burning stare melted holes in the fellow.

"Anything you ask, Lord John." Jim said with some conviction. He needed to convince them he was with them, not against them. He wanted to walk out of that room without a death warrant on his head.

"That's right. Lord Seneschale, pour us a libation would you?" John held up three fingers. Mark poured three shot glasses with a smoky tan liquor and passed them out.

Jim took the glass and said, "I don't drink alcohol."

"You will do anything for me. Drink it as a symbol of our loyal bond," John said flatly.

Jim waited a moment, then downed the biting alcohol. He looked out from his teary eyes to see John waiting for him to finish.

John sat still for a few moments, then said to Mark. "Seems safe enough." Then they downed their shots of twelve year old whiskey.

Mark blew a stream of air and puckered a bit. "Whooooo. Good."

"Smooth." John agreed.

Jim's eyes were big as saucers. It could have been poison. They tested him.

John started as Mark poured them another. "You're going to work. You're going to work for me. You are going to be my ... lessee, what'll we call you. Batboy?" John threw out. "Valet? Butler? I know, my man Friday. That's it, you're going to be my valet, butler, chauffeur, security, laundry man, food taster and personal shield until you show me that you are worthy. The beauty of this is if anything happens to me, you will be blamed and beaten to death as the prime suspect. As long as I am happy and healthy you live in relative ease, fuck-up or fuck me over again and your ass is grass. We'll make sure of that."

Jim was relieved beyond saying.

He stared up at the man's thick unshaven face.

For the first time he saw Sir John as not just another person out there. John had power over him now. He felt the man's charisma pull him into his service. He would do whatever this man wanted, to please him, and atone for whatever slight he had committed.

Jim was still unsure just exactly what his infraction was.

He thought it was because he took the credit.

Regardless, he was now in the household of the leader and not out running around in the woods.

"When do you want me to start?" Jim asked.

"Right now." Mark said firmly. "It's about time for supper and we have a meeting. You go get us a couple of plates. We're starved," and turning to John, "and we need to leave them alone tonight," referring to the populace.

Jim snapped to, "Yes sir, coming right up. Any drink with that?" Jim fell right into the waiter job. It was something he knew, how to wait on retail customers.

He had to force himself not to bolt out of the room. The second he was through the door, relief washed over him, he had gotten his promotion, just not the way he thought.

As he rounded the corner he ran right into Brick.

"I gotta' get 'em supper. You can ask." Jim almost pleaded with the heavy square-chested carpenter.

Brick said, "Then you better get a move on. And bring me some too."

Jim's heart pounded and he hyperventilated on the way to the serving board.

He felt like a pinball, bouncing off of cutthroats and thieves and executioners. Keeping in the good graces of all the tough-guys who killed for John and Mark was going to be harder than he first thought.

He felt more and more like a little kid, threatened by the big kids on the bus.

This growing up stuff was hard.

20

The Pit

A.Q. Second Month

Sally watched the filthy barefoot young man asleep on the floor of the crude dirt pit. He fell at her feet earlier that day. It was the only entertainment since her internment in the muddy bottomed hole.

He fell in a most dramatic fashion; bouncing off the wall and flopping in front of her like a sack of potatoes, then he shit himself loudly and long, shivered and went unconscious.

The smell of his excrement mixed with her own foulness, as she hadn't been given the opportunity to leave the well of despair to tend to her daily ablutions. She'd dug a small hole in one corner to house her filth.

Now, this interloper had spoiled her housekeeping arrangements by filling his drawers and stinking the place up. She watched him and pondered whether he was an ally or a foe.

He had certainly invaded her private boudoir and come a'calling unannounced, 'how gauche'; no call ahead, nor introductory note of reference, not even a business card. She was tempted to call management and complain.

Sally's mind was playing some pretty strange tricks on her.

Since she lost Garnet, her horse, and somehow ended up in the custody of children in a hole in the ground, she had seriously begun to doubt her world-view.

Georgia Stapleton, the leader of the County Council and instigator of this mission to these farthest ends of the realm, kept appearing in Sally's mind. She could hear the conversation that put her here in this place.

—

The back room of the council chamber was filled with all sorts of living accoutrement: sleeping bags and kitchen camp gear and piles of papers and even a large plastic construction style porta-potty adorned one corner of the formerly austere and elegant meeting room.

"My dear it's so good to see you again, please come, sit. Tell me all about what is going on?" The crone implored of Sally when she reported.

The old woman had taken a shine to Sally and depended on her to be her eyes and ears on the outside.

Georgia was confined to the halls of government and forced into being a decision making fiend. She was busy all day handling the affairs of the county people and administration. Court was held every day, twice a day, to hear petitions and reports and make snap judgments about important matters concerning the populace and their well-being. The pace was grueling and Georgia Stapleton, Chairwoman of the County Council, lived for these small moments of respite when she could just sit quietly and talk to a compatriot over tea.

Sally slunk into the thick-aired space deferentially and took the old woman's hand in a gesture of supplication. "Yes, Ma'am. Thank You, Ma'am."

"Oh quit all that and get in here. You are a sight for sore eyes. I tell you girl, these people are going to be the death of me, I tell you." Georgia beamed at her protégé.

"Hello, Georgia. It's good to see you. A lot is happening out there."

"Tell me about it, Sally. I can hardly get a moments rest." Ms. Stapleton reached a pipe and filled it with some dubious green smoking product.

"Now," she struck a match and puffed the blue smoke up and away from Sally's face, "what's the haps?"

"Uh, well. Let's see. Coldman's just about got it all sewed up out there at the airport. He has an army now. There must be a thousand people at the stockyard."

The old woman half closed her eyes and looked off into the distance as she digested Sally's report and inhaled her 'analgesic'.

The Sheriff had done his job and taken orders as best could be expected. She was pleased.

"We cleared all the cattle on the north and west sides, and livestock all the way to the forest."

Georgia nodded as she looked up from puffing.

Sally went on, "we were working on the southern side, toward Eggtown, when Three Stones' compliance was assured. Then it was a cluster-fuck shuffle-up. Excuse my French."

"How so honey?" Georgia beamed a pleasant accepting aura of trust to Sally and waved her pipe.

Sally continued unbroken. "Well, Coldman mobilized several hundred men and all of his machines to go back-up the coasties …"

"And so …?"

Sally's tone gossiped, "Things started changing. A boatload of Latinos and other hangers on, who couldn't get in earlier, they've been camped outside his gates for two weeks, were his new conscripts, so he filled the empty spaces made by the Three Stone mobilization, with them."

"So he increased his army by sending men into the field?"

"That's right."

"Well, unintended consequences. Seems all I have to deal with anymore are unintended consequences. No matter what I do, honey, I get some weird feedback that we hadn't counted on. Go on." She burned the remains, smacked her mouth and spat her tongue tip as she put the pipe down in finality.

Sally was getting a contact high from the close quarters and the thick pot smoke the old gal was exuding. For a moment Sally wondered if a stoned little old lady should be deciding the fate of the county, but she dismissed this thinking, as there was no one else leading. At least no one with as steady a head on her shoulders as this ancient, wizened, woman in front of her.

Georgia Stapleton had risen to the challenge and met it on every level. No one was more qualified, nor had the downright courage to make the decisions she had. She had led and molded the rest of the council to a consensus and pushed the middle of the road politicians to take a hard stand with her on issues that affected peoples' lives. She was the lead Goose in the 'V'. Everyone else drafted her wake. She was rigorously logical, practical, and tough, and by being so, led the way.

Sally continued, "Well, I am pretty much out of a job right now. We gathered all the livestock in our grasp with the database I had and now it's basically all done. I am a third wheel out there. I sure did have a lot of fun riding with the men though."

"The men, eh?" Georgia lowered her head and looked up at Sally with a slightly naughty insinuation. "I bet that was some tough duty."

Sally got the innuendo and blushed a little at an old woman's hinting of hanky-panky. "Oh, nothing like that." She denied almost too strongly. "Strictly business."

"Of course, my dear. I would never think that you would take advantage of a situation like that. You have much too much integrity. Besides, keeping them chasing is better than getting caught." She puffed her pipe.

Sally was a bit aghast at the old woman's brashness, but there was truth to Georgia's observation. She had flirted a little, and maybe cajoled the deputies with temptation a tad, and possibly pushed her feminine charms to the limit on one or two occasions; but always only just enough to get the desired result of obedience and acquiescence to her plans for mission victory. The old woman saw that Sally had a way with men and she didn't fault her one jot for it.

"I am your representative. I maintained my professional demeanor at all times." Sally asserted professionally.

"Well I hope not at all times. That could get tiring. I know there are some pretty choice bits of beef on the hoof in the Sheriff's Department and a girl has to do what a girl's got to do." The elderly woman smiled enigmatically, the beauty of her youth shown through her ancient face clearly. There was lust in her soul.

Sally was unzipped by the blatantly honest assertion. Her cheeks reddened as her face admitted as much.

Just then the door opened and Georgia's grandson, Georgie, entered with a tray.

"Ah, tea time." The lady clapped her hands.

George set the tray between them and proceeded to scold his grandmother. "Doggone it gran'ma. You can't be smoking all day long. Give me that." He collected the now spent pipe and her pouch. "She is just incorrigible I tell ya'." He directed at Sally. "Now you drink this tea and have your cookies. It's almost your nap time."

"You'd think I was a child the way he treats me." Georgia said with a loving tease in her voice. "Thank you Georgie, now get out, so us girls can talk."

As soon as he left, Georgia started in. "What do you think about him?" She gave a look.

Sally's eyes widened at the implication that Georgia was suggesting Sally consider nailing her grandson.

"He's un-married and cute and did you see his tushie when walked out of here? Uh, huh?" Her almost non-existent eyebrows went up and down like Groucho Marx.

Sally, red faced, wide eyed, frozen in place, almost spilled the tea she was pouring. "Georgia! He's young enough to be my son. Oh for heavens sake. He's right, you are incorrigible."

"Great ass though?" Georia chirped in.

"Yes ..." Sally nodded and couldn't contain herself.

They burst into laughter. They howled as a couple of teenage girls.

Tears rolled down Georgia's cheeks. "Haaa ... I'm crying for you girl," and laughed harder.

Sally completely lost it and they cackled and guffawed; spilt their tea and dropped the very rare chocolate chip cookies.

Georgia popped his head back in.

They stopped.

"Are you all right?" He commanded from his granma'. The women each looked at him, then at each other, then exploded in hilarious sea gull cackle.

Georgie glared at the loony, stoned crones and harrumphed.

The door slammed and they were left in their fun until they used it up. The quiet after laugh vacuum left them in a giggly state. They each quieted, as their desires reminded them of lovers and times gone by. They very much enjoyed each other's company.

Finally Georgia took a solemn tone. "Sally? I have a new job for you."

Sally looked up from her steaming cup of softly scented civilized bliss.

"Here's the deal. West County has a fire chief out there who is handling things just wonderfully."

Sally listened.

"Almost, too wonderfully. We get regular reports of how well things are going and how they don't need any help and all."

"That must be a load off your mind. At least one area is working the way you'd planned out," Sally congratulated.

"Well, most of the kitchens here in town are doing well and our volunteer response has certainly been greater than we anticipated, but, well you see, the reports from West County are too good."

"What do you mean, too good?"

"Well, let's see ..." she thought for a second. "Their bike messengers are always on time and although they perform their duties well, well, they don't act like the others who come in."

"What do you mean?" Sally asked.

"It's just a feeling I get. When we get messengers from other towns they are spotty and late and always real talkative about what's going on with them and their town. You know what I mean?"

"Hmm." Sally slurped tea.

"These West County bike guys are always on time, like a clockwork schedule and pretty tight lipped. And the reports are just perfect."

"So, someone is actually competent and you're skeptical?"

"They already sent their volunteer firefighter and their families to help. No one else sends in offers to send people into town to help. They are all asking for some kind of assistance. Sentimental is the only area that doesn't ask for anything at all."

"So, you suspect something?" Sally was dubious.

"That's right. It's creepy when you can time the day by their bikers' arrival."

"Oh, come on, you exaggerate."

Georgia wagged her bony finger, "I do not. It got to where I was expecting them, they were so prompt."

"Well, what could they be up to, really? I mean, so one group was more prepared than the rest, what's the worst they can be doing?" Sally shrugged.

"Something fishy is going on. I just know it."

"Well, what about it?"

"I need to find out what they're up to."

"Ok."

"You can go out there."

Sally froze at the suggestion.

Georgia continued, "now that you're done with the livestock, you can take a couple of your favorite deputy-dawgs on a little ride out there and see if I'm all wet or not."

Georgia turned to her cuppa' tea and savored the brew.

"Well, what will I do? I mean you just want me to go out there and poke around?" Sally asked.

"Yeah, sort of. Don't get all official on them or anything. Just visit and bring them greetings from the council. Observe and report back." Council Leader Stapleton said.

"Ok. Observe and report back."

"And go on a nice camp trip."

"With some of my guys." Sally clarified.

"Mhmmm." Georgia confirmed.

"You are incorrigible." Sally joked and they laughed and laughed.

—

Observe and report back. If only she could have observed anything. If only she could report back. If only she had kept her big mouth shut in the first place. Why did she think she was one of those who could, or should, make things happen? It always ended up like this. She put her efforts out there and it all turned to shit. She should have stayed quiet and hidden in the crowd, like the other office workers who were safe at home with their people.

The young man groaned and rolled to face her. He was filthy and battered and looked about as bedraggled as a guy could.

She noticed that he sported a bulge in his pants.

"Uhhhn," Sam moaned, opened his eyes, smacked his sticky dry mouth loudly. "Oh Jeez." He rolled away from her and slowly, in what looked to be great pain, he levered himself up, walked to the wall and leaned against it. After a little fumbling, he pissed. His water plowed a muddy trickle down the loose dirt wall and a rivulet flowed to his bare feet.

He didn't seem to notice he was standing in his own urine.

Sally wrinkled her lip in disgust.

The fellow shuddered and jiggled and put himself away and with a zip, he turned to her.

"I beg your pardon, I was unable to find the men's room." He stood in the puddle of his own making.

"I understand. Perfectly all right. I wish I could offer you some cleaning facilities, but as you see, we are a bit lacking at this hotel."

Sally sat huddled on her side at the bottom of the hole.

Sam swayed a little and looked up at the lip of the pit above them. It was only about twelve feet in diameter and maybe ten deep. It was freshly dug and the sides were loose dirt and would crumble down the moment it was disturbed.

"Quite a little garden spot you have here. How's the room service?"

"Spotty, to say the most of it. I was waiting for my fresh water when you arrived."

A trickle of dirt cascaded from the surface.

Sam looked up into the bristly muzzle of Attila as he sniffed at his master in the hole.

"Attila. You piece of shit. Why didn't you help me? Ya' friggin lousy dog." Sam waved a finger up at the dog and tugged at his sticky drawers.

"Bucket of water eh? You normally get one?"

"Yeah, well, the kids guarding me aren't so very dependable." Sally shrugged.

"How long have you been in here?"

"A few days. I think three, maybe more. But sometimes I am not too sure. I haven't seen any grown-ups, but I'm hoping that someone will come soon and get me out of here. What did you do to get in here?" Sally asked.

"Nothing really, I went for a walk in the woods and they snatched me. I did meet some grown-ups though. It was weird."

"Weird?"

"Yeah, the kids called them 'Lord' and 'Sir John,' and stuff like that. They said I was a slave." Sam said.

"A slave."

"Yeah, well they took all my stuff and here I am. What else am I?"

"You're not dead." Sally informed him solemnly.

Sam conceded her logic. "Yes. I am not dead, yet." He looked up at the circle of light above him. Tall trees loomed at the edges, pointing at the center of his sky.

"If they wanted to kill us I think we wouldn't be having this conversation," she added.

"Not too tough to make this a grave," Sam said.

He noticed Sally's khaki shirt and signatory patches. He didn't recognize any. At first he thought she was some kind of park ranger. On closer look he saw courier and animal control stitched on them.

"What's with the uniform? You some kind of dog-catcher?"

"Funny you should ask. I'm the County Animal Asset Allocation officer and County Council liaison to the Sheriff."

"Well, laa dee fucking da."

"You have heard of the Sheriff right?"

"Well, I've heard of Sheriffs, but 'THE' Sheriff. Can't say that I have."

"The County Sheriff."

"Well, OK, the County Sheriff." Sam gave in to her assertion.

"Where did you come from?" Sally asked.

"I came from the City."

"The City?" Sally was little aback. He had news from outside the area. She was now interested in this guy.

"Across the frontier. The border." Sam made air quotes.

"What happened? Was it a bomb?"

"What?"

"What happened to the world?" Sally stared, beseeching.

After a moment he said, "Fuck if I know. No body knows. It all just stopped. Who the hell are these people?"

"I don't know … they're not the Sheriff, believe me. How did you get here?" Sally asked.

"Uh, well, I got my ways." Sam recalled in his mind the moments of terror and hiding under a bush while the border guards chased Attila around in the dark. Sam slunk past them and crawled for hundreds of yards like a snake to elude them. The dog didn't reappear until the next day. "It wasn't easy. So, does this sheriff run the border or something?"

"Something like that."

"I mean he's the law right?" Sam queried.

"Yes, the law. He answers to the council. The County Council. They're the ones in charge now. Since things got dark, they're the ones who've been keeping it all together. They saved us all from chaos."

"So, you work for the law, and you're in here, with me, an illegal immigrant."

"Seems that way." Sally responded flatly.

"Sooooo ... who are these people that have us? They aren't the law?"

"Definitely not." Sally stated firmly.

"OK, I am not getting a very clear picture of what's going on here, but that's nothing new these days. Hell, the gangs run the city now. The whole structure collapsed. So, why am I surprised that the Sheriff has a little competition."

"The city collapsed?" Sally had heard nothing from outside her immediate world.

"Yeah. They torched city hall, someone closed the golden gate bridge, but we ran across anyway, they blew up some ships in the bay, it was all a real mess. I mean for the first couple of days it was OK, and everyone tried to be nice, but they couldn't keep it up. They got hungry."

"What do you mean you ran across anyway?"

"Some assholes from Little Willow tried to break the bridge. They destroyed the road, but they left a little piece intact. Then the bastards shot at anyone who came close to their end of the bridge. We finally stormed it and they couldn't stop us."

"How sad."

"Yeah, sad. So, now Slocoma County has a border set up, huh. Same thing, except you guys somehow got machine guns. You and your council did a good job too. Crap, now I'm stuck in here with one of the murdering bastards." Sam moved back against his side of the pit, accusing.

"I'm not a killer." Sally asserted.

"Maybe that's why they put me in here. I got plenty of reason." Sam's voice lowered.

"What reason?" Sally was now on guard and backed into her dirt corner.

"I saw where it happened. You're one of them. Mowed down, hundreds. And you sit there, all innocent and tell me you are a part of the law. No wonder you're in here. Machine gun Kate."

"I tell you I didn't kill anyone. You've got it all wrong. No one has used machine guns. You make me sound like some Nazi or something. The border is a guidepost to the valley, that's all."

Sam was head down and glaring at her.

Sally insisted, "no one is being shot like you think. It's just not the way we operate."

"You're a fucking Nazi. You all say it was legal or you didn't know about it or some such drivel. I saw it! I heard it."

"I'm not sure I understand you," Sally cowered.

"I crawled through piles of dead bodies to get here. Do you think they just piled themselves up in burnt bloody heaps of their own accord?" Sam leaned into his accusation.

He was angry now.

His power was restored by the prospect of being able to exact a little payback against the unassailable forces that had been ranged against him. His modern pacifistic upbringing washed away with the patter of machine gun fire and the screaming of humans trying to get away from the conflagration that drove them to their deaths. And here, right in front of him was one of the perpetrators. Now he understood why he was in the pit with this person. He was there as an instrument of revenge. He could at least make one of them pay.

"That just can't be so. I can't believe it. The border is supposed to redirect the overflow from down south to the central valley where there is enough food for all. It's not what you say it is. There never was any intent to …"

Sam laughed out loud, cutting her off. "You are some kind of bureaucrat lackey who has her head in the sand. WAKE UP!!! You are a fucking NAZI murderer!" He puffed up in indignation.

Sally stared at him in fear. This guy was about to tear her to pieces over things that she unaware of; things she couldn't believe, things that weren't her doing.

She knew about the border.

She was there when the council sent Dave Putnam to coordinate with Eggtown and the Three Stones Coast Guard Training Base.

She delivered the messages to the Sheriff calling for the mobilization of sign-making teams and trucks and the men to get them there.

She was in the middle of it, but there was no hint of massacre. There was no intent to kill people en mass; just the opposite.

"The border was to be a barrier to funnel the refugees to a more productive area where they could sustain themselves. The county just doesn't produce enough food. Only in the central valley could the city find enough sustenance for any kind of prolonged stay." She pleaded her case.

The county was strapped to the limit and the influx would destroy that delicate balance.

She thought back, and although she knew they mobilized armed men, she just couldn't imagine that they would fire on people in general. She could certainly understand if there were armed threats to the Sheriff's men by the wanderers, but wholesale slaughter was not in her picture of the world-view portrayed by the leaders.

Georgia Stapleton would have been appalled if that were the case. She would never allow such an action to take place. She was a good woman with compassion and good intentions.

Sally was horrified and didn't want to believe this fellow.

Sam stood staring through hate filled eyes.

"Listen. I am not a part of any organized effort to kill people. I was responsible for cows: cows and chickens and sheep and goats, and horses. I've been in a cattle stockyard for the past month. I don't know anything about any machine guns or the awful things you are telling me." Sally pleaded.

Sam took his turn. "You know, when I was a kid, there was this little old lady who lived in the house behind ours. She was a sweet nice German woman who made really wonderful cakes. The thing was, she thought Hitler was the greatest man who ever lived. She said he saved their country from ruin. That he was the one who helped Germany become great and that all the stuff about the holocaust and the camps was all made up propaganda the allies put together to discredit him. The victors write the history books. Well, lady, I'm telling you that you are that woman. You think you are innocent and there is blood all over your hands. Your Sheriff and his guys have killed hundreds if not thousands. I was there. I saw it. Believe it."

Sam's legs and ass itched from the drying shit smeared all over them. His feet hurt, his back hurt, his head hurt, and now his heart was in pain at the thought of being captive with this stupid woman.

Linking the person in front of him to the memories of falling people and rotting corpses and the nasty flies that swarmed everything with their blue shimmering color and their buzzing insensitivity to life was making him sick to his stomach.

He had put the thoughts away for days.

This conversation was bringing back the vile memories that he knew he would carry forever inside him. He didn't know what else to say to her. He wanted to smash her face in, but he couldn't. His rage and temper were dulled by his state of filth and degradation.

All Sam wanted was to wash up and find a dry comfy spot to sleep, to sleep for a long time.

Sally watched the man's rage drain away and he slumped into the dirt.

They were both hostage to forces that obviously didn't give a hoot about their enmity.

They were being held for a purpose.

Something was coming to them. It wouldn't be too long as exhibited by the temporary nature of the muddy hole they were quartered in. They surely could not be expected to live in here for any prolonged period of time and this pit was only a super cheap security cell. Their captors must not have many facilities to spare if this was where they housed their prisoners.

"My name is Sally," she said softly.

For a moment Sam didn't move. He breathed deeply and raised his head to look at the woman. She was in her forties or early fifties he guessed, trim and fit and not a total desk-monster. She was an active person and had the lean look to prove it. Her graying hair was cut in a sort of page-boy style and framed her face in a nice oval. Her eyes were wide set with high cheekbones and a mouth with full lips that under different circumstances he might have called luscious. She wasn't bad looking and her expression wasn't hard or mean.

She was trying to bridge the gap.

They were in the same boat at the bottom of this hole and although they may have their differences they were, for the time being, allies.

"Sam," he croaked. He realized that he had little to drink and was parched.

She nodded and they sat in silence for a bit.

It was darker and cooler, the sun was falling.

Sally stood up and hollered at the surface. "Hey! Hey, up there! We need water. Hey! We need water!" She stood quietly waiting for a response.

The old dog, Attila, had been there the whole time and when she yelled, he lumbered his big body up and loped off. "Great I chased the dog away."

"You never know with him. Stupid creature does the damndest things," Sam added.

"Hey!" She yelled some more. "Hey you guys! We need water!"

A puff of dirt flew down on her upturned face and stung her eyes. Sally crouched away and cowered from the onslaught of dirt in the face.

'Roof. Roof, roof ... roof,' Attila stood on the lip and barked, deep and gruff, down at them as the bucket descended.

"What'd I tell you?" Sam said.

In a moment a scraping sound and more dirt fell as a five gallon plastic bucket lowered on a string. It jounced down the side and dislodged dirt that fell in the water.

Sam was up and reaching. He held it stable, took the bucket, reached in and dipped a small aluminum camp cup tied by a string into the muddy stuff. He drank two or three before he got his breath. He held out the cup to Sally.

She slowly stepped to him on the neutral ground the water conferred and took the cup from him.

Their fingers touched only briefly and she drank.

Sam stood back and gave her room.

After she had her fill she said, "We need to get you washed up. You'll get sick like that."

"What? So you want to help me ...?"

"You can't be comfortable. That you relieved yourself wasn't your fault, but staying that way ..." she reasoned. "I'll turn my back." She did that and walked to her side and leaned against the dirt wall.

Sam pulled his trousers and began the yucky task of washing his shit from his body. He was very judicious with the few gallons they had.

"Um? I kind of need to wash my pants and there isn't a lot of water here."

"You get cleaned up. We'll get more, I have a feeling."

He turned them inside out and dribbled water on them. "Uh … could you help me? I need to rub while you pour."

"OK." Sally came and took the cup and ladled onto the jeans while Sam massaged the filth from his pants. Sally didn't notice at first but he was doing his filthy holey underwear also. She glimpsed, his cock dangled comically as he scrubbed. She poured and kept a straight face.

"There, that's enough." Sam declared.

"Here give them a good rinse. Hold them up." Sally dictated.

Sam stood and held the jeans, in the dark pit.

She took the bucket and splashed the remaining water all over his legs and the clothes.

It felt fresh and cool.

He shriveled and puckered and wrung out the water to struggle his way back into the garments.

"Thank you." Sam said in monotone.

"You're welcome. You'd have done the same for me." Sally replied.

They each moved to the driest spot and squatted down together.

There wasn't much else to be said between them. They had both learned things that changed their outlook on the way things were.

Sam had thought he was past the idiots with the guns at the border and if only he could get far enough north he would be safe. Sally thought that things were under control and going to get brighter and that the people she was working with were honorable and decent folk.

They were both wrong.

21

<u>Court</u>

Sam and Sally waited. They hadn't heard much of anything from the surface all day. In the late afternoon light their outlines faded into the soil walls of their prison. A gloom descended and the chilling blanket of night fell. The pit became black as pitch. After a bit, stars appeared in the round window to the cosmos above. They sat quietly and peered up at the cold reaches of space.

In the quiet darkness of early evening they heard people laughing and horses clumping around.

Attila scurried from his post of watching over them and vanished.

More sounds of people moving and some commotion filtered down into their trench. It sounded like commands were being given and soon a flicker of firelight reflected off the one tall redwood tree that could be seen from their limited vantage.

Strains of a chorus, singing, filtered down. The tune was melodic and repetitious.

Sam asked, "What are they singing?" He didn't recognize it.

Sally listened with her ear cocked upward, "Something about, nobody's home, hey ho, something."

The droning round rose in volume and pitch as more voices added to the chant.

Smells of cooking meat drifted on the air with the unholy sound.

There had been so little sound since the quiet, that singing affected the captives deeply. They were rapt at the sonorous humming roll of many voices in cadence. It sounded alien and yet, comforting and familiar at the same time.

"Meat nor drink or money have I none …" Sally repeated, "Yet I will be happy." They stared at the open sky from their dark hole and listened to the singing group.

"Great sentiment." Sam commented dryly.

The singing continued for quite awhile, the firelight grew brighter, and the impression of a large gathering above them became clear. The tune changed and another unfamiliar song washed the night. The chorus sounded happy and was joined by occasional laughing and sounds of a people having a party.

Sam felt utterly dejected. He sat in wet pants in filth while folks had a good time above.

Sally listened carefully and tried to fathom whether the party goers were even aware that two human beings were starving and cold and dirty in a pit nearby. Could people be so callous?

The singing stopped.

'Roof. Roof, roof, roof,' Attila reappeared above and barked down at them. He kept looking back over his shoulder.

The clatter of an aluminum ladder reached over the edge and clunked down beside them.

"Ladies first," Sam said.

"Gee, thanks." Sally shakily mounted the wobbly thing and they climbed into a scene from antiquity.

A large bonfire was roaring in the main compound and was surrounded by a hundred or more people. They looked like something out of a fantasy novel: cloaks and staffs, spears and not a few swords as well as plenty of sidearms and rifles, horses pawing the ground behind a small raised dais with a big throne-like chair.

A gauntlet of folks in a line, guided them from their cell to the edge of the fire pit. They stood in a cleared space surrounded by armed people.

The whole thing was exactly what Sam had avoided for weeks, being the center of a scene.

Sally straightened herself up as best she could in the few moments it took to walk to the fire. Sam minced on his bare feet and gladly took a place in front of the drying flames. His ass was frozen.

They were alone standing near the fire.

The crowd stood back silently. It seems they were all waiting for something to happen.

While Sam's pants steamed, it occurred to him that they might be about to be burned at the stake, or roasted for supper. Maybe they were the dinner guests. As soon as he thought it, it put a chill in him that the fire couldn't chase away.

Sally stood with her back to the fire and looked openly at the crowd surrounding them. She scanned the people for any recognition of civility or acceptance and found none. They weren't mean-looking, but there was no friendly nod or pleasant eye contact to be had in this crowd. They were a solemn bunch. That did not bode well, for Sally felt they knew what was coming, and it wasn't a celebration of joyous abandon.

Attila had joined them and lay at Sam's feet to snooze. He thought the dog would sleep all day long if he could.

Sam was gratified to smell cooking meat and realized there was a fire spit going off to the side and fellows attending it were ladling coals from the big fire with long handled shovels. His stomach growled. The only thing he had eaten were those old grapes and he ended up wearing them on his leg.

Whatever was going to happen was about to commence. The mob turned as a small retinue of men came into the light and surrounded the dais.

A large man, dressed fairly normally in trousers with suspenders, a plaid shirt, belt with holstered pistol, and the brand new lace-up steel-toe work boots that Sam owned earlier that day, stood in front of the big chair.

The round, heavy-set man with the large fu Manchu moustache and black rimmed glasses stepped forward and bellowed out. "The court of the Shire and Sir John is now in session. Draw nigh. Draw Nigh. Come on; get in here folks so you can hear what's going on." Mark waved at the people at the far edges of the fire.

The large man on the dais sat down on his big chair.

"Is there any business before this court that is not on the agenda?"

From the side, a thin man came forward. He bowed uneasily and made his case. "Uh, I am Glen Thomas, I live on Happy Road, just down the way. I have a request."

248

"Come forward, Glen. Go ahead," Mark Young, the seneschal for the Shire and acting court herald bade him approach.

Glen stepped in front of the dais where Sir John sat and made a slight nod of a bow. "Well, John, I was hoping that we didn't have to burn my place down. See, it's a perfectly good house and we'd like to make it available to be used by the group somehow."

Mark responded, "Glen, the law is clear. It was found to have no value and be a haven for foes and a danger to us if left. We talked about this."

"I know Mark, but I want an exception. What about it John? It's a good house. We can use it."

John Ritter, Sir John, the leader of the Shire, held up a hand. When he had several moments of silence he asked some questions. "Has the house been cleaned?"

"Yes Mi'lord it has." Mark responded.

"Has it a position of strength?" John asked.

"No, Mi'lord." Mark said.

"Is it a stick or stone building?"

"Stick, Mi'lord."

"Any solar? A woodstove? A shallow well?"

"All gleaned Mi'lord. None of those things are there now."

"The well?"

"Deep, Mi'lord."

"Is the roof shake or tile, Glen?" John directed at the owner.

"Shingle, John … Mi'lord," he whispered.

"Have the trees been cleared?"

"They have Mi'lord." Mark answered.

Sir John stood up and spoke. "Glen Thomas. I give you the right of the torch. You will burn it. It will be done tonight. Our good Lord Joe, will go with you."

From the sidelines a woman sobbed. "But, it's our home. It's ours …"

Glen went to her and held her tight in his arms. "It's OK honey, it'll be all right."

"But why do we have to burn it? It doesn't make any sense. It's not his or any of these peoples'. It's ours!" She was getting loud.

"Shut-up. Just shut-up and come help me. We have to. It's the law." He led her away.

Lord Joe Billsop, and two of his burly men were close on their heels.

Glen knew what Joe was. He knew that people could disappear when Joe was involved.

She yelled at her husband. "We don't have to! It's our house and he's just some low life piece of …" A smacking sound resounded. "Aaargh," she screamed at the hard slap her husband gave her.

"Come on, Joe we'll do it now. She'll help." Glen's voice rang out as they left the firelight and he dragged his stunned and sobbing wife away from court.

Sam and Sally exchanged glances.

Sam wrinkled his brow and made an 'oh' shape with his mouth.

"Now, to the agenda." Mark announced.

Sam took a deep breath and was sure their turn had come.

Sally was watching Sir John. She thought he was quite a handsome fellow and he spoke with a calm confident air that belied no malice. His voice was soothing, even when he was commanding a man to burn down his own house. She couldn't help herself. She liked the look of him, but he was obviously powerful and dangerous.

Mark called out clearly. "Will the Lords present please come forward."

Three men emerged from the crowd and stood in front of John.

"I call to this court, Squire Dave Nickel. Present yourself."

Long legged, dark haired Dave, had been standing inconspicuously near Sam and Sally, at guard. He strode by Sam to stand in front of the men waiting for him.

John stood. "Kneel, good Squire Dave," he said. The teenager knelt in the dirt. The men stood towering around him.

Mark unrolled a sheet of paper and read. "It has come to our attention that through diverse great efforts, and in unbending service to us and the people of the Shire, that I, John, Lord of this realm and servant to the people, and with the unanimous assent of the Lords of our protection, do, with great joy and gratitude recognize Dave Nickel as … a Lord in his own right. Stand and be accepted by your peers, Lord Dave."

Dave stood and the men clapped him on the back.

Mark called. "Three cheers for our new Lord Dave, hip-hip,"

The crowd cheered. "Hurray!"

"Hip-hip."

"Hurray!"

"Hip-hip."

"Hurray!" They continued. The forest rang at the resounding yell of the crowd as one. Silence fell like a curtain as the last hurray rolled out and into the void of dark absorbing woods.

"Do you, Lord Dave, wish to take a squire at this time?" Mark went on with their ritual.

Dave was red-faced at all the attention and when confronted with the question he dug his toe in the dirt and rubbed his mouth. "Well," he began softly.

John said. "Speak up Mi'Lord. Let all hear your voice."

Dave raised his head high, looked out over the assemblage and proclaimed. "I wish to take for my squire ... Jimmy Carpenter, if he'll agree."

"Whoop!" Jimmy yelped and jumped up from near Sam. He was also quietly standing guard on the prisoner. "Heck yeah, Dave. Cool." He held his fist in the air.

"Let all recognize our protective Lords and honor their houses." Mark concluded. "That is all gentleman."

The older Lords rejoined their people.

Dave and Jimmy clasped briefly and took station on guard near Sam.

"Thanks fellas." John added as he sat down. "What's next, Mark?"

Mark Young, fumbled with some papers to find his agenda.

Just then, two young teen girls in sheer diaphanous gowns ran up to Mark and clung to him briefly. Every eye riveted to their loveliness, backlit by the bonfire, as they both whispered in his ears. If they weren't barefoot and clearly naked under their sheet, they would have never gotten close to the chief.

"Of course," Mark said out loud."

They turned and ran off into the darkness.

Mark licked his lips and loudly announced, "Bishop Jonas, of the Enclave." He turned and shrugged at John.

A moment went by before stirrings from the side drew everyone's attention.

From the forest trail, eerie glowing shapes appeared amongst the trees. Strange ghostly flowing forms of ethereal light wound their way toward the gathering. As they came closer the firelight lit them and an entourage of people in long white gowns manifested from the strange into the real.

Each of their gowns glowed from within, from flashlights underneath.

They filed in slowly and collected in a wide semi-circle in front of Sir John. Their lights all went out. They set three folding chairs in front of the dais.

They formed a ring and then came the young girls leading a beautiful man in a blood red robe. His long blonde hair flowed onto his shoulders. His blue eyes glinted with intensity. His long aquiline nose pierced the darkness with glowing confidence and surety of purpose. He sported an attractively trimmed beard with a jaunty moustache that was turned up at the tips and waxed to points.

He was flanked closely by two shorter, and identically red robed assistants and they strode a flashy red curtain of pomp onto the padded dirt space at the great fire.

They marched regally to the steel folding chairs.

He arranged himself and the three sat in unison.

"Welcome, Jonas." John said right off the bat.

Jonas gestured and his paramour Becky, leaned close. Jonas whispered in her ear.

"Our spiritual leader wishes to be addressed as Bishop …"

"Mi'lord." Mark instructed her as to John's position.

"Mi'lord," she finished nervously

Mark and John stared stone-faced. Several moments passed in nervous tension.

The fire collapsed into itself and a shower of sparks rose to the heavens.

Sally was fascinated at this power-play being acted out in front of her. She had seen none of this feudal theater while she'd been in the pit. This was new to her. Obviously there was a power structure that the Sheriff and the council knew nothing about and it was already orchestrating a society far removed from what they had all been used to; a lord, a bishop, and a village of people who were willing to burn down their own homes on command. These people were making up a whole new world.

"Welcome to my court, Bishop of the Enclave, is it? My heart gladdens at your presence," Sir John said.

An audible collective sigh went around the congregation.

It was an unprecedented request from Sir John to have a title conferred by mere desire. No one had thought to be so brash; except Jonas. Until now, everyone had been given their titles. Most were titles they never imagined. It impressed people when John and Mark created a hierarchy of power and included people at all levels. They had made lords and ladies and squires and pages and journeymen and created scrolls to recognize people in their jobs, such as: acaters in the storerooms, groomsmen for the stables, and burlers for the women sorting clothes. Folks had no idea that they would get a title for their job. To have it conveyed by the leader and be publicly recognized gave people purpose. They had taken on menial labor chores and owned them as important. They were important. The smallest employ was vital to the society's survival. They were rewarded by pro-active gestures implemented by Mark and John and the creative people they surrounded themselves with. It worked, everyone felt entitled to respect for their position, no matter how small.

Jonas, had solidified the encampment at the old Christian youth camp and collected a large following.

A lot of the townspeople who were not jolly on the spot when the quiet came and didn't join John and Mark at the start were left in an organizational vacuum. They held on to the belief that things would return to normal. One thing that came out in common was their propensity to fall back on old tried and true beliefs.

The Christian umbrella was wide and people could cling to it in these times of trouble. Even if the power was off, the church was not.

Jonas used the lure of Christian belief to bind these people together. They weren't very powerful in terms of resources; the Shire snatched up loose and easily attainable assets early,leaving the Christian kids behind the eight-ball, but they were strong in their beliefs. They stuck together and relied on the magical and divine. Electricity was divine magic that god had taken from the sinful of the world. The Enclave had obviously been keeping batteries and direct-current light technology going as was evidenced by their glowing entrance. They clung to the light as their scriptures verified their deity to be of the light.

Sir John and Mark had collected quite a large array of solar cells and car batteries. They were in the secure sheds in Brownsville, the machine shop armory, on the far ridge. They were being used there to provide headlights and to heat the starter glow-plugs of the diesel battle tanks and trucks.

The Shire looted all in the first two days. They were tasked to chase electrical resources early, but who wanted to lug around heavy batteries, that slowly charged by solar cells and the power could only be used to make light. It wouldn't turn a motor or make a pump go. Lights were nice at night, but they attracted attention. Everyone was way too busy working on food storage and sequestration of new assets to spend much time on maintaining lights during the dark hours. That was when you slept. The day was long enough. There was no need to extend it.

The average Shire resident had such limited luxury. Night fell, it was dark.

Jonas apparently thought otherwise. He was of the mind that the power should be used in religious dramatics.

John was impressed at the show. Their entrance was indeed spectacular for the times. It wasn't the strip in Las Vegas, but it made everyone gasp and pay attention. He would have to watch this Jonas kid from down the hill more carefully.

"What may I ask is the reason for your visit? … Bishop." Sir John inquired with a smile in his voice.

A lovely woman's voice rang clear.

"His Excellency wishes you to bestow the sacred artifacts, that rightfully belong to the church, to the church."

"I am afraid I don't know what you are referring to." Sir John said, and smiled openly.

She spoke again for her lover and spiritual leader.

"Uh, I am the light, sayeth the lord." She said in a matter of fact tone.

"And that means?" John wrinkled his brow, smiling patience.

Jonas leaned over and whispered to her.

"We are the holders of the light and must keep it sacred for his return." She parroted.

"What light?" Mark tried to clarify.

From the other side, the third red-robed one, Apostolus, spoke up. "We're collecting solar panels and batteries and stuff to keep the lights on, you know? If you got any we'll add 'em to ours."

John scanned the three. They were devoted to the pleasant faced young man putting on airs between them.

- I could disappear him in a heartbeat, John thought. 'Just what does this whippersnapper think he is doing? He is in my camp challenging me for my batteries and solar panels? In the name of Jesus? He is one brazen little shit.'

However, Jonas had about four hundred people under his sway. That was what Mark's spies reported. John didn't want to alienate the local zealot populace. He didn't have to feed them or let them into his Shire, except by dribs and drabs depending on need and their qualifications. John felt no obligation toward the people who had turned a cold shoulder to him. He was loyal to those who were loyal to him at the first.

Jonas' parish consisted of people who thought the world would return to its former state. They prayed for a second coming of the light and the magic. It fit neatly into the Jesus message touted by modern bible-bangers. Jonas was one smart cookie to merge the message of old and the current hope for a return of the wonders of electricity. Their minds clung to the memory.

There was an angle to this that John hadn't considered. He had basically ignored those who hadn't followed him. He had set them aside by momentum of his societal juggernaut to make the Shire. He hamstrung their efforts at organization by precluding their contact with the authority of the county powers back in Saint Rose and also by tricking the volunteer firemen to move to Saint Rose to assist the county.

The only other players of any note were the ranchers and vineyard owners. The Shire had either co-opted the ranchers' livestock by mutual agreements or stolen them outright and left the owners without much clout. With no food to offer people it was hard to convince folks to help retrieve lost cattle from an armed and organized authority. Only a very few felt they had cause to dispute the Shire's power, some mysteriously vanished.

John and Mark carefully nurtured relationships with the vineyard owners who needed labor to get in their harvests. The Shire was, as yet, unable to provide any work crews for the winemakers. John wanted to assure their crops got in and their product was put up. Alcohol was going to be the new currency in the coming year. The Shire needed to get a hold on the supply in West County. Not only did they need the vineyard owners for their grapes, but to learn their methods. It wouldn't be long before the need to kowtow to the arrogant wine snobs, who normally used desperate low paid people from a foreign country to make their egregious profits, would end. There weren't any of the vineyard owners who had come to the Shire. John and Mark needed to bring them labor. Showing up with willing well fed people to do all the menial chores that machinery had done would be a godsend to the vintners. A godsend.

John pondered how he could utilize the parish of the Eternal Light to further this cause. Their teachings were well steeped in concepts of subservience and poverty and service to a Lord. The whole concept of a 'lord god' was borne out of a hierarchical need for a power structure that was ruled by the top. Christianity was a religion based in slavery and sacrifice and bearing the sufferable burden.

Apostolus continued, much to Becky's aggravation. "It's not like you've been able to keep the lights on, so we were just wondering if you had stuff you weren't using that we could have?"

John was liking this more and more.

Becky was flushed.

Jonas beamed dull-witted radiance.

John licked his lips and began slowly. "I am gratified that the Eternal Light shall be held in such sacred and secure hands as yours, Bishop. I shall see that you receive the artifacts, so you may preserve our heritage and carry the light of the world into the future, for us all."

Mark turned and cast a sidelong glance at John for his eloquent agreement. 'Diplomacy can be learned,' Mark thought. Not for an instant did he imagine John was going to give Jonas their batteries and solar panels, though.

Jonas felt in power. He had shown he had the support of a more populous, albeit weaker, in terms of raw power and resources, community. The energy of his ritual and strength of the lord-on-high at his back pulled Sir John Ritter into his web of influence. These rough backwoods pagans couldn't even get the lights on. It was the right thing for John to follow him.

The enclave was the only deserving group who could manage the light and electricity properly. It was obvious that the Shire was lost in the darkness. Their compound was dark and they showed no ability to keep the fabulous electricity alive. Jonas' camp was strung with lights; as many as their few car batteries and solar panels could keep going. They had the technical edge they thought.

"For these things I ask a boon in return, Bishop." Sir John kept on.

"What's that John?" Jonas squeaked, in his eagerness he forgot to use his go-between, and spoke directly to John.

"Sir, John." Mark interjected lightly.

Jonas was embarrassed at having the aura he was trying to maintain be broken so easily. "Sir John," he said more calmly.

John's voice stayed cool and soothing. "Now that I have given you a boon you shall give me one in return. I wish for you to start a university; a college of sorts, to study the eternal light and look at ways to regain the power."

Jonas couldn't believe his ears, he was stunned. Sir John just suggested the very dream that he had of starting a place of study to preserve the knowledge and find ways to rekindle the magic electricity.

The power of the Lord made him shudder in realization of this miracle of fulfillment. Jonas was now, more than ever, convinced of the divine avocation that had been set in his lap. He was the one to lead the people. He would be, the college.

The Lord God, had made a test and his divine placement, here in the wild coastal redwoods of West Slocoma County Northern California, was where his destiny was to be fulfilled.

He, Jonas, would fill the darkness with the light.

That stiff old geezer's petty attempt to lead the will of the people away from the light of the lord. This was proof that God was working through him and that this crude knee-jerk old man would always be his spiritual inferior. Jonas would lead the people out of the darkness. The shire would serve the Enclave.

God interceded on Jonas' behalf and, as the adage always said, worked his mysterious ways.

John strove to clench his face into a pleasant and neutral accepting look of kindness to the blonde hippy in front of him. He had met a lot of Jesus freaks in his life and could see that this Jonas kid was really putting some effort into it. He laughed heartily inside. That made it easier to show a pleasant face. John wanted to clap out loud and hoot and holler that the show was great!

As their eyes met, John, nodded slight deference with a downcast glance.

Jonas stared a moment. He moved his hand, ring extended for the mountain man to kiss.

Becky, moved fast from under his elbow, grabbed his hand, and guided it up and not down.

Jonas followed her every move, always.

They stood and she danced him, arms held high and turning toward the crowd.

"Welcome them!" She forcefully breathed up into his ear, "wave your hand."

It was an artful bit of deceit. Becky, was from the start, invisibly hooded under his shoulder. Her sable hair merely peaked out and shrouded her face. Their dark red shimmering gowns made her vanish from the back as she and the other acolyte formed a large flowing red curtain around Jonas.

She held her arm right against him in a Tango move, guiding her marionette. To the crowd, it appeared as if Jonas was standing and waving his beneficence to them.

As they turned away from the dais, Mark held up his hands and did a little semaphore wave at the Shire.

Mark bellowed, "Hail the Bishop! Hail the Bishop!" He kept arm signaling 'cheer for the putz', over and over. They picked it up and cheered for the 'Bishop'.

The shire started chanting, 'Hail the Bishop.' They wore huge grinning cheery faces as they laughed out loud.

"Hail the Bishop!"

John turned to Mark with a silly puzzled look of 'what the..?'

The Shire dutifully continued cheering at the church folk. 'Hail the Bishop' rang in parody.

Mark smirked at his buddy and let them drone on until it was nice and uncomfortable, then he made a large final sweep of his hands to end it and the cheer snapped to a halt.

Jonas' people were quite unnerved at being yelled at so vigorously, then by the abrupt end to the noise.

The silence chased the chant into the darkness.

"And now, on to other business, Mi'lord." John barked at Jonas. The kid had his fun.

John was completely convinced that the power was not coming back on. He knew that there had been some fundamental change in physics. Magnets didn't allow the invisible flux to flow in smooth controlled lines any more. He had put one of Jack Brown's buddies, a retired electrical engineer, on the task. The result of those experiments yielded nothing. A big fat nothing. They couldn't induce any metal to hold magnetic properties. It was as if all metals had suddenly become non-ferrous. The D.C. power flowed along wires from positive to negative poles on a battery and that would warm a wire or light a bulb, but no magnetic force could be induced to hold onto a metal, nothing could be magnetized. Therefore no magnetic field could be generated. It made no sense at all, but there it was. Magnetic fields in lumps of metal were magic and they were gone. John fully believed it was a dead-end exercise.

He was more concerned with getting this power hungry upstart busy doing make-work, and keeping the outside of the Shire rabble under control and hoping for things that would not be, than any real anticipation of a return to the way things were before the quiet came.

It would cost the Shire nothing to distract them and let their cult flourish. A cult that could make a little show with a few strings of x-mas lights and train its followers to be servile would be very useful in John's schema of new societal norms. Let them believe and hope and pray and pay tithe and provide labor. Let them revel in their sacrifice to a greater good and bow their heads to the concept of a supreme being who ministers to their needs and who supports someone who cares about their eternal souls.

John was up to the task for that role. He and Mark could keep an eye on them and use them to do rote menial tasks and free his people for management and planning. Then his people could concentrate on more crucial and productive activities than picking the grapes that would adorn their tables as wine.

"A monastery perhaps, Mi'Lord?"

"Yes, Mi'lord." Jonas found himself saying.

"Anyway, you work on the details for our next meeting." John said generously.

Sir John stood again and proclaimed to the whole crowd in a ringing voice, "I, Sir John, servant of the peoples, and benefactor of our Bishop Jonas, declare that the Enclave of Eternal Light shall be under our protectorate and beneficence. Are there any dissenters to this ruling in this court now?" John asked them plainly.

None said a word.

"Are there any who assent this proclamation?"

The Shire sang out quickly, "Aye!"

Two men dragged more wood to the fire and stacked large Douglas-fir pieces, tepee style, onto the blaze. Sparks flew high into the night.

"Hearing affirmation, I, Sir John, assign the Enclave and its university to be so."

Mark jumped right in. " Hip hip …"

The crowd yelled "Hooray!"

"Hip hip."

"Hooray!"

"Hip hip."

"Hooray!"

Even the somber acolytes were caught up and cheered as loudly as any in relief of being spared their lives. There were a lot of rumors about the motley Shire that surrounded them.

There was a post cheering rustle as people made little comments to one another about how snazzy Jonas looked or about how generous Sir John was and how the Shire was more powerful now than ever, etc., etc.

Jonas was more than a little at a loss over how to react. He had anticipated resistance to his demands for the solar panels and batteries.

Sir John caved in and then went one step further by introducing the concept of a school that was only a dream in Jonas' mind when he prepared for the visit to court. He hadn't actually thought to bring that subject up until after the argument about the artifacts was won. He won it all though. He got what he wanted and more.

Jonas, with a flourish of his rich red robe strode out of the encircling firelight.

The Trinity of Jonas, Becky, and Apostolus, and with his almost clothed girls at their heels and white robed acolytes following, left the bright blazing firelight for the long walk home. The tiny flashlights under their white bed-sheet garments flicked on and their ghostly glowing figures wound through the woods and away.

Sam and Sally were mesmerized by the whole proceeding. They had just been privy to some pretty astounding developments in a world that they had no idea even existed. They were both impressed.

Sam had seen nothing so solemn nor ritualistic except in the movies.

Sally was bowled over by the strong presence exhibited and supported by the company of all. The county council was dry and boring compared to the high drama of this court.

Sam had been turning like a roast on a spit the whole time in an effort to dry out his wet jeans. Sally was scorched by the large fire and sat to the side with her teenage guard and his ever present hammer.

During the drama they had briefly forgotten why they were there.

Mark called, "Bring forth the chaff." He referred to them as the unusable portion of grain. They were not the kernel, but the dry useless husk on the grain known as the chaff.

Sally was prodded with a spear butt by the fat teen boy, Half-ton. Sam found a dark metal spear point poised by him. He followed the shaft to the wicked looking face of Jim the thin. Sam didn't like the look of him one bit.

They each strode in front of the dais and stood at Jonas' chair marks.

Sir John held his fingertips together like the steeple of the church and looked down upon them with cold scrutiny.

Mark spoke. "Why have you come to our realm?"

A moment passed before Sam felt the small point of the spear behind him niggle a little at his lower back.

"Speak thrall." Jim said from behind him.

"Uh, well ... I wasn't really coming to your realm, so to speak. I was, uh, well, I was just heading north, with my dog. Your guys attacked me." He felt the spear tip again.

He whirled and slapped the point of the deadly thing away from his back.

"Hey, just quit it kid. I've just about had enough of you and your little spear crap."

Jim pulled back in a defensive posture. The tip of his spear hovered in tiny circles pointing at Sam's face.

"Stand easy, Jim. We want him to talk. You can skewer him later if that's the verdict," John said with a dismissive flourish of his fingers.

"Aye, Mi'lord," Jim said. He took a couple of steps back and leaned on the spear.

"Why should we spare you?" Mark asked.

Sam was at a loss.

This was the job interview from hell. 'And what positive attributes would make you right for this job? In your own words.'

"Uh, well I'm pretty smart. And I know how to hunt ... and um ..." he scuffed his bare toe in the dirt.

A muted chuckle arose from the crowd. He wasn't making a very good case for himself.

"I'm still alive," Sam chirped.

"Aye. That you are." Mark conceded. "So far."

"He's a good guy." Sally piped in.

"Really?" Sir John got into the act now. "You know him from before the quiet?"

"No, not really, but I spent time in the pit with him and he's OK."

That got a good round of laughter from the crowd.

Mark held the palms of his hands down to quiet the people.

"And who are you to vouch for him?" Mark inquired of her.

"I am Sally Reynolds, the Animal Asset Officer for Slocoma County." She proudly announced.

"Ahh, The confiscator," Sir John said, "and I take it, you know the Sheriff?"

The crowd grumbled.

"Yeah, I know him," Sally admitted.

"I see. And you think that this creature has redeeming qualities? Enough to spare his life?"

"He's a human being. He did nothing wrong. Certainly nothing to be killed for."

"You are quite the little lawyer." John toyed with her. "You are an animal expert and a human expert also. You have no idea what he has, or has not done and you conclude that he should be spared on that basis."

"I'm just saying you can't just kill a guy for stumbling into your territory," Sally backpedaled.

"He defied the border. He trespassed without permission. He ignored the signs and the warnings. He ate fruit that wasn't his and which wasn't offered to him," Mark said.

"None of those things are death sentences."

"So, what would be a death sentence? Invasion of property to take food from people and starve their children? Or gunning down heroes trying to reclaim their property unjustly taken?"

"I don't know. I ..." Sally stammered realizing she was caught in a snare of her own actions.

"You have done those things confiscator."

She had been key to the round-up.

She knew that the Sheriff had summarily executed more than a few who had tried to enter the airport perimeter to steal cattle.

She knew that her deputies fired first on the men on the road when told to stand down.

"At what point do we allow strangers to dictate authority over us? When they come here guns blazing? I think you have defended this fellow enough and should keep quiet before you get him burned at the stake."

Sam thought she was doing a pretty good job until then; burned at the stake sounded pretty drastic. "Uh, excuse me. Sir John, Sir?"

John looked at him and raised his eyebrows.

"I really like your new boots, sir."

"Don't be impertinent." Mark snapped from the side.

John raised his hand slightly. "I do too. They fit like a glove. Seems you have an interest in shoes I hear."

Sam saw his out. The shoes. He knew where the shoes were. He glanced around and realized the majority had worn out footwear. The cheap Chinese shoes from before the quiet had reached the point of needing to be replaced. These people needed his shoes.

"Yeah, well, I've been meaning to talk to you about that. The shoes I had on me, weren't the only ones."

"Go on." John was having fun with these people. He knew the guy had a stash somewhere. The boots found on him were brand new. One pair even had the tissue paper from the factory still in them. Not even a whole day in the pit and this guy was ready to tell all.

"I know where there's more."

"Do tell?"

"Yeah, and there's lots more, not just a few pairs, I mean hundreds." Sam gushed.

"Hmm. I see. And you were hoping to trade this knowledge for … your life?"

"Well, yeah."

"Is that all?" John gave the guy a hint. He could gain status in the Shire with his kind of donation. "Just your life?"

Sam looked from side to side. His mind whirled. What else could he get? He didn't know what to ask for. "Well, her life too."

The crowd gathered close around to hear the proceedings and they murmured their interest in the implications

"I don't know what kind of bond you two have, but loyalty is a virtue. You do know, she is a criminal. Probably responsible for hundreds of deaths."

Sally couldn't hold her tongue. "I am not. I'm only a dog-catcher." The politically incorrect and not wholly truthful words fell around her.

The crowd laughed. They knew of the livestock confiscations. They knew the Sheriff's reputation and approval by the County Council of his extralegal actions.

The sound of machine gun fire from the border couldn't be completely muffled.

Recon teams had heard it and seen the deployment of the Coast Guard and the Sheriff's army and even though the border gave great benefit to the Shire, the methods were still appalling to the people.

Young William and three of his recon team were still missing. She was the first uniformed goon from the thieves and scoundrels of Saint Rose that they had caught and brought to justice.

"So, you tell us where the shoes are and we let you live here as a thrall."

"What's a thrall?" Sam wanted to know.

"Well, it's a step up from chaff. We have no use for chaff. Thralls are very useful indeed. Thralls are able to work their way up. You will survive, room and board, medical benefits, vacation time and a retirement pension." The crowd laughed at John's joke.

"How do I know that you won't just kill me after I show you where they are?" Sam asked.

The crowd murmured again, this time in disapproval. Sir John giving his word, in court; to the Shire there was no better guarantee for anything. His honor was sacrosanct. Without it their whole society would collapse in a heap.

"I promise you will live. There, I said it out loud." John stated.

"Her too." Sam insisted.

"Her too."

Silence fell over the assembly. Sir John had no idea where to go from here.

Sam got what he wanted and didn't know what else to say.

Sally wanted to say something, but a part of her counseled restraint and she also remained silent.

Mark pondered the affair for a moment and finally broke the reverie, "Be it proclaimed. Sir John acts in the favor of us all. Long live our Barony!" He shouted it fervently.

"Hip hip ..."

The crowd yelled "Hooray!"

"Hip hip."

"Hooray!"

"Hip hip."

"Hooray!"

"Barony?" John asked as he and Mark walked back to the house.

"Shires don't own monasteries." Mark replied with a smirk.

22

Nomads

The heavily armed dump truck squealed its brakes as it came to rest in front of Alice's cottage. It sat rumbling noisily in the settling dust as three men jumped down; two ranged out with drawn rifles, the third strode onto her porch.

"Alice." John called. "Alice, are you here?"

The roar of the clanking loud diesel truck woke Alice from her fitful hot afternoon nap. Salty spit rose in her mouth and she felt nauseous. Morning sickness had plagued her the last couple of days.

She rubbed her eyes and rolled to greet Sir John, the Baron, coming through her bedroom door. He loomed large above her and she felt frail in his presence.

"Sir John? Welcome." She tried to rise, but doubled over and reached for the bedpan to cough out wretched bile in her throat.

John felt at a loss for the girl. As she curled over the edge of the bed he poured water from the pitcher and offered her a glass.

"There you go." He waited for her to respond. He didn't know what to say to the sick girl.

She coughed and spit and wiped her mouth, "thanks," and took the water. It was warm and tasted of dust. She slurped it nonetheless, washed the acid taste from her and leaned against the older man on her bed.

"We gotta' go." John said.

"Go?" She looked up into his stress lined face. "I just got here. Where're we gonna' go?"

"We have to go deep into the woods. The hordes are coming. We don't have much time."

"Oh." Sweet, blonde Alice Gunderson, looked around her immaculate bedroom: chintz curtains, lace coverlet on the bed, perfectly arranged dressing table with antique mirror. She got a forlorn look in her eye.

"I just got here." She had dolled the house up nicely for her and Bill. It was the perfect romantic white clapboard honeymoon home. There was even a white picket fence in the front surrounding some rose bushes, in bloom. She was waiting for Bill to return from his recon. She had made the place a nest for them and their coming baby. This was to be their home.

"Come on. Get your bug-out bag. The truck is waiting." John gently coaxed her to her feet.

She stood shakily and moved to the closet where Bill had left the knapsack all ready. She had buried it under rolls of fabric that she intended to make into clothes for their child.

As soon as John saw where she headed for the bag he dove on the closet, grabbed her fabric and her essentials under arm. He lead her into the main room where she slowly put on shoes and groped around a bit trying to remember things she might have forgotten.

"I have to write Bill a note." She declared.

John handed her personal gear to the house guard, Bob, who stood on the porch. "Yes, that's a good idea Alice. Write him a note. Let him know you love him and that you are OK."

She sat at the dining table and penned a nice letter to her love. 'Bill my darling. I am with Uncle John. There is jerky in the jar in the cupboard and pickles. I wait for you to catch up. Know I am waiting. Love, Alice. P.S. Hurry.' Her flowing script was beautiful and artistic. She folded the paper and set a vase full of the morning's wild flowers on it.

One last look around so she could carry the memory with her until she came back. She clutched her bulky sewing basket and turned from her hope of a home. She was lifted into the sky by thick masculine arms at the back of the dump box.

John took Bob, who had been watching over her for the last few days, to the side. "Soon as we're out of sight, torch it."

"Yes my Lord." Yeoman Bob confirmed. He was one of John's first men and he would do exactly as told.

"Work to the Jenning Bridge. That's where we're crossing. We've already dropped the River Mountain bridge. Get your horse there and help drive the cattle. I am going to re-establish up north. Any stragglers you see send them on."

"So, I'm the rear guard?" Bob asked with a crooked enigmatic smile.

"Yeah, you're the rear guard, Yeoman. The most important one. Brick's got the last of Happy Lair to deal with and the rest are on the move. Meet up with him and join us."

"I'll have news for you on whatever follows." Bob said with a gleam in his eye.

The dump truck roared as the driver gunned it impatiently. John clapped Bob on the arms and they nodded to each other.

He clambered onto the truck and yelled "Heeyaw, Joe, Let's do this!"

The hammering of the roaring engine echoed off the trees and left only a cloud of dust as the only sign of its existence.

Bob calmly walked into the house, found the jerky, pickles, and some good leftover bread. He poked around for any other useful items, and then he spilled the kerosene lamp onto the sitting chairs in the living room and flicked a match onto them. He strolled out, stored his loot in saddle bags, mounted, and rode off in the direction of the noisy truck.

—

Donny Stuart had been torn between coping with the lack of electricity, a vehicle to get to town, and the desire to get the grapes harvested and into vats. An entire crop was ripe and bursting with sweetness. The grapes needed to come in and be processed.

He was having a devil of a time trying to reconcile his want for them to be turned into wine and the amount of back breaking labor that it was going to entail without mechanization. The fact that he didn't have a crew of men to harvest it all at once was relieved by the fact that he didn't have the mechanical capability to process it all at once, either. His role in management was being expanded by his desire to get the grapes in.

He thought he and his wife and their few remaining neighbors might get it done, but it was going to be a lot of work. None of them had done that much physical labor, well, for their entire lives up to this point. They were the kind of people who drove miles to go to the gym or carried their bicycles with the SUV to the bike path. They were exploiters of people. They rode on the froth of the waves of commerce. They hired other people to do the grueling and boring work. Sometimes they assisted, and they knew how to do it, but as a rule, they did not perform the act of labor from dawn to dusk like the field hands

Now, the crop was waiting for them and there was only a handful of local Hispanic pickers around. Most of the Latinos disappeared right after the power failed. They had scurried off to be with their families nearer to town, he assumed.

Donny had only: two Guatemalan fellows, his wife JoEllen, Helen Nessler and her husband Roscoe to help. A couple of people wandered into his yard last week with news of the Christian Camp down the ravine on the other side of Sentimental.

The Christian strangers stayed in his barn one night and although they vowed to return with help, Donny wasn't counting on it. That made six people to do the work that a crew of twenty, with machinery, normally did.

Donny and JoEllen sat at their picnic table under the oak tree in the yard. The lawn sloped down to the edge of a field of grape vines. The vineyard was spread out before them to the limiting redwood trees in the distance. The vineyard comprised the entire top of the hill that surrounded their house and barns.

"I talked to Helen and she and Roscoe can come help. At first Roscoe wouldn't leave the house unguarded, but lately there's been no one around. It's like everyone left, or is staying home." JoEllen said.

"Thanks honey. I got the tubs ready on the wagon and our amigos are cleaning the vats." Donny shared.

"How are we going to separate the stems?" JoEllen asked her husband.

"Well, I kind of got a big hand-crank fashioned onto the pulley of the machine, We can turn it but it is going to need some muscle, a couple of big guys, who we don't have. The amigos are tough but they're small. It's gonna' take some beef. I don't know if it's even worth the effort."

"Donny." JoeEllen squeezed his hand and looked into his eyes. "We have to try. It's the only thing we can do."

"I know, but it's a huge job," he sighed.

"Look, my family came here a hundred and fifty years ago and they didn't have any power. They did it. We can too." She squeezed his hand.

"Yeah, but …"

"No buts. We'll do as much as we can. Maybe we won't get the whole thing done, but we're gonna' harvest this crop. The grapes are the best they've been in years, you said so yourself. It may be a small batch, but it'll be a great wine. Hell, we'll stomp it the old way if we have to, barefoot." She rubbed her foot up his trouser leg.

Donny looked up at his wife. She had given him a family, both their kids were grown up and far away with big city jobs. She had helped him plan and manage the vineyard from the start. They had been good partners for many years and she was now doing the one thing she was really good at, inspiring him to move mountains. He was enthralled with the woman in front of him. She was his rock, and he was hers. They were going to go forward even if the world wanted to stop.

"Halloo." A ringing voice from the redwood grove nearest the house called out.

They sat up and saw the two Christian strangers waving. After a moment a crowd of people appeared with them and Donny and JoEllen Stuart rose to greet a hundred fresh faced vineyard workers.

"We couldn't let our neighbors go wanting in their time of need." The black man said as they came close. "We're here to pick your grapes."

"You were so kind to us the other day when we needed shelter, we thought we would repay your Christian charity with a little of our own." The middle aged white woman said.

"Everyone," the black man turned and waved them to gather round, "this is Don and JoEllen, our Samaritans."

The crowd swarmed the couple and it was a veritable love fest of greeting as if they were long lost friends. Everyone introduced themselves and the Stuarts were lost in a sea of names and friendly faces. These were people from the local surroundings whom they had never met. A lot of people had moved into Sentimental in the last few years and unless one made a big effort to go to Church or hang around the grocery store, or linger very long at the post office, one just didn't meet new folk.

The village of Sentimental was more of a tourist hangout than a place where locals shopped. Modern lives were exclusive and driving alone to hit the big box store in town was the norm. Before the quiet, people spent their leisure hours online or in front of the TV, not hanging out in the village. Donny and JoEllen's circle was with the other big grape growers and a few of the older families. There were events, but they were exclusive and many of the local denizens fell outside of the loop.

At the rear of the crowd stood a tall imposing young blonde man. He waited until last. Jonas stepped forward with raven haired Becky on his arm. He sported a beatific smile. The crowd fell silent and parted as he glided forward. He offered his hand in a strange effeminate way.

For a moment Donny almost laughed at the kid. It looked like he was offering his hand to be kissed. He put away his impression and grabbed Jonas' hand in a firm handshake.

"Pleased to have you all here. Like ah …?" Donny groped for the black man's name.

"Floyd." Floyd piped in cheerfully. His teeth flashed bright against his light coffee colored skin.

"Yeah, Floyd, and … oh crap … I'm sorry." Donny stammered.

"Sharon," Floyd volunteered again as he put his arm around the woman.

"Floyd and Sharon, may have told you we need a little help here. I want to thank you all for coming. Please forgive me, I am not going to remember all your names." Donny dug his toe a little.

Becky moved into Donny's space. "This is Jonas, our Bishop." She bowed a bit and moved aside as if to reveal the man he was standing on front of. Jonas tilted his head and radiated his pleasant loving smile.

"Yes, Jonas. I think I can remember that. Uh, like I said we're glad you're here, but I don't know what Floyd has told you. We need labor, nothing glamorous and, well we don't know what we can pay you." Donny groped for the right words. He wasn't entirely sure how to accept their offer.

Jonas spoke again. "Donny. My enclave is here to save God's bounty from the scavenging birds that ravage the land. There is nothing you can offer us to do the work of the Lord. Render unto Caesar what is Caesar's and unto God what is God's. Please tell us what needs to be, and it will be done."

Jonas thought back to the secret meeting with Sir John to arrange all this.

—

John sent word for Jonas to meet him privately in the woods near John's old house for delivery of the promised solar panels and batteries.

John culled the most damaged panels and weakest batteries for the enclave. He brought a small cart of the stuff.

Jonas was disappointed at the meager offering. He was sure that John was holding out and had much more in the way of D.C. power resources. Jonas' disgust at John's obvious short-changing him on the solar panels was tempered by the cow John included.

"Bishop, friend. I bring tribute to help you start the university study." John waved as he approached on the deserted trail.

"It is a gracious offer John, uh, Sir John, and I accept it in the spirit that it is offered." Jonas replied.

"I also bring you this animal. It is another symbol of our mutual respect. Take it, slaughter it, feed your church." John handed the rope lead to Jonas.

Apostolus, Jonas' hired man, stepped forward and started the cart down the path to the enclave.

Jonas was about to turn away when Sir John said, "Jonas, I know this one cow won't feed your people long. I can supply you more, but uh, I need a favor."

"A favor? What kind of favor?" The hair on the back of Jonas' neck stood up. He could feel the ax about to fall. This man was going to ensnare him into some deal. Jonas did not trust Sir John.

"The grapes are ripe. They need to be harvested." John said. Brick stood aside and nodded agreement.

Jonas asked, "grapes?"

The cow belched up and chewed its cud.

"There's a vineyard on the other side of the creek from you, on the hill, Donny Stuart's place. He needs to get his grapes in."

"You want my congregation to work for you?"

"Jonas, the grapes aren't mine. Donny isn't even a part of the Shire, but it serves the whole community if the harvest happens and wine gets put up."

"Why don't you get your people to do it? Why us?" Jonas wanted to know.

"We're stretched thin managing our affairs and can't do both. We don't have the people to do it, but you do. That gives you an advantage. You have people who need work and who are hungry. I just want to do the right thing here."

"So ... what? You feed us if we harvest some other guy's grapes?"

"There are other vineyards too, not just Donny's." John continued, "And you have a lot of people down there in need of righteous labor."

Jonas chewed his lip. The sound of crying children and the grousing about meager rations had already become a threat to his camp. People were grumbling. They were protein starved, hungry, and bored.

"Come on. What do you say?" John smiled.

The memory of his hungry parishioners nibbled at the edge of Jonas' mind.

It was difficult not to be enticed into the deal. Jonas knew there had to be a catch, but he was compelled by practicality and reason to comply with John's request. Beef was going to make him powerful and John was giving him beef.

—

Jonas and his hundred workers had fire jerked beef in their lunch sacks and were ready to work as God intended, harvesting grapes for wine.

Donny was torn between laughter and reverence for this kid. The offer of labor was overpowering and Donny held his mirth. They needed this. He looked around at the surrounding crowd. These were serious folk who had hiked up the hill and it looked like they expected to work: gloves, jeans, long sleeve shirts, and hats for the ever-present sun.

"Ok, then. I can't turn down an act of faith like that. Thank You. Thank you all." Donny misted over as soon as the words came out of his mouth.

JoEllen came and hugged her husband in joy and the moment they looked up they realized all people were kneeling and facing Jonas. The peer pressure was great, and even though Donny wasn't an especially religious man he and JoEllen bowed their heads.

"In the name of the Lord who has come again, and he who has blessed us all with this opportunity to reap God's work, we beseech affirmation of your word, oh lord, to us all in our task…"

"In Jesus' name." The crowd echoed.

"Under the guidance of our brother Don and his wife, Lord, give us the strength to make your fruit into wine. We praise the Lord." Jonas finished.

"Praise the lord." They repeated.

Floyd piped up, "OK, let's do it."

—

"Where are we going?" Sally asked of the woman pushing on the pipe next to her.

"You ask a lot of questions." The sweating middle-aged woman leaned into the pipe sticking out from the side of the box truck.

Rows of pipes stuck out from both sides of the engineless truck. It was full of food and supplies and being pushed by a swarming crowd down a dirt road through the forest.

Since her reprieve at the bonfire, things had moved fast for Sally. A group of older women had swarmed around her and led her away from the fire. They took her to a barrack in a sprawling house and bid her sleep. She was surrounded in the bowels of a dark house somewhere in the woods. It was a harem. It wasn't the fantasy filled 72 virgins harem, it was the ancient order of women banded close for protection. There was a phalanx of crone aged females. They were done with having kids and knew all kinds of important social stuff. She was kept in the center by constant contact in this exclusively woman's household group. Escape wasn't an option.

The next morning she awoke in a dormitory of women.

"Get in line." The middle aged and thick limbed woman told her. She wended her way out of the gloomy bowels of the large home toward thin daylight at the head of the line for a small bowl of naked oatmeal on the flagstone patio of the sprawling mansion. Shortly after her meager meal she was slapped in the face with a thrown towel and directed, "Wash. The dishes won't do it themselves."

Sally spent her first morning in the Shire with her head in a steaming haze of soap and clattering pots and bowls, surrounded by women.

Soon, men lined up and were served by women who had finished their early breakfast. The men came and ate and left. They didn't linger. Next, came the kids who were motivated enough by hunger to get up and at 'em. The women were the kitchen. They boiled pots of water and oatmeal and worked the breakfast for the community.

To the side, a couple of chosen women fried up a few eggs and bacon and tortillas. Sally saw them make a nice set of plates on a tray full of the premium breakfast, red jam and coffee included, and take them to whoever deserved such extravagance.

Sally washed dirty dishes and kept her head down.

Her first day was filled with laborious tasks. She had no time to think about where she might be or how to get away. The other women were always close by and busy themselves. It seemed a very egalitarian society. There was no grand director who did nothing while the others toiled. They all seemed to work equally hard. There were definitely task makers, but they too got into the chores to complete them. The work was done quickly and with gusto. These people were doing things that needed to be done to ensure their survival. No one was getting paid. They were not employees.

They acted like owners and when Sally handled a sack poorly and spilled a small amount of rice, she was sharply challenged.

"Hey! Be careful or you go hungry tonight." Lois chided. Two other women knelt with Lois to scoop up the dirt and spilled rice. A plate appeared and they winnowed the grains from the dust and returned a good two handfuls back to the sack.

"Look, you may be Miss High and Mighty in Saint Rose, but here, you're the same as everyone else confiscator, about to starve and thankful as hell we let you be with us." The slightly heavy-set Nancy, arched her eyebrows and threw at Sally.

Sally didn't try to argue. There was no point. She spilled and they caught it. She understood the seriousness of their situation and knew that she might well be hanging from a noose. She had to earn some place amongst these people or escape, and escape seemed impossible as she was constantly surrounded by dozens of women and girls. They all seemed loyal to the Shire and she got no hint of dissension. These people were wholly committed to their cause and their community.

Each of the older women was attended by younger females. It looked like an intergenerational mixture. A post-menopausal lady and a thirty something woman interned by one or two teenagers or young girls and they in turn were followed by a couple or three tow-headed children. It was a mutually symbiotic relationship: the older woman knew a lot of things, but hadn't the get up and go, the middle aged ones could see the point and had energy and strength enough to work and the younger girls had exuberance and their youth to put any labor issue over the top. The young learned from the old and the old got to lavish praise on bright women of the future and were in turn revered for their knowledge and service.

Sally worked alone. She wasn't 'in' yet. She was watched by all and had no protégé to help her. Being middle aged she certainly fell in the category of the elders, but she was a solo slave. That's how she felt. She was trapped here and forced to labor for people she had no connection with. She kept her head down.

She watched and observed the social construct of this new camp. The dormitory setting was a communistic structure and no one seemed to have anything of their own. They all shared everything. It seemed that most of what they had to share was work.

The world she was imprisoned in, was wholly of women. There were no men in their area. The men came for meals, but none stayed. The women decided how to attend to the chores before them. No man directed their show. It worked smoothly and with little fuss.

Sally was impressed by them. She wondered if they shared their men too.

"Hey rustler," someone shouted at her, "keep moving, we have to bug-out because of you, so the least you can do is help get us out of here."

Sally trudged into the dark house for another sack of rice, or toothpaste and toiletries or whatever the storeroom had left.

That had been her entire day; hauling goods to the truck, and now she was pushing the truck.

The entire cluster of women worked at keeping their truck moving. There wasn't room for all of the women on the push-bars, those not pushing were in front heaving on some big ropes, or walked behind and waited their turn to lend weight to the endeavor. As each tired, they stepped back and another filled their place.

The large box truck had all of their worldly needs inside. They had spent the last hour of daylight getting the thing down the ridge and away from the Happy Lair, as it was called. When only a few hundred feet down the road they clearly saw smoke behind them from the conflagration that was their shelter the night before. They turned away from the destruction behind them and diligently pushed the thing deeper into the woods.

Scorched earth was the policy. Let there be nothing behind of use. Invaders would find nothing to sustain them or encourage them to continue.

These people were not planning on revitalizing society or keeping anything from the past unless it served them immediately. Sally was a little stunned at the thought that so many people had bought into the idea that things were not going to return to normal. These people aimed at the darkest and most difficult scenario for the future that one could imagine. They all believed this awful situation would last and nothing from the world before, would return. It was hard for her to swallow that idea, but they seemed to have gotten a jump on preparation for such a dismal world.

She leaned into the iron pipe sticking out from the truck. She grunted and groaned with dozens of others who earnestly threw their shoulders into the weight of the machine. It had done such massive amounts of work moving their food and their furniture and everything that made up their long gone world, now they were returning the favor and forcing it down a dirt road by sheer might.

Sally toiled alongside other women. Some were near her age, some were young and fresh. The girls were in high school only a month before, and were planning for mid-terms and the upcoming prom. The football season was in full swing and high school teams in rural America were battling it out. The cheerleaders and ingénues hollered their support of the young men carrying the ball in mock battle against a manufactured enemy represented by another high school. Now there were real battlefields.

The world had twisted around on itself.

Sally had gone from being a nobody temp worker to a very important cog in the machinery of a disrupted society trying to get back on its feet. Serendipity had allowed her to wheedle herself into a position of power where none had existed and fate had yanked it away just as quickly. She was again, a nobody in a crowd of competitors trying to shove an old truck down the road. It was as ignoble a fall as one could imagine. She commanded and was now being commanded.

The end of the world had been a boon to Sally. Long hidden talents had risen to the fore and her attitude of getting things done had served her well in that environment. Now, she was merely one of the masses again. She was a bit relieved. She could just kick back and do her job here. She didn't have to put herself on the line. No one really depended on her. She could coast along as a laborer and get fed and be amongst people of similar circumstance. She didn't go to bed at night thinking of the next day's strategy. She didn't have to manage teams or think about logistics or reports or curbing her opinion. She now had no opinion about her day. She did what she was told.

Leaning into the bar with others to move the truck was strangely gratifying. She was working together with other women for a common cause. So seldom were there occasions where one could find common goal to ally one's efforts with. This new world had hidden positives. She slept and ate well and although her body was achy from disuse, she felt exercised and slept peacefully.

Sally fit into the regimen and the bug-out progressed. The shire wound through west county hills and filtered deeper into the heavy thick redwood forests of the Pacific coast.

Occasionally teams of cavalry charged by on some urgent business. She spied one of the deputy's mounts, under a fierce looking youth with a helmet-like shock of raven black hair, and her thoughts lingered on the fate of her friends who had been cut down during her capture. The horses clattered by and vanished quickly. Maybe she could get a horse.

Lois, the small jowly jewish woman called out from the cab, where she steered the engineless truck, "Come on you bitches, put your backs into it."

23

Waterboyz

A.Q. Second Month

Two weeks unwashed and unshaven, Wayne lay on wet jagged rocks, plunged his arm into the tide pool, and scrabbled in a crevice for the cold sharp mollusks that would feed him. It was hard to make his stiff fingers work in the frigid water. His arm was numb from repeated dunking in the cold sea water. The good side of it was that he barely felt the jagged rocks and stinging things in the water. His hands were like wooden tools. He was grateful for the momentary relief of chill immersion. When his hands warmed up he would pay the price with nettle stinging, itching and sharp pain from numerous scrapes and cuts.

He tugged at the cluster of small black mussels. They didn't want to die. They wanted to stay clinging to the wave washed rocks. Battered by the incessant movement of the cold Pacific they were well suited to holding fast with a myriad of tiny black root-like tendrils. Wayne's unfeeling fingers gripped them tight, his face near the surface of the water; he rocked them back and forth, pulling and focusing his energy into that small spot of leverage that would loosen them. With a tearing feeling they let go and he pulled a handful of the inert black creatures up into a pile in front of him.

He rolled to his side, flexed his arm, rubbed the bare tender pink skin with his other, relatively warm hand, and sensation returned–painfully. Out of the corner of his eye something glinted. Wayne focused.

He glimpsed movement in the bushes of the gulley above him. Quickly he gathered his hard won protein for the day into a kerchief and stuffed the wet bundle into his jacket pocket. He made for the cover of the thick brush. He didn't want to be caught unawares with his dinner out where someone else could get at it.

Wayne was now concerned that someone was pilfering the few items of value from where he had left them. His blanket and few tools could not be replaced easily and he would be hard pressed to continue on without them. He made for his hidden cache of paltry, yet valuable goods.

He slipped the worn canvas jacket on as he loped up the steep slope and leaned into the scratchy clawing branches of the thick brush that grabbed at him. He wasn't so concerned about stealth at this point. If someone was stealing his stuff he wanted to get there and stop them.

He clambered up the last bit of the bluff before the depression where he made camp last night. He came over the lip of the low spot and his fears were justified. A lone figure was hunched over and rifling through his gear.

Wayne launched himself onto the thief.

Neither said anything. It wasn't like the movies where the guy screams his intent and they holler things at one another while they fought. There was only grunting as the two wrestled. Wayne was two hundred fifty pounds of tough old carpenter and the thief was a slight fellow who wriggled and squirmed more than fought back. In only a few moments of thrashing in the gorse, Wayne pinned the intruder down.

He looked at the face of the little guy and realized it was a woman. Her hair was cut very tight around her face. She wore combat boots and camo uniform trousers under a long dirty blue pea-coat.

She started crying, and just as expected he relaxed his grip a bit. She moaned and tears flowed.

"Please, don't hurt me. I'll be good. Just do it, I won't fight, just please don't hurt me," she pleaded.

Wayne glared into her face, "You are a thief."

"I didn't know … I thought it was loose stuff … honest."

Wayne loosened his grip more and sat up on her.

She looked up at him and her tears abated. "Aren't you going to rape me?"

"Rape you?" Wayne was a little disgusted at the suggestion and he let her arms go and sat off her to one side. "Nooooo ... I'm not a raper ... rapist ... whatever. You were stealing my stuff," he accused.

"I'm sorry. I didn't know it was someone's. I didn't see anyone, I thought it was loose."

"Well it's not. It's mine."

"I'll go. I'm sorry." She crawled out from under his leg and made to leave.

"Wait." Wayne knew he was going to regret it, but he had been alone since he crossed the bridge and when he looked into her face he could see her intent wasn't malicious and she was just trying to stay alive. Maybe a little company would be good and she might have information that could help him. "OK. Apology accepted."

She made to move off.

"Stay. Have you eaten?"

The question stopped her in her tracks. Big round eyes broke through the dirty savage exterior and showed her longing for food. "I ... uh, no. Not lately."

"Not lately huh? Does that mean there was no croissant with this morning's coffee?" He put on a light face and smirked a bit.

Dirty white teeth broke the grimy façade for a moment as she caught the joke. "No, they were all out of croissants this morning."

"Well, I don't have any pastry, but I do have some mussels I could share." Wayne was already collecting a little pile of twigs into the burnt hole in the loam for a fire. "Here, go get some water. There is a little spring just down there." He tossed a jumbo-sized steel can that once held stewed tomatoes at her feet. "Be quick, I don't like to let a fire go too long. It attracts ... attention."

She stared at the fire blackened can for a second, then with a nod and a hopeful look on her face she sprung at it and lurched over the edge of the depression and down the hill. In only a few minutes he had gotten a fire going with his disposable lighter. When she returned he emptied his pockets of the mussels into the can and they lay close around the tiny fire feeding it twigs and minding the simple shellfish stew.

"What's your name?" Wayne asked.

"Kit, what's yours?"

"My name's Bruce, but they call me Wayne."

"How do you get Wayne from Bruce?"

"Wayne, it's my middle name, but I like it better. Just call me Wayne."

"I don't like Kit that much either. Maybe since everything else has changed it's time for me to change it too."

"It's not like anyone is going to be checking up on you. So, if you don't like Kit what would you like to be called?"

"I don't know. I always liked Whitney. You know, like Whitney Houston?"

"Ok. So be it. You're Whitney. So, Whitney, which way are you headed?"

She just stared at him. A far-away look crept into her eyes; she teared up and buried her face in her hands.

Wayne Nickel, scowled and fed more twigs under their meager steaming soup.

She had obviously been through some trauma. He could only sit and let her sort through her angst. Nothing could be said to mitigate the change they had all endured the last few weeks. He had an idea what she might have been through. Her immediate readiness to be subject to rape in order to prevent being hurt told a tale. Since society had come apart at the seams he could imagine what she had done to stay alive.

She composed herself, wiped her face and looked up at him. "Do I have to be going somewhere?"

"Uh, well, I just figured you were on your way somewhere."

"Why? Because you are going somewhere doesn't mean everyone has somewhere to go." Her chin quivered.

"Look, I don't want to upset you, I was just making conversation." Wayne said.

"Just making conversation? What do you want from me?"

"I've been alone for a few weeks and I thought a little friendly talk would help us take our minds off of … make things a little normal. You know?" Wayne said.

She felt contrite and nodded knowingly. "So, are you going someplace?" She asked.

"I'm going home." He looked up and his face lightened.

"Where is home then? Not many people live up on the beach."

"I got a house up near Sentimental. Ever hear of it?" Wayne said.

"That's past the border." Whitney got a scared look on her face.

"Not that far north, just up in Slocoma County."

"I know where Sentimental is." She let her words hang in the air.

The mussels boiled over and Wayne used a pair of pliers to fish the can of steaming froth from the flames.

"We better let them cool for a bit." He stated as he shook his hand from a scorched finger. The heady aroma of fishy ocean food made their noses twitch and their mouths water. It smelled wonderful.

"There's a breeze inshore. I sure hope no one else can smell these." Wayne said as he pushed the last of the twigs deeper into the fire to consume them.

"Good thing we're way up here on this hill. We'll be done before they get here." She said.

"Yeah, this little dip is pretty good cover."

They were completely obscured in the small depression at the lip of the hill. Wayne had to stand up to look out over the top of the prominence.

The view inland was rolling hills and scrub brush all the way to the two-lane blacktop, State Highway #1, which ran up and down the coast. A few scattered clumps of coastal cedar and closed cone pine trees bunched up here and there as dark forest blobs. In the distance, inland, were straight rows of wind-break Eucalyptus trees delineating the edge of cattle country where a black patchwork of scorched earth scarred the prairie. Wayne had seen the smoke a couple of days ago and worked west to avoid the grassfire.

A brownish-red raptor hovered above them; its head swiveled to give them the eye as it soared past. They were perched on top of the bluffs overlooking the rugged California coast. The bird discounted them and zoomed away on the updraft as it hunted for smaller prey.

Wayne would eat his dinner, nap until dusk and then risk another night hike north. He knew that as soon as he got past the bay town of Bowditch he could turn inland and follow Oldman Valley Road almost to his doorstep.

"What do you mean, before they get here? You expecting company?" Wayne was suspicious.

"No, I mean that if there were anyone …" she backpedaled.

Wayne fished a steaming glob of the black mussels from the can with his pliers and a screwdriver and put them in front of the woman.

"Dinner is served."

She picked at the mass of partially opened shells attempting to get one apart from the rest and to her mouth. They were still pretty hot and she picked and dropped them repeatedly.

"Give them a minute. They're not going anywhere." He could tell she was famished by the intensity she focused on those little shells. She kept sucking her breath in little shushing sounds each time she burned her fingers and let go of her potential supper. Wayne let his clump lay on some sticks and steam. He waved his hand over them and inhaled deeply.

"Half the meal is the savoring of it." He smelled the seafood steam and seemed to get great sustenance from it alone. "Mmmmmm." His stomach growled audibly.

She finally got one of them pulled free of the rest and sucked the little mollusk from its home. Her eyes rolled up and her face was a blissful countenance of joy. She chewed the super tough muscle from the shell and licked it completely clean before she went for another one.

"You said something about the border. What was that about?" He asked her as he pried loose one of his treats.

She looked up from her carnivorous exultation with a mean and scared look. "You really don't know, do you?"

"Know what?"

"About the border."

"No. I guess I don't. I was unaware of any border north of here until you got to Oregon, or Canada."

She sucked at her supper and eyed him as she formed her words. He couldn't tell if she was so hungry she couldn't reply or if she didn't really want to tell him. Wayne wrinkled his brow and looked at her expectantly.

"They set up a border. You can't go there," she said.

"Who set up a border?"

Her eyes wandered from side to side. She didn't want to tell him.

"Look, I catch you stealing from me and then have the heart to feed you and so, I figure you owe me a little something. So, tell me about what's ahead," Wayne insisted.

She held the mussel she was chewing, away from her mouth and licked her lips. She was troubled about relating the story.

"Well?" He looked her in the eye.

"Well ... there was this sign; it said, 'Go no further', 'food is in the valley', 'go east', 'or else'." She went back to chewing her mussels.

"A sign?"

She nodded.

"That's it, a sign?"

"It had a skull and crossbones on it," she said quietly.

"So that was all there was?" He asked.

Her teeth scraped on the mussel shell getting the most out of it. She looked at him with a scared look.

"There was more wasn't there." Wayne asserted.

She nodded slowly.

"Maybe you need to tell someone your story. It might help." Wayne led her softly.

Whitney's face broke and fell into itself as her emotions took over her features. Her eyes filled with water again and she started looking around for a way out of telling him what she knew.

"It's all right. I won't judge you. I'll listen. You are not alone. But, I need to hear what is ahead. If there is danger you have to let me know." Wayne spoke softly as to a child in pain. "You can tell me."

Her eyes brimmed over and she wiped the back of her hand across her face. She took a couple of deep breaths and looked off into the distance. Then she looked him dead in the eye.

"They shot them. They shot them all." She was working very hard not to break down.

"There was a fire and everyone ran, but they couldn't run fast enough and then they kept shooting and shooting and they didn't stop. I ran. I couldn't help them. I wanted them to stop, but I couldn't do anything. I saw their faces. They were ..." she lost her composure and wailed out loud.

The few mussels in her hand she tore at with her other hand as she cried. "They didn't do anything. They stood together and went down there to get away from the fire and they shot them. They shot them!" She screamed. She broke down into a blubbering ball of woe.

Wayne came across sat next to her and held her tightly. He stroked her hair. "It's OK, it's all OK. There, there, now. You're safe now. It's OK. Let it all out."

She continued to blubber for a bit and then started to talk through the sobs. "They thought the signs weren't real. They said we were just trying to scare them and they had a right to march down the hill. They said we wouldn't shoot citizens …" she wailed. "But they did! Then the fire came and it was everywhere. They all went down there." She fell into another fit of heaving and crying. "They burned up and the machine guns kept making that awful noise and they shot and they shot. They wouldn't stop!" She looked up into his face. "I wanted them to stop. Really, I did, you've got to believe me."

Wayne looked down into the face of true terror. She was horrified and scared more than he had ever seen anyone. Her entire body shook and trembled at the memories in her head. The nightmare wasn't play-acting or a movie horror flick it was a real dirty bloody massacre. She had witnessed a slaughter.

She sobbed for a bit longer and after some heavy sighing she finally regained some composure. "You can't go there."

He left her alone and she went back to chewing the last of her mussel meat.

Now he was really curious. Where was this border and could he avoid it?

"So, you wanted to know where I was going. I am going away from the border. Where that takes me I don't know. I have nowhere to go. And I am telling you now, that you can't go there. There's no way to go north, unless you want to join … them." She informed him with a stiff upper lip.

"I see."

They ate the rest of their supper in silence. When the can was cool enough Wayne sipped the salty stew juice and offered some to Whitney. She gladly took the can and drank.

The fire burnt out and a little spring water cleaned the can and snuffed out the last of the telltale smoke. The afternoon sun was warm on them and the hollow shielded them from the incessant ocean breeze.

After a bit he lay down for a little nap. It was a while until sundown and Wayne was content to rest in preparation for his upcoming night hike. He slumbered. He felt her lie next to him and snuggle into his arms. They spooned innocently and napped the afternoon away.

He awoke alone as the sun fell towards Japan and China. The cool breeze chilled the air and he knew it was soon time to get a move on. He held his hand up horizontally and counted the widths of the sun's height. Only one hand high told him it would be about an hour until it set.

Wayne wondered where the woman had gone. She must have decided to move on.

He lifted his fifty-five year old body, up. The creaking of his joints and the pain in his back from sleeping on the ground indicated his age more than his driver's license. He gathered his few belongings, the cook can, his one piece of blanket, and the plastic bottle canteens. He strung it all together and rose above the lip of the hill.

He scanned the horizon all around. A few minutes of watching had kept him from running into trouble more than once so far. He stared out at the rolling hills for telltale movement.

A crunching sound behind him startled him and he whirled around. Whitney clambered into view carrying bottled water and some greens. Wayne felt some relief at her not having left, but he didn't know what he was going to do with her. He couldn't watch out for her very well. He could hardly keep his own back covered, much less some woman who was a basket-case.

"Oh, you're up." She smiled brightly as she entered the camp spot. "I was getting water for supper and I found some miner's lettuce."

Wayne watched her plop down. She looked like she was settling in for the evening. He scanned around again then crouched by her.

"I'm about to go."

"Go?" She looked up with her big eyes. "You can't go. It's almost sundown. It'll be dark soon."

"That's when I move," he said.

"But, there's no where to go to. We're safe here." She pointed out.

"I told you, I'm going home."

"And I told you, you can't go there. You just can't."

"I heard you, but I have to try. It's where my life is. My family." Wayne countered.

"Don't you get it? There is no more 'my life'. It's all gone now. It's all changed. It's all new now. Like my new name. We start over. We start over right here."

"Look …"

"We can live here, we have food and water and it's safe here and …" she prattled on.

Wayne pressed his lips and shook his head slowly at each thing she said.

"Look I found miners lettuce, and got water, and we can build a little shelter here with drift wood, and I found an old surfboard. You could use it to fish. And …"

"I'm sorry Kit … Whitney. I'm going north. I leave soon. You can stay here or come with me, but I am going." Wayne asserted.

"You can't just leave me." She started to cry again. "I can't stay alone anymore. I need you. You have to help me. I … just can't … anymore …" Tears ran down her cheeks and she hugged herself tightly.

Wayne stood up, turned and climbed out of the low spot, He strode through the tough bushes to the beach. He was crying a little too. The world was a very hard place now.

He couldn't let the tears of one woman turn him from his mission to reunite with his family. They were all he could think about. They were his reason for living before the quiet and now after the quiet that had not changed. His entire life was based around making the world for them. He had sacrificed many things to continue down that path and one woman that he gave mussels to wasn't going to influence his resolve. He broke out of the bushes and stepped across the tiny rivulet of muddy water at the bottom of the gulley as he came out onto the beach. He looked up and froze.

He couldn't move as he watched a sailboat pointed directly at him come inshore.

It was under full sail with a bone in its teeth, white froth curled away from the bow.

Wayne saw movement on deck and it prompted him to action. He plunged back into the gulley and dove under cover. He lay still as a rabbit with an eye out to the vessel.

The boat was unusual in that it was a dark color. It didn't have the normal white hull and sails. It was entirely a mottled grey brown, perhaps thirty or forty feet in length and may have been the pride of the marina before the crude camouflage paint job.

The sloop turned into the wind, sails flapped loosely, a figure moved forward, crouched, and an anchor fell into the water. It trailed a short length of loudly clacking chain then fell silent as the rest of the rope anchor line threaded into the water. The figure secured the anchor rode and jumped up to the mast where lines came loose and the sails sagged down to the deck in a flapping mess. The boat drifted backward.

The crewman scurried aft and yanked the sails into a bundle as they came down. He worked alone. The sailor was silent and knew exactly what he was doing. The bow lifted over a wave, the anchor line came taut and the craft stopped drifting backward. The mariner bundled the sails up and lashed them. He bent again and let out more anchor line, then froze at the very front of the bow with one hand out and holding onto the line, testing it. After a few waves washed under he seemed satisfied went aft and vanished below.

Wayne scrambled out of the gulley worked his way out of sight and crawled up to where he left Whitney. She was gone. He lay down in the low spot and made a little head-dress of brush. He slunk forward and peered over the lip of his hide-out at the boat.

It wasn't long before the sailor was rhythmically kicking something on deck. He was blowing up a small inflatable boat with a foot-pump. The little craft folded out of its bundle into a recognizable shape. When fully charged, he tossed it into the water and snubbed it with a small line. In only a few minutes the lone fellow was rowing to shore with a load of empty plastic water bottles and it was evident he was after fresh water.

Wayne watched and his mind whirled as to what he might do about this obstacle. He could bypass, slip over the top of the hill, and move farther north before venturing back to the beach for his evening trek. Maybe he could show his hand, greet him with a friendly smile, and see if he could hitch a ride up the coast. He couldn't be sure if the sailor was alone or not and it didn't seem likely that he was anchoring as a favor to passing strangers.

While he pondered his options the dinghy landed under him out of sight. Wayne moved down the exposed slope and risked being seen to continue his surveillance of the guy. He climbed down to the top of the steep vertical bluff. At the lip of the dirt cliff he spied the small boat beached below.

Whitney appeared on the rocky tide pool shelf and ran to the grey inflatable.

Wayne wanted to yell at her to stop. But he couldn't. He could only watch in amazement as she dragged the boat to the water. From under him the sailor came running. He tackled the woman and they fought.

Wayne couldn't believe she was trying to steal the guy's boat, and now she was fighting for her life just below him. He didn't owe her anything. They had only just met.

She was stealing, again.

He jumped up and fell, skied, tumbled, and flailed himself down the sandy broken rock embankment to the rough rocky ledge at water's edge. Orienting himself he found the two rolling on the ground and then, into a tide-pool. He came upon them, scraped and bruised from his descent as they sputtered up out of the icy cold bath.

He intended to stop the rough and tough seaman from hurting his thieving companion out of a sense of shared food loyalty and nap-time pal.

The icy water dousing and the reality that they were both very well matched women left him helping each of them, bedraggled, from the pool. They both sputtered their indignation as he pulled them to relatively dry ground and they each sat aside.

"You fucking bitch!" The sailor girl hotly yelled.

"Bite me cunt." Whitney replied more controlled.

The sailor girl appeared only eighteen or twenty and although cute and skin soaked like a wet rat, her sweater loose and hanging wet, draped and clung to her. Her hair was in a tangled mess of comical shape and she was seething angry. She started to get up and go at Whitney again but Wayne put a hand on her before she regained her balance and she almost fell back into the pool.

"Sit. Stay." It sounded like he was commanding his dog.

Whitney started to rise, "Good, keep her ..."

"You too." He put a hand on her as well and she half-fell/lay down on his other side. He had them both at his feet. Together they didn't weigh as much as he did. And soaking wet they were constricted by their tight jeans and clinging clothing. They glared at each other.

The sailor said. "So, what the fuck is this? A stick-up? You'll both be sorry when my guys get here."

"Oh yeah, like you have 'guys'. Right. I could have taken her Wayne. You should have let me alone." Whitney threw at him.

"When they find out what you've done to me you're both gonna' get it ..."

"Kick her Wayne."

"Shut up. Both of you," he scolded.

The last of the sun dipped its warm yellow happy face below the horizon and his glowing fatherly face was the last clear view the girls had of that day. They soon started shivering.

"Look, I ... we ... she tried to take your boat on her own. Get it? This is not a stick-up. We are not 'together'," Wayne tried to explain.

Whitney whined at him, "We're not? I should have known. The way you left me. You don't care about me any more than any of the others. Well, fuck you too Wayne Nickel. Sleeping with you was a big mistake."

The sailor threatened. "Let me go now and we won't kill you. Just walk away, both of you. Don't say anything more, just leave me and my boat alone and you will live. Otherwise ..." She made a gesture of drawing her finger across her throat. She looked at Whitney as she did it.

"Piss on her Wayne. Come on, we have the boat. All we have to do is sail away. What's she going to do? Huh? What are you going to do bitch?" Whitney started to get up again.

"Sit!" Wayne yelled. "Shut up both of you!"

The low swell washed the rocky shore with a shushing sound as the light of the day waned and the world became a monochrome black and white before the darkness of night.

He reached down and grabbed the sailor by the scruff of her neck. She was shivering quite violently by now and he led her to the small inflatable.

Whitney rolled over, crawled to her feet and followed them.

"Get in. We're going aboard." They shoved the dinghy to the water and with careful dancing, the three of them balanced inside and rowed to the bobbing sailboat.

They were at the limit of the tiny tender's capacity and a few times the cold Pacific sloshed over the collapsing rubber sides to soak their feet thoroughly before they made the side of the mothership. They clambered aboard and huddled in the cockpit. Wayne put his beefy hand on the sailor-girl's shoulder when she tried to lead the way inside and went below first. The two shivering and teeth chattering females sat in the cockpit and glowered at one another while he inspected the cabin. He waved from the dark cave of the cabin and they gratefully found their way below. By now they were shivering so violently that they shook like neurotic puppies.

The cold breeze and chilly dark early evening gave way to the calm warm feeling interior.

"Light." Wayne said.

Sailor-girl's quivering fingers found the matches and lit a small kerosene lamp.

"We don't light often." She huddled around the tiny lamp for a meager ration of heat. Whitney joined her and they begrudgingly shared the miniscule amount of heat the lamp gave off.

"There is a heater," she said.

"Light it," Wayne commanded.

Sailor-girl worked at an ancient looking polished brass affair hung on a bulkhead forward. She pumped and lit and coaxed the thing to life. In a few moments a tiny wave of warmth radiated out into the cabin.

Wayne sat on the engine cover at the main hatch. He closed the main companionway hatch and door behind him. The inside of the sailboat was now a cozy glowing refuge of warmth in a world of biting cold harsh reality. The soothing plip-plopping sound of water against the hull melded with the creaking of the anchor-line and the clacking sounds of rustling rigging as the cold awfulness of the outside world was held at bay.

"You have dry clothes?" Wayne asked of sailor-girl.

"Yeah." She turned to go forward.

"Hold it!" He barked. "Tell Whitney, where." He nodded at Whitney and she shook her head 'yes' in between her still shaking hypothermic shiverings.

"My stuff is forward, to the right, the big red bag …" Sailor-girl looked after Whitney rummaging in the dark. "In the overhead … up high, higher …"

Whitney dragged out a bright red sail bag. Sailor-girl dove into it and pulled out dry clothes.

"Change out." Wayne told them. "Where I can see you."

Sailor-girl gave him a nasty look.

"Don't worry, I have a daughter."

"Yeah, right." Sailor-girl scoffed.

"He doesn't care. Really." Whitney confirmed. They exchanged glances of feminine camaraderie and stripped their wet things off.

"Wring 'em out. Hang 'em by the heater." Wayne advised.

The girls pulled their tight wet clinging things off and swapped them out for clammy, yet dry clothes from the big red bag.

"What's your name?" v asked of the sailor-girl.

She was peeling her jeans off and in the middle of what she considered the most sensitive portion of the procedure.

"Kristen," she said.

"Undies too, young lady. Get dry. I don't want any one to get a chill over this. I won't look. I promise."

She pinched her face as she blushed. She had a dilemma for a moment about whether to face him or turn her behind as she changed.

It didn't matter. It was all in her head. Wayne had a wife he loved, a daughter in college, and was truly more concerned about her health than the look of her bum.

She flushed a bit and finished fishing out new and dry undies from the bag.

The young women finished the procedure and their wet things were strung in front of the little kerosene stove when bumping sounds from outside resounded through the hull.

"You're going to get it now," Kristen said, "the boys are home."

Whitney's eyes got huge and she cowered in the pilot berth as her emotions took over and survival mode kicked in, but this time she was trapped, no where to go. She looked about to burst into tears.

Muffled talking from outside filtered into the space. Wayne moved to the side and freed up the entryway. He sat calmly and waited for the 'boys' to come home from their day.

Kristen rushed to the companionway, opened the door and scurried out.

"What the hell bitch? You got the lights on and what …?"

"Pirates Casey, I swear, they attacked me. When I got water, I couldn't …"

"Shhh, quiet down please." A young man's voice said calmly. There was whispered talking topside that neither Wayne, nor Whitney, could hear clearly.

After a moment two long, black, neoprene covered legs snaked their way into the cabin as a tall thin young sailor flowed into his familiar space. He sat on the engine cover in the entryway.

He looked like a Greek god in his black wetsuit. His tawny, wild, flowing hair stuck out at crazy angles as if permanently wind sculpted. The wetsuit clung to his full beefy chest muscles and his rippled six-pack abdominals.

He glanced at Whitney cowering on the settee and then fixed on the old guy sitting in the starboard berth. The scruffy old man was wearing rough worn canvas construction clothes. She, was surprisingly, wearing Kristen's dressy clothes. He saw and smelled the drying laundry and felt the scared and intruding vibe the two interlopers exuded. These two weren't threatening in any way other than being inside his house where they didn't belong.

Wayne liked the look of the young man right away. He was strong and handsome and after the long windswept day his cheeks were pink and his blood was up. He was at the peak of manhood, in his element, and in complete control. Wayne could relate. Wayne leaned back and relaxed. The worst was he would be thrown overboard and be delayed a bit more. He could swim the one hundred feet to shore.

Whitney was scared out of her wits. She was going through a whole series of concocted stories in her head that she could try and tell to get out of the predicament she was in. She had tried to steal their stuff, she attacked Kristen and she would pay for this, no matter what she said.

"Kris, get in here." The young Captain said over his shoulder. In a moment sailor-girl, Kristen, slithered past him in the narrow companionway and stood inside the cramped space.

Thumping and scuffling on deck told of other crew working at getting their gear stored. Wayne was pretty outnumbered here. Her guys were a reality.

Whitney was about to jump out of her skin. She was sure she was doomed. Her hopeful thought was that the other crew on deck were all men and that this Kristen bitch was the only competition she had to contend with. Maybe she could find an in with her womanly wiles. At least she was on the water, she could use her nautical skills to advantage. Use what you have.

"So just what the hell happened here? I leave you with a simple task and I come home to a boat full of hitch-hikers?"

"I was getting the water Casey, and this bitch here, tried to steal the dinghy. I fought her off, but then this goon came and beat me up. I couldn't beat them both and they …"

"Did you scope the shore?" Casey looked her in the face.

She looked away, "It was late. The wind …"

"You didn't scope did you?"

"I did everything Casey. Honest." Kristen pleaded with the young man. "They jumped me. It was a trap."

"OK. Go help put away the gear." He glared at her.

"It's not my fault …"

"Go." He commanded.

She dropped her eyes and squeezed by him and went topside.

Captain Casey sat and stared at the visitors. He turned and pierced the woman with his passionate blue eyes. "Did you try to steal our boat?"

Whitney was disarmed by this gorgeous sun kissed guy. "I didn't know it was yours, and I thought that …" she trailed off.

He didn't move a muscle.

She stopped her plea. "Yes," she replied.

He turned and looked at Wayne, who met his gaze, "Did you beat up my crewman?"

"I did not. I stopped the fight," Wayne replied.

The boat rocked with the weight of the crew on deck moving around as they stowed their gear and the evening swell lifted and dropped the bow in regular cadence. The slight corkscrew motion and close quarters worked on Wayne and he swallowed his salty queasy discomfort. Thumping and clattering of topside rigging echoed loudly inside the confines of the vessel.

Casey sighed deeply. He opened a cupboard at his elbow and looked inside. "Kris!" he yelled.

"Yes Casey?" She appeared above his shoulder. "Did you finish the water?"

"No, Casey, they jumped me … and …"

"All right. All right. You and Rob go ashore and finish."

"Now?" She asked.

"Yes, now. Get moving." Casey snapped.

"What about Oliver? Is he coming …"

"Now!" He barked at her.

She turned and went.

"My dilemma is what do I do with you? Pirates we hang," he said, "thieves we cut off their hand." He looked at Whitney and she pulled her hands in tight.

"Do you know about the border?" Wayne asked.

Casey just stared at him stone-faced.

"I live near Sentimental. My family is there. I'm just trying to get home. I don't want to cause you any trouble or take your boat or anything like that. I just want a ride past the border."

"Why should I give you a ride?" Casey asked. "What's in it for me?"

"I don't have any money or anything, but what I carry. I've got stuff, a house full of stuff. I could go get it when we get there."

Casey laughed. "Really? I give you a ride past the border and you go get stuff for me. Funny. Like a loan ride or something?"

"Something like that." Wayne realized it sounded pretty lame.

"I can get stuff. How about diesel engines? You know how to make them run?" Casey was clearly trying to make something out of nothing with the scruffy old guy from the shore. He could have them both tossed over the side in a heartbeat. In this new world there were deals that had to be teased out of every situation. Opportunity was in every strange encounter. Some paid off well and others returned only the slimmest of reward, like escaping alive. Maybe this guy could help.

"I have a pretty good working knowledge of them. Why? You need a mechanic?" Wayne asked.

"He can do anything." Whitney added hopefully. "I've seen him. He knows his stuff." She lied.

Casey focused on her. "And what do you have to offer for her ride?"

"Oh, she's not really with me. I mean, we're not together … per-se," Wayne said.

"You're not together?" Casey looked back and forth.

"I just met her. Like I said, I tried to stop the fight." Wayne said. Whitney looked down at the teak floorboards.

Casey started to chuckle. "So you just happened to see two girls fighting on the beach and you decided to stop them. Chivalry is not dead, I guess."

"I guess not," Wayne agreed.

"And you brought them both here to my boat to … what?" Casey wanted to know.

"He made us strip." Whitney barely whispered.

"I can see that." Casey said. "You're wearing Kristen's nice things. Even she never wears them. She's saving them, and now a pirate is wearing them. So who made who do what?" Casey prodded at the edge of Whitney's veracity.

A gruff looking and very hairy surfer-dude finished stripping off his wet-suit in the cockpit and tapped Casey. "They're coming back," he said.

"OK, Brandon."

The surfer-dude bent, stared straight at Whitney, and whispered in Casey's ear. Casey's eyebrows raised and he glanced at Whitney and nodded. Brandon stood up and left to tend to the returning water taxi.

Whitney put on a slightly more hopeful look. If these guys are lonely with only that Kristen girl for company she could make a place for herself here. Although hairy as an ape, that Brandon guy was a hunk. Underneath all that fur she could tell he was built like a truck. Although she preferred women she could charm a guy to save her life. She might get out of this after all. Or get into it deeply.

The dinghy bumped against the hull and muffled voices combined with the sound of the water jugs clattering onto the deck.

"Don't move, and don't touch anything. I'll be right back." Casey commanded.

Wayne looked sideways at Whitney. She was as malleable as soft clay. She flowed in and out of truth and lies effortlessly and would form herself into any situation easily. She was quite a manipulative artist. She was a true survivor.

Whitney had found a small hand mirror and was checking her face.

Wayne could almost hear the gears in her head whirring.

Casey re-entered sans wet-suit. He was more impressive in only short pants. The man was lean. He was chiseled. His skin was taut and glowing. "Here's the deal. You help us get this engine going and we run you past the border," he addressed Wayne.

"What makes you think it will work, I mean, the power is out. The world quit working, or, hadn't you noticed?" Wayne smirked a little.

"Yeah, I noticed, but I heard that diesels can run though."

"Who told you that?" Wayne asked.

"Can you get it going or not?"

"I know how, but it kind of depends."

"Depends? On what?" Casey asked.

"Depends on whether that engine has been run and whether there is any juice in your batteries. Depends on whether there is fuel. Depends on whether you got a crank. Depends on … a lot of things."

"You get it going. We take you north."

"And if I don't?"

"We put you ashore here. Byby." Casey made a little wave.

"Nothing ventured, nothing gained." Wayne shrugged and smiled. "What about her?"

"You're not together. Remember?" Casey pointed out.

"I still care what happens to her."

"We have another offer for her. Nothing to concern yourself with."

"I see." Wayne closed his mouth.

"You, pirate," Casey directed at Whitney, "out."

She went on deck leaving the men below.

Casey turned and flipped some hidden latches and uncovered the small two cylinder diesel engine he was sitting on. They moved the cowling aside.

"We got fuel. The heater is diesel and the sight-tube shows it's got plenty," Casey pointed. "It must have run recently because the engine log said he went on some short trip last month." Casey fished a small log-book from a cubby-hole and fingered to the page he referenced.

Wayne nodded and asked. "Crank, have you got the crank?"

"Uh, crank. What does it look like?" Casey wondered.

"This isn't your boat is it?" Wayne asked.

"Uh … well, it is now. But, no."

"You don't know anything at all about this thing do you?" Wayne accused.

"Not really. I never ran a diesel before. I'm a wind-surfer, not a sailboat mechanic."

"I see. Most of these small motors have a hand crank that we can turn it over with. See, here is where it fits." Wayne pointed to the nut protruding from front of the engine case. "If we have the crank we might get it going. Do the batteries have any juice?"

"I've tried and it won't turn over, man."

"Not to turn it over, to heat the glow plugs."

"The what?"

The hairy guy stuck his head into the hatch. "We have to make way Casey. The wind is backing on us. We gotta' go."

"Allright, Brandon. Let's get this back together. You can make it go while we're under way." When they put the engine cover back on, Wayne spied the hand crank clipped inside.

"Here it is," he said. "I'll check out the systems and in a bit we'll try it out."

"I gotta' make sail. Do what you have to. Just get it going or you're going to have a long swim back."

The two girls and a third fellow, older, bearded, and thin as a rail came below. Wayne and Whitney sat aside as the skinny little fellow donned clothes and Kristen stowed gear. She attended to the thirty-something man closely, helping him with his clothing and handing him his deck shoes.

"Thanks doll."

"I missed you baby." Kristen said.

He gave her a big fat kiss.

"Where is Oliver? Did something happen?"

"He was …" he struggled to tell her, "I don't know. He got taken."

"Taken?" She wrinkled her brow. "By the Sheriff? What?"

"No, in the water. We were sailing back and he just … got taken."

"A great white!?"

"It wasn't a shark, it was … we all saw it, right in front of us. It was some kind of big jellyfish squid thing. I don't know. It was weird."

"So, he's dead?" Kristen's chin quivered a little.

"He got taken, OK? Board sail and all, a big tentacle and these jelly things swarmed him and well he vanished and we sailed away as fast as we could." Rob was visibly upset by having to relate the sea monster story.

The two hugged and she caressed his anguish away. "It's all, alright now, baby. You're safe now."

He sniffed a wet nose and blinked back tears. "I know, everything'll work out."

"I hate it when you go ashore without me. It's so dangerous and look at what I have to deal with." She gestured at the disheveled land-girl, Whitney, and raised her eyebrow dramatically.

Thumping on deck and an uneven whirring sound from forward told him they were pulling anchor.

"Bilbo, get your ass up here and lend a hand," sounded from above. He gave her a parting squeeze and fled topside.

Kristen sat with her back to the bulkhead and eyed her two intruders. "Now you're in the soup." She smiled enigmatically.

The boat's motion changed as the anchor broke loose and they floated free. Whitney looked up at the overhead as strange clattering and rubbing sounds came from the deckhands setting sail. In only a moment the cabin lurched to port and Whitney leaned back. The cabin appeared the same, but it tilted until all the little things on shelves and in cupboards slid to rest against their holding door or railing. A whole symphony of sounds clicked and clacked all around them as the boat heeled over and soon a whooshing sound pulsed up through the hull. They were sailing.

Wayne was duly alarmed at the attitude change of his body in the small cabin. He held one hand on a center post to keep from being thrown across the tiny space into Whitney's lap.

Kristen nonchalantly pulled out a journal and began noting their departure. She moved around the cabin and noted certain compass headings and tapped on a barometer for its reading.

Wayne controlled his queasy stomach and removed the engine cover. He busied himself to pay for his ride home. He was on his way to see his wife and teenage son, Dave. They had been alone for weeks and Wayne was very worried about their well-being.

He had to get home and protect them.

24

Baroness

A.Q Year Thirty

"Why didn't you kill her?" asked the dark eyed pixy faced girl.

"Because, she was ... cool." The old man answered.

Amber looked sideways at the old coot. She couldn't swallow the reason. "Since the woman was a part of the problem, then there was reason to dispose of her." That made sense to the survivalist girl.

The old guy wheezed a little as he tried to formulate an explanation as to why he hadn't ended the bitch when he had the chance.

The bitch was part of the Sheriff's department and led the posse to forcibly take property. She rode with the most heinous of criminals and was, therefore a part of the greatest massacre in known memory. Yes. All of those things.

Yet Sam hedged. "I held her in reverence. She helped me in my lowest moment."

The bitch Baroness had stooped to his low and filthy level to make his lot better. She found reason to do so. She had no incentive to give him water. She was a prisoner, as was he, but had no compunction about risking her precious resources to better him. He had done nothing to merit kind treatment. Yet, she had done so.

"Gawd, Sam! You let her go! She allied with the Baron and betrayed you. She hung you out to dry." Amber, the usually sullen girl, blurted out her exasperation at the old man's reticence. "I mean really, dude," she used the ancient fellow's slang against him, "you barely knew her and yet, you helped set her up. Man. What a douche." She wagged the black swath of hair that hung over her eyes.

Sam shrank into his bed covers a bit. Most of him disappeared beneath the layers, chastised. The young girl was right. He had set up Sally, to take over. He had saved a monster.

"How was I to know she and the Baron would hit it off? She was a prisoner like me, I was just trying to repay her a little for her kindness."

"Well, you repaid her all right. That's the first time you ever told us that the Baroness ever did a good thing in her life. I mean as far as the stories go, she's the wicked witch of west county." Amber threw at him.

The old man looked through his bleary eyes at the stern teenager who challenged him. He tried to think of a comeback, so as not to put her off. He wanted to pass on wisdom that he had acquired over the years. He did not want to drive her away. He wanted her to listen to him.

"Amber, listen. It was a brief moment in our lives." He waited for the grown up looking youngster to see him.

"Yeah, so?" Amber's piercing eyes peered from under her long bangs.

"I was captured, she was captured, and we found each other, in a pit. Oh, crap you'll never understand." Sam sank further into the bed. His mind slipped sideways into thoughts far from the topic.

Sam felt the cloth in his fingers and luxuriated in it. The old style sheets that surrounded him were the last of ancient and long gone technology. No one had produced a two-hundred strand per inch sheet for decades. Yet, Old Sam had been humored by his tribe and was bedded in the best cloth from the past that their scavenging in the old buildings could provide. Unused cloth from tumbledown ruins had found its way onto his bed. Those who tended the old man were respectful and found things to foster a lifestyle that comforted him, no matter how antiquated or precious.

The remains of the tribe had all watched the old man shrivel into nothingness. Sam was the 'Old Sam'; the one. He was the one who told all about what was, the one who told how to go forward, and the one who knew what had passed and might be again.

Amber now saw him for what he had become; a dying old man with nothing but stories about a long dead world. Did this burnt-out creature really have anything for them? The world was completely different now. What did he have to tell that would make any difference at all?

Amber was alone with him. It was late morning and the elders and hunters had gone out for the day. Their scavenging and foraging took first priority and watching the old fart who was going to die any minute was last on the village's list of priorities. Amber drew the short straw and was relegated to watching the nasty smelling fellow.

She couldn't help but argue with the guy. She was in a foul mood from not being able to go on the hunt and took it out on the old man. It was totally boring to sit and wait for him to die. She prodded him for some interesting story or tale to pass the time.

Sam had acquiesced. He loved a captive audience. He felt it was important to let them know what he had been through. He vented his personal and internal story in order to get it all out there and hopefully pass a few wise tidbits on to his twice removed granddaughter. He was making legacy with his saga.

"So, why?" Amber insisted.

Sam peeked out from under the long unlaundered sheets, "I don't know. There's something that happens when you are in a bad place. Other folks can be good ... even when they're bad." It sounded wrong as soon as he uttered the words.

How could Sam explain the bond he formed with the woman in the pit who helped him clean the shit from his ass with her drinking water? How does one convey the compassion that is bestowed out of a sense of mere decency in a gesture of humanity? It was a concept that was lost on a youth whose entire existence was based on 'get to it and take it before someone else does'. Sam groped for the right words to help her understand empathy.

The youth understood 'get back' something for what you give. Giving for no guaranteed return or for no deal at all was an alien concept for the lass.

"We went from the pit to a tribunal, and then into leadership. It was crazy. One minute we were about to be burned at the stake and the next we were leading teams of men to get shoes." Sam paused and looked hopefully from under his sheets.

She sat quietly, her head slightly down, her dark eyes glaring up through her bangs, fixed on the old man. The look was accusing.

"You see, the only thing I had was shoes ... get it? Shoes?" Sam poked his foot out from under the covers as an exhibit.

She didn't look at the ugly appendage.

"See, there were no more shoes. The Chinese, they made all the shoes and we didn't. And, well, I knew where there were lots and the Baron didn't. He needed them. Get it?"

She pressed her lips tighter. "So." Amber stared at him. "What about her? Was she or was she not a bad person? Wasn't she Sheriff?"

"Yeah, she was part of the Sheriffs department and yeah, they killed all the city people, well, they didn't kill 'em all, they started a fight with them, well they didn't start it, but … there was this big fight, see? And well, after the city people went to Saint Rose they were a threat to the Baron, see?" Sam poked his head further from the sheets and took on a supercilious grin as he nodded.

"Well, she was …" words failed Old Sam. The woman he was trying to describe to this kid, thirty years removed, was a mish-mash of conflicting descriptions. On the one hand she was a conniving and manipulative siren who cut the throat of anyone who stood in her way. On the other hand, Sally was the unwitting victim of unforeseeable circumstances who rose to the occasion in order to get through the darkest of days as best she could.

Sally Reynolds, had proven herself to be a versatile and flexible creature. She had risen to the top when Sheriff Coldman commanded her to direct the livestock confiscations. She didn't bat an eye at the taking of citizens' livestock for the good of the whole. Her position as consultant evolved into commander of the deputies. She filled the mold as expediter for council edicts with a passion. She was the golden child of the militaristic renaissance fostered by the collapse of the electric grid.

Before the quiet, she was a nobody.

She became a force to be reckoned with. The council expressed their whims and she fulfilled them. The amount of power she wielded was awesome.

She didn't know that. She didn't see it. To her, she was only doing the 'right thing' and 'helping out'. From the other side of the spectrum she was the Nazi Queen who could destroy on a whim, or save with a gesture.

Sally and her trusty steed Garnet rode into and overcame innumerable obstacles. They took what was needed for the community to survive. When the council proposed, she and the

Sheriff disposed. The execution of orders were more often that not, at her direct behest. When cattle and livestock were herded away from their homes to less desirable pasture under the Sheriff, Sally was the image embossed on peoples' minds.

Sheriff Coldman sat hidden inside his tower-bunker at the airfield while Sally brazenly showed her face to the ranchers of the county. She was the one responsible. She was the one who held the papers. She was the one who spoke words of kindness and reason whilst their livelihoods were publicly rustled from them. The papers meant nothing to the ranchers. It was the image of a smiling, and oh so reasonable sounding Sally, that persisted. Sally, the taker. Sally, the woman who held in check a small army of gun wielding fascists. Don't cross the woman, or else. She took cattle and sheep and horses and pretty much everything else.

Sally was oblivious to the enmity felt about her. She was entirely clueless regarding peoples' hatred for her. She didn't give them a second thought. Sally had been steeped in the bureaucratic stew for so many years that it was business as usual for her. She ended each day with a smile and a feeling that she had done her level best to fulfill everyone's needs. Buying into the bureaucratic mind-set alleviated her conscience. She slept well.

Sam didn't think that she fully understood her power before her time with the Baron. Once she got the Baron's eye though, she changed.

Sam couldn't put all of this into words for the girl in front of him. He knew what Sally went through and where she had ended up, but to try and bestow that to the girl was beyond him. Sam was old and tired. He didn't want to have to justify the insanity of the past.

His mind wandered from the vile story and filled with joyful fantasy. He wanted tasty food to suffuse his senses and he dreamt of having naked young girls in his bed. He imagined soft nubile things and how they would make him hard and pleasure him to ecstasy. Sam pictured the beautiful dark-haired morsel in front of him there. He wished the lovely young thing would miraculously find him attractive and enjoy him as much as Paris did.

Paris was his companion, like it or not. She had stayed with him through thick and thin. She was the one who ended in his bed. Sam acquiesced to her late night naked invasions and pleasured the old girl's treat. She worked him up and gave him relief. Paris knew how to please a man. When she wanted him to stroke her to climax she tempted him with prolonged prick-tease and after he had gotten her to joy, she finished him. She treated his cock as a temple to be worshipped while the young could barely tolerate his presence, much less fulfill his fantasies about them enjoying him. Paris got what she needed from him and he from her.

Sam drooled a little at the thought of Amber. His mind undressed her and explored her nubile body. It would never be.

Amber stared at the old coot and saw that his mind was working hard on some puzzle.

He kneaded his hands and licked his lips as he thought.

"Sam. What are you thinking?" She demanded.

He blurted, "Sally was a great woman. She helped more than she ever hurt. But, when she had a job, that was her priority." Sam said with finality.

Amber looked at the old man and tilted her head to the side a bit. "Really, Sam? You can't kid a kidder. Just tell me what happened after the shoes. What about the evil dark Baroness who ate the hearts of children." Amber sat stiff in the chair next to the redwood carved bed. Her buckskins squeaked when she shifted in the polished hardwood chair. Her thigh exposed in a flashing sliver as she shifted her weight and her bare knee protruded from the leather skirts.

Sam felt exposed. He couldn't just gloss over history and let Sally die. He had to tell this gorgeous young brunette the story. She was forcing him to perpetuate Sally's memory into the future, into the girl's story. He had to tell her story and in doing so he would dredge up his own forgotten past.

The old man began again. "Baron John was angry when we showed up. There was no good news. Things had gone from bad to worse." Sam emerged from his bed-nest a bit, but hung his head as he told the story.

"The massacre had happened you see; the Baron was appalled. There were thousands who died ... he didn't know what to do."

Amber stared at the old man.

He was staring into the bedclothes.

She thought it ludicrous that the Baron might be appalled at death.

"See, the fire drove them into the guns and the Sheriff's guys didn't know how to react and ..." Sam was trying to voice the horror of a history that people didn't talk about. The disaster of the city folk trying to come north and the county's efforts to repel them had collapsed into a slaughter instead of a persuasive effort to send them to more fertile land. It was an enormous failure. Here he was trying to justify it, for Sally's sake.

"See, the county council got the Coast Guard to enforce a border, of dubious demarcation, in order to ensure proper accommodation." He glanced at her.

Her face twisted into a question mark. He was using big words.

"The county could not enjoy all comers. The border," Sam made quotes marks in the air, "was being overrun with tens of thousands of hungry people."

The girl hadn't a clue what tens of thousands meant, but she understood hunger.

"They spilled into the farms at the edge of town, and when they found them empty, they marched, like army ants, into Saint Rose itself. The town knew they were coming. Word spread fast. Folks fled. It was an invasion. All them people at the edge of town who stood their ground were run-over. Nothing stopped 'em, they were really pissed off. They were mad about the unwelcome they got at the end of a gun. A bunch had weapons from the coast guard."

Amber was listening to him now. She understood pissed off people holding their ground to survive.

"The zealots rained lead on the first few holdouts trying to defend their houses. When they got into town, crowds filled the streets, fleeing. There were thousands of city folk driving them. At least, that's what I heard. We bugged out too. The other way."

—

The bug-out was a chaotic affair. Piles of goods and half prepared food stuffs were hurriedly crammed into any and all conveyances that the Shire could muster.

Brownsville, the motor pool and fabrication shop, run by Lord Jack Brown, a fire plug shaped man with a flat topped skull, mobilized their moving stock: dump trucks and front-end dirt loaders and tanker trucks and a few tractors pulling strings of hay wagons like trains, snaked out and through the hilltop mansion forts where they were loaded up with just, everything. The entire Shire pulled together and fled their new communal homes on the hilltops. They liked the mansions they had commandeered and were now abandoning them.

The first part of the journey was to skedaddle down a state park back road. The county had encouraged a deal to purchase a huge piece of property from a timber company and turn it into a park. The idea was good, but the park part never really materialized and the property remained undeveloped. There was a good dirt road that cut through tough back country of the west county on this property. It was the only way to access the north coast without traveling on either of the two main roads. Maple Creek road crossed the largest parcel of undeveloped land in West County south of the Rushing River. This was their back door.

Heavy steel pipe state park department gates were sprung and re-closed after the passage of the convoys. The slow moving get-away rumbled at a walking pace down from the high ridges to meander around the tortuous terrain to the sea. A rally point near the bottom of the first big hill filled a meadow with the machines and encampment.

Late in the afternoon the box truck pushed by the women's auxiliary and hospital came bumping down the road and rumbled silently to the edge of the camp by the creek. The seventy-five women accompanied their truck and came straggling in. The down slope let the truck roll on its own and the footsore women gladly let the thing roll as far as it would.

Lois, the driver, muscled the steering down the pot-hole filled track. She was in a state of frantic action trying to keep the thing from the ditches and missing trees. She pumped the brakes and ham-handed the steering wheel until she was near exhaustion. She asked to drive because she was small and weighed very little and her reward was that she got the hell beat out of her as the old truck jounced down the rough logging trail.

Sally had grabbed a handhold and swung up into the open box as the thing rolled by, and so she rode most of the last down the hill. She had time to rummage through some of the collected clothes before enough other women arrived to push the thing again. She found some fun things that she stowed in her sack. Sally hopped out and they leaned into the heaving-pipes and rocked the box-truck until it splashed through the creek and with a final cheer the women swarmed and kept its momentum going, up the opposite bank and into the meadow encampment.

It was all so anticlimactic. There was no sound other than the huffing and groaning of women insisting they were good enough to carry their own load. The engineless truck found its place at the edge of the other machines and camp was made.

They weren't finished with their day. Fires were started, a couple of steers slaughtered and the evening meal got underway. Boxes of potatoes and other leftover vegetables and soon to perish food appeared. When cavalry horsemen arrived from their rear action patrols, the feast ensued.

The sun fell behind the heavily forested hilltop that loomed above the deep cut of the valley. The cattle were driven ahead and the machinery in a ring of the camp was the guard stockade. The majority of the Shire was camped in the meadow and only a few cowboys and cattle-kids were ahead and ranging to the next hopeful home.

Sally ladled a vege-meddly onto the plate for a lean young man. "Sorry, there's no bread."

He looked up and smiled a thank-you to her, "That's OK. Maybe when we get settled." He moved on down the line for his cut of beef.

Protein kept them going. These guys were up at dawn and rode all day long to fulfill the recon needs of the Shire. They didn't fight, they observed and ran. The Shire was not interested in confronting the hordes of hungry, nor the Sheriff's men, they were only interested in avoiding conflict and surviving.

Sally admired the tough fellows, with their hard leather chaps and smell of horses and the trail mixed with their natural workingman odor. It was the deputy corps all over again. Sally liked men. Men had been a bane and the joy of her life, and she found them impressive. Whether she was on the positive or negative receiving end of them, they were a challenge. She desired to be in their company. It wasn't rational, but it sustained her and had, on occasion, ruined her.

She found satisfaction in feeding these men and they found her joy in service a loyalty. Sally wasn't 'Glamour Girl' pretty, nor overly endowed in any way, but men liked her. She exuded a genuine liking for them and their needs and they responded. It was all quite subtle, but heartfelt none the less.

The cadre of women ranged from the pale white with age to red-cheeked toddlers running around camp naked . Teenagers and young girls did most of the toting and fetching at the direction of the older women. The younger girls had the energy to do the chores. The older women knew what needed to be done with the least amount of waste. The girls needed confident overseers to give them the backbone that wasn't built-in by modern society, and the crones needed to feel that they knew something and were of value.

Many of these mature women had ended up alone, practicing new age and supposedly progressive thought, they had been left at the side by the mainstream. They had been left behind by the beautiful and perfect images of youth that dominated modern media. Young ingénues ended up as the paramours of older movie stars in romantic movies. Magazines were filled with the airbrushed images of creatures that were now, merely remnants of those once young beauties. They had become old. They had sagged and gotten thick and grayed and strange growths had appeared on their skin in the form of skin flaps and floppy arms and tits to their bellybuttons. Double chins sprouted when they weren't looking and bellies struck out over their pants. Their asses got wide in spite of their best intentions to keep from stuffing their faces with bread and ice cream. They couldn't help themselves. The only real joy they got out of their lives was to cram sugar and wheat and instantly gratifying garbage into their maws and their waistlines showed it. They were ready to leave modern society for the new world because they had lived lives that left them with no children or men or ability to motivate their heavy bodies to lives more meaningful than cat caretakers.

The younger girls were in a world of unknowns. They were texting and flitting from moment to moment and constantly able to connect with their friends and whatever community they thought they had and then ... they couldn't. Four of the teenage girls were backwoods hippy kids and didn't even have cell phones. They were the outcast weird girls in the old world and were now the ones who knew how to do the tough chores that needed doing. They were more attuned to being left in their heads and were comfortable in their own skin. The entire lack of electricity and disconnect didn't throw them. They were already there, they lived off the grid, they made their own music, they knew what they could do and they exuded a tangible confidence.

The four, two of them sisters, became leaders among the females by dint of their character. They fell into the lifestyle of gleaning fruit and gathering wood, right away.

The other modern girls spoke too often and too loudly. When they refused to follow the lead of the tough girls and balked at working so hard to accumulate a basket of walnuts, the older women chastised them right away and got them to get in line to do the work necessary. The girls had the energy to do the chores and in the Shire, no one lounged during the day. There was no 'survivor' TV show vote off the island here. Popularity based on beauty and your ability to fool others and lie wasn't the model. These were the real hunger games. Do your job well and you got to eat. Expect special treatment because you were cute and you found no shampoo for you and your hair got cut off to prevent lice. Do or die.

The lifestyle everyone was thrown into was dull, monotonous, slow moving, dark at night, and quiet. There wasn't any radio or i-tune or albums or cd's on the stereo to mollify their attention deficit disordered brains. People were left to their own thoughts. People thought they had been free thinkers and that they had thoughts of their own. They discovered that they hadn't. Practically everyone found themselves, at one time or the other, zoning out in fantasy daydreaming while humming some jingle or pop tune.

Media images that were, for years, repetitiously hammered into their brains rose to the surface: content thrown up on you-tube, stories and characters from programs that were fed to them through television and movies, and of course, songs sayings and ideas from commercial advertisements. Non-existent characters were their internal measure of behavioral normality.

Pro-actively motivating a community agenda forward was not what people were used to; at least not with people they didn't have history with, those who were now close around them. They had grown up in a society where other people did things and they watched them. Celebrities were the ones who had great ideas (even if they merely portrayed the ideas of writers) and were the leaders. Regular looking people weren't the ones who led the way. It was exceptionally photogenic people who knew what to do, not the unkempt homely looking ones.

If it weren't for the laborious demands of the daily chore schedule, their despair at being alone in their heads might have incapacitated them. Apparently it was work that was setting them free, at least during the day. While toting wood and hauling goods, or raking seeds to dry, or gathering fruit, the tasks kept their minds busy.

The night-time was different. After supper, when the sun set and camp settled into a brief respite from the day's work, they fell into old thought patterns, brought about by years of consuming provided content, the wheels turned silently inside, their minds started working to fill the quiet dark void. They thought of all the things that were no more. Silence allowed them to hear sounds in their heads. Night became the old bogeyman of the past. It was dark and scary out there. The walls of the forest closed in after the sun fell and it made people feel very small in a world that was a very big place. The faces of strangers in the firelight were the entirety of those who now mattered.

Joe Billsop, one of John's first Lords, quietly appeared at the main fire with a guitar in hand. His daughter Zoey, one of the tough hippy teenagers, arranged a heavy blanket so her old-man could lean against a log and play.

Joe rolled into soft strumming and soothing sounds rose up to join the crackle of the firewood.

An audible sigh rose at the joy of the familiar sound and smiles shared all around. The music was calming and uplifting. There had been little entertainment since the quiet came. There hadn't been time to sit and enjoy any cultural activity. There was too much work to be done, and by night-fall people crawled into their beds to hide from the dark cold quiet of their terrifying new world. The soft music, up to now, was all in their heads.

Joe instantly connected to their love of delightful sounds.

Brick, his grizzled beard accentuated the already hardened face, strode into the fire ring dragging a large chunk of wood. He dumped it into the fire and the crowd widened out as the blaze grew. More wood and more people grew the fire into a light that drew in the moths of the Shire.

This was the first time the whole group was in one place since the start. Faces loomed from the darkness, where they had retreated after a hearty supper, and the space around the blazing furnace grew.

They huddled under blankets together around the bonfire against the unusually early chill and crept as close to the heat and light as they could stand. The ring expanded and more guitars showed up to join in.

Beatles' songs became sing-along tunes and the community jelled. People found common ground in harmonizing the old tunes. The few songs that were simple enough and had memorable words that could be sung were from the sixties. It was the last era when there was universal acceptance of musical melodies that could be sung to. The youngsters followed as best they could and learned the words to 'Hey Jude', and 'Back in the USSR', the elders got loud as they remembered the words.

The singing voices of free people rang out over the still cold woods and drove fear away. It was warm and joyful and felt secure. They had no qualms about attracting attention, they were miles from the border hordes and had burned every house in their wake. No one was on their heels. The Shire-folk took their space back from the uncertainty of darkness and quiet. They gained power by merely singing old folk-rock songs together.

Baron Sir John's convoy of two box trucks and a large battle-rigged front end loader bumped and rumbled down the last long hill, splashed through Maple Creek and rolled to the edge of the camp. They were returning from an expedition for goods. They had fuel and the shoes.

John saw the bonfire from half-way up the valley. It was gratifying to have a light to guide him home. His nomads beckoned to him. For only an instant did he have misgivings about the light and its possibly advertising their position. He put those thoughts away. They had meticulously blocked the road behind with fallen timber. There wasn't an unblocked road for miles. Not even bicyclists made any time against the scores of fallen trees across roadways that the Shire left in their wake. John was confident they were the only ones moving that night.

His expeditionary force parked the ever-idling loader and secured the trucks in tow-ready positions for starting in the morning. Guards were posted on the machinery with assurances of relief and supper soon coming.

Half a dozen women jumped up from their spots at the cozy fire and ran to get hot food ready for their returning men.

Sally followed the teenager Zoey back to their station in the serving line to help.

Mark Young heaved his bulk up and strode his prodigious bulk from the comforting fire to welcome his Lord and men home.

John greeted Mark Young in a brief embrace and whispered the 'all clear' and they filed to the food line.

"It was good Mark. Just like our Sam said." John nodded as he briefed Mark openly. Sam was close at his heel, where he had been commanded to stay all day. John wanted him within reach. Sam wrinkled his brow and shrugged a smile.

Mark held out his plate for Sally's vege-goulash, "We are out of the forts. We found space for most everything and the livestock are ahead around the bend about a half mile. They'll move at dawn. We can delay a bit and let them get ahead before we mobilize camp."

"Excellent, my friend. I see the folks are feeling OK, nice of you to keep a light burning for us." John realized the woman facing him with the big spoon was the 'confiscator'. "Any trouble?" He asked, staring at her.

"Not a whit." Mark said.

John didn't move down the line and Sam, hungry and eager for his portion bumped against him. John looked Sally in the eye and asked again. "Any trouble?" He cocked an eyebrow.

In the flickering firelight he looked as sinister as the devil himself: road grime lined his face, his thinning curly hair stuck out in tiny horn-like points, his lowered chin and arched eyebrow twisted his apprehensive smile into a grimace.

Sally's eyes widened and she gulped a little trying to muster enough spit to talk. "No trouble ... my Lord."

John pulled his plate back slowly and nodded slightly. "Good, glad to hear it. Sam," John gestured him forward, "get your grub man, you deserve it." John stepped aside and Sam sheepishly held his plate to her.

Sally bowed her head in almost imperceptible obeisance. She ladled her medley of vegetable glop onto his plate. "Thanks," Sam said.

John turned back to Mark, who had watched the interaction with interest, and said. "The border's a mess. Those idiots started a friggin' war out there. We had to go almost all the way to Tamale-ville before we could cut back to the warehouse. How this Sam-guy," John gave him a glance, "ever got through when he did, was a miracle."

Mark wanted details. "So, were there as many as he said?"

"More, the place was a distribution facility for 'The Shoe Place', it was packed. We got more than we hoped for."

Mark beamed. This was good news indeed. "Fabulous. That'll be one of the more difficult things to replace. We'll use every one of them." He referred to the shoes.

"Hmmmm, I smell beef." John smiled.

Zoey, at the end of the board, held up a haunch of beef skewered on a pole, so Gladys, her elder mentor, could hack off a slab for their leader and his men. Joe's daughter Zoey was a nubile young teenage girl who hadn't yet fulfilled her role as a woman, but who had left childhood behind.

Sam was transfixed by the lithe form framed in the firelight. Zoey's hands were up above her head, holding one end of the six foot pole that spitted the roast. She stretched taut, almost on tip-toe, in a loose full length frock, surrounded by a heavy denim apron, grimy from food preparation, belted at her waist, it accentuated her blossoming figure. Her hair was imprisoned, hidden under a bonnet, very old timey-like. She was not in the least, a picture of femininity or glamour or anything that the modern world gone-by would consider as pretty or attractive.

Sam was smitten at the sight.

She stood fast and focused on the upheld meat the older woman hacked.

"Rare, or an end?" Gladys asked John and Mark.

"An end for me, I've had enough raw meat for awhile." John said.

"I'm going rare, Gladys. The only pity being, no bread to sop the juice." Mark veritably slobbered at the prospect of a hearty piece of meat. He had waited until everyone else was fed before he even considered eating. He had just about reached his level of patience when John's convoy arrived. Mark was past his suppertime and his girth wasn't happily tolerant of delayed fulfillment.

The older woman bent into her work, cutting slices from the slab of meat, Zoey watched intently. The girl learned all she could from her mentors. They surrounded her. There was so much going on, things were happening, people were doing things for one another and making do with little. Zoey was enthralled with the exciting action of the new world. It was real. Things were happening.

Zoey's formative years had been spent mostly in solitary instruction with her sister at home. Her father, Joe Billsop, home-schooled them, so their social interactions were limited. Joe's wife had died in child birth when her little sister came. Zoey had always looked to her father. Now she was ready and eager to join the women to do what they could for the community. When she jumped up from the campfire, two of her contemporaries huddled more tightly together and pulled the blanket up to hide their faces and thereby get by without helping. It was noticed by the crones. Pecking order was very important to the social structure and the gals would remember who helped and who didn't.

Lois hinted in a discreet whisper to the pert blonde girl at her elbow. "Why don't you go help Zoey?"

The teen put on a pitiful face of one put-upon, and said. "I don't wanna'." She thought better about it and added quickly. "I am so cold and we just got comfy." She whined a tiny bit.

Lois nodded and let it lie, for now.

Mark and John entered the fire light.

It quieted as they came close. One of Mark's assistants opened a canvas director's chair for his boss, the Seneschale, their administrator, plopped his fat ass down.

"Please, don't let me stop the fun, for crying out loud." John took a spot offered on a prominently placed log, "What was that I heard? 'Let it be'? One of my favorites. Let's sing! It's our forest we can make as much noise as we want and the neighbors won't complain. Haroooooooo!!" He howled at the frigid stars above while waving his fork in the air and beamed a huge toothy grin as he sat and dug in to his supper.

People around the fire laughed nervously at their leader. They knew him as a very serious man and no one except his personal guard had really spent much time with him. It wasn't well known that he had a great sense of humor and a passion for life that was, in the modern world, seen as just a rude loud guy.

Joe played, other guitars followed, logs were dumped on the blaze and the hundred and fifty Shire folk, minus the guards at post and the cow and goat herds sang. They sang at the heavens above. The clear stars looked down at the small group of creatures defying the darkness and quiet with raucous music. Some folk took up sticks and tap tapped drumming and percussion accompaniment. The mood lightened and the people became one and were glad.

Sam stood to the side and gobbled his plate of food.

Sally touched his elbow. He looked down at her and could tell she was happy. She was stranded here in the middle of the woods, no one her friend, having to play kitchen servant and yet, she seemed pleased with herself and her day's accomplishment. Her face was golden in the firelight. It wasn't the only light she had, she was beaming as she watched the good folk of her new community come together.

Sam was a little amazed that she showed little or no animosity and was joining in so fully with these weirdos. They were making a feudal world and happy to do so. It was antiquated, but it seemed to work. People wanted to be told what to do and where to go, otherwise they floundered around and scattered in all directions. It was, as he just discovered, gratifying to fulfill a Lord's wishes and be praised for it. It felt good to be an asset that mattered and be respected. He had worked years for people who, although they paid him, never really respected him or made him feel that he mattered. Their disdain for his ilk showed through their thin veneer of tolerance for working people who were stupid enough to be used up in the name of profit. John wasn't like that. He seemed genuinely loyal to his acceptance of Sam, the shoes not withstanding. Sam saw the egalitarian effort by the rulers of this strange society more as partners than as bosses.

Sally marveled at the scene. These people were uprooted, fleeing into an unknown future in the cold woods, and they were as happy as could be. There was no grousing about the difficulties, nor was there any doubt in their minds about following the man, John, who had just howled like a dog at the sky.

Who was this fellow leading them? He had appeared to her as both repugnant and attractive. He scared her and gave her heart. The people rallied to him and he followed their desires by leading them to a method for fulfillment of themselves. He was a nobody who rose to the occasion at the collapse of civilization, just as she had done, and found himself in a commanding position. He found a niche to be filled and stepped into the vacuum easily and without visible effort. He was propelled into it. She wondered how he accrued such a large group of friends so quickly. He must have had an entire society of militia minded survivalists already organized when the power-out occurred, a long-time leader of disgruntled back woods folk. It turned out she was way off-base on some of her assumptions.

After the terrifying moments at the court that decided her fate, she was guarded in her enquiries. She was a prisoner on parole. Sally thought long and hard about how to broach the subject of loyalty, in fleeting hopes that she might foment revolt and lead a freedom loving cadre of people back to the Sheriff and the praise of the county's officials.

The sweating, thirty something gal next to her in the slave-galley like rows of women trying to keep the truck rolling, seemed a perfect candidate for insurrection. So Sally stuck her neck out. She ventured an off-hand comment to the woman, as they struggled to push the heavy truck along the dirt road, "where do you think we're going with this thing?"

"You just never mind and push." The woman replied and bent her head down into the weight of the machine.

"Why didn't we just stay where we were?" Sally pushed.

The closely cropped brunette threw a glance up from her head-down toil at Sally, "John knows, he's ahead of the curve. You want to live? Get your head in the game. There's no going back, confiscator. Now heave!" She grunted as they leaned into the pipes that stuck out from the truck to force it over the rocks in the road.

'Get your head in the game,' she'd said. The words rang in Sally's ears. The game had changed so drastically in the last few weeks that she wasn't sure what the game was. It was unknown territory.

The campfire burned hot and the folk sang a few tunes.

John jumped up from his seat and ran off into the dark. He had a gleam in his eye and jogged away from the firelight with a hitch in his gait. A few moments later he returned with three hourglass shaped hand drums. He gave them to a couple of his men and soon there was a quite a hullabaloo of noise coming out of the camp.

John was, it seemed, quite an accomplished belly-dance drummer. He pitty-patted the thing into life.

The others followed and in only a nonce, a girl, probable fifty-five if she was a day, swished her flat-tire middle, cottage cheese thighs, and pendulous tits in cadence with the rhythms of the drum skins, around the fire. They thumpita-thumped middle eastern dance rhythms to the gyrations of the over-the-hill belly dancer.

People slapped their thighs, banged their sticks and strummed their guitars to make a noise. Faces, upturned in glowing joy and yellow orange flames of the primeval light, radiated gaiety and joy. They were making music from nothing and danced around the fire; it was ancient, it was spontaneous, it was wonderful.

Sally found her moment. She knew the rhythms from an almost forgotten hobby of belly dance classes, pre-Jazzercize. It was all the rage a few years back, before the middle east became a battlefield full of terrorists.

Sally darted to her sack and dug out the bits gleaned from the truck earlier. In a few moments she was half stripped and bedecked in a scarf around her top and a swishing skirt of alluring gauze-like material. She ululated a lilting and foreign hy-ly-ly-ly sound from the farthest realms of the planet and from a long forgotten past into the thumping male chorus of drums as she joined the music-filled space around the fire. Her lilting high-pitched trilling tongue added feminine rills to the deep masculine throom of hands on goatskin drumheads.

She couldn't help herself. She was taken back. Taken back into the far past of her youth, when she hung with hippies who drummed around firesides and danced at the slightest inclination. She loved the free form grace that rose to the surface, so long cemented over by the confines of proper and appropriate society at large. One just doesn't dance when one feels like it. In order to stay out of mental health, or police scrutiny, one suppresses the desire or the compunction to let loose. Peer pressure from perfect examples that media bombarded us with, inhibited everyone. If you weren't as good as the people on TV you shouldn't do it. It had all been poppycock. Everyone can and should dance whenever they felt the urge. Sally felt it. She hadn't danced in front of people for the sheer joy of it in decades. Here was her chance. She couldn't help herself.

She had to dance. Her feet knew where to go. Her hips felt the air around them where they belonged. She swayed and flowed into the rhythms and her body moved. The pounding of drums and sparks flying into the sky reminded her that there may not be a tomorrow and although today was tough, it was good reason to celebrate. They had escaped, and she was of them.

The dirt around the fire pit became dust as several women jumped to their feet, not to be outdone by the confiscator. They precessed around the flames in languorous hip swaying and thigh jouncing. These girls, in ancient wore out bodies, were the skinny gorgeous hippy chicks and go-go dancers of the past. They had gotten soft and fat in the world of largesse. They had, for too long, suppressed their joy of flaunting their sexuality through dance. Now they were uncovered. They flocked to the light and the deep hammering sounds surrounded them with acceptance by their community.

These rejuvenated crones became girls again and found themselves shimmy and shaking in the faces of the men. It was an unconscious tribute of obeisance and service that they paid to the men. They knew it pleased the fellows to have a dancing girl, regardless of age, shake her stuff for him. Only a few weeks before and none would have considered acting so brazenly towards men leering in the firelight. The times had changed. These men would kill for them, it was rumored. These men would die for them, some had. These men would do all the things that women could not, or would not do without serious trepidation. The women danced the pain and sweat and grime of the day away.

Around the camp fire, led by their Lord, a humble drummer who sat a simple log, eyes rolled into his head in a chanting trance and projected staccato rhythms with the caressing of drum-skins a humping-thump of a primitive beat by the light of a blaze, the women teased their long forgotten youth back to the here and now through joyous movement.

Golden orange flames lit the women from behind and licked at them as they shook and shimmied and stomped the dirt into dust and raised a cloud of primordial haze to mix with the combustion that pierced the night. They gathered, hooted and clapped and hollered and trilled and drummed anything they could get their hands on. The guitars clustered and wailed their strummed moaning strains and a kid whistled a high-pitched flute into the mix as the party worked itself into fervor.

Sally felt unlimbered. She felt freer than she had in years. Her body responded to the sound. Her desire to move and shake among those around her rose high. She cavorted and twitched her hips. The heat of the blaze forced her to keep moving and turning.

The vibration of the scene elicited a momentary coincidence of dancers. The other dancers swayed together for brief seconds and competition and cooperation came together for women, together, holding the fire-ring captive in their entrancing and whirling embrace.

Sally whirled around and glimpsed Zoey, the teenage meat holder from the kitchen, as she followed her example and was next in line. The girl emulated Sally, the confiscator, in dance.

Sally moderated slightly and repeated moves more often to allow the nubile youth to follow her. Very shortly the two of them were hip shaking, stepping together and writhing their arms in cadence. Sally smiled broadly and caught the girl's eye.

Zoey was game and they danced to the delight of all.

The line of women joined in the unspoken competition and they began to emulate one another in sashaying and swirling and jumping and cavorting around the consuming and eminently dangerous bonfire that licked at their feet. They flew and twirled about and raised their arms in swaying graceful arcs and swirls of accentuated symbolism only deciphered by emotion.

Sally danced, they followed, she fell into the joy of unconscious ability and found acceptance among the people of the Shire. She was the confiscator one minute, and the dancer the next. Her past was no longer in the fore, as so many other pasts were supplanted by new behavior in these times of the new world.

A crescendo of drum-thumping and the cacophonously uncoordinated noise that emanated as music from the lone ring of firelight in that meadow, many miles removed from any other, in the cold black expanse of thick forestland, echoed a final doom-doom-doom, as Baron Sir John, stood and with an exaggerated nod signaled them all to a climactic end.

Silence followed the sound as it rolled away, into the still woods.

A few moments passed, crackling fire and heavy breathing of dancers the only sounds, folk looked up from their drums and feet and strumming fingers to gaze into the eyes of their fellows in community and a roaring cheer filled their throats.

An accolade of joy and appreciation and gratitude and camaraderie echoed and bonded them to the moment.

They laughed and stood and stomped their sleepy legs awake and stretched their tired overworked backs and smiled and hugged and complimented one another and everyone congratulated everyone else for the wonderful few minutes of sheer uninhibited outpouring of unbridled energy that they created, shared, and immersed themselves in. They had pulled joy from thin air and bathed their senses in the fullness of the moment. No one directed it, there was no plan for it to occur, it was a completely spontaneous collection of talent and desire to do something together for no other reason than, it felt good.

The shire-folk were happy to be with themselves and getting over their reticence to dance in front of others, or play music, however unpracticed, or just howl at the sky. They worked, foraged, cooked, ate, washed their clothes, slept, fought, and watched each other's backs, together. Now they played and danced together. They were building family, a family of persons whom hadn't even met just a few days previous.

The night's activities forged a unique bond between the people. Toiling in kind was one association, sharing food and the old adage of breaking bread, even though there was no bread, was another connection, but making music and dancing with joyous abandon was a unique relationship that would bring a smile for years to come.

Mark, their administrator and back office planner, couldn't have orchestrated a better bonding exercise for the Shire. He tapped his toe, clapped his hands with the beat and ogled the women who gleefully pranced about in front of him. His mind worked on the event and the power it created in the people. He was already scheming about getting rugs for the dancers, making more drums and flutes, and singling out those who seemed to have enough knowledge to teach and foster the dance and music.

Damned if it wasn't that confiscator woman, who showed a. repertoire of practiced moves. The younger girls followed her moves right out of the gate. She was a natural leader.

Mark pondered how was he going to play her for the role. It would give her power in the group and he certainly didn't trust her. He had cautioned John about letting her live long enough to get to the open court, much less giving her amnesty. Mark had no less than ten different people scrutinizing her every move. He knew when she took a piss on the roadside. His people were coalescing nicely as a community, but she was finding popularity, and that was dangerous.

John rose and held his hands in the air. "Hello all," he called, everyone quieted and he continued, "that was wonderful, the first guard-shift is over so, sentries please report and relieve your comrades. Now, on to more serious business," John got a stern look on his face and lowered his head as if there were bad news to share. The crackling fire seemed loud in the expectant quiet. "It seems … we found a case of wine,"

"Really? You 'found' one?" Mark asked loudly interrupting John.

"Well it, uh, fell off of a truck …"

Many smiled and several laughed at the joke.

A cavalryman wearing tall boots set the case down and John pulled a bottle. He fumbled for a moment and then swore. "Oh, crap." He looked a little lost for a second then looked up sheepishly. "Anyone got a corkscrew?"

The crowd laughed heartily as someone handed him a Swiss army knife.

He uncorked it, took a swig and declared, "Subtle, with a hint of blackberries, a soupcon of poison oak and a smoky burnt tire after taste."

More laughter.

"We can sleep in a little tomorrow. Let's celebrate another day alive!"

The bottles went around as John took up his drum and started a slow and deliberate beat. Others joined and inadvertently tried to speed up the pace. He held his hand, palm down and kept them at the slower pace. He knew some fairly intricate mid-eastern rhythms and it became the first lesson as his guys, using his other two doumbek style belly dance drums mimicked his moves, and he taught them the strange mixture of deep doom-doom beats with higher pitched tekla-tek accents in between.

The slow unhurried tempo gave everyone a chance to reflect a little. The guitars found plenty of room to fill and the sound rounded out pleasantly.

Sally had stepped aside and readjusted her flimsy garb. She returned to the ring undulating a dance that was more interpretive and modern. She moved around the fire ring, seemingly unaware of any one else as she slipped into the mood and into her own world. She moved without hesitation; flowed smoothly around the fire as if choreographed. The music moved her and she let it. Her mind left their awful reality and she floated in the joy of her dance. She trailed a long strip of light veil-like material that streamed like liquid from her fingertips and peered through the tips of the orange flames to see Zoey on the opposite side, mimicking her.

The girl's bonnet was gone, her hair cascaded over her face and shoulders, down. The heavy work clothes shucked, she wore only a clinging and very short slip and pranced barefoot. She looked for all the world like a woodland sprite.

Sally pulled loose another veil, gave it to her, and they played with the light floating material, streamed it behind them, swirled it in loops and draped themselves suggestively. The women highlighted femininity: youthful, nubile, unsure, blossoming, alongside mature, practiced, fully-grown and experienced. The steady languorous beat was hypnotic and their sexually charged movements caused trails of glowing firelight to follow after their sinuous bodies as they circled wide-eyed faces.

The bottles were soon emptied. Magically, another couple of cases of wine appeared. Some folk had other bottles or flasks they were sipping from. A few folk stepped outside the ring and were smoking, some tobacco and some not. A quiet peace settled on the Shire folk as dancing women wove a spell of peace over the group and moved to the insistent throoming and clicking of the drums.

The evening wore on and more drumming ensued, with more dancing. The wine lubricated their society and inhibitions fell. The folk had a darned nice party.

Mark, always watching and scheming, slipped away and made his rounds. Without prompting, one of his ever present clerks fell in step behind and followed quietly and invisibly. Even the outer most sentries, who weren't found, but who surprised them in the dark, said all was calm except for occasional curious woodland critters wondering what the noise was all about.

The ever-idling front end loader chuff-chuffed at the end of the line of machines that outlined the perimeter of their circle. Mark had to work a bit to get the driver's attention. He was sealed inside the enclosed cab with ladder plates in place which prevent access to the operator's position. All Mark could get from the man was an OK hand-signal and a smile, he would not open up, even for Mark.

He walked down the road until he found Jorge and his gauchos watching over their wealth of livestock.

"Hola senor Mark." Jorge said as he led him to their awning lean-to. Two of Jorge's Hispanic cowboys lounged around a small fire. They looked startled to have one of the bosses show up. And put down their guitars guiltily.

"Evening Jorge. How are you boys doin' out here tonight?"

"Ebery ting ees goot, Senor Mark. La fiesta es grande, eh?" Jorge asked about the ruckus from the campfire.

"Yes, it is a good time at the old campfire tonight." Mark agreed.

"Well, there is a little vino there for you and your men when you get relieved. You boys go on up there and play them a little music, eh?" Mark smiled broadly. "They need some good music, all that amateur drumming got everyone all riled up and they need to calm down a bit."

The cowboys looked at one another sheepishly. One of their main leaders was encouraging them to play their guitars and join the group.

"Really?" Jorge asked with an American sounding twang. "Chew bon us to go play dere?" He pulled his Stetson and scratched his head.

"Of course. You boys need a break as much as anyone. Besides I think the folks'll like your music. It's honest and it aint' the Beatles. I mentioned it to Sir John and he's expecting you."

Jorge was flattered. "OK, Senor Mark. Eef chew say so."

"Yeah, Jorge, I do say so. Lot of folk don't know you boys and that's a good way to show 'em who you are. Whadda ya' say?"

Jorge rattled off a couple of phrases in Spanish and his guys nodded, smiled and chatted for a moment while making gestures out to the darkness. They had wanted to go to the party, but were stuck taking care of the cattle. This was a welcome invitation. They were separated from family and found good occupation doing what they loved, working with livestock; they were cowboys, mariachi cowboys. They were of the old world and made music when they could for entertainment. It seems they were discussing getting all the boys in to make music for the Shire.

"Si, senor, Mark. Mi compañeros want to do det. Tenk you."

"They'll love you guys, I know it. Anyway, we'll send relief soon, and you guys can get up there and kick-it a little. Eh?" Mark said. " I gotta get on with it. See you boys later." He waved and waddled off into the darkness with his unseen, dark robed, clerk following him closely.

All was well. Mark found his tiny teardrop trailer. At the door he said to his shadow. "Go tell John them Hispanic boys need relief right away and they gonna come play some good old fashioned mariachi for everyone."

The skinny helpmate said, "Yes Lord," and scurried off.

Mark crawled inside the tiny trailer. He congratulated himself on another successful day managing the Shire and soon fell into a fast sleep.

John watched Sally emerge from the crowd and take the dance ring. At first he didn't recognize that she was the confiscator, but when he finally did, he felt gratified she hadn't escaped to warn the Sheriff, and also pleased to see her dance. Apparently she was fitting in nicely.

Although a fully mature woman, she was trim and fit. The uniform khaki was gone and replaced with a simple band around her top and an ankle length, almost see through, skirt. She had slit the skirt and fixed it to her ankles like some diaphanous pantaloons. She swirled a veil gauze in hypnotic weaving in the air as she cavorted around the roaring bonfire. It was only a few moments and she was leading a troupe of dancers around the blaze.

Each time she danced by him, John had to force himself not to stare and gulp, or lose the beat. He took to closing his eyes so he could focus on his drumming. He was leading it mostly and they needed a clear rhythm to follow. This confiscator woman was the most distracting woman he had encountered in a good long while. She wound her spell of feminine moves around him and the Shire. Mark had left for the night and she came and sat in his seat, right at John's left elbow. John spent energy ignoring her. He felt a magnetic attraction to her presence.

Sally found Mark's empty seat by the fire next to John. She sat close to him and watched his Lordship in the midst of his people.

Jim the thin, hung in the shadows behind John, at the ready, where he always was. He fingered a wicked curved knife, as he glared at the evil bitch who sat next to his Lord John. He ached for her to do something threatening.

John was stern-faced with a prominent brow and small eyes. He sported a slight smile in drumming concentration. Much of the time his eyes were closed and he looked to be in some joyous trance as he played. The music wove around them and Sally felt safe and secure at his side as well as trembling trepidation at being so close to such a dangerous male. He was strong, powerful, artistic and loved. She caught a whiff of his manly aroma and veritably gushed. His smell was primitive and lusty. The peppery tinge tickled her long unfulfilled desire for male attention. Some men just smelled right, even unwashed. He was robust and exciting and in charge of everything in his world. She was smitten. At the court that decided her fate she had liked the look of the guy, and now she was drawn to him like a bee to honey. His pheromonal allure infused her senses and added an intoxicating sensual layer to the wine. She gulped a hearty swallow from the passed bottle and smiled her intent up to him.

Sally had been held at arm's length by all the women. She had no companion or even civil associate who she could even sit with comfortably. The open loathing the other women exhibited towards her forced to sit by John. He was the only one in the Shire who was non-plussed at her presence. Everyone else made her felt dirty and shunned. While at his side she felt the defense of his presence deflect the icy glares.

The drummers found wilder loud beating to be popular and the thumping rose in tempo and decibels.

Sally couldn't help herself and jumped up to join the wild and primitive scene. She cavorted around with the other gyrating folk, as some men now also danced up a dust storm. The fire roared high into the night as writhing bodies leapt and stomped a celebratory outpouring so long denied. The mass of people around the yellow fire made joyous noise and their exuberance filled their hearts and the night.

John drummed more intently, keeping his hands busy. The magic of the fiesta was tangible as the entire Shire at the fire danced and drummed and chanted and sang and hooted and hollered their joy as the beat rose to crescendo of hammering and cacophonous fervor.

John could feel the end coming as the climax peaked and sustained to its point of diminishment. He got the eye of the main drummers and with a signal they finished the next round and with a wave of his hand, stopped. The drums fell silent and the crowd took the cue as if of one mind. Echoes of their noise rolled away and filtered into the dark quiet woods. The folk stared across the flames for a couple of beats, then another cheer and clapping thanks to one another.

Sally fell onto John's coat at his feet and draped in his lap, exhausted.

John sat there for a moment, this exciting woman, breathing heavily, leaned on him, almost throwing herself to him. He was afraid to touch her. He hadn't been with a woman in over a year. She was sweating and trembling and he felt her heat on his leg. He stroked her hair lightly. His only thoughts were of this fabulous creature bestowing herself on him.

She turned her face up and smiled at him alluringly. She was making eyes at him and he thought for sure he detected gratitude. That's when he got a whiff of her. Her arousing female scent clouded his head and drilled a poignant signal to his loins. His skin became hyper-sensitive and her heated arms, where she rested on his legs, burned strong sexual attraction. He was immediately embarrassed that she was touching him so close. He couldn't stay seated comfortably any longer. The constriction in his jeans made it impossible. He took her arm gently and rose.

John stood and raised his drum over his head. "Now, that's what I call a campfire!" he hollered above the crowd. More cheers followed and, "Yeah!" from several replied.

"A long day tomorrow folks. Thank you. Thank you all very much for the party! The Shire!" He called.

"The Shire!" his people yelled back.

"You can stay up, but no more drums tonight. I need my beauty sleep." John called and waved his hand as he turned to find his bunk.

Plenty of good-natured laughing and "Goodnight, Sir John."

Sally had disappeared.

Jim the thin took his other two drums and they juggled the instruments and a bottle of wine as they trod the rough grass to his rig. A pickup truck cab-over style camper was lashed to the bed of one of the older trucks. It was small and cramped, but it wasn't a tent or on the ground and had an actual mattress and sheets and his private gear. John climbed up. Jim handed the drums up to the shoulder high truck bed, Sally appeared from the darkness behind John, already onboard, and took the drums from Jim.

Jim flared his nostrils at her and scowled.

John watched the two dark forms and half-smiled at the interaction between them. She was being subservient and helpful.

John stopped and looked at her in the dark for a moment. She stood silently. Both her hands were full of his drums. She was dressed quite scantily and concealed nothing except her charms. No weapons. He fumbled for a key, opened the door fetched his other drum and ducked inside. Sally followed.

Jim the thin crawled under the truck and unrolled his scant bedding in the grass. He lay awake, surrounded by the sounds above.

—

"That's it?" Sharp nosed Amber, skewered old Sam with the pointed question. "That's all it took for her to become Baroness? She fucked him?"

"It was a hell of a party." He whined a little.

"Unbelievable! The lengths men will go to get their little head massaged. I mean that is about the dumbest reason for trusting someone in the whole wide world. Especially her!" Amber berated the old man.

"Hey, don't you get on your high horse little missey! That's the night your Grandma and me hit it off. Zoey was the greatest woman that ever came down the road. Your best blood is from her."

"Granma … Zoey!? The hippy girl holding the beef? Oh my God. I can't believe half of what you tell me." Amber stomped her foot on the floor to emphasize her exasperation with him.

"Yeah, well not that night, but we hit it off. So you better watch out girly. One day you're gonna meet the right fella and …"

"And I'll," Amber pulled out a wicked looking knife, "cut off his balls and feed 'em to the cat if he's a bastard like that witch the Baroness. I'd never let someone like that live long enough to seduce me into giving away everything. How could you people go along? I'll never understand the old world. Good thing it's gone. Crazy people. That's all there was back then. Crazy!" She swirled her finger in circles next to her head.

Sam was nostalgic, but he had to admit she was right. From their perspective the old world was an insane place. Even the depredations of their current situation fell under rationality when compared with the world that had magical power for all and death dealing forces at the fingertips of unworthy people. At least in the present day you knew who you could and couldn't trust and if you made a deal with someone the payment was straightforward and honest.

Sam sighed. "Yeah, it was a crazy world back then."

25

Halor

In the nineteen sixties, when farmer Bill Ames grew up, the town of Halor was a busy and vibrant farming community. It took fifty years for it to become a shell. All that remained were empty storefronts, boarded up buildings, county offices with no employees, and weeds growing in the streets.

In his father and grandfather's time it had been a real going concern. They worked the rich Iowa expanse their entire lives. The farms were productive, modern and fruitful. It took a robust population of folks to support them. In turn it secured them all with a simple but prosperous living.

However, the twentieth century agribiz paradigm finally dictated a different economy of farming and the small town's social economy eventually suffered. Corporate and machine efficiency didn't require so many people. The town of Halor emptied out and dried up.

When the quiet came, Halor could barely be called a town. The buildings were still there, but they were mostly vacant. The few remaining people lived and worked miles away out on million acre corporate corn fields. Modern farmers had vehicles that whisked them the fifty-plus miles to town in less than an hour. In only two hours they could be at the big box stores near Iowa City.

The local grocery and hardware sat empty and rang hollow as the winds of the Great Plains dusted them to a monochromatic collection of boxy buildings filled with nothing but memories.

The nature of mega farms revolved more around their utility as marshalling yards filled with steel buildings sheltering fleets of modern farm machinery as anything else. The locations of the monster farm distribution hubs were based on economical reasoning. They were located on good supply roads and had nothing to do with heritage. Incorporation ruled the landscape. The days of farmers tending their own land were gone They were replaced by institutional farm factories tending genetically hybrid crops and livestock.

Legacy farms were very few and far between. A few old farmers held on, but even they worked for the monstrous companies that now owned the land their fathers had tilled and brought under cultivation. The only vestiges of family farms were an occasional old homestead where heirs had hung on and retained the forty or one hundred and sixty acres around the house. The rest was internationally controlled agri-biz.

When the quiet came, whether they were old farm families or corporate crews, the people were out, trapped on their expanses, stranded on the thousand mile sea of a gently undulating plain of green, a hundred miles or more from any active town.

It was impossible to work the great expanses of corn from an agri-biz designed oasis without electricity or a modern transportation system in place. They realized this at once. If things stayed quiet, without electricity working, then they would soon starve in their desert of inedible industrial corn.

In the first thirteen days the outlying enclaves of humanity sent couriers into town. Most everyone had some old, pre-computer-controlled-injection system diesel, tractor or truck, rusting out back.

The creative old-timers jury-rigged their diesels and putt-putted to civilization. Without electricity they improvised manual fuel pumps and turned the ancient engines over with compressed air. Ingenuity was in their blood and if it was possible to make it work, they did.

The diesels ran, but fuel was dear. The quiet brought people's interest in the ghost town of Halor, back into focus.

After the quiet came, temperatures soared during the day, and plummeted unseasonably at night. In two weeks it was regularly above one hundred and ten degrees each day and frost coated the land at dawn. Under these extreme drought and freeze conditions, the corn shriveled to tinder. Instead of a fall harvest that year, a breeze came up and there was the thousand mile fire.

The first farm crews and families huddled on their oases compounds. It's all they could do. They weathered the fire storm on tiny islands of dirt in a sea of flaming corn. The barren parking lots for their machines allowed them some fire break and if they shielded a pit where they could hunker down, some survived. They lived, but were left in an absolutely barren burnt landscape that stretched beyond the horizons.

Caravans of trucks roared into the town of Halor warning of the impending conflagration. They thought they had a two day lead on the fire. The town filled with folks from more than two hundred miles away. The incoming messengers and bearers of the coming bad news were at the end of their meager remaining fuel reserves.

There was a little lake right near the town central green. It beckoned to the farmers for them to take a stand there. The last of their fuel was spent defending the town. The refugees and local folk chopped down and disked everything that grew for a mile around the perimeter of the town of Halor.

Flying embers and looming smoke forced every person in Halor to be pro-active in the fire brigade and, so the town survived the conflagration that would become an apocalyptic story of legend. The quiet was of course one thing, but the thousand mile fire that finally destroyed it all was the story of saga and of hell come into reality.

That was on the fourteenth day after the quiet.

Bill Ames was fifty five years old. He had reached the double nickel, it was his birthday. He wasn't celebrating; he was burning a perimeter around the homestead with his son-in-law, Rick.

Rick heard the first news yesterday of the coming fire while in Halor and had beat his old horse almost to death trying to get back to the farm to warn Bill.

There was already a periphery of an ancient fruit orchard around their home and tourist truck farm. The grassy freeway off ramp next to the old homestead gave him a nice fire break to work from.

Rick and Bill started back-burning from the freeway and worked southwest along the fruit trees, little patches at a time. The corn burst into flame at their torch, and the almost imperceptible breeze was, in those few moments before the main fire, in their favor.

Bill had followed his grandfather's lead and left a large fallow field around the wooded lakes on the south and west; a several hundred foot wide shoulder of native grasses stretched from the woods to the edge of the volatile corn. Bill remembers the arguments he had with the Agra people about not planting that little swath. They had demanded he utilize every inch of available acreage, he had desisted. Old Grandpa Ephraim's method was correct.

They burned the grass uneasily. It was unnerving to tend a fire in such dry conditions. A slight wisp of air at their backs kept them out of the smoke and sparks. When they reached the corn, rolling clouds of sooty overcast from the coming fire threatened, the breeze had freshened, and its direction had changed out of their favor. They steeled their nerves and flamed the main body of corn as far away as possible from the woods and the main homestead. It sparked easily and embers flew onto them into the already burnt grass.

Bill stood at the edge of his small woodland. Embers floated down. Choking smoke wisped around him. Corn crackled and roared as it tried to burn upwind toward the oncoming inferno.

The woodland defined the edge of the original homestead and Bill watched the flames leap up in the corn he had so industriously tended earlier that year. He fretted over the flammability of his trees and nervously kept an eye out. He watched the corn burn, into the wind, toward Halor, and away from him.

The little bee-boy helped them. He stayed alongside Bill and Rick, ready to reach and grab. Once the teenage boy understood the back burning tactic, he stayed close to Bill and helped as best he could. He wasn't afraid of the fire. He was afraid of being alone. His grandpa died and the electricity stopped on the day they arrived to work the bee hives. Ben, the bee-boy, didn't know what else to do, but to follow the farmers' lead. For the last two weeks Ben had followed farmer Bill and Rick wherever they went.

Later that night the big fire came and ringed the old homestead. The entire horizon glowed red. The speed of the roaring conflagration caused its own wind and the inferno loomed over their heads like a monstrous dragon intent on consuming them. Sparks and embers rained down on them. The family stayed busy with backpack pump sprayers and wet blankets chasing through the grounds putting out embers. The house, barns, orchard, and woods were spared, but only after enormous effort. Dawn found them exhausted filthy and praying their thanks. They were reborn that night, reborn into the new barren burnt world of after the quiet.

There was no authority, transportation, or communication after the quiet came and Bill and his wife, Jill, took the bee-man's orphaned grandson into their home quite naturally.

Just before the awful corn fire Rick, Jillian's husband, fetched her and their little girl from their small ranch home down the road. The three of them joined Bill and Jill and the thirteen year old bee-boy on the old family homestead. It was quite a family affair and for the next five years they survived there; tending the ancient apple and pear orchard and hauling water up from the lakes to keep the small truck farm productive enough to sustain them. They also dealt with the riff-raff and long range migratory folk who travelled the great interstate highway by their home. It was a wild and sometimes violent five years, but they abided, and time passed.

Bill and Jill both passed away in the seventh year of the quiet. That year Jillian, her husband Rick, and Lizzie, moved into Halor. They felt a need to be in the company of society. Their little girl, was growing up and they wanted her to know what it was like to live around other people in a more civilized manner. After Jillian's parents died, the allure of living on the old family farm was gone. Church and community drew them away from the desolate periphery farm at the freeway. They left for town and bequeathed it all to the strange bee-boy who loved the place.

Ben the bee-boy's hives flourished after the quiet. He found himself in the enviable position of being the 'go to' guy for sweetening honey and bees for pollination. He loved the dilapidated orchard and the old homestead and would not relocate to the safer town.

Things had happened on the day of the quiet that held him there. It wasn't just the graves of his old grandpa and his new parents, the Ames', although he tended them carefully and kept them proper, there was something else that held him. He could not shake the image of the thing that landed in the pond. He had seen it clearly and it was, to him, a divine vision. It was a moment of reality that he couldn't explain or tell any one about. No one would understand or believe him. It snapped his desire to leave or try to find his way home, alone, across thousands of miles of open country back to California. He loved the bees and his new home and the mystery life held for him. Ben, grew up to become 'The Bee-Man'.

For as long as Ben the bee-man could remember there had never been an empty storefront on the Main Street of Halor Iowa. The town was rejuvenated after the quiet and the buildings filled with life. Ben never saw the dilapidated and forlorn town that died. He had never visited Halor before the quiet. He was with his grandfather doing his bee keeping busy-ness when the quiet came and he got stranded with the Ames family. He only saw the new town. He was now a part of that new town.

Today, Halor was awash in horses and carts and people and dust and goings on. It was downright bustling. Most everyone lived pretty close-in to town and managed the surrounding farm parcels at the edge of the open plain.

It was fifteen miles from Halor to the great east-west abandoned freeway where Ben's place lay. He lived by the remnant of concrete interstate that stretched from the dawn to sunset across the gentle rolling plain.

The entirety of Halor's populace had turned out for Ben and Gloria's wedding. There were five hundred people living in town and not many single young folk of marriageable age. It was a celebration that everyone wanted to take part in. Ben, the Bee-Man, was well liked and more importantly, necessary to every person.

The great fields of pre-quiet corn had never come back. For the last ten years emphasis was on diverse staple food crops. Drought resistance was a key factor and the availability of good reproducible seed. In the first year folks grew any and everything from left over seeds in the fruit on their shelves. Unfortunately, many of the simplest of foods had been hybrid and the seeds refused to germinate. They were patented genetically modified 'perfect' fruit that sat unblemished in the market and had a huge shelf-life. Cantalope, watermelon, tomatoes, apples, cherries and every kind of easily attainable fresh fruit, which looked fabulous, would not reproduce. The staples of potatoes, beets, kale and similar 'boring' foods could be grown. Very little of the diverse, before the quiet, food-stuffs existed.

Ben held the monopoly on bee technology and sweetener. His life was moving his hives to assure that the community was serviced with pollinators. He produced honey and there was no other source for sugar. He had not shared his knowledge of bees and made himself inexpendable. Ben had even gone to the lengths of searching out all the books in the tiny local library about beekeeping and making them his. He had the knowledge and he kept it close.

The wedding was well attended. Not showing up and paying one's respects at Ben's wedding might have grave repercussions. If, heaven forbid, Ben took offense and overlooked your need for bees, your food crop might fail, or your chicory coffee wouldn't get that tiny bit of sweet adulterant that made it palatable. So, everyone was there, feasting, dancing, making music, getting a little drunk, and sharing anything they had to make the party a success. Everyone needed everyone else.

The ceremony was early in the morning on the first day, then a feast lasting all that day and into the first night, and finally an old fashioned shivaree. The townspeople banged pots and pans and drums and made merry, well into the night, keeping the poor newly-wed couple awake. Ben had generously provided four barrels of mead, honey wine, and the folk got quite happily soused. He regretted giving them the mead and feeding their uninhibited clamor; as he got no rest.

The townsfolk, and the blissful couple, were bleary eyed on this, the second day. Ben and Gloria were fed a sumptuous brunch and then led a parade through town to be presented gifts at each persons' house.

Their horse drawn wagon, festooned with flower decorations and loaded with hand made gifts for the newly-weds accompanied the obligatory visits to each house for blessings. A retinue of all the prominent citizens surrounded the wagon and led the horses to each scheduled stop. The couple sat politely on the wooden cart bench as speeches were made and gifts proffered through the mid-day.

Ben and Gloria humored the crowd politely and eagerly awaited their chance to get away and begin the long ride back to their farm.

"May the Lord shed his bounty on you, Ben, and you Gloria, who are now sanctified by holy matrimony and may you bless our community with many dutiful god fearing children to help us build a world of peace and strengthen our fold. May the Lord bless you and keep you. Amen," old reverend Fuller's voice sang out at the edge of town.

Ben couldn't help but fidget just a little. He was tired of all the folderol and just wanted to get home with his new wife.

Gloria beamed her broad smile at the few teenage girls in the crowd. She was the one who got the catch of the town.

Ben was wealthy in terms of status and holdings. Ben, the Bee-Man, was sole heir to the north sections between town and the old interstate highway. He had everyone beholding to him for his bees and their fruit creating abilities. His apples and honey products were precious commodities in a land that had returned to pre-corn plains since the quiet.

The bee-man had been the most desirable eligible bachelor and Gloria had him by the arm in a marriage cart. She was the envy of every young girl and she knew it.

Ben stood and waved. Everyone became quiet in anticipation of his speech. He gave none. When everyone was quiet, he sat back down, clucked at the horses, flapped the reins and the newly made wagon rode out of town. The crowd stood silent for a few moments then cheered and waved good-bye to the couple.

After a few hundred yards Ben said, "God, I sure am glad that's over."

Gloria was shocked. "Ben, don't be profane. They are just wishing us the best."

"They just want to stay on my good side, you mean. I saw how Howard Steel was falling all over himself to be extra nice. If he said how happy he was for us one more time I was gonna sock him."

"Oh Ben, don't be like that. Besides, it's over and look at all these wonderful blessings they gave us." She softened her tone and snuggled against him. "We are going to be alone at home soon. We are not going to be bothered by that shivaree tonight." She hugged him closer and gave him a come hither look.

"Gloria, and here I thought you were such a pious girl," he leaned back and said sarcastically, "they warned me that a woman would change after the wedding, but I had no idea." He smiled the smile of the cat that got the canary.

She nuzzled his neck and cooed, "I have some ideas."

"Giddup there!" Ben flapped the reins and the horses broke into a trot.

They rolled into the farmyard where Ben had been stranded by the quiet so many years ago. The fruit tree orchard had been expanded and covered quite an expanse around the old farm house. Most of the windows in the house had been replaced over the years, mostly through the wheeling and dealing of Ben for used glass in exchange for his honey products. The paint was old and peeling and the house and barn looked the worse for wear.

The corn had burned up and could never be grown in great quantities like it was before the quiet. The fire after the quiet crushed the huge farms and sent the people back to the towns and to a time of an older more sustainably managed paradigm of farming. Diesel machines were difficult to fuel and the systems that supported the agri-biz ways were gone. Vast stretches of the mid-west plains returned to native grasslands and woodlands. A man could cultivate only as much as he could comfortably work by hand, or with horses, or if he was lucky or wealthy enough to have them, oxen. Towns became closed communes of closely shared resources. Ben's farm was not close to town and the amount of labor available at planting or harvest didn't allow him the luxury of farming large acreages. He turned to the apples and his bees. They were a rarity and he made the most of them. If he hadn't, he surely would not have gotten a wedding party in town.

They unloaded the wagon and Gloria busied herself right away with finding a place for everything. She was raised a good Christian girl and knew her place and duties as a wife. Ben put the horses away and found Joe, the young teenage boy they hired to watch the place, sleeping in the loft. Ben checked on the few animals they kept, paid Joe his pot of honey, and sent him on his way home. Joe hitched his loose britches, bed roll, clay jar of honey, and loped down the lane at a mile eating pace. It was a long walk back to town. It would take him until midnight.

Ben found his new wife, Gloria, in the kitchen working the fire in the old square iron wood stove. She was heating one of the pots of food they had been given as a gift. They had gotten such a grand array of smoked meats, cheeses, and premade food that they wouldn't have to slaughter anything for quite a while. Gloria assembled a selection of delicacies from their loot and Ben fetched a bottle of his best honey mead from the locked cellar.

The chores done, they settled at the kitchen table, lit some beeswax tapers and savored the fine treats and wine. There wasn't much to say. They ate in silence and fed each other tasty bits: pickled pigs feet, canned mushrooms, sweetmeats, sharp cheese and crumbly rough grain sourdough breads. They washed it all down with honey mead and before long they lounged in a happy and contented haze.

It had been a whirlwind few days. Ben didn't go to town very often and having Gloria come back to the farm with him kept him on the edge of anticipation. There was no way they could have consummated their marriage in that dusty hotel room, not with all those noisy, drunken people around and shouting and carrying on all night. It was an exhausting celebration and they had only been able to sleep fitfully, but tonight was different. Tonight Ben was on his home turf. He felt comfortable here. It was quiet and safe. They had time for each other and they were alone.

The newly wedded couple sat close together and Gloria ran her hand up his leg and caressed him.

"Ben?" Gloria asked through pig-grease smeared lips.

"Yes?" He looked up from his almost empty glass of mead.

"Honey." She cooed and gently took his hand and placed it on her bare leg.

"Yes … honey?" he wrinkled his brow quizzically and gulped a little.

"Honey balm. I want … some," she said in a breathy voice.

He knew what she was talking about. He made a honey balm that was a soothing salve. There was only a little bit that ever made it into circulation of the general population. Ben could only make a small quantity from the royal jelly. It was very expensive and dear. He commanded and got a high price for it. It was surely something Gloria had never really experienced, but only heard about. It was reputed to be an aphrodisiac. Even in such a strict Christian community as Halor, girls gossiped about such things.

Ben dared not move his hand. He felt the warmth of her flesh and it stirred him. He knew about the birds and the bees, but the last five years he had been raised at the edge of the strictly fundamentalist Christian community of Halor. There was no hanky-panky in his history.

When the quiet had come, all the prurient interests and images of the modern age were stripped away. He had seen pictures and some pornography as an internet literate kid, but that was a long time ago and he had never experienced anything so sensual as actually having his hand on the warm soft flesh of a girl's thigh. He had seen the rabbits and the horses and the cows do 'it', but none of the feelings he was experiencing were remotely similar.

The rushing blood in his head and pounding in his ears was more like the hot sweaty dreams that had occasionally woken him. Only now, it wasn't dark, and he wasn't asleep or alone. He was with his wife, the girl he was supposed to do 'it' with, and she was leading the way. His head spun a little from the mead. Her hand moved up into his crotch and he squirmed a little at the blatant forthrightness of it.

She was a good girl. This wasn't what he expected. Of course he didn't really know what to expect. He sort of envisioned the rabbits, but had no idea how that came to be. They didn't stroke one another. They just got onto one another and did it. Gloria had a strange mysterious look on her face and was biting her lower lip softly. She leaned over and kissed him on the lips, slowly.

They had kissed before. They had kissed when they were officially betrothed by the town elders, as a sign of commitment. They had kissed when they were married, perfunctorily in front of the whole town. It was all so quick and chaste. They had not kissed like this before. She flicked her tongue and licked his lips lightly as she kissed him. His mind focused on the warm soothing motion. He parted his lips and let her. It was warm and luscious. His head was roaring with a thunder he had never heard before. His eyes were closed, but streams of light and pictures flooded his mind. He found his hand had snaked its way between her thighs and for a moment he was embarrassed and started to pull back. She grasped his wrist and held his hand there.

"Honey balm," she whispered.

He licked her taste from his lips and gulped. "Uh, yeah. Sure. Here have some more mead," he stammered, "I'll be right back." He didn't move.

Gloria stood up; her legs wide, hands on her hips, her shoulders square and dominating. "Honey balm," she commanded softly, but firmly pointing her long white arm at the door. "Now, Ben!" Her tongue poked at the inside of her cheek.

He rose and backed out of the room as she took a good long swig from the mead bottle and batted her eyes at him.

"Go on. Go get it." She smiled and teased. Her candlelit image, hoisting the bottle, and her skirts, draping her full glowing legs were likeably lascivious. He beamed and blushed at the scene as he tried to focus on getting the balm.

Ben swallowed in a gulp, "Uh ... yeah," turned and stumbled into the doorjamb. He felt like he was in a place he did not know. It all seemed a little blurry. When he reached the front door his mind snapped into focus. He felt strong and powerful and on a mission. He bounded out the door and across the yard to the store cellar with a wry smile on his lips. He fumbled with his keys and opened the ancient padlock, plunged into the darkness of the cellar, his fingers found the small pot of jelly in a moment and as cobwebs clung to him he extracted a pot of the smooth slick stuff.

He strode across the long-grown lawn as a victor with the spoils of conquest held triumphantly on high to find that Gloria had cleared away the food from the table and was sitting on its edge. She was holding the bottle of mead in her crotch. Her full skirt was hiked up around her knees showing her calves and now bare feet. Her bodice lacing was loose and her young pink bosom peeked out from the top.

"Come here husband," she smiled.

Ben clutched the little pot of honey balm to his chest and crept to his wife.

"Help me with this," she indicated her bodice and lacing.

He put down the pot and fumbled with the long laces of her garment. She reached out and started to undo his shirt buttons and pulled the suspenders off his shoulders. It felt funny having her touch his clothing. No one had ever touched his clothing but him in his memory, but shortly after she began, he thrilled at the tickling and things started getting looser.

Gloria pushed him a little and he sat on the edge of the table. She took a long gurgling swig and gave him the bottle of mead. She straddled his leg, her behind to him, and bent to put his boot on the chair. She held his thigh up into her as she undid the laces. Ben couldn't move a muscle. He almost dropped the bottle of mead then took a huge drink himself. She pulled his other leg up onto the chair and sat on that knee as she fiddled with the elaborate boot laces in the candlelight. He felt her heat on his thigh. He swallowed with a gulp.

Ben looked down at her bare shoulders as she worked over his feet. Great desire for her welled up inside him. Her bare shoulders and the curve of her back narrowing to her waist made him want her. He could feel her fingers taking his boot loose and then his sock and she firmly rubbed his naked foot. The sensation was too much and he started to pull his foot back and laugh.

"Oh? So you're ticklish eh?" She held his foot tightly and stroked the bottom.

"Ach! No!" He laughed.

Gloria picked up his foot making him lie back on the table and held his foot between her legs and tickled him mercilessly.

"No! No! Don't…" he laughed and squirmed, "Ahhhhhh!" he screamed, "Not fair! Not fair!"

Gloria giggled gleefully. She turned, laid on him and writhed against him.

"Not here! This is the kitchen!" Ben pleaded, worriedly looking around.

"What? It's our kitchen isn't it?" she asked. "No one else is here. We can do what we want."

Ben felt it was almost sacrilegious to be so naughty in the old family kitchen. It was his adopted mother's kitchen. He had never in his wildest imaginings thought he might be doing it there.

Gloria pulled his shirt fully open and kissed him on the neck and the mouth and they both fell into a frenzy of kissing and pulling at their clothes. She reached down and grabbed his pants and with a few yanks pulled them right off him as he lay back on the table. She stepped out of her skirts and with only petticoat underwear on her lower half, hovered over him in all her glorious young womanhood.

He gazed up at her bosoms in wonder and marveled at the round plump beauty of them. They hung like ripe fruits in the soft glow of the candlelight. He gulped as he reached out his hands to pluck them. He dared let his fingers linger on her nipples and their hardness pulsed in anticipation.

She bent and slid off her last garments and then she reached his underwear and pulled them off him like shucking a cob of corn. She stood at the edge of the table and bent over him. They kissed in fabulous naked trembling excitement in the sparsely lit farm kitchen. Their flickering shadows jumped on the walls. The final glow of the setting sun and the bright candles bathed the kitchen walls in a strange shadow dance of their burning red passion.

They slobbered on one another for several minutes. Gloria came up for air, reached into the honey balm pot and took a generous scoop of the expensive stuff. She slowly smeared a little line of the goo on his chest and down to his lower tummy.

Ben gasped softly, "Oh, oh, oh, oh …" as her fingers toyed with the top of his pubic hair.

"Me too," she begged.

Ben gulped deeply. He reached out clumsily, took a scoop and slowly smeared his wife with the single most valuable, by weight, substance in their world. His fingers slid along her shoulders and down onto the rise of her breasts. The jelly was sticky and his fingers found the edge of her aureoles and then her nipples and delicately tested their tolerance of his touch. Her breasts swelled and the nipples hardened under his fingers and in turn caused him to harden likewise.

The smooth honey balm flowed on their skin and melted into them. Its sweet smell filled their senses and invaded their minds. It was a warm and luscious feeling. It spread out onto their skins like a slick moist coating. They took their time.

He followed her lead. He feared to upset her by pushing his desires beyond her comfort level. Each place she smeared the gel on him he did the same to her. It flowed on their chests and nipples and under their arms and on their necks. It smoothed onto their stomachs and down to their thighs, carefully avoiding the most sensitive places and worked around their legs and on their behinds. Ben stood up from the table and they languidly worked the salve onto each other in the middle of the family kitchen. They stuck together as they massaged each others' back and shoulders and when they had finally used up all the obvious places where the cream could be easily and not too embarrassingly applied they lingered, toying at the edge of their most private places.

They hugged each other tight and their bodies slid smooth and sticky on the lubricating glue of the sweet stuff. Ben was hard and pressed himself against his new wife's tummy. She did not shy from him. Slickly her hand found its way between them and she massaged the ointment into his pubic hair. He let her apart from him and followed suit. Gloria got a fresh scoop on her fingers and moved quickly, as if afraid to linger. She slathered a healthy portion on his manhood. She did not belabor him, nor repeat the move. Ben gasped at the immense sensation. He found his focus and did the same to her. When he did, she grabbed his wrist.

"Do that some more Ben. Make me feel I am yours." She guided his hand to continue to rub the sweet smooth creamy stuff on her puss.

Ben held her in one arm and worked the gel on her with his other hand. She stood, legs slightly apart and moaned. Her fingers entwined his hair. She held his head firmly against her breasts as he massaged her womanhood. She moaned more intensely and Ben felt his own sexual pressure pounding. Gloria panted and moaned in earnest and would not let his hair go. He tasted her sweet honey tipped nipple mixed with the slight salt of her body as she pressed his face to her chest. His rod was hard and pounding and he could see she was engrossed in his ministrations and he was getting none of it. He wanted her to hold him so badly, yet he did not stop masturbating her. She rocked back onto the table and lifted her legs allowing him to hold her from falling down.

"Yes. Don't stop, yes. More Ben, more!!" She grasped his knob so tightly he gasped. He massaged the royal jelly between her legs as she writhed and yelled at him. "Oh God! Oh God! OH GOD!!!!!!!!" Her juices flowed onto his hand and the hot fluid from her surprised him.

She slid her hand up and down him and he came instantly.

The hot semen jumped out of him and splashed on her. "Oh God!" he blurted, embarrassed at their profanity and his ejaculation.

"Oh gawd. You're my lord." She sighed and they both fell in slow motion back onto the table, smearing their love juices between them and all over the hard-wood kitchen slab.

They both lay still and panting for several moments. She clutched him close to her and trembled. A sheen of sweat glistened on her in the candlelight.

He had no idea that it was going to be like this. It was not like he imagined it to be at all. He was embarrassed and elated at the same time. He was happy to be with her and ashamed at their animalistic situation. They hadn't even coupled. He knew he was supposed to have put himself inside her, but it hadn't happened. Had something gone wrong? It felt wonderful right up to the moment when he squirted. As soon as that instant passed it didn't feel right for some reason. He didn't know what it was he had done wrong, but it didn't feel completely correct. Gloria did not seem to mind in the least. She had a happy contented look on her face and was holding him as if everything was perfect. Ben did not really understand. Women are strange he thought.

After a few minutes Gloria sat up and drained the bottle of mead.

"I want to wash," she said, "Come on." She got up and tugged his hand. She crossed the kitchen, looked back at him to make sure he was following her, and went through the door.

"Wait." Ben called after her, but she was gone. He couldn't believe it. She was in the yard, naked. He rushed to the door. In the early evening gloom he could just see her ghostly white form going down the hill towards the pond.

"No! Wait!" He called to her. She spun around, dancing and skipped away through the orchard down the hill. She was laughing.

"Gloria! Stop!"

"Catch me if you can," Gloria called back. Her wispy milk white form disappeared into the trees.

A shiver ran down Ben's spine. She was heading for the lake. He shuddered at thought that she might be going there to bathe.

Ben screamed after her, "Gloria! Come back!," he stumbled at the foot of the wooden steps of the back porch.

He was torn between his pious upbringing, the wrongness of his nudity in the open air and the care he felt for his new wife. It was a dangerous and brazen act for her to run around naked. Besides the uncommon frivolity of her running around with no clothes on she was headed for the water.

The waters were forbidden, left alone since that tragic day of the quiet. Things had gone on down there, things no one really knew how to explain, things that had scared old Bill Ames; especially at night. It was a place that they had avoided for years at the old man's warning. Something crashed there the day of the quiet. Something evil.

The lake was off limits and left alone and now, his new wife was running down there for a bath.

The star-filled night cast a glow on the orchard. Her pearly white form flitted amongst the craggly old rows of trees. The grass was cool thick and soft.

Gloria felt wonderful and happy and exuberant in her nudity as she pranced through her new orchard. This was all hers now. The house the orchard the farm and especially her bee-man were hers to enjoy. She danced and spun around as the down slope carried her through the carefully tended apple trees to the edge of the shimmering expanse of the dark lake. The summer had been warm and the cool waters called to her. The dilapidated old dock shone clearly as a dark walkway out onto the star reflecting water.

Here in the midwest there was nothing for her to fear in the water. The largest thing in the lake might possibly be a big bass or lake trout. She had a clear view in her mind of the waters from the picnic she and Ben shared earlier that year. She didn't swim then. It wouldn't have been proper. She loved to swim. She had spent many hot days with the other girls on the river bend below town, splashing and carrying on during lazy hot summer days.

She ran to the foot of the rickety dock and turned to wait for Ben. She saw his fish belly white form appear and come running down the slope. She turned and gingerly stepped out onto the old dock.

She minced to the end as Ben yelled, "Gloria stop! Wait!"

She struck an alluring pose at the end of the dock. Ben stopped at the waters edge and pleaded, "Gloria, come back, please! For the love of God!"

"Come to me. Come to me," she crooned in a fake accent like a movie vampire, "I vant you to come to me." She licked her lips slowly and held her hands to cover her assets.

"Gloria please … " he pleaded. Her body was clearly framed against the glowing water.

Ben gasped and almost swallowed his tongue as she turned and dove into the lake. Her white body disappeared into the strangely glowing backdrop of the lake water as she plunged out of sight.

"NO!" Ben screamed. He found himself running down the rickety old grey boards and flinging himself into the water to save her.

The water was cool and brisk. He floundered a little to get his bearings when he came to the surface, "Gloria!" he yelled, spitting water. He could feel lake-bottom as he kicked.

Her tinkling giggle rang out behind him, "I'm right here silly." She spat a stream of water at him as he turned to her voice. She swam away from him easily.

"Please Gloria, we have to get out of the water." Ben pleaded as he tread water.

Gloria swam around him. Her smile beamed out from the early evening darkness.

He circled in place to keep his eyes on her. "Come on Gloria. We have to get out."

"Whatever for my love? This is a dream. Our lake, our farm, our love. Come to me." Gloria cooed at him as she touched him under the water with her toe.

Ben nearly jumped out of his skin when her foot slid up his leg. He could barely swim. He was sure there was something in this lake that was going to 'get him'.

She swam close to him and gently touched his bare goose-bump skin under the cover of the dark cool water.

"Gloria …?" Ben whined as she lowered her head and peered at him with dark sultry eyes and a cat-like smile. Her arms found his thrashing limbs and pulled them to her as they came together and floated in a love embrace.

The touch of skin, the caress of water, the ethereal view of millions of stars hovering above, put Ben into an unreal frame of mind. His mind swam in the heady influence of this woman in his arms. Gloria delighted in the sensual excitement of the moment with her man.

They floated effortlessly. The water around them warmed. Their minds melded in love and joy and peace.

Ben's frantic anxiety about the lake faded away into the night.

Gloria exalted, in tremendous feelings of power and love, in the arms of a strong lover in charge and responsive to her every quivering and sensual thought.

The water enfolded them and held them up and together. They could only see and feel each other. The lake enabled their lovemaking. It caressed their skin and stimulated their senses. The water rolled around them and kept them together in a shared embrace of spiritual and sensual journey together. Their minds linked and fused in mutual joy and caring and sexual desire and fulfillment. They came together and their minds soared above the earth and seemed to be looking down on their bodies in the lake. Orgasmic waves welled up in them and carried them beyond the moment into the vast uncharted places of the spirit.

Their coupling was held and prolonged in the warm water of the lake.

Every inch of their bodies were massaged and stroked by the balmy soothing lake.

Gloria roiled in complete satisfaction and fulfillment, "Oh God! Oh God! Oh God! OH GOD!"

Ben felt touched in places he never imagined could give him pleasure, then he convulsed in another stupendous ejaculation and felt as if milked as he lost control of his bodily functions. The sucking feeling of his orgasm felt wonderful. They reveled in divine ecstasy as their conjoinment lifted them to the heights of pleasure and consummation.

Their minds filled with images of strange and wondrous visions. They saw stars and galaxies and knew memories of things they had never experienced. They each saw and felt things they never imagined. A psychedelic imposition of memories, not their own, floated through their intense lovemaking. They drifted into delightful orgasmic oblivion.

Groggily, they awoke, cast up onto the cold mud and grass of the shore, under a newly rising sun.

"Uhhhh. What happened?" Ben groaned.

Gloria rolled against him softly and moaned, "It was wonderful Ben. It was divine. I saw God. You are my Lord."

Ben rubbed the thick coating from his eyes. He didn't see his wife Gloria. He heard her voice and saw her talk to him, but the girl next to him was not his wife. The woman in the muddy grass was covered in filth. Beyond her silty exterior she had no hair. She was pink and naked and hairless and sludge covered filthy. He leaned on his elbow and stared wide-eyed at the muddy albino salamander next to him.

Gloria rolled over and discovered herself in a mire of bone-chilling grass. Her elbow sank into the saturated ground as she turned and was slapped by the view of a gross troll laying next to her.

"Aaaaaaaaah!!" Gloria screamed at the top of her lungs as she recoiled and tried to stand in the thick ankle deep ooze by the lake. Her escape was thwarted by the sucking glop.

"It's me. It's Ben!" He pleaded.

As the realization that her husband was the awful, dirty, grass slathered gollum-like monster next to her, she froze. Her eyes-wide, as she stared at him, as he stared at her.

They were both completely hairless, pink, finger and toe nails almost gone and feeling quite empty.

"Oh My God. I have to wash," Gloria declared.

She looked at the lake, shuddered, then turned and ran up the hill to the house. Ben followed her lead and they ended at the large hand-pump in the yard. She started to pump and he took over when he arrived. They pumped and washed the muddy filth from their bodies and then, without another word ran into the house.

26

Honey Bliss

Years of languishing in the alien prison had lulled Sloodin into a state of quiet acceptance. He busied himself with endless days and months and now years, of cleaning the damned pond of its toxins. Each evening he worked at encapsulating the poison laden mud in mucous envelopes and setting them out onto the dry shore of the little lake.

During the hot bright days he slept, deep in the bowels of his ship at the cooler bottom of the lake. It was a simple life in this jail. Each evening, as the burning fierce orb above fell near the horizon, he ventured out from his wreck of a spaceship, to work at cleaning another seemingly endless expanse of the nasty sludge that lined the lake floor. The toxins that fouled this planet were pervasive. Intellectually he knew he was making headway. The pond was only so big and although the artificially synthesized compounds were slowly breaking down, it seemed never ending.

"Why am I worrying? I knew the cleansing period would be at least twenty years. It's only been ten solar turns and I must temper my impatience with a long view. Old Uncle Sloodat spent fifteen years' time working the Heyameyt cloud clusters to prove them. I can at least hold myself to task in order to re-certify my own planet." Sloodin vocalized his convictions as he lay just under the surface of the lake. To an objective ear his poorly articulated verbal frustrations sounded like a dull, pulsating, thrumming, machine. His entire body throbbed an echo of his thoughts and it merely made a muddled 'throom' sound. No one, snood nor human alike, could decipher it as intelligible language. It was just noise.

In the early evening dusk, before he began his evening chore of encapsulating the toxic muck, he floated thin as a sheet of plastic just at the water's interface with the gaseous atmosphere. He floated as thin as his mood dictated. Even though he languished on this alien planet in a dirt bound cell of containment he found a strange bit of peace.

He enjoyed looking. His love of the visual world served him well at these times. His protruding eyestalk stood up from his flattened body and pierced the water. He gazed at the cosmos. He enjoyed the sparse star view punctuated by the huge glowing guardian moon.

His planet had a friendly and over powering sister planet of a moon. It hovered impossibly close as it rose above the craggy, rough, land growths that stuck so incongruously up from the ground toward the sky. The moon was a wonderfully cold and bright beacon of light streaming through the branches of the strange trees. He loved to look at it all.

"My alien prison with a view." He sighed a rumbling boom into the water.

Sloodin pondered how different it all was, now, so close to the dry land. He was surrounded on all sides by deadly territory. His little lake was only safe as long as the land stayed out of his space and didn't crash down into his prison pond. It seemed dangerous to have all that ground so close and looming above him, threatening to cave in and inundate his life station of water. His fears were unfounded as the land seemed to magically hold itself out of the lake and allowed his prison to remain. Nature was wonderful and terrifying. It was still a reminder that this was a prison and he must endure his accidental sentence however long it may turn out to be.

He had observed the land and its weird growing things for all these years and still had little understanding of how they defied gravity and thrust themselves up and away from the ground into the sky. What an impossible world. Things that he initially counted as assets of this rich planet were still a mystery to him: continents, greenery, land animals and the rich flowing rivers of fresh water enriching the oceans with delicious minerals and organic matter. He had taken these things for granted and never deliberated the strange reality that made up the planet's land part. He hadn't imagined that there was anything to learn about the land that could enhance his kingdom. The ocean was far larger than the bits of land and life ashore was minimal compared to the diverse riches of the sea. The land was miniscule in comparison to his great oceans and hadn't seemed to be of any great consequence.

Then, the land creatures made war against him and his kind by poisoning the sea. How had they come to be and why they had acted so irrationally? Their reason for driving snoodkind away was still an unanswered question in Sloodin's mind.

Sloodin lay still. He spread out obscenely flat and thin at the lake surface. There was no one to embarrass or chastise him for his slovenly and self indulgent shape.

"Maybe I am going mad, reverting to my youth. This endless monotony of cleaning and waiting for rescue is making me into a crude child." He let his skin project reflections of the stars above.

"Who cares? I am planet lord and I will do what I want. It doesn't matter. I can't insult or embarrass anyone here." He mimicked the light patterns of the sky and displayed the entire viewable cosmos with his emotional chemical body light.

"There is no one to see me. Hah! I can flash all I want. I can see the world as it really is. I can be as thin as I wish. It may be kid's stuff, but I like it and it makes me feel good." It elated him to wallow in the juvenile habit of fluorescing star patterns and viewing the world with his one eye. He flashed colors across his one half acre of floating skin and rippled the water of the lake with his unabashed humming monologue.

"Thrroommmmm ..." He vibrated shimmers of his mood into the water.

Sloodin was perfectly happy with the world and felt only a slight vibration before he was violently punched in the gut.

Something had plunged into the lake and landed right on top of his outstretched fabric thin body.

He felt the splash and wave radiate across his body as he contracted.

Instinctively he flinched his eyestalk closed.

The weight of the body falling onto him pushed him down and repeatedly punched at him.

He hung between fear and surprise.

Being jumped on was unusual. He could recall a branch or two, and leaves from the trees, and the momentary flicker of small fish feeding at his fringes, but never had anything so large attacked and punched him.

Sloodin convulsed in alarm at the uninvited intrusion. He contracted to surround the intruder just as another object fell onto him near the first. Now two attackers forcefully hammered at his vulnerable thinness.

His fight or flight reaction enfolded the two intruders as he synthesized deadly paralyzing stingers to immobilize the thrashing kicking things. He predatorily pulled himself around the threat.

This was an invasion of his space and evening tranquility.

'Every time I let my guard down this hostile planet assails me with danger!' He thought as he prepared to sting this threat to death, surround with mucous mesh, and hold for food or disposal as mood dictated.

They attacked him, but he had them. They weren't going to escape.

Then, he tasted the sweet.

Delicious sweetness flooded his senses.

Luscious, savory, succulent, deeply satisfying layers of mouth watering sweetness bathed his minds and flowed across his skin.

Sloodin reeled at the intense and heavenly taste of the things on him. Each kick and movement sent plumes of fabulous tastes to him.

He folded himself around the two animals swimming in the lake and formed a cup around them so none of the fabulously delicate sweetness could escape.

He wanted this stuff.

It was good.

It was delectable.

These animals assailing him were coated with the most fantastic stuff he had ever tasted in his life. The sugary goodness was mixed with an equally tasty sheen of their body sweat and organic wastes. He drooled and put away his stingers as the wonderful taste calmed him.

Sloodin held them in a cup of his body and savored the mix of their bodily secretions and the sweet covering they offered up to him.

They did not seem to be pursuing any attack. The two animals gyrated their strange shapes to stay on the surface of the lake.

Sloodin slowly enfolded the swimmers. He filtered out water and concentrated the tasty brew of them. When he was close enough to touch them on all sides he thickened the water to provide positive buoyancy for them. Their thrashing and kicking slowed to more relaxed movements as they found it possible to float effortlessly. They clung to one another floating in Sloodin's body formed pool. He matched their temperature and warmed himself to hold them. They seemed completely oblivious to his presence and were engrossed in themselves. Sloodin tentatively enclosed the things and held them as they floated together under the stars.

Their shape was alien and strange to Sloodin. They had a soft covering over hard stick structures inside.

'This must aid them in their difficult struggle against gravity on the dry,' Sloodin thought.

They had the consistency of free swimming vertebrates and not that of the hard-shelled fleeber, but they lacked many of the attributes of fish. No exterior scale armor and entirely internal oxygen filters. Every part of them was soft except for the stick structures inside. It seemed a very odd configuration for a creature supposedly evolved enough to aspire to waging war against the supreme race of snood. They seemed fairly delicate and easily killed.

'Lucky for them galactic registry law protects them from my wrath,' Sloodin chuckled.

In spite of their strange composition they were flavorful. Sloodin delicately licked their bodies. It made him shudder in rapture and he held them even closer. The musky flavor of them seeped through the covering of honey sweetness. Sloodin was now of the mind that they were not attacking, but offering themselves to him. Their sweet exterior only tempted a tasting of their true deep nutty aroma. He could now taste their saltiness mixed with tangy and almost pheromonal fecal flavor. The beings were like candy, sweet on the outside while rich and satisfyingly complex underneath. Sexual perfume floated through the other aromas and added another layer of choice and mouth watering tastes to the mix.

Sloodin, in gratitude, exuded sedative, calming and slightly hallucinogenic chemical compounds.

Sensing they breathed the dry air, and could not go under the water, Sloodin manufactured an oxygen rich mixture of liquid for them. They dipped below the surface unaware they were submerged.

They all clung feverishly as their ardor increased. He soothed them as they made love in his encompassing embrace. As each wave of fragrant delight washed over him, he responded chemically with peace, joy, love and lust. Their coupling ritual formed juicy odors that sent Sloodin to the edge of ecstasy.

He enfolded them tighter and more closely. His fluid body wrapped around the two animals making love in him.

He insinuated his tentacles into every crack and crevice of them. They were quite entangled and similarly inside one another.

He flooded them with chemical thoughts of passion and sexual hunger.

He fed them a heady mix of thought provoking chemicals that let them see him in their minds.

He prodded gently and followed their appendages with probing fingers in a warm slithery and caressing embrace.

He generously shared love and held them floating inside him bodily as he melded his thoughts with theirs and his body with theirs.

He read the simple animalistic pulse of sexual focus in their minds and in turn they received strong infusions of Sloodin's long pent up desire for touch and companionship.

The aliens tasted so fine. Their minds opened to his spiritual power.

He couldn't get enough of the delicious nature of their exotic tasty bodies. Their minds sucked in his offered thoughts of holy mantra and group love and communal belonging.

He bathed them in sedative and kept them alive and semi-conscious as they copulated. The three of them mingled and flowed into and surrounded one another in a floating, cuddling, stroking embrace.

Sloodin felt their warm pulsing bodies as he inserted his fine tentacles deftly alongside, and in time with, their own intertwinings.

They shivered in delight at his enhancement to their lovemaking.

He gently explored each orifice as they lost themselves in carnal ecstasy. Their four pulsing hearts pounded a melodic drumbeat rhythm in alien, amoeba-like, and human fornicating harmony. Their tangled writhing mass of flesh danced the tango in triplicate. They felt to their core. They experienced joy and a rapturous upwelling of quivering corporal lusty engagement. Their swirling probing bodies swarmed in erotic private acceptance of the other. They floated freely and were mindlessly propelled by their writhing mass around the pond. In and out of each other's forms they went as Sloodin's chemical compounds melded the emotional consciousness of them all together into one seething humping, sucking, feeling, fucking, bundle of unbridled thrill.

The final reward came.

They reached climax simultaneously. Bodily juices flowed.

He spurted, she squirted, and Sloodin spewed in orgasmic fertility. The animals arched their backs and silently screamed their release into the liquid pool that was Sloodin.

He held his pets tightly and enfolded them in a complete warm slithering embrace.

"Blisssssss," Sloodin hummed vibrations out to the world he owned.

The vibrations of him quivered the soft flesh of them and they soared into rapture with him.

He caressed and petted his scrumptious land animals. It had been so long since he had experienced any joy or any hint of shared pleasure.

He convulsed in tune with their thrashing. Through secretion of focused slimed lust and fulfilled desire he shared his intimate thoughts as all three shuddered together in sexual joy.

They shared a chemically induced ménage-a-trois session of fervent passion. The creatures rolled in gravity-free warm water, every inch of their bodies caressed by his delicate slimy body, intertwining wherever there was space. Their efforts reached another fervent and chaotic moment together as sexual orgasms overcame them.

Sloodin climaxed with them, again.

He joined in the consummation with his seed.

He couldn't help himself.

He spewed his long held juices on and around the funny feeling and sexually serious creatures of the land. The thick ooze from him filled the space in his body that he held them in.

Their orgasms continued as hormonal glop coated them and bathed their senses with intense emotions of lust and desire and fulfillment and they each convulsed as their eyes rolled up into their heads and they fell into a surreal world of incredibly intense pleasure.

Time stood still.

He held them firmly and carefully as the three of them succumbed to the intense and repeated orgasms. They all three trembled through waves of immense and unbounded joy. The animals floated, vibrating with unending delight inside the envelope of Sloodin's warm enfolding body. They all shuddered and shook as the intensity of the moments overcame them all together again and again … and then they relaxed into a huddled group of mutually spent lovers. He kept them alive and oxygenated when they lost consciousness.

"You're so fragile … and so good tasting."

"I am glad I didn't destroy you." Sloodin choked back a tear as he held the helpless things.

In the course of their intercourse he had stripped them of every last bit of their savory coatings, and their contents. He had sucked out every bit of dgested nutrition and cleaned the yummy organics from their systems until they were quite hairless, pink, naked, and empty.

Sloodin forced himself to the raspy greens at the edge of the land where they could breathe on their own and recover. He did this with great love and happiness.

These strange alien beings had brought him the great offering of themselves. They had shared the ultimate treasure of themselves with him.

He still did not understand the motives of the land creatures on this planet, but he was grateful they had come to him.

He steeled his nerve and placed them in the muddy, grass verge at the pond's edge where they could recover in their own time and in their own world.

Sloodin unfolded his eyestalk and dared a look at them. They were totally hideous white blobby looking things. Their appendages were queer stick like protrusions. The main sensory input part was an odd growth out the top of the body. He shuddered a little at the thought of having made love to such awful looking things.

'I am stranded in prison on this hostile world, love the one your with, I guess,' he thought. 'What ungainly beings,' he clucked at them.

"Now I see it."

"The life-preserver suits."

"That's what they are."

"Hah!?"

"Monkeys with machines."

"Dangerous, yet curious." Sloodin marveled at the hideous things on the grass and tried to place them with the memories that his Uncle Sloodat had ingrained in him about similar monsters. "Well, you're gruesome, but not totally evil." He smiled as he spoke to the lake.

Sloodin squirted a slimed thought of gratitude onto them.

"Thank you for the happiness, creatures."

"I see how you get around on the land."

"You crawl on those stick arms."

"It must be clumsy on this planet."

"You would have sunk into the poison if I hadn't kept you up."

"Do you normally mate in the water?"

"Why did you come to share your sweet and luscious bodies with me?"

"I still understand so little of this planet."

"Eighty thousand years I have owned this place and it is still a complete mystery to me." Sloodin sighed deeply and remembered the odd internal skeletons he felt inside the animals.

"You are not very sturdy and I almost killed you."

"You should announce yourself before you offer yourself to me."

"I was startled."

"You taste very good." A little flattery couldn't hurt, he thought.

"I know you live in the gas, and on the dry land."

"I will never understand this place I fear." The edges of the lake rippled and thrummed at the vibrations of his crude sonic speech punctuations that he peppered in with the slimed thoughts that he bathed the animals with.

Sloodin fulfilled his need for pillow talk as he rambled incoherently to the sleeping creatures.

"I know you are only crude primitive animals and I bet you haven't the faintest idea of what I am saying to you."

"Anyway, thanks."

"I really enjoyed it all." He slid back to the center of the lake and folded into a dense mucous covered four armed mass.

Sloodin fore-went his evening chore of collecting the bad concentrations of mud, rolling them into balls and placing them on the little dam near the tiny trickle of the outflow; a day off. He drifted into the depths, found his ship, crawled inside and went to bed. It had been a special day for him in his prison pond, crash-landed and trapped on his alien planet.

27

<u>Mekhedz</u>

A.Q. Year Fifteen

The bald headed monk yelled across the top of the dust covered personnel-carrier at the grizzled Baron; he hollered to be heard over the tire-roar below, above the deep whirring 'waow' sound of the heavy central flywheel between, through the shrill high-pitched turbine engine behind, and with the whiney whistling wind reflected from every sharp edge protuberance on the steam driven Kommandercar.

"I told you we shouldn't have gone down this road!"

Although twenty three miles in one daylight hour showed very respectably on the log, the Bishop took it as miles into an error.

Baron Willem, squinked his eye and turned only slightly to glance at the pasty-faced little twit. Bishop Justin, had been a thorn in his side since day ... one hundred ten? 'That's right, it's been an entire season that I endure your twaddle,' Willem thought to himself, as the Bishop, normally ensconced below, intruded into the Baron's pilot space on the riding deck and spewed his 'I told you so' vitriol.

"The road is clear," Willem called back, "perfect recon report," referring to heliograph signals acknowledging a go-ahead for the group.

It was the best case, in practice, scenario for the recon-motorcycles. They expedited convoy movement. Until now, fail-safe (something is fishy), and hazard (ambush), indicators prevented the bikers from ranging too far ahead.

Something always happened; seldom had there been so much clear roadway since the start of the crusade. For the last three days the convoy had moved hundreds of miles. Only at the start of the trip, last year, on their way through the Nevà-desert and Yoot-lands, had they gone so far each day. This was the first time in months they traveled into the afternoon without incident. Open roadway of the best southwestern kind: vast reaches of nothing-land that stretched to horizons viewed in the morn and possibly gained at dusk, places one could view only from a rapidly moving vehicle, because if traveled any slower one would die of thirst and want. It was country to be crossed, not lingered in.

The Baron perched solidly in his pilot blister and glared sidelong at the Bishop clinging to the edge of the co-pilot's hatch opening.

Down the ancient cracked asphalt the massive iron land-yacht rolled. It had large diameter wheels and a heavy, impossible to dent, body. It was hard to get rolling and hard to stop. Its attendant cadre of rolling stock followed: a bob-tail water-tank truck, four tractor-trailer tankers with large bladder methane digesters inside them, three remaining shuffle-bins (i.e., dump trucks, the largest held the sphere of God) carried the camp accommodations, and one remaining front end loader that was rigged as a battle-tank brought up the rear. They had started with four times the number of vehicles. The Baron tried not to think about his losses as the Bishop nagged him. These few machines were the whole of their surviving crusade convoy and they must succeed.

Baron Willem turned away from the nasty little bishop. He bore forward into the future on his mighty steam-turbine powered conveyance.

He peered into the desolate country ahead. 'What in the hell is this priest talking about?' he thought. 'This is the best time we've made in months and we've got the Lord. If only this priss Bishop would just let things be.'

He commanded the course, felt the wind in his teeth, and kept moving ahead on the only way available to him.

The Bishop looked at the sun-baked commander in what he thought was a withering gaze of disapproval. In his ranks he had always gotten acquiescence and compliance with that look.

The unkempt leader, in his googly-eyed goggles and leather tank helmet sported a long moustache that whipped in the wind, ignored the Bishop's clean shaven godliness,

The bishop's thoughts hung in the air, 'How can this man take us further into the desert? There's no water there. God would not approve. The sea is the other way.' Justin lamented internally. How could he convince this insane headstrong man to stop going toward ruin?

The machines rolled inexorably into the dry hot wasteland.

Strange and looming formations of red rock paraded by as they crept along flat valley floors. Twisted rock and plateau sculptures told of violent days past: forces long absent from this dry desert land had torn and ripped the land from itself and left fantastic shapes to frame the highway they traversed.

The two opposing minds bent into the dry warm wind that pushed against their faces. Their tiny heads stuck up from the surface of the lumbering fifty-five ton land-yacht/personnel carrier.

The Bishop felt compelled to make the Baron reconsider his course. The man was determined to take them into harm's way at every turn, and now, he was driving them into hell itself. He had to convince the crazy Baron to turn back. He stared out at the never-ending landscape and tried to frame a strategy of persuasion. Surely the immensity and futility of trying to cross this immense desert would be eating away at the man's confidence.

The Baron couldn't believe the gall of this replacement priest. The acolyte had replaced old Bishop Elder, who was killed by Yalls during a parlay. This was a whippersnapper who had no experience beyond catering to the twisted whims of the older monks of the order. The only reason the Baron tolerated his presence was because the Bishop had swum with god. He supposedly knew the Lord's wishes and promises. The people believed in the priesthood and the god they transported. The light of the world was with him and he was necessary to perpetuate the belief of a second coming and keep the simple minded rabble servile.

The convoy of machines rumbled along at a mind boggling 20 M.P.H., southwest, up in altitude, yet on a path of least resistance. The kommanderkar led the convoy and kept pace with their slowest vehicle, the loader tank in the rear. After months of delay, trying to go the shortest way and fighting to get away with their prize, this moving along, unhindered, felt good. The whole convoy was enthusiastic.

Open road was far better than the mountain snows that stranded them for the last four months. Their retreat from the eastern plains into the western mountains had depleted the expedition physically and morally. They could repair most anything, but bad weather, constant breakdowns, and battle damage had whittled away at the armored column.

They had encountered enormous obstacles in the east. When they neared the great rivers, recon reported the bridges gone. They tried south, but the highways were dead-ends and the people there, known as 'yalls', were hostile and couldn't be made to understand how important their mission was. The Baron's plan was turned back and they ended in the big mountains during winter. They toyed with the idea of again fighting their way back through the Yoot-lands, but discarded that idea. They were now less in numbers and far weaker than during the battles that they had barely survived the first time. It was almost catastrophically disastrous then and it would be their end if they tried to go back the same way they had come.

The Bishop insisted they make it to the sea where god wished to be. The lord would save the planet. He would fix his mistake. He would make it all right again. If only the convoy could get him to the ocean, the people would have their magic again and the prophecy of the second coming would be fulfilled.

It wasn't an easy route. Their hope was to make it all the way to a tropical shore, but they couldn't go east, or back the way they came from; it wasn't survivable. The great Rocky Mountains had forced them into the southern deserts. Here they found their way, the great American southwest, lots of open road and a glimmer of hope to complete their crusade.

"We can't keep going this way," Bishop Justin shouted above the din.

"Which way then?" the Baron threw back and gestured at the single asphalt line that stretched ahead across the open expanse.

The bishop's eyes quickly watered. He hadn't any goggles and the hot wind forced him to abandon the pilot space. He yelled a final instruction. "Keep an eye out!"

He fell below into the calm atmosphere of the yacht. 'I told him,' he thought self-satisfied. Justin contemplated how he could possibly tell the Lord about their predicament. He dreaded the thought of communing with an unhappy god. God had always been so loving and accepting that Justin was afraid that the never-ending desert hell on their agenda might turn the deity against him. Justin was sure that the god in the sphere they carried could give pain as well as pleasure. The little bishop shuddered coldly in the stifling heat at the imagined wrath of his lord god.

Baron Willem nudged the driver under him with a knee, shook his head and chuckled knowingly at the ridiculous bishop. The loyal young machine-driver, Joe, looked up and smiled at his fatherly master, then corrected a jot on the outstretched highway to stay in the center of the worn ancient road.

They lived on the roll. His people were wheel-mounted and ready to go, or fight. Willem had devised a motorcycle recon relay to maximize his mobile village. Triplets of diesel powered recon motorcycles ranged ahead; they signalled safe passage ahead with semaphore flags and heliograph mirrors and the camp rolled. They had finally gotten onto these desolate unguarded back-highways and rolled a phenomenal hundred miles in a day. Until now, to avoid ambush and road hazard, recon frequently forced a halt to the mobile village, but now they were making time.

The Baron was ecstatic at finally being in the groove. He rode on his kommanderkar as a flea directing the beetle under him. He loved the feeling that roaring machines gave him; the movement, the power, the experience of going somewhere with intent, unstoppable. He floated, grinning, on the wings of joy, perched on his lumbering monstrosity while the endless landscape flew by.

As the sun fell and threatened its orange-red demise on the horizon the tiny flapping stop-flags of the motorcycle recon team came into view. The convoy slowed to a crawl as they circled around the three men standing next to their two-wheelers in the center of the road. When the encirclement was complete and the Baron was satisfied, he stopped and the incessant noise from the machinery fell quiet.

Ringing the wagons was their first defensive posture and it had served them well over the last year. Although each unit was well armed, no single car was ever caught out alone, except of course the recon bikes. All of their heavy losses had occurred during running pitched battles and due to mechanical failure. Ringing the wagons presented a defensible wall of iron.

People tumbled from the machinery and camp awnings appeared from the sides of the trucks and cooking pots full of dinner were pulled from hot engine compartments. Venison was served up with rationed portions of mead (honey-wine from the Beeman's farm) and roast onions from the low wet-lands at the base of the great mountains they had left the week before. No fires were started as there was no wood to burn, nor was there a need for heat, the desert floor radiated the warmth it stored from the day. A general feeling of contentment lay over the company. All was well. They felt safe.

Their iron ring of machines enclosed them. Their field of fire was complete. The range, endless. They could literally see for miles. Unless the enemy was invisible they were secure in the vast open space of the desert. There was nothing but small rocks and gravel as far as the distant white cliffs on the horizon.

The kommanderkar's boiler tinked loudly as its metal skin cooled.

Willem lounged with his crew as the sun settled brilliant and flat on the Earth; fallen from a crimson sky.

"I must report sire," Bishop Justin broke into the Baron's dinner conversation.

The Baron looked side-ways at him. He sat with some of his chosen men at a table under the small tarpaulin awning stretched out from his kommanderkar.

"Yes," he said curtly.

"My liege ..." he didn't want to say it, "There is a shortage."

"Shortage, now what?" The Baron grunted through a meaty mouthful.

"Well, Milord, the breakdown in the colo-raydo land hurt us. We have ..."

"Really?" Willem replied sarcastically. "I am not unaware. You bring nothing new to me."

"Milord, we have diminished output." The Bishop left it hanging.

"Diminished?" The Baron asked.

"Yes, milord, that colo-raydo incident hurt us badly. We may not have enough methane to sustain this ... desert," he strung-it out.

The Baron hated when the mealy-mouthed priest brought things up. They were almost invariably bad and occasionally true.

'Damned, if the little guy didn't pop his head above the hull today in order to inform me that we were short on organics for the digestors,' he thought.

That is what it really came down to. The scientific constraints on methane and fuel oil production were limits on the Baron's physical power. He couldn't burn fuel that wasn't there. He had to try to match his energy usage to production. Their capabilities denoted their limitations. Not enough gas, not enough travel. Now, this priest, bishop, magic-believer, was hinting that he should do something against the only course of action that was available to them, which was to keep heading south through the desert.

"Listen, priest," he prodded at the little fellow with a meat dripping deer bone, "make more gas or I'll digest your ass to get across this desert. You and all of your swishy little sycophants …"

The bishop peered nervously at the warrior. He nodded his acquiescence and nibbled at his pinky fingernail as he paced in the uncomfortable space around the man.

'God-damned little shit.' The Baron thought, then said, "This is the only way left to us. There have been things that you didn't screw up. I admit. Draining the lake to retrieve god's orb worked. Blinding the yalls with your light, again you saved yourself."

"Thank you milord," Justin said quietly.

"Too bad you have no idea about which way to go. Your old maps said east. Logistics and deadly obstacles refuted that idea." He spat. "The bridges over the mighty Miss are gone. Blown. Your predecessor, Elder, led us to ruin!" The Baron was on a roll. "Then, we retreated and left your well intentioned leader, martyr Elder, in his grave. We let you fill his place and the first news I get is the man you insisted drive our main digester, put it off the road into a gulley!" The Baron leaned forward his mouth agape, eyes fixed on the bald bishop as if waiting for an answer.

The weasely looking man made the excuse, "an unfortunate mis-hap, milord. The grueling journey, the escape, perhaps he fell asleep milord."

The Baron pierced the fellow with an angry glare that shut him up. "And now, you tell me you have failed to make enough fuel?"

"Milord, we counted on trees and shrubs to supplement …"

"Enough! Why do I allow these geeky little pimpoids to control our gas?" Willem asked of his driver who sat aside quietly munching stale bread and hot stringy venison.

"Our most valuable resource?" the Baron reiterated.

The young driver wrinkled his brow and shrugged at his leader's question.

The tough Baron turned back to the bishop, "Your brotherhood is responsible for keeping the cold light of the dee-see, but you and your little friends are not competent to manage the fuel. You crash my trucks and fail to store enough for our trip. You sing about the god in his egg, but have no idea where we should take him. Perhaps the priesthood is fine for the village at home, but our army of machines needs strong results. That is where you are a weakling." The Baron practically spat in the monk's face.

"Yes, milord." The bishop said as he rose and excused himself.

"That's par for the course. Run you little shit. You can't solve a problem so you flee." Baron Willem took a swig from a flagon of sweet warm wine.

Bishop Justin scurried across the open space of camp to be near his acolytes. He could hear the Baron cursing behind him.

"Figure it out bishop, or I'll boil all of you to get across this waste." The Baron laughed. His men joined in with cackling taunting laughter that rang out across the high dry desert.

Justin headed for his brothers near the shuffle bin that held god's egg. They huddled under a tarp stretched around the warm engine compartment of the ancient truck. Desert temperatures fell quickly when the sun took the light and left them in darkness.

He adjusted himself after the humiliating kowtowing to the insufferable macho Baron; puffed out his chest, threw back his shoulders and broke into a purposeful stride.

The shuffling clump of bald dark-robed men looked up expectantly as he approached.

"I told him. I told him before we left the mountains and today and again just now. I told him." Justin declared boldly.

The ten acolytes, brown wool robes covered them but for their hairless heads and cleanly shaven faces, nodded sympathetically. These were his brothers. He had grown up with three of them and knew them intimately. Seven of the group were new initiates from the town of Halor, where the convoy found god. They were already acolytes to the lord, and were bound to protect him on his journey to the sea. Their leader was Ben, the bee-man.

The armed convoy had invaded and insisted on extracting god's egg from the lake bottom. Halor's residents were left out of the process. The sphere had been loaded onto the truck before the townspeople could mobilize against them, as if they could have put up much of a fight. They were not nearly as well armed as the Baron's company. Halor's defense had mainly been its location, away from the main freeway in the middle of the great plains.

The Beeman's farm, where god lived in the lake, was close to the interstate and relatively easy pickings. The Bishop Elder had swum with god and the seven boys who lived with the Beeman on his farm had attended the old man, as he entered hirsute and full and emerged bald pink and empty, from the lake. The brothers were the guard and servants of the lord. They knew his joy and had each been with their god at least once.

Justin melded into the group hug as they commiserated with him. The boys and men huddled in a breathy and close embrace under the warm tarp that reeked of hot diesel engine. They held each other tighter and tighter as they sighed away the tribulations of their day.

Justin's excited breathing found some calm as his brethren pulled him into their core. A soft moaning lament of prayerful chanting rose unbidden from them. A low growling mantra they had been creating floated out from deep within them. The chant flowed from their hearts and souls and was driven by their desire for intimacy. Being in the lord was preferable, but since he was entombed inside his egg, unreachable, they found their closeness in other ways. Hands probed into the folds of one another's tunics as the song of spiritual connection emanated from their throats. They reached and petted one another under the veil of their hymn. The gentle touching and fervent caress of each to one another, no one knew to whom, was soothing and supportive; they held onto whatever sensual feedback that could be gotten. Their lord god had taken them to such extreme pleasure and delight that the bar for gratification was high and their reticence to reaching joy was gone. In the company of their own, like minded humans, they found the most meaningful recreation of their spiritual experience. The touch of man was paltry compared to the all encompassing experience of god, but their desire for it was unabated and pursued. They chanted the mantra and practiced their sensual art of pleasure with their Bishop Justin at the center, writhing in supportive joy.

The tarp at the front of the truck undulated, amoeba-like, over them all, standing and massaging one another. Their robes moved up and over their shoulders as a layer of thick floating cloth that held their heads above and distinct from the fish-belly white skin and naked scrawny legs underneath. Their bodies molded together and rubbed against one another in a seething attempt to recreate the lord's touch. Their shuffling dusty sandals bumped, delicately refraining from crushing their neighbor's toes, as they upheld the mass of writhing men against the filth of the desert floor. The tarp coated their heads and they breathed in their own exhaustion and rolled their skulls in mantric chanting.

"Ohhhhmmmmmmmmmmm."

The church of the magic light, the church of the second coming, the church of something better is ahead just wait and see, groped and pleasured one another and chanted and breathed into each other's faces. When one opened their eyes, the sight was as awful a shock as the lord god himself, so they closed them and listened to their internal voice about the sensations of their bodies. Blind, they rolled back into their heads as their bodies smashed together magnetically and their writhing appendages entwined into and around the bodies of their own, they found connection to god. They found the sensation that god imbedded in their minds of his reality; the reality of being a god and swimming in the great sea of spirituality with your fellow gods, the flow and ebb of the current flowing with the collective body of us, the writhing and seething, pulsing harmonic oneness of the mass. The great feeling and orgasm of being with an other.

Two convoy sentries peered out from their perches. They ignored the Baron at feast and the incestuous priest grope and the various scuttlings below as tenders were stoked, tanks filled and engines were checked and readied for the night. They hunkered close to their ancient machine guns and scanned for coming danger from out there in the endless moonlit desertscape.

The hot day turned into bone chilling night. As night wore on, their breath steamed as they watched the emptiness for enemies. Nothing came, coyotes howled in the distance, guards dozed fitfully and the moaning priestly brothers went at it again.

In the middle of the night, the Bishop stumbled, naked, from his tiny berth under the chassis of the great shuffle-bin where god reposed, to relieve his bladder. He stood shivering at the edge of the vast enormous open expanse, ten gazillion stars above and the yip-yip of some desert animals in the distance, when he heard it. He heard thumping. Faint and very far off, but distinctly there, thumping. It was another mystery of the desert. He turned and scampered back to the iron cubby and snuggled against his warm acolyte, Benjamin.

—

The young hunters had heard them first. They heard them coming the day before. The walls of the surrounding vertical canyons acted as enormous echo reflectors and the strange whining noise reverberated faintly. The hunters sat on the edge of the great cliffs looking out to where the sound came from. They didn't know what it was.

The rumbling whine of the convoy could be heard above the natural sounds of the desert for miles.

The old men listened and they knew what it was.

Machines.

They knew when the machines stopped and when they started again.

When the silence fell, at the end of the day, the wise old men convened in the dirt kiva in the ground and decided their plan of action.

The white man's evil was again coming to enter their sacred world. They had kept the stories of the white men alive. They warned their children to be on the look-out for the sounds of the devil from the past. And now, the sounds were real and the entire village heard and was afraid.

All knew the strange tales from the past around the evening campfire: men who flew in the air, moved at great speed, talked and saw each other from miles away as if they were in front of you, and an entire people who cared little or nothing for the spirit of the world.

The old wise men had waited for the return of these white devils and now they were coming. They all heard them today. All day the sound came.

The young braves were fired up at the sounds that echoed down the plains. They had been wakened to the truth of the old men's stories by the strange sounds. It had only been a fairy tale before and was now a reality.

The old men met in the quiet underground kiva and gently discussed their options. Peyote was eaten and sacred visions came. The pipe was passed and the meaning of existence revealed itself. The young warriors danced around a blazing piñon fire above, painted their naked bodies, chanted sing-song mantras loudly and worked themselves into a frenzy. The tribe was abuzz over the sounds that rolled from the north all day. They were coming. What should be done?

The drums pounded into the night and the entire tribe slept little as they decided how to meet the end of the quiet and the coming of the devils.

—

Another day and another piece of the journey unfolded. Boilers were fired, steam got up, and the wagon turbines whined their flywheels to speed. The older, slower shuttle-bins waited until the last moment and then, a hissing whine of compressed air motors and the old trucks roared to life. Their ancient internal combustion diesel engines sucked precious oil and made forward momentum. The convoy rolled.

Lamar clung to the handlebars of his hurtling motorcycle. He gripped the deteriorating rubber handles firmly as the machine rattled at high speed down the hot brown highway. He hunkered into position behind the small square of scratched windscreen. His body molded onto the seat of the two-wheeled thing and gripped it tightly with his legs. He hugged the warm machine in the early morning cold and snuggled against the chill penetrating wind that tried to bore through his leathers and reach into him. As long as there weren't any road-cuts or mechanical failures to stop him from his sprint across the open plain, he went, hell-bent, hunched over and flat-out. The vast expanse of flat strait roadway let him open-up and ride-out. He flew to the edge of the machine's stability. It started to wobble in front and only then did he pull back a hair and find the sweet spot of maximum speed. His hands itched from the vibration. He had no meter to tell him how fast he was going, but he ate the road rapaciously.

Lamar's second, followed close behind, or so he hoped. 'Let him try to catch me.' He wouldn't take away one bit of his focus to look behind to see if his bike-mate was there. On this unending open road he blasted faster than he had ever gone before. The center of the antique asphalt had held up very well in the dry desert and was smooth and unbroken. He was exuberant in clinging, absolutely still, to the racing bundle of metal bits that sped straight ahead into the future.

The hammering of the ancient two cylinder diesel deafened him. It yammered at his consciousness and rang in his ears. Lamar was having the best ride of his life. He was the tip of the spear, the leader into the unknown, the most susceptible, the most revered and intrepid man in the convoy.

Big Roy, the newest and least experienced rider in recon, watched the little man pull away from him. 'Damn that guy's going fast. No wonder he's the best,' Roy thought.

Roy was a large fellow and not eager to go faster than he felt comfortable. Lamar had told him to keep up and so, Roy pulled on the throttle of his rickety two-wheeled machine and sped to an uncomfortable pace.

Lamar, his leader, continued to vanish ahead.

Roy pulled harder on the throttle as tears streamed from his eyes. He couldn't really see his recon leader clearly. The scratched goggles made it hard to see anything other than the edge of the road. Roy mostly saw only where Lamar had gone and smelled his oily exhaust. He followed bravely after his hard bitten motorcycle leader.

There was only one road.

Roy clung to the wind buffeting contraption and held on for dear life as his speed increased to catch up to his mentor. They were supposed to travel together. Lamar had left him far behind. His only choice was to try and catch up. He held on tightly and prayed the bike didn't explode under him.

Lamar flew by the two young Native Americans in a blur. They were surprised at how fast he came around the bend and didn't have time to loose their arrows at him. His machine vanished past them.

Little Horse ran out onto the roadway and aimed after Lamar, but he was gone. Scared Dog saw the other motorcycle too late. He yelled at Little Horse and aimed at the machine bearing down on his friend.

Big Roy slammed into the teenaged archer from behind. They exploded in an uncontrolled unzipping of stability. Little Horse catapulted into the air, Roy tumbled, the motorcycle fell over and bounced into a somersaulting whirl of flying pieces. The three objects scattered together down the hard asphalt.

Scared Dog ran to his friend who was a small heap of broken and twisted buckskin. Little Horse was still and obviously dead, his head lolled at an angle and bones stuck out from the side of his legs. He had a look of surprise on his face.

The motorcycle lay a hundred yards farther on the road. It made a rattling noise as its wheels whirred slowly to an unbalanced stop. The rider was nowhere to be seen. Scared Dog ran to the edge of the highway and found the rider at the bottom of a sandy wash. The man was moving and the fact that he had survived the crash and Little Horse had not, infuriated Scared Dog. He nocked an arrow and placed it into the man. The fellow squirmed, rolled over and pointed at Scared Dog.

Angry bees buzzed by his head as strange popping noises came from the man. Scared Dog nocked another arrow as his left leg burned and buckled under him. More bees and popping as dirt puffs flew up around him. Scared Dog tried to get up and loose another arrow, but burning in his chest made him curl up and crawl back from the ravine edge. The bees stung him worse than ever before. The man's bees were mean and very painful.

Scared Dog lurched across the road as his blood moistened him and filled his moccasin. He stumbled to where their shared horse was tethered and could just barely climb up and spur the mount. He rode for home. He had to tell his tale to the elders. The white devils were here. They were fast and they had angry burning bees.

Draco lay on the bare dirt hillock and watched the riders speed out of sight. He was in the third recon motorcycle position and his job was to monitor the riders with binoculars for the one mile leg of advance. Draco watched Lamar speed away from the simple-minded galoot, Big Roy.

Lamar was the older and more experienced rider. He was a lean, well built man with a pointed cleft chin, sharply defined cheekbones, and a pencil thin moustache. Lamar was as sharp of mind as the chiseled features of his permanently wind-burned face. He moved in quick flitting motions that had served him well in avoiding injuries of pitched battles past.

Big Roy was new to the recon team and less confident on the two-wheeled machine. He was at least six and a half feet tall, weighed an eighth of a ton, had huge hands, an overhanging brow, and a lumbering gait that belied the moving of a great mass when he walked.

Lamar and Roy vanished around a bend in the otherwise straight road. They should have stopped, re-established the chain of communication with their mirrors, and let Draco catch up to them. The bend in the road was so slight that it may not have seemed enough to drop from his line of sight. Lamar knew better. They were moving faster than Draco had ever seen them. The ride must be exquisite. Flat open road beckoned for full throttle and a chance to unwind the beasts.

Now, Draco, was in a quandary. Should he chase after them or wait until they reappeared to make contact? He peered through the glasses at where they ought to have emerged from the bend in the road. He scanned the area and finally caught glimpse of a man on horseback riding away at breakneck speed.

Draco jumped up, stuffed his glasses in the rider's bag on his bike. He coasted to the bottom of the hill where he dropped the clutch and the thing pop-popped to life. He roared down the road after his team.

Draco violated protocol. He was supposed to report back that the team was lost. The convoy depended on the recon warnings to assure their survival. Draco thought he might save the day and his pals if he could get to where they left his sight.

Roy had an arrow protruding from his left shoulder. His right arm was broken in more than one place and could only flop against his likewise broken ribs. A searing white-hot wipe of pain covered the right side of his face where he was road-rashed from pate to chin. He wasn't fully aware that his face was half gone, he only knew that the savage archer was still alive because he could only use his left hand to wield the pistol.

"The little shit shot me with an arrow! An arrow?!" Roy yelled out at the multiple pains that were just now beginning to be felt. His face was on fire and his shoulder dug a point of deep throbbing as his ribs and arm ached at each slight movement. He had to get out of this gulley to a defensible position. He holstered his pistol clumsily. To get into a semi-standing position he levered himself up slowly and crawled out of the gravity well holding him to the earth. He lurched to the side of the steep sided dry wash and leaned against the protruding arrow. Now he really felt the damned thing in him.

"Arrghhh." He blanched at the refreshing wash of pain and banged his head against the flaking dirt wall. "Don't bang the arrow!" He said out loud to himself as he stumbled along the wash to somewhere other than where he was.

Draco roared up on his machine and slowed as he neared the bend in the road. He could see it would have been easy to think it was a straight shot. The bend was slight and at speed would have been indiscernible to a rider.

A small cluster of things in the middle of the highway prompted him to stop and dismount, pistol at ready. He crouched and scanned. Nothing moved as he deciphered the scene: a foreign body, one wrecked motorcycle, and nothing else. He looked for the recon uniform that belonged to the machine and the other rider.

A slight breeze whipped a bit of dust across the scene. The hot sun bore down on him and demanded he make a decision. Draco ran across the road and scanned about for the rider of the fallen bike; nothing but an empty gulley,.

He had seen one man ride away and it wasn't his recon. The motorcycle lay broken on the road and the only person he could see, wasn't his crew. It was some savage in buckskins who looked liked he had been stepped on.

Draco realized he had failed to notify command about the danger here and the convoy was stumbling into this trap. He ran to his idling motorcycle and with a roar, fled back to his people.

Roy heard the receding motorcycle and tried to yell out. "Hey! I'm here." It stabbed him to yell. He moved along the dirty wash, away from the ambush.

Lamar realized too late that he had gone too far. The joy of the ride was great and he sported an immense shit-eating and dirt stained grin. Never before could he push it to the max. He now knew what the machine could really do. 'It'll go faster. The suspension needs work. More balance of the wheels,' he thought.

Lamar pulled up and slowed to turn around. A clattering from underneath him caused the motorcycle to lurch, as arrows flew into the spokes and struck all around him. His momentum faltered, he put his foot out to get balance at the now, very low speed. Three young men sprinted out and tackled him and his bike.

Draco felt the chill of sweat on his spine. He ran from the danger, as was proper. He was scared. He thought a bullet would hit him in the back at any second. He pulled the throttle to maximum. The heavy home-made diesel motorcycle screamed its throaty bellow. He flew faster than ever before. The wind forced him to lie down, his eyes watered, vibration stung his hands and itched inside his thighs, a high speed wobble pushed down against his flight. He blinked often to get a vague, slide-show idea of where the road ahead was. A fat desert bug drilled a painful hole in his forehead, just below the leather skull cap and above his inefficient goggles. Yellow goo dribbled along his hairline. He flew on. He must warn the Baron.

Ben, the bee-man, insisted on traveling with his lord god. He was a willing accompanist. He had convinced the baron and his weird priestly followers to obey god's wishes to take his lord home, to the sea. They gladly followed Ben's suggestion to return god to the ocean. They were on a crusade to acquire the lord and take him back to the west coast. They wanted the magic back. The Pacific Ocean was near where they came from, it was perfect. Once they realized that Ben had tended the lord for years and knew him intimately they bundled him into the mix.

The fly in the ointment had been that they couldn't return to the west coast. Vast deserts and the savage Yoots barred the way.

So, here they were, heading south from the Kolo-raydo country to what was hoped were tropical waters south of the yalls who had plagued them so terribly in the east.

Ben sat, strapped into the hard seat on the side of the flatbed that carried the lord's egg. Ben knew the egg was a space ship, even if it didn't look anything like a vessel that could go into outer space.

The baron had drained the lake and dragged the growth covered sphere out and loaded it onto the truck.

It was god's house. He was inside. At least they assumed he was inside. He wasn't anywhere in the slime and muck of the lake bottom. He was sealed up tight and although no one had communicated with the Lord since before the move, they believed he was still in there.

Ben endured the warm air blowing on him as the convoy rolled on.

This was his mission; to assure god made it to the sea and restored the magic so, he could have back his internet, his cell-phone, his texting and connection to the rest of the world that in his juvenile mind, he was once dependant upon. TV could once again flicker in every home and lights would drive away the night. Ben loved what God had done for him and believed that if he fulfilled this one task, then the world would be made whole again. Electricity would return.

That was why Ben, the bee-man, sat perched on the edge of a flatbed truck in the middle of nowhere going no place. He was trusting the brotherhood and Baron Willem to finish the journey at waters edge and everything would somehow, be magically all better.

When the convoy slowed to intercept the recon rider hurtling at them, Ben sighed at yet another delay.

The line of machines ground to a halt on the expanse of asphalt as Draco breathlessly recounted his intel to the Baron.

Ben stood off the road and peered forward in hopes of understanding the delay.

The Baron waved his arms and remounted. The convoy roared to life and proceeded on, but with the front end loader tank in front.

The Baron knew that they couldn't turn, or go back, or camp and wait it out, he had to drive them to the hills ahead. That was where sustenance lay. Cool water and trees and game filled the hills ahead. The gun mounts came alive and each truck bristled with weapons. They knew how to deal with small bands of brigands and primitive savages. Smash and slash. The convoy rumbled on.

They stopped at the ambush site. Infantry squads swarmed from the trucks and secured the area. They retrieved the wrecked motorcycle, mounted the Indian's body on a cross at the front of the Kommanderkar like a hood ornament and in only a few minutes found Big Roy in the gulley. He was pretty beat-up, but was a wealth of information about the primitive nature of their enemy.

They bore on at a moderate pace, ten miles an hour, and were poised to fire. The country became sparse hills and deep gullies as they neared the towering white cliffs that announced the edge of the mountains and the end of the open road.

28

High Priest

A.Q. Year Three Hundred

Tall, freckled and bronzed by the desert sun, the most intrepid speaker to god, Jerome, strode through the dirt courtyard of the adobe brick and mud monastery. He was on his way to see the Abbot and demand more tribute for god.

Ancient dirt buildings rose around him in ungainly and mishappen two and three story blocks: tiny doorways, few windows, exposed hand hewn viga poles sticking out from near the roof-lines, each festooned with all manner of drying food and clothing. The bright red ristras of chili peppers hung alongside strips of salted animal flesh and carefully laid out strings of fruit to dry in the hot desert air. The walls were mud-molded by human hands and there was not a hard square edge or corner. What he had first distantly seen as a fabulous glimmering city of gold glinting from the center of a white arrow wall of rock above, he now knew as a shabby mud village at the foot of a scarred cliff.

Jerome marched with an air of confidence. He had achieved his goal and considered himself to be a High Priest.

The old abbot had seemed so strong and powerful when Jerome first arrived, now he was just a tired little man trying to hide the truth of his abbey's poverty and foul duty.

The abbot was afraid of Jerome. He avoided Jerome because he'd asked for tribute every few days since his first return from the cave and it was taking a toll on the resources of his brotherhood. The abbey did not make a habit of supplying god with any of their larder unless it had been paid for. They took the pilgrims' money for food, stuffed them full, sent them up the cliff and then scraped their smashed bodies from the base of the mountain into shallow graves. Initiates didn't normally return and had never insisted on going back up. The few that didn't end up as piles of smashed wreckage at the foot of the cliff babbled and were too crazed to understand. They usually ran away across the desert. The brothers at the abbey did not bother to chase them nor to minister to them. The only two pilgrims that had ever made it down alive and stayed at the monastery were so insane that they were babbling idiots who stared from wide afraid eyes; they were kept as pets and did slave work.

Jerome had not only returned sane, but insisted on going back up the mountain. He had demanded tribute to god from the brothers. At first they didn't want to comply, food was scarce out here at the edge of the nothingness desert, but Jerome berated them and forced his will. Now he was going back for more.

Jerome was determined to hear the rest of the lord's story.

The old abbot was determined to get rid of the young man, somehow.

"He is coming brother." The weasel nosed monk, Fiodor, rasped at the old abbot.

"Damn. Why so early? I am still abed." The fat fellow heaved himself up from he smelly straw bed and reached for his rough spun robe.

"He catches us unawares. He knows we avoid him." Fiodor said.

"I am not going to let him take our food to that monster again." The abbot said as he threw on his robe and stumbled out of his chamber.

The abbot's mud apartment was perched upon the incongruously out of place structure of the ancient tank of Baron Willem. The ancient rusted Kommandurcar comprised the first floor of the building's foundation and presented a metal wall at ground level.

Jerome moved quickly up the steel ladder and appeared at the tiny doorway as the old man came out onto his patio roof.

"Good morning brother abbot Bryan. I come to seek tribute for our lord." Jerome said a bit too airily for that time of the morning.

The abbot snarled at the bald pink young man and headed for the ladder. "I have no time for you today Jerome. I must go to vespers."

"Yes, we must go to vespers." Fiodor chimed in and stepped rudely in front of Jerome to take the ladder behind his abbot.

"I understand Brother Abbot, but I must have tribute so I may leave early, in service to our lord." Jerome followed them down the ladder.

The abbot and Fiodor had already made the ground and were scurrying away as fast as their legs would carry them across the courtyard.

Jerome scurried after them. "Abbot Brother, I must ask only this one last time. I believe the story is almost complete. I can go home after today if I can get our god, the lord of the cave, to speak his last tale to me."

The abbot came up short in the chill shade of the sacristy porch.

"You will go home?" The old abbot scratched his ass and adjusted himself.

"Yes abbot, I am almost finished and can leave. I must take the word of god to my people." Jerome reasoned.

"If we give you more food for … that cave, you will leave here? And not come to bother us again? The last time?" The abbot asked.

"Yes abbot. I will fulfill my duty for the end of the story." Jerome begged a tad.

Fiodor shrugged and gave the abbot a knowing look suggesting an easy solution.

The old abbot scowled at him and asked Jerome. "What part of the story don't you have? I mean, you have been up there dozens of times since you got here. That's more than … well, more than anyone. What more do you want to know?"

"I don't know how our lord came to be here, in the desert. How did he come to be in there?" Jerome asked innocently.

The abbot pursed his lips and Fiodor looked away. "Well, it's not a story I suppose he could tell. The founders of our order risked everything for the task."

"The lord reveals all to me. I know the tale of it all, except how he ended in the cave." Jerome said matter of factly.

"And yet, you go back to … it, you are drawn to it, you want more. Haven't you enough of it? Always one more time. Don't you yet see why we are here watching that it stays where it is?"

"I see him for what he is." Jerome said, knowing that the 'God' in the cave above was truly a supreme being and not from this earth and that he held the secret key to the world. "I understand all that. He will tell us how to restore the magic."

The abbot rubbed around his face in exasperation.

"All will be revealed to me." Jerome smiled nicely.

The abbot pulled his chin and peered from his tiny eyes at the ambitious young fellow; they had some antique solar panels, and batteries and lights for yearly rituals, what else could he possibly learn?

This boy in front of him was the only one who visited it repeatedly and was the only one in memory who had gotten anything coherent out of the creature.

Even so, Jerome was stressing their comfort levels, driving the abbey into poverty with his demands for free tribute, and for no visible return. No one was thrilled by anything he brought down from the mount. There was no huge revelation or joy for the monastery. Nothing the thing might say changed their lot. The monks were men stuck in their circumstance by their fear of change. They stayed and lived at the edge of the desert because they liked to hide and didn't know any better.

"One last time. That is all." The abbot demanded sternly.

Fiodor pursed his lips as he dug out a chit for a ration from the cook and tossed it at the beggar.

Jerome backed away to go collect what he could from the kitchen to feed the insatiable story-teller in the pool above.

"Thank you brother. Thank you." He turned and scurried off to the kitchen.

Fiodor looked askance at the abbot. "Brother? He is more than we can bear."

"Easy Fiodor. What can he do? God wants out, we hold God sacred and secure. There is no way to move the Lord, he is constant."

"He could fail to satisfy and be devoured." Fiodor chimed in cheerily.

"At worst, if he fails to leave we can drive him naked into the desert as a heretic and liar and be rid of him."

"He pledged he would go on his own." Fiodor affirmed, nodding.

"Our conscience is clean either way."

They watched Jerome disappear in the adobe maze then turned to their smoking parlor for morning vespers.

Jerome stuffed a couple of rabbits and slop from the garbage bucket in a goatskin. He knew god cared little for fresh foods, the more rotten the better. The hard part of the order to fill was the honey. Brother Ben, the cook, had been getting less and less open to the young man's pleading for the stuff.

"You, again?! Get out of my kitchen you rat, you vulture, you coyote." Ben raved at Jerome pilfering his honey pot.

"Brother Ben, I have the permission of the Abbot for this tribute to our lord." Jerome explained as he held up the ration-chit.

"This is not brother Bryan's kitchen. It is my kitchen. I am the one who says what can go on here." Ben pulled out a large wooden spoon menacingly.

"I have all I need for our lord, Brother Ben." Jerome backed towards the door.

"Yer damned tootin' you got all you need. You're done in here. Do not feed my prisoner any more … unless you pay. You go out and hunt for it if you want to be so damned friendly to him." Ben brandished the spoon.

"Brother Ben you don't mean that. He is our lord. Our Planet Lord." Jerome took a reverential tone.

"It is evil infernal boy. Don't you get it, yet? We don't worship the thing. We keep it so it can't get out. It is our foul prisoner." Ben sneered at him.

"Brother Ben, if only you could feel the love … the truth and compassion in him. You would help me feed him and help me get him back to his true home, the sea." Jerome implored.

"Hah! Help him escape? You are truly crazy. It destroyed my world. Don't you read the scriptures of the brotherhood? No of course not. You only listen to the monster and its lies." Ben accused him.

"God, Sloodin, only tells me truth."

"HAH!"

"What 'lies' then, Ben?" Jerome asked.

"Unbelievable!" Ben shook his giant spoon towards the mountain. "Listen boy, this entire monastery is a prison. We are a long line of men, dedicated to holding the heinous creature that ripped the glory from man. A single creature took all the light from the world. He is responsible, don't you see? He is the reason there is no more magic in the world and he refuses to give it back. He keeps us in this state of primitive existence for his own selfish greed." Ben shook the spoon in Jerome's face.

"But, he was only trying to protect the oceans from the ignorance of our ancestors. We must learn not to poison the world. Our ancestors were bad and thoughtless and for that we were punished, and rightfully so," Jerome pleaded with his only friend in the entire village.

"That's what he says. It isn't up to some other creature to pass judgment on us. All I know is we were great and glorious and the world was full of light and wondrous things and now we live in mud huts and scrabble in the darkness. Multiply and subdue the earth was our creed. It was all ours. Now it's, go softly, go quietly, lest we invoke the wrath of a foul god. No Jerome, you don't know what you're talking about and you are a fool to go back and feed it any more."

"You think as you will Brother Ben, I must go, this one last time. I must learn the secret." Jerome argued.

"You don't get it boy. There is no secret! He is a prisoner and evil beyond compare. Ach! What's the use, here, take the honey. Get out of my kitchen and don't come crying to me when you learn that you are wrong … Just go." The fat brother sadly turned away from Jerome.

Ben had seen the wrath of the creature. He was a boy when the quiet came three hundred years previous. He was there when the thing fell from the sky. He had lived with the thing. He had made love with it. He had been made an accomplice to its vile plan to enslave mankind in a world bereft of electricity. He knew it better than any human who had ever lived. Ben, the bee-man, monk-cook, living in a dirt house at the base of a desert cliff, knew the truth of the monstrous alien that they kept captive in the cave above. He had bathed with the creature and heard its entire story, about how he found our planet and made it his own, about how he hated the land animals and their vainglorious pursuits and how he had disseminated the magnetic bacteria to cure the humans of their addiction to electricity.

Ben knew. Ben knew all about the 'evils' of electricity. He grew up with TV and lights and music that filled the day. He knew what joy could be had at a touch and he hated the monster trapped above. He was forced to live without power and then again, he was forced to endure the greatest hardship man had ever encountered, longevity. The damned creature had loved him and somehow, made him live longer than any man ought to. Ben had endured three hundred years of no magic, and was now being asked by this upstart pilgrim to help him 'save' the creature that had damned him to eternal poverty and seemingly endless life.

Let the kid go.

Jerome stared at the broad back of the heavy-set cook for a moment. Ben had been the only monk that befriended him and told him anything truthful or useful about 'God' in the cave above.

"He says he'll turn the power back on. It'll all come back on." Jerome said simply.

"He can't reseed the magnetic bacteria." Ben said.

"How do you know that?" Jerome stopped.

Ben turned slowly and looked at the piebald red man, splotched from the harsh desert sun and the repeated acid washings by the lord, square in the eye. "I found him. I am the bee-man. I'm the first to swim with him."

Jerome stood agape.

"He made me live forever."

"Then you understand!" Jerome cried.

"No!" Ben turned away, so he wouldn't strangle the kid.

Ben turned back to him shaking his head. "Don't you see, it's gone. The world ended. Just as surely as the prophesies of old foretold the collapse of the Roman empire." His arms were open, palms up. "Once it's broken, it is very hard to fix. Nothing will change for us."

"It might for you if, as you say, you live forever." Jerome cajoled with a smile.

"Oh, come on. You really think if, and I do mean with a lot of doubt here, if he turned it back on, and if I could cobble together enough old junk to make the world run again that would be a valid future picture …?" Ben stopped spouting.

"What if?" Jerome put to him.

"Listen carefully now, I will tell you." Ben spoke more quietly and sat at one of the long wooden tables. "When I was a boy I had the magic. It was wonderful, yes. There was a thing called TV. It was pictures and stories. Some of the stories were about beings from other worlds. We knew all about the cosmos and the planets and the vastness of space. There were shows about UFO's, that's what we called them, spaceships and aliens from out there." He pointed the spoon at the ceiling.

"You knew about him? But how …?" Jerome sat down.

"Just listen, we thought we knew a little bit. They never talked to us. They never showed themselves. They were just a fantasy borne on a statistical probability of the sheer numbers of other worlds that someone else had to be out there too. No one could prove they existed, but everyone speculated. People always asked, 'why don't they contact us? Why don't they ask us about things? Or show themselves.' The reason was, we are cockroaches."

"Cockroaches?" Jerome parroted.

"Look, when you find roaches in the kitchen, do you try to talk to them? Or look for cockroach art? Or cockroach literature or theater or dance or music? No, of course not. You ignore them until they get into the larder and then you try to get rid of them."

Jerome was confused by the concept. He was thinking about its implications to him and the creature in the cave who had been so loving and soothing to him. He thought he was a partner with god.

"We are not in their world. Any more than they were in ours. They live at the bottom of the sea, as far from what we might consider an intelligent space-faring being as they could be. They don't breathe air, they don't talk or walk or do anything like we do. They are more alien than any TV show or movie and more foreign to us than the great minds of the world ever imagined. We are dry. They are wet and have no need for us or our culture. That's why it's useless to assuage him. He won't do anything. He can't. We killed his ship, so he certainly can't turn the electricity back on. He made that clear to me hundreds of years ago, when we threatened to drop him into his prison unless he did, he refused."

"He preferred to be in the cave?"

"That's not the story. The story is that we are small minded vain creatures that are stuck on this tiny planet in a huge galaxy that we are not suited for, except here. We have to live here and take care of what we have, here. There is no, 'out there' for us no matter what 'Star Trek' says."

"Who are star trek?"

"A TV… just a story, about how we could leave our world and go out there for something better."

"Sounds heavenly." Jerome smiled beneficently.

"That's all bullshit!" Ben rubbed his face in exasperation. "Look, the snood are fluid creatures that can withstand the stress of acceleration and, ummhh…" Ben raised one eyebrow, "mutation and long hibernation. They do it naturally." He was excited about telling him.

Jerome touched his arm. "Easy Ben."

"But you can't go out there in space with him, Jerome."

"I don't want to go out there, I just want the power of the magic and better lights."

Ben snorted laughter. "Yeah, well one follows the other. As soon as we got electricity we thought we were pretty smart and next thing we thought we could mess this planet up and just go get another one to live on. That just isn't practical. Can't be done. So get over it."

"Star Trek?" Jerome queried.

"Whatever, go on, be his pet cockroach. It won't change anything."

"I just want to be a bishop." Jerome said plaintively.

Ben looked up into the youngster's eyes. "You already are ya dit! You did it, you saw him. Go home, be the bishop. Get your reward 'cause there's nothing more here for you."

Jerome hugged the honey pot tight. "I told the abbott I would go one last time."

"You got everything you came for." Ben rose and shuffled back through the dirty curtain to his quarters.

Jerome sat alone and pondered his choices. He just wanted to be respected, to have others serve him and live rich. He didn't want to carry the weight of the world on his shoulders or colonize other planets. He just wanted to show off fancy lights and be respected, awed and live an easy life. He thought he could get a secret from God. Turns out he already had all he could have; direct current. He felt deflated. Ben had burst his bubble and the quest was over.

Jerome embraced his inner cockroach.

He grabbed some bread and cheese, walked out of the dining hall, turned left, away from the steep cliff, away from the dirty village and the cynical old bee-man, and into the great desert;

homeward to claim his bishopric. Ben was right. Jerome didn't need God anymore.

Ben sank onto the well padded Ironwood chair in his den; the backroom of the kitchen. As was his usual habit he pulled a small curtain, flipped a couple of switches, pushed a button to read the solar battery meter for the day He dug out his paraphernalia box: made a notation, strewed two wire-wrapped bars with dangling auto battery clips on the table, then slid a small hidden panel exposing two terminal ends of his chemical lead-acid array under the floor, and clamped the three-hundred-year-old car jumper-cables to the powerful knobs of the battery. It sparked. He dug a small vial from the plain hardwood box and spilled a little near the apparatus. He felt the ghostly hummmmmm, he was pushing current. The iron filings did his bidding and a neat circle of opposing figures on the poles aligned and made a round pattern on the table.

Magic. Electromagnetism.

Ben drew himself a beer and waited. He picked up one of the dozens of open books scattered about his homey cubicle and killed fifteen minutes reading.

He read the meter and decided to give more charge. The bars sat in charred holes on the table indiscernibly vibrating with magnetic potential.

He could afford fifteen minutes more, but he couldn't concentrate on Marx's evaluation of labor. That damned kid would not leave his mind. Ben had already resigned himself to Jerome's death, since day one, and he just sent him off to his demise, yet again. What was there to think about?

"Sigh."

Just another damned pilgrim. His mind swam with the little guy's sincerity and fervor and visions of them together.

He tossed the unread book, unclamped the power and slid one of the bars out of the coil of wire, as he did once a week, or when he got a new test bar, to see if the metal was ferrous-like enough to retain a magnetic field. He swiped the bar almost disdainfully through the now relaxed iron powder on the table.

He held the bar close in the candle light and squinted peremptorily.

It was always clean.

He blinked hard a couple of times, then fluttered and refocused on the blurry thing in his mitt, it was still blurry. He leaned forward and brought more candles to looked hard at the bar.

It was fuzzy.

For an instant he felt to disconnect the wire, but he knew there was none and he froze; he rotated the blob of tiny particles, stuck together magically at his fingertip. He pulled a small magnifying glass and peered at the miracle at his touch. The little iron lines were standing on each other all minutely stacked up.

The bar was magnetized.

His heart skipped a beat.

For three hundred years the electromagnet would make a weak field, but the metal bar would never retain magnetic character. It always vanished with the loss of electrical current, but now it held the force.

'The Kid! I have to tell him! Tell him he was right.' Ben thought, 'but he's already gone.'

"I'll tell him when he gets back. It's his last time up there. Just a routine visit." He said to no one. Ben leaned back and sipped beer as his blood pressure reflected the adrenaline rush from the magnetic test results. He twirled the rod slowly in his fingers and watched the blurry glob.

He breathed deep, belched and smiled.

ABOUT THE AUTHOR

Ray Morgan is an accomplished story teller and stage actor. He is a western man having made North America, west of the continental divide, his stomping grounds. He adventured by dog sled in Alaska and sailed the Pacific Coast to Baja in a small sailboat. He's fought the frost giants of the North Slope oil fields and resisted deep-sea sirens who wished to drag him to a watery grave. An ardent fan of the science fiction genre he's happy to finally put a little of it out there from his desk.

Made in the USA
Columbia, SC
16 December 2018